Cat Laughing Last

ALSO AVAILABLE IN BEELER LARGE PRINT BY
SHIRLEY ROUSSEAU MURPHY

Cat to the Dogs

Cat Under Fire

Cat Laughing Last

A JOE GREY MYSTERY

SHIRLEY ROUSSEAU MURPHY

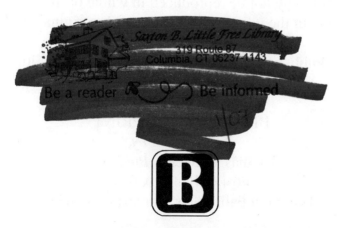

BEELER LARGE PRINT

Hampton Falls, New Hampshire, 2002

Library of Congress Cataloging-in-Publication Data

Murphy, Shirley, Rousseau.
   Cat laughing last a Joe Grey mystery / Shirley Rousseau. Murphy.
      p.   cm.
   ISBN 1-57490-438-8 (acid-free. paper)
   1. Grey, Joe (Fictitious character). 2. Garage sales—Fiction. 3.
Cats—Fiction. 4. Large type books. I. Title.

PS3563. U355 C3 2002b
813'.54—dc21   2002011463

Published in Large Print by arrangement with
HarperCollins Publishers, Inc.

BEELER LARGE PRINT
is published by
Thomas T. Beeler, *Publisher*
Post Office Box 659
Hampton Falls, New Hampshire 03844

Typeset in 16 point Times New Roman type.
Sewn and bound on acid-free paper by
Sheridan Books in Chelsea, Michigan

*To the memory of Joe Cat,
a debonair fellow of wry dignity whose creative
manipulations shaped his world pretty
much as he chose.*

I would like to thank soprano Barbara Brooks for escorting me through Carmel's Golden Bough Playhouse. While I have not drawn a mirror likeness, I hope to have captured a small portion of the magic presen between performances in the dim and empty theater.

No other animal has managed to get itself tangled up in as much legend, myth, symbolism, religion, history, and human affairs as the cat. From the time it first appeared upon the scene some four thousand years ago, it has played its part in almost every age . . . Black magic, white magic, good luck and bad, a hundred superstitions covering every aspect of human life and condition, are ascribed to the cat . . . Here is a compendium to attract mere mortals . . . there is a magic about it overall, and what we would dearly love to be is magicians with supernatural powers. The cat would seem to have retained some of these occult faculties. Let us therefore be friends to them and friends to their friends.

—PAUL GALLICO, *Honorable Cat*

Cat Laughing
Last

1

THE MAN LAY FACEDOWN, BLEEDING INTO THE BRAIDED rug of Susan Brittain's breakfast room, the fallen keyboard of Susan's computer dangling from the edge of her desk and dripping blood onto his face. The sliding glass doors of the large, bright room stood open, admitting a damp, chill breeze. The white shutter doors of the floor-to-ceiling cupboards had been flung back, the contents of the shelves thrown to the floor, a jumble of office supplies, boxes of costume jewelry, and ceramic dishes. Susan's prized houseplants were crushed beneath broken ceramic planters and heaps of black potting soil; every surface was dusted with soil and with clinging black powder where a plastic bottle of copier toner had burst open, the inky haze charring a blood-splattered doll and crusting the lenses of Susan's good reflex camera.

One shoe print was incised in the toner powder but had been partially smeared away. The computer had been turned on, the program on the screen a list of eBay auction items showing photographs of each offering with its price. The time was 6:30 A.M. Susan had been gone from the house for half an hour. As the victim lay committing his blood to her hand-braided rug, across the village three seemingly unrelated events were taking place, three small dramas that might, at a future date, help construct a scenario of interest to Molena Point police—and to one gray tomcat and his tabby lady.

At the south side of the village, in the old mansion that housed Molena Point Little Theater, a young tortoiseshell cat prowled alone among the sets, her bright, inquisitive mind filled with wonderful questions. She was not hunting mice or snatching spiders from the cobwebs that hung in the far, high corners of the raftered ceiling. Her curiosity centered on the theater itself. She had watched the sets being built and painted, marveling at the green hills that looked so very like the real Molena Point hills over which she ranged each day. When she backed away from the sets, as the artist often did, the rolling slopes seemed nearly as huge and throbbing with light, the land running on forever along the edge of the Pacific. Only these hills didn't smell like green grass and earth, they smelled like paint. And no houses nestled among them, just scattered oaks, and wandering herds of longhorn cattle and deer and elk, from a time long past.

"Did Molena Point truly look like this?" she whispered to the empty theater. "All wild and without people? And such big animals everywhere? Were there no little cats then? And no rabbits or gophers to hunt?"

Every wonder that the kit had encountered in her short life had demanded vociferous response. She had to talk about each new event, if only to herself. She stood watching the hills, filled with questions, and she looked above her, too, at the ropes and props of the theater, at the catwalk where she liked to prowl, at the electrical buttons and cords that operated the various curtains, and at the overhead pulleys and lights, all complicated and wonderful. Muttering among ragged purrs, she sat admiring the set of the Spanish hacienda, with its deep windows and ornamental grills, and its broad patio with masses of roses blooming. The long, painted tables seemed very real standing about the patio with their white cloths and silver and crystal and vases of flowers, waiting for the wedding party—for a bride and groom

2

two hundred years dead. And the sadness of the love triangle sent a shiver through the kit, as if Marcos Romeros had just now been shot, this early dawn, as if at this moment he lay dying and betrayed.

The kit relished the stories that humans told—but especially she loved the ancient Celtic folklore that spoke of her own history. She had never seen any kind of play being made, she had never seen any story brought alive, onstage. This new kind of storytelling filled her with wonder almost greater than her small, tortoiseshell body could contain.

While the tattercoat kit dreamed alone in the empty theater, and the morning sky over Molena Point brightened to fog-streaked silver, the man who lay bleeding in Susan Brittain's breakfast room stirred. His fingers twitched, his hand moved. His eyes opened, his expression puzzled and then afraid.

And across the village in a handsome stone cottage, a phone rang. One ring, two. On the third bell the system switched to an answering tape, recording a long message from a New York literary agent. Ten minutes later the instrument rang again, and an equally terse and irritated communication was committed to the machine from a prestigious New York editor. No one emerged from the bedroom to check the messages, certainly not the handsome, silver-haired author, a man one would expect to stroll out garbed in an expensive silk dressing gown and hand-sewn slippers. But it was, after all, only 6:50, California time. A writer who worked into the small hours had no desire to rise with the sun.

Several blocks away, in the crowded front yard of the Roy McLeary residence, as villagers gathered for the McLeary yard sale, an altercation was about to erupt over a small and unprepossessing wooden box that lay half hidden among cast-off household accessories and scarred furniture. A clash of emotions that would amuse and surprise the dozens of early bargain hunters, and would sharply alert the two cats who lay draped over the branch of a huge oak at the edge of the yard, greatly entertained by the intense atmosphere of the early gathering.

Joe Grey and Dulcie, having come from a predawn hunt up on the open hills, had arrived before daylight prepared to enjoy the bargaining. Though most of Molena Point's yard sales started officially at 8:00 A.M., by 6:30 or 7:00 they were well under way, every shopper eager for the best buys.

Among the dark, prickly leaves, Joe's sleek silver gray coat blended so well that he was hardly visible. But one white-booted paw hung over the branch, and the white strip down his face and his white chest might be glimpsed among the dense foliage by an observant visitor. His yellow eyes gleamed, too, watching, highly intrigued by the human passion to possess another person's broken cast-offs. Beside him, Dulcie's green eyes were slitted with amusement. The tip of her dark tail twitched, and her dark brown stripes blended with the oak's shadows. Neither cat anticipated the trouble that was about to explode below them; neither was prepared, this morning, for the innocent gathering to turn violent.

And while the three events were yet to merge into an interesting scenario, six blocks to the west, out on the wide, sandy shore where the breakers rolled steadily like an endless heartbeat, Susan Brittain and her big black poodle turned to head home, following their own double trail of footprints back toward the village.

4

Susan's short, white hair was covered by a baseball cap, the collar of her faded jacket turned up against the sea wind. On Saturdays she walked Lamb very early so she could get to the yard sales, and could beat the other first arrivals who would snatch up all the best items. This morning she had left the house at 5:30, heading downhill from her apartment toward the heart of Molena Point, the village rooftops and oak trees massed below her, like black cutouts against the silver gleam of the sea. She had passed only a few cottages with their lights on, and then the shop windows softly illuminated—little lighted stages showing off bright jewelry and imported sweaters and fine china. Susan didn't need to urge Lamb along; knowing the Saturday routine, he leaned his strong ninety pounds on the leash as he did at no other time, looking back at her urging her to hurry. Heaven knew she moved as fast as she could, considering her seventy years; but not fast enough to suit Lamb.

There was nothing lamblike about the big dog. A standard poodle was not a cuddly playtoy. Her daughter had called him Lamb when he was six weeks old, a small bundle of fluff then, and the name had stuck. Now, Lamb's long aristocratic head and his muscular body beneath his short-clipped, tightly curled black coat showed clearly his power and dignity. Susan felt bad, sometimes, that he had never been taught the formal rituals of retrieving, of gathering in game birds, working with a human hunter on California's lakes and rivers, that he had never been allowed to develop the instinctive art that ran so powerfully in his blood. He was a companion dog, forced to trade his wild yearnings for home and fireside.

Around them as they headed home, the village was waking, cottage lights popping on behind curtained windows, the smell of freshly brewed coffee warming the damp sea air. She never tired of the village's diverse architecture, the small houses and shops an amazing and congenial mix of Bavarian, Swiss, Mexican adobe, California contemporary, Mediterranean, Victorian, all softened by the richly flowering gardens for which Molena Point was known, and by the dark and sprawling oaks and cypress trees that stood guard over the crowded rooftops. Somewhere ahead, a dog barked counterpoint to the sea's steady thunder. She'd had a lovely, quiet ramble with Lamb along the empty shore, looking away where sea and sky stretched forever, and she felt at peace. She had no clue that when she arrived home, her life would be precipitously altered.

Hurrying up Ocean between the shops, she saw only a few other dog walkers, saw none of her dog-owning friends; nor did she encounter the quiet New Yorker, Lenny Wells, and his sad-faced dalmatian. The young man was new to Molena Point; she had stopped with him for coffee several times, sitting at a sidewalk table, their two dogs lying quietly by their feet. She had suggested several congenial groups that Lenny might join, to get acquainted. He seemed so shy and uncertain; that was little enough that she could do to help him get settled. He was years her junior, quiet and respectful, very gentle with the young dog.

By the time Susan and Lamb reached home they had done two miles, a distance that Lamb considered trifling, little more than a warm-up. They were back at the house at 6:40, the sky cream and silver above them over the Molena Point hills. Starting in through the side door of the garage, Lamb growled and lunged through ahead of her, his ears back, his teeth gleaming as fierce as the fangs of an attacking wolf.

Alarmed, she pulled him back forcefully, shut the door, and moved away, speaking softly to Lamb. Someone was there, or had been—the big dog was not given to flights of fancy. Snatching up a sturdy, five-gallon plastic pot that had come from the nursery, she turned it over beneath the garage window and stood on it to peer in.

She no longer kept her car parked inside; it had sat out on the drive since she'd converted the double garage into a neat and efficient workroom for the storage and shipping of yard sale purchases. Looking in, she caught her breath.

The three big work tables had been overturned, and one of the legs broken. Shelves were ripped from the wall, cupboard doors torn off—and all the carefully cataloged treasures that she and her friends had purchased at countless yard and estate sales lay broken and scattered across the concrete.

Stepping down from the makeshift stool, feeling more angry than afraid, she retrieved the short-handled shovel from where she'd leaned it against the wall last evening when she'd finished planting some lavender bushes in the side yard. Holding the shovel like a battering ram, and speaking quietly to the growling poodle, she flung open the garage door.

2

"LIKE A COLONY OF PACK RATS," JOE GREY SAID. "Such an appetite for other people's possessions, it's enough to make a possum laugh." He turned to look at Dulcie. "Humans are as bad as you, when you steal the neighbors' silk undies."

7

If a cat could blush, Dulcie's furry face would be red. She didn't like him to laugh at her. But it was true, she'd been driven by a longing for cashmere and silk, for soft, pretty garments, since she was a kitten. Such a keen desire that she would slip out of the house in the small hours, and into her neighbors' homes, pressing in through a partially open window or swinging on the knob of a back door left unlocked. Slipping toward the bedroom, she would depart moments later dragging a silk teddy in her teeth or a sheer stocking or a bright, soft sweater, taking each lovely item home to roll on, to sleep on, to rub her face against. And how else was she to have the lovely garments that she so coveted, except to borrow them? She was a cat. She couldn't indulge in shopping sprees at Lord & Taylor's or I. Magnin's. She only wanted to enjoy those treasures for a little while before the neighbors came to retrieve them. Well, she *had* kept Wilma's good watch for over a year, hidden under the claw-footed bathtub.

As the sun rose beyond the cats' leafy treetop, the crowded roofs of Molena Point caught gleams and flashes of light. Shingled roofs and red tile, sharp peaks and slanted were soon all aglow. The time was not yet 7:00. In the distance a dog barked, an insistent staccato against the soft pounding of the sea. The morning air smelled of pine, and iodine, and of multitudes of small, dead shell-creatures. Out over the Pacific, dawn was reflected from the sea like burnished metal. But beyond lay black rain clouds—they might blow away north toward San Francisco or might creep in over the village and rain on the McLearys' sale.

Slow-moving traffic filled the narrow street as new arrivals tried to find parking places, so many eager shoppers that the lane was choked with vehicles. And the lawn was crowded with folks wandering among borrowed church tables piled with toys and clothes and baby garments, with bent silverware, outdated golf clubs, tarnished jewelry, with dented cookpots and old handbags and faded Christmas decorations. Between the tables stood scarred dressers, beds, breakfast tables, and toy chests.

Watching folks argue over prices or haul away chairs and tables and broken toys, jamming their newly acquired treasures into cars and SUVs and pickups, watching all the little dramas, Joe and Dulcie, replete with a breakfast of wharf rat and young rabbit, were of much of the same frame of mind as a human couple who, after a satisfying supper, had settled down in a front row at the theater to be entertained.

"The McLearys must have cleaned out not only their own attic," Dulcie said, "but the houses of all their cousins and uncles." Indeed, the Molena Point McLearys were a large clan. "An anthropological treasure trove, an artifactual record of four generations of McLeary family history."

"Four generations of bad taste. A microcosm of useless human consumerism."

She stared at him.

He shrugged his sleek gray shoulders. "Look around you. Abandoned projects, thrown-away intentions, broken dreams, soured ambitions. Relics of human disenchantment."

Easing his position on the branch, he looked at her with tomcat superiority. "You don't see a cat going off on a dozen projects—golf, snooker, Chinese checkers, paint by numbers, needlework, photograph albums. You don't see a cat tossing away one craze after another. Look at the wasted time and effort, to say nothing of the wasted money. And then they have to get rid of it all. And their neighbors grab and snatch, until their own closets are bulging."

"You're in an ugly mood. What happened to live-and-let-live?"

Joe Grey shrugged.

"What you see down there," she told him, "is a lifetime of magnificent intentions. An incredible richness of human endeavor and imagination. You're looking at dreams down there—at the products of creative human energy. At happy, vital, and endlessly diverse moments in McLeary family history."

Joe Grey snorted, his ears and whiskers back in a derisive cat laugh.

She widened her green eyes, but kept her voice low. "I've never seen you so sour. Are things not good at home? What, Clyde's messed-up love life is making you cross? Or," she said, "is Clyde still thinking of selling the house? Is that whats eating you?"

"My mood has nothing to do with the house, or with Clyde's love life. I am not driven by Clyde Damen's vicissitudes. I am simply making an observation about the confusion of the human mind. You don't see a cat throwing out the living-room furniture every year and buying all new stuff. Look around you. Why would—"

"Cats don't have living-room furniture."

"I have an easy chair." His tone was so pompous that they both laughed. Joe's upholstered chair, which sat in the Damen living room by the front window, was so ragged and faded it resembled nothing as much as the hide of an ancient and molting pachyderm. "You don't see me tossing my good chair away at some yard sale."

"If that chair's a prototype of the quality of your life, that clawed-to-rags, fur-matted, stained and smelly horror, then you, my dear tomcat, are in trouble."

Joe nudged her playfully; but soon they peered down again, fascinated by the bargain hunters. The locals were dressed in jeans and sweatshirts, some folks freshly scrubbed, some still uncombed as if they'd just rolled out of bed. The conviviality of neighbors brightened the morning with friendly talk and wisecracks. Here and there a weekender wandered, just as eager for a bargain, a tourist dressed in brand-name shorts, starched shirt, and Gucci sandals, or golf or tennis attire. Some shoppers carried nonspill coffee mugs that they had brought from their cars. Two were munching on breakfast rolls, wrapped in squares of waxed paper, that they'd picked up at one of the bakeries on the way over. At events such as this, one saw a true cross-section of the village. Besides the rich and comfortable, and the famous, who "did" the yard sales for a lark, one saw clearly the Molena Point residents who lived on limited funds, people trying to stretch every dollar. The inveterate bargain hunters, rich or poor, showed up at every such event. The cats watched a portly, bleached blond lady in walking shorts, a blue sweatshirt, and red tennis shoes try to fit a six-foot wicker bookcase into a small Jaguar sports car. She had wrapped the bookcase carefully in blankets—whether to protect her ten-dollar bargain or protect the hundred-thousand-dollar jag wasn't clear.

Nearer to the cats' oak tree, two women stood arguing over a glass-topped patio table that both claimed to have spoken for first. And directly below, a huge-bellied man, stripped to the waist, carried a ruffled, flowered chaise lounge over his head, in the direction of a battered pickup truck. The cats watched a tiny little old lady precariously juggle a glass punch bowl of such proportions that she could have used it for a sitz bath. Maybe that was her plan. Fill it with champagne, and voilá, just like the old Harlow movies. The sight of her prompted Dulcie to quote to herself, *When I am old, I will wear purple, and bathe in French champagne.* She caught her breath when the lady nearly dropped her gleaming treasure, and before she thought, Dulcie reached down a paw as if to offer assistance— but drew back quickly, glancing at Joe with embarrassment.

No one looked up to wonder what that cat was doing. No one had seen the two cats in the tree or, if they had seen them, no one would imagine their conversation, or dream of the thoughts churning through those sleek feline heads. Their human neighbors would never imagine that cats might discuss human frailties—though they might allow that cats didn't give a damn about human foolishness.

Of the residents of Molena Point, only four people knew that Joe Grey and Dulcie could speak, that the two cats read the *Molena Point Gazette* far more perceptively than some human subscribers, that they liked to frequent the village news racks perusing the front page of the *San Francisco Examiner*, and that when there was nothing more interesting at hand, they watched prime-time TV. Only four people knew that Joe Grey and Dulcie were not your ordinary, everyday kitties or that they had, during various criminal investigations by Molena Point PD, not only pointed a paw at their share of killers and thieves, supplying critical evidence to convict the miscreants, but that they had spied as well on any number of villagers, in the comfort of the villagers' own homes. No one knew that, posing as stray kitties, the two were adept at passing on sensitive information to police detectives. Not even Max Harper's own cops, nor Captain Harper himself, knew the identity of their best informants; Joe Grey and Dulcie were far too smooth to blow their own cover.

But the two cats had other human friends besides the four who shared their secrets. Peering down, they watched three of their favorite senior ladies making their yard sale selections with careful judgment—and with huge dreams. These three women weren't shopping for fun, they were searching out purchases to secure their own futures.

Mavity Flowers, small and sturdy in her threadbare maid's uniform, perused a display of china and crystal about which, through necessity, she had come to know quite a lot. Cora Lee French, a head taller than Mavity, a lovely, slim Creole woman with graying hair, slipped lithely among tables of needlework and linens, touching the stitching with gentle, experienced hands. And tall, blond Gabrielle Row checked over the clothes that hung on long metal racks, looking not only for resalable bargains, but for anything useful to the little theater costume department.

Gabrielle was still elegant, despite her sixty-some years. Her short-clipped gray hair was skillfully colored to ash blond, and the cut of her cream blazer was long and lean over her white slacks. Working full-time as seamstress in her own shop, she had for many years been wardrobe director as well for Molena Point Little Theater. And now, frequenting the yard sales, she was not only hunting for costume material but was planning, too, for a time when she would be less active.

Five ladies made up the Senior Survival Club: Mavity, Cora Lee, and Gabrielle. And Susan Brittain, who was not to be seen this morning, though Susan hardly ever missed a sale. Susan's garage was headquarters for wrapping and shipping the items the ladies sold on the Web. She handled, on her computer, all their eBay sales. The fifth member was Wilma Getz, Dulcie's housemate, retired parole officer, gray haired, in her late fifties. Wilma might be called a silent partner, agreeing with the women's plan, meaning to take part at some future time, but not totally committed.

The ladies were looking toward buying a communal dwelling that would accommodate them all plus a housekeeper and a caregiver when that time arrived. All of them had some savings, or home equity. And the cats were amazed at how much money they had set aside by hitting the yard sales and selling at auction. So far, it amounted to over ten thousand dollars.

Senior Survival's plan for mutual security and comfort, in a world of dwindling incomes, increasing taxes, and the possibility of deteriorating health, seemed to Dulcie infinitely courageous, a bold alternative to the ladies' separate interments in retirement or convalescent homes—a plan of mutual cooperation but individual responsibility. These ladies didn't like conventional institutions.

Slowly the sun slid higher above the hills, slashing through the oak leaves into the cats' faces, making them slit their eyes. Joe's white paws and chest, and the white triangle down his nose, gleamed like snow against his smooth gray fur. As Dulcie backed along the branch, her dark stripes cloaked in shadow, she resembled a small, dark tiger. Only her green eyes caught the light. A breeze fingered into the tree, to rattle the leaves, a chill breath that, by its scent and direction, promised not rain as the marine clouds implied, but a warm day to come. Perhaps only a cat would be aware of the message—how sad that humans, trying to assess the weather, had to read barometers and listen to the questionable advice of some book-educated meteorologist hamming his way through the morning news. Such dependence left one open to innumerable misjudgments in attire—to getting one's head and feet wet; while all a cat had to do was taste the wind and feel in every fiber of his body the changes in barometric pressure.

The sun was returning to stay, no doubt of that. No more tearing March storms with winds wild enough to jerk a cat right out of his own pawprints. Spring was settling in at last, the acacia trees exploding with brilliant yellow blooms that smelled like honey. All the early flowers were opening. Village cats rolled with abandon in the gardens, and the outdoor cafés were filled with locals and tourists—a perfect spring, in the loveliest of villages. Who needed to travel the shores of Britain and France, Dulcie thought, or trek through Spain and Africa? Molena Point was so beautiful this morning that Dulcie's purrs hummed through the branches like bumblebees.

But suddenly an unease touched the cats, a foreboding that made Dulcie stiffen and sent a chill twitching down Joe Grey's spine as sharp as an electric shock.

They studied the crowd below, puzzled and alarmed, their ears flicking forward and back, every nerve on alert, as they tried to figure out what had alarmed them. They were crouched on the branch, wary and keenly predatory, when sirens sounded: a police car leaving the station, they could see beyond the treetops its red whirling beacon heading away through the village, in the same direction where, a quarter hour earlier, an ambulance had departed.

An ambulance, alone, was not uncommon. It could mean severe illness, a heart attack, the agony of a broken hip. A squad car alone could mean anything—a strayed child, a driver ramming into a tree. But the two vehicles together, the law and the medics, were inclined to mean trouble.

The cats had crouched to leap away across the roofs to have a look when Joe saw, in the street below, the source of their sudden unease. A growl rose in his throat as a petite young woman stepped out of her black Lincoln. The cats watched Vivi Traynor cross to the McLeary yard, trampling through a flower bed, shoving a child aside as she hurried to the sale tables. She was small and curvy, her black tights, plaid miniskirt, and black sweater clinging, her black hair teased into a bird's nest around her thin face, and held back with a red bow. As she rifled through assemblages of household cast-offs, the village locals, who had not yet seen the author's wife at a yard sale, watched her with interest. A portly tourist whipped out a scrap of paper as if to ask for Vivi's autograph. Did the wife of an internationally famous novelist rate the status of autographs? Certainly Vivi always attracted attention. The couple had been in town barely three weeks, Elliott Traynor having come to oversee a little theater production of his only play, an experimental form that the *Gazette* called innovative and exciting.

Word had it that Elliott was fighting cancer, that this theatrical production was a project he longed to enjoy while he was still able. The play was set in this area of the California coast where Molena Point now stood, and the musical score had been written by a well-known composer who made his home in the village. The cats watched Vivi wander the garden intently searching—for

16

what? Perhaps looking for some stage prop? Slipping between a stack of used windows and a flowered couch, she performed a theatrical little hip wiggle to ease past a rusty barbecue, then giggled shrilly as she shouldered aside a portly lady tourist. The sight of her made Joe's fur twitch.

Since their arrival, Elliott Traynor had kept largely to himself as he finished the last chapters of *Twilight Silver*, the third novel in his historical trilogy. But Vivi had made herself known around the village, and not pleasantly—as if she enjoyed being rude to shopkeepers, as if she took pleasure in being abrupt and demanding.

The Traynors had not wanted a staff for the cottage they were renting, but had hired the cleaning service provided by Wilma Getz's redheaded niece, Charlie. Charlie tended the Traynor house herself, early each morning, then left the couple to their privacy.

Molena Point's residents, numbering so many writers and artists, were not put off by Elliott's reclusive ways. They talked among themselves about his books and about the play, waved when occasionally they saw him on the streets or in the black Lincoln, as they headed to the theater; otherwise they left him to his own devices. The presence, alone, of the prestigious writer, seemed adequate enrichment to their well-appointed lives.

But no one had warmed to Vivi.

Traynor's previous wife had died three years before. Six months later, he married Vivi, a woman forty years his junior. Besides her loud, rude ways, something else about her made the cats want to back away, hissing, a chill that perhaps only a cat would sense. Whatever reason she had for appearing this morning in the McLeary garden could only, in Joe Grey's opinion, mean trouble.

17

3

THE LIGHT IN SUSAN BRITTAIN'S GARAGE WAS DIM. Standing in the doorway, again peering into the gloom, the first rays of sun striking in past her shoulder, she searched the shadows among the overturned shelves and tables, looking for someone perhaps still crouched there among the ripped-off cupboard doors and scattered empty shipping boxes. An unwound roll of bubble wrap lay twisted across the fallen shelf units like the cast-off skin of a giant snake. Susan could see no one standing silently, waiting for her to enter. Had the vandal been after something he imagined was secured behind the cabinets? Why else would he rip them from the wall? What could he imagine she had, of enough value for him to go to all that trouble? Her instinct was to run, to get away from the house, to call the police from her neighbor's.

Was the vandal in the house somewhere? Had he broken into her home as well?

The door from the garage to the breakfast room was closed. She couldn't see whether it had been tampered with, but when she headed further inside to try the lock, Lamb lunged into her path again, snapping at her leg and growling. She backed out of the garage, her hand on his head, grateful for his protection.

She didn't want to go around to the patio entry. If someone was inside, she would be easily seen through the glass doors of the breakfast room before she could reach the front door.

Carrying the oversized plastic nursery pot from the side of the house, she stood on it again, to peer through the high windows into her bright breakfast room.

The cupboard doors stood open, their contents pulled out in a mess on the floor among the overturned dinette chairs, her watercolors jerked from their hooks, and the glass broken, her expensive ceramic pots thrown to the floor, spilling their delicate plants in heaps of black soil. Her heart was pounding so hard she felt faint. Both anger and panic blurred her vision—and fear.

A man lay sprawled beside her desk, facedown and unmoving, his blood mixed with spilled copier toner, the toner floating on top the viscous red pools like scum on a stagnant pond. She couldn't see his face. What had he wanted? What had happened to him? She owned nothing of great value. Was this simply vandalism, senseless and cruel? Not a burglary at all, but someone mindlessly stoned and intent on destruction, who ended up harming himself?

Whatever had happened, she felt totally violated, felt far more wounded than she'd ever envisioned when she'd heard about others' break-ins. Reading those accounts, she'd tried to imagine how one would react, but she hadn't had a clue.

She wondered, sickly, if he had trashed the whole house. Maybe he'd already made off with her TV and CD player, maybe with the few pieces of gold jewelry she kept in the top drawer of her dressing table, then had returned to see what else he could find. Had someone else been here, and hit him? He was very still, though from the way the blood and toner were smeared, it looked as if he had moved, maybe tried to roll over.

This was the stuff of some lurid movie. She needed the police, she needed someone. Her pride in her independence didn't stretch this far.

Beside her, Lamb looked up at her with solemn, dark

19

eyes, alert and questioning. Reaching down to stroke him, she tried to reassure herself, to take herself in hand.

Why had the burglar turned on her computer? Its light shone faintly across the man's body, reflected from the eBay auction lists.

And *was* there another vandal? Was he out here in the yard somewhere, watching her? Looking in both directions along the side of the house, she knew she should get away.

None of this made sense. Could that man in there be lying so still to deceive her, wanting to lure her inside and grab her? Someone who would hurt her simply for kicks? Lamb continued to watch the window, the gleam in his dark eyes hard and alert like a snake ready to strike.

Certainly, with Lamb by her side, she would be safe going in. If she went inside, she could see better what had happened, could see if the man was dead, then call 911.

Oh yes, she could do that. And maybe she should take his pulse, she thought, disgusted with herself.

Hands shaking, she stepped down off the plastic planter and backed away. Pulling Lamb's leash tight, she slipped around to the drive where her car was parked. Unlocking the door, she signaled Lamb to get in. Following him, she locked the door again and used her cell phone, which she kept plugged into the dash, to call 911, her voice shaking so badly she could hardly make herself understood. That surprised her, that she would lose control. She managed to tell the dispatcher there was a man lying wounded in her house, bleeding and possibly dead, that there must have been two men. After she hung up, she wondered if she should back out of the drive, get away from there, even if the car was locked.

But it wouldn't be long. She would wait in the drive until the police came.

They arrived within five minutes, a patrol officer— one of two new rookies, she thought. And the new detective from San Francisco, Detective Dallas Garza. She was aware of Garza from her friend Wilma, who knew most of the officers in the Molena Point PD. She wished that Captain Harper himself had come. The captain had a terse but comforting way about him. During all that trouble up at the retirement home last year, when she'd been staying there recovering from her car accident, and those people were killed up there, Harper's laid-back, quiet resolve had made everyone feel easier, had kept the elderly residents from panicking. But the department was growing, and Harper didn't go out on many calls anymore.

Detective Garza was a squarely built, solid man in his late forties, dressed in slacks and a sport coat, his short black hair neatly trimmed, his black Latin eyes unreadable. The uniformed officer with him was young, with dimples and a cleft chin. Susan gave Dallas Garza her house key, and remained in her car with the doors locked, as he instructed, while they cleared the house. Garza had told her to be ready to drive away if anyone came out or if she felt threatened.

He was in there a very long time. Through her slightly open driver's window, she heard the glass door of the breakfast room slide back, as if they had gone out that way and were looking over the patio. Then she heard the back patio gate creak open. Beside her, Lamb listened, following every sound.

Maybe ten minutes later she heard the gate shut again. She sat in the car feeling useless and uncharacteristically frightened. She didn't approve of such fear in herself; she wondered sometimes if this Senior Survival plan was simply a sign of weakness—a gaggle of old ladies who felt they couldn't cope with life alone? Looking over at Lamb, she was mighty thankful to have him. The big poodle, sitting erect in the passenger seat, watched the house as intently as if he could see through the walls. Another police car arrived, parking on the street. Garza came out of the house to confer with the officer, then walked over to her car, looking down at her as she rolled down her window.

"There's no one in there, Mrs. Brittain."

"That's a relief. Is the man dead?"

"There's no one in the breakfast room. There's no body." Garza looked at her carefully. "There's a lot of blood. Detective Davis is on the way. She'll photograph, take samples, and lift prints. Do you want to tell me again what you saw?"

Her hands began to shake. She couldn't believe what he told her. Reaching to Lamb, she clutched her fingers into his short dense curls.

"You couldn't have mistaken what you saw? Saw the blood, perhaps, and imagined . . . ?"

"Of course not! Are you sure there was no one? You're saying that man got up and walked away?"

"There was no one in the breakfast room. The glass door was unlocked and ajar. Did you leave it that way?"

"I left it locked. I would have heard it open. I looked in the window, standing on that plastic pot, and he was there. I came right to the car, locked myself in, and called you. Well, I guess he could have opened it then, when I was calling, and I wouldn't have heard. But he was so still, and so much blood . . ."

"Could you describe again exactly what you saw?"

"A man. He looked dead. Lying on his stomach. Denim shirt and jeans. Lying in blood. His own blood, I supposed. Spilled printer toner mixed with blood, floating on top. Blood running into the spilled potting soil. He . . . the man was turned away, I couldn't see his face. He had short brown hair, and he was thin." She closed her eyes, trying to bring back the scene, then looked up at Garza. "I think he was young. Smooth neck, smooth hands."

"Was he wearing rings or a watch?"

She closed her eyed again, but she couldn't remember. Just kept seeing the blood.

"Did you notice anything else? His shoes? What kind of shoes?"

Again she tried to bring back the scene. "Blood and potting soil, or toner, on his shoes. They must have been jogging shoes. Yes, white. Blood and toner staining the white."

Garza nodded. "There was a blood trail out the glass door and across the patio. But no one in the house. Your keyboard is filled with blood and could have prints. May we take it as evidence?"

"I have another, I just recently bought that curved one—to help prevent wrist problems, you know."

Garza nodded. "And you're all right waiting here while we finish the initial investigation?"

"I'm fine." But, *I'm hungry*, she thought. *I want my coffee.*

She could go to the neighbors, beg a cup of coffee. But she didn't want to talk to anyone, didn't want to answer questions. And she didn't want to ask to go in the house while they were taking evidence. They wouldn't want her there getting in the way, maybe destroying something they felt was important.

As Garza turned away, a plain green Chevy pulled up the drive, parking beside Susan's car. Detective Juana Davis got out, a squarely built Latina woman in her mid-thirties with short black hair. She smiled and waved to Susan, and went inside with Garza. Susan sat in her car thinking about having to clean up that mess, and about this loss to the Senior Survival club fund. They'd had no one item of value, but many small treasures that altogether would have brought a nice sum on the Web— now all shattered and destroyed. And she thought about the five members of the Senior Survival club buying a house together, wondered if five women living together might be more secure, maybe take better precautions— or if five lone women in a house would be sitting ducks for anyone who wanted to harm them.

I'm getting paranoid, this is crazy, this is not the way I look at life. She stroked Lamb and looked into his eyes, and saw such steadfast courage that she was ashamed of her own cowardice.

It was half an hour later that Davis came out to tell Susan that the trail of blood led across her backyard, across her neighbors' side yard, and disappeared at the curb of the street below her house.

"The victim may have gotten into a car. Do you remember a car parked down there?" Davis pushed back her short hair. She was in uniform, though usually the detectives dressed in civilian clothes.

"I didn't come home along the lower street," Susan said. "I came up the other way, directly from the village. Walking. I'd been walking Lamb, on the beach."

Davis nodded. Her dark Latin eyes warmed to Susan, and she reached to pat her arm. "You'll continue to wait until Detective Garza can talk with you again? Are you comfortable?"

"Of course," Susan said, badly wanting her coffee.

The detectives spent nearly two hours going over the scene, photographing, dusting for prints, taking blood samples from several locations, and taking Susan's own fingerprints for comparison. After about an hour, Davis asked her if she wanted to come in and make coffee.

As she sipped that first, welcome cup, Detective Garza sat with her in her living room, refusing coffee, asking endless questions. She allowed him to examine her hands and arms for any cuts or scrapes or bruises. She tried not to let that ruffle her. This was part of his job, to be sure she hadn't been involved, that she wasn't holding back information.

"Who knows your routine, Mrs. Brittain? Who would know that you are in the habit of walking early in the morning?"

"All my neighbors know that. And my women friends. Wilma Getz . . . Shall I give you a list?"

"Yes, with addresses and phone numbers, if you would. Anyone else?"

"Other dog walkers would know. Anyone used to seeing me and Lamb in the village or on the beach. This is a small town, Detective Garza. Everyone knows your business." Garza had only been in the village a few months; but surely even working in San Francisco, he'd be aware that some of the neighborhoods were like a small town, where everyone knew everyone else. And Garza knew the village, he had vacationed here for years.

"When can I begin to clean up?" she asked. "Do I have to leave that mess?"

"For a while you do. We'll be putting up crime scene tape, we'll want everything left untouched until we notify you. Can you stay with a friend for a few nights?

25

Stay out of the house until we're finished?"

"I'll call Wilma. I'm supposed to meet her and some friends for brunch, but I . . ."

"It might help to have friends around you. And please don't leave your dog here, for his own safety."

"No, I wouldn't leave Lamb. He'll go with me."

"He's a fine, dignified fellow. Does he hunt?"

"No. My daughter never trained him. She got him for companionship. She's working in San Francisco now, so I inherited Lamb. Do you have dogs?"

"I used to raise pointers. I have two that I'll be bringing down later, when I get the backyard fixed up for them." He smiled. "Go on to brunch, Mrs. Brittain— you and Lamb. I'll wait while you pack an overnight bag."

She gave Detective Garza her spare house key that she kept in her dresser, and packed a bag while he waited. His presence in the house was reassuring. Before she left, they checked the doors and windows together. As she drove away, she saw Detective Davis canvassing the neighborhood to see who might have been at home, who might have heard or seen anything unusual. The disappearance of the body—of the wounded man—distressed her. She didn't like the idea that he might return.

But, comforted by the officers' thoroughness, she began to feel easier. She was not a flighty woman, she was not going to get hysterical over this. After the wreck that had left her so crippled, which had taken a year to recover from, she had been able to keep herself together. So why go to pieces over something so much smaller? All the time she was in the wheelchair she had not lost her nerve or resolve—at least, not very often. She told herself that this break-in, this ugly invasion of her privacy, was nothing compared to that nightmare. Yet she couldn't shake the sense of being totally violated.

She supposed everyone felt this way when such a thing happened, felt incredibly angry at their own helplessness. If she could get her hands on either of those men, even the hurt one, and if she was strong enough, she wouldn't answer for what she might do.

Parking a block from the Swiss Café, she smoothed her short hair and put on some lipstick. Detective Garza was right, she needed her friends. Clipping on Lamb's leash, she let him out of the car and headed for brunch, praying that she wouldn't end up crying in her pancakes, making a fool of herself.

4

WHEN THE AMBULANCE SCREAMED AGAIN THROUGH the village, Mavity Flowers jumped, startled, dropping the handful of old beaded evening bags she'd been sorting through. That violent noise tore right through a person. She never got used to it, not since the ambulance came when her husband died, when Lou was taken away.

Pushing back her kinky gray hair, she knelt to pick up the little old purses, clutching them against her white uniform. Rising, she laid them out across the cluttered table atop a mess of other bargains so she could choose the best ones. You'd think she'd be used to sirens at her age, and with so many older folk in the village. The ambulance went out often, even if only for some poor soul who had taken a bad fall—went out more frequently than she liked to think about. She felt uneasy

27

suddenly, thinking about her Senior Survival friends. But Cora Lee and Gabrielle were right there at the sale. Wilma never came to these events—but Wilma was healthy as a horse, working out twice a week and walking every day.

She hadn't seen Susan, and that was strange. Susan got up so early, she was always among the first, eager to get the best buys. Looking around for her, Mavity wanted to use the McLearys' phone, see if she was all right.

But that was foolish, that was the kind of fussing that would deeply annoy Susan. She was too independent to tolerate her friends' checking on her for no sensible reason.

Mavity knelt to pick up the purses, selecting the nicest ones, and looking to see if any beads were missing. She hoped that when her time came to depart this world, there would he no need for sirens. That she'd go fast, that she wouldn't have some terrible, debilitating stroke to leave her lingering. It terrified her to think of growing weak and helpless, of being unable to care for herself.

Even though she was getting up in years, she felt young inside, and she kept herself in good shape, cleaning houses all day. She could still walk a mile into the village, buy her groceries, and carry them home again, and not be breathing hard when she plunked the bags down on the kitchen table. Still wore a size 4, even if all she bought was white uniforms in the used-clothing shops. Only when she looked in the mirror at her wrinkles and crow's-feet did she see the truth about her age.

She had no children to look out for her if she got sick. Now that her niece was dead, she had only her brother

Greeley, and what good was he? Older than she was, and he'd be all thumbs, trying to care for a person. Irresponsible, too. Living down there in Panama like some foreigner. The last time he flew up to see her, look at the trouble they'd had, him stealing, right there under her nose, robbing from the village stores.

No, she couldn't depend on Greeley. When her time came, she prayed for one massive stroke. Zip. Gone—to whatever lay beyond.

Maybe she'd see Lou again, maybe not. Two old folks wandering hand in hand again. Or maybe they'd be young again. No aches and pains. Wouldn't that be nice.

She hadn't been to church for years, didn't remember how a priest described Heaven. Well, if there wasn't any Heaven, if there was nothing after this life, she wouldn't know it, would she? Might as well think like there was, and enjoy the promise.

Anyway, now she wouldn't be alone if she got decrepit, now she had a new kind of family to depend on, and to depend on her.

She'd balked at first at the idea of the Senior Survival club; it had seemed silly, and she'd never been a joiner. But maybe it would work. They were committed now, the five of them set on making their lives easier by their own efforts, not depending on some agency that they had no control over. Susan said they were reinventing their futures. Well, they weren't planning on nothing fancy, no grand cruises or flights to Europe. Just a way to grow old with more security, by helping each other, using the money they were making right now as they picked over the McLearys' cast-off junk, plus the money they'd all make selling their houses.

Mavity had to smile. This all sounded like a

confidence scheme. Except there was no outsider to rip them off. It had been their own idea, the five of them, all friends for years. Four of them widowed, and Wilma divorced, all alone now and tossing out ideas for their futures. She paused a moment, looking across the garden at her friends, at Gabrielle, and at Cora Lee. And for a moment, she couldn't help it; she felt a nudge of envy.

"Mavity's daydreaming again," Dulcie said. Wool-gathering." She watched Mavity, who was watching Gabrielle and Cora Lee, and she could almost guess what Mavity was thinking—a little of Mavity's indulgent daydreaming.

Across the McLeary garden, Gabrielle was inspecting a tableful of silverware, her tall slim figure handsome in her pale blazer, her short, soft blond hair catching the sunlight. Beyond her, Cora Lee French sorted through some boxes of books, her café-au-lait coloring and long white sundress making her look about seventeen, despite the salt and pepper in her black hair.

"What are you grinning about?" Joe asked, cutting her a look.

"About Mavity—at what she's thinking."

"What? You're psychic suddenly?"

"She's thinking, *In my next life, I'll be tall and willowy like Gabrielle and Cora Lee.*"

"Come on, Dulcie . . ."

"She is. I've heard her say it often enough, rambling on while she's helping Charlie clean someone's house. It's Mavity's one discontent, that she isn't tall. *If I was born again tall and slim and beautiful, and with a little cash, I'd know I was in heaven.*"

"You're making fun of her."

"Not at all. I love Mavity," Dulcie said, her green eyes widening, her tail lashing. "But that is what she's thinking. And probably thinking, too, *Well you can't have everything . . .* And maybe, *I'm healthy and independent. I can outwork most women half my age.*" And the cats looked down fondly on little Mavity Flowers, hoping she'd be tall in the next life, the way she wanted to be.

They watched her select a pearl-beaded bag and tuck it with five other evening bags into her two-wheeled, wire mesh cart, laying half a dozen hand-embroidered hankies on top so they wouldn't wrinkle. All would bring a nice profit on eBay. Amazing, the things people would buy on the Web. They'd listened to the ladies tell how they'd cleaned out their own mother's attics years before, and sent to charity items they wished they had back. Old Sandwich glass, Dulcie remembered, that Gabrielle had once thought was so tacky. And the old brass binoculars that Wilma said would now bring eighty or ninety dollars.

Water under the bridge, Mavity would say, and that made Dulcie purr. *What's gone is gone.* She could just hear her. *Look at what's right here under your nose, don't be crying for what's lost, that you can't bring back.*

"You *are* making fun of her," Joe said. "You're smirking like the Cheshire cat."

"I'm not. Anyway, Mavity doesn't care what anyone thinks—she wouldn't care what a cat thinks. Look, she's going to buy those used uniforms, too, like she always does."

Joe didn't reply. He was watching an old man try out a set of golf clubs. Old guy had a real hook. He ought to take up checkers.

Dulcie smiled as Mavity held a white uniform against herself for size. Mavity bought the generic uniforms that would do for any trade, beautician, waitress, or her own job of housecleaning. The little, spry woman was proud of her work. Her square, blunt hands were rough from scrubbing, but gentle when they petted a cat. Her face was brown and lined from the California sun and from the sea wind that blew down the bay into her small house when she left the windows open. *Fishing shack*, Mavity would say, *if the truth be told.*

But now Mavity's house was called a bayside cottage, and worth half a million. Mavity said that she and Lou had paid thirty thousand for it, forty years ago when they were first married. Just a little house on stilts, at the muddy edge where the marsh met Molena Point Bay. Amazing, everyone said, what had happened to the Molena Point economy—to the whole country's economy. Mavity was, through no effort of her own, a well-to-do property owner.

Except that soon the house wouldn't be hers. The home she'd kept dear since her husband died was, the ladies said, about to be gobbled up in the all-powerful sweep of village politics. About to be condemned, as was the whole row of bayside houses.

"Well, Mavity has a good job," Dulcie said. Working for Charlie's Fix-It, Clean-It, she couldn't have a better boss. Tall, redheaded Charlie Getz was such a no-nonsense person. And now since Charlie had bought that old rundown duplex, she and Mavity were working on it, painting and sanding the floors. Mavity liked working in an empty place more than she liked cleaning while someone was in the house. She always said she didn't like anyone looking over her shoulder, and Dulcie understood that.

Vivi Traynor was still picking and poking, now among some stacked boxes. When Charlie cleaned for them, she'd told Wilma, she had to be really quiet. She said Elliott was the temperamental kind of writer, couldn't stand noise. She said less complimentary things about Vivi. One thing was sure, Vivi Traynor was young enough to be the novelist's granddaughter.

Snippy, too, Dulcie thought. *With a giggle like a freight train whistle.* And Dulcie had seen Vivi flirting with the village men. Though if her famous husband was too busy with his writing to care, why should anyone else? He stayed at home in the afternoons and in the evening, shut up in his study, but most mornings when Charlie did up the place, the Traynors were at the little theater.

Vivi, having apparently found no treasure worth purchasing, rose from the clutter of boxes. She stood glancing around her, jingling her car keys and jangling those bangle bracelets she always wore, then she moved on again, looking, slipping among stacks of broken toys and used clothing. Dulcie watched her lift a folded bedspread to see what was underneath, then rifle through a stack of suitcases, shifting the dusty valises and opening them. She was very focused, as if she were looking for something special. As she pried and prodded, never stopping to admire any item, her face was frozen with distaste—maybe she couldn't bear dirt or the smell of old things; but her black eyes darted everywhere, looking. And across the yard, Gabrielle had stopped collecting sale items, and stood very still, watching Vivi.

Strange that Gabrielle hadn't greeted Vivi, that the two women hadn't acknowledged the other. But Gabrielle was like that, she wouldn't press their brief acquaintance. Despite her look of smooth sophistication, Gabrielle was shy and reserved—she had met the Traynors during a trip she'd made last fall to New York, one of those senior tours. She had gone to school with Elliott's sister, and had called them, then stopped by their apartment to extend her condolences for the sister's death, a year earlier.

Gabrielle stood frowning uneasily toward Vivi, as if puzzled or, Dulcie thought, almost uncomfortable because Vivi was there. But when Vivi glanced up, Gabrielle turned quickly away.

And here came Richard Casselrod, getting out of his Mercedes SUV. Casselrod always seemed a bit seedy, his tweed sport coat worn and wrinkled, his black hair mussed. His pockmarked complexion made him look like a street bum—yet he did keep an elegant shop, two floors of lovely antique furniture and accessories. Wilma had bought several nice pieces from him, including her cherry desk where Dulcie liked to sit in the sunshine, looking out the front window. Strange, in Casselrod's sour face, how his black eyes were always smiling—as if he loved everyone he met.

He showed up at all the yard sales and estate sales. The ladies of the Senior Survival club said he was always buying, and that they'd see him in the consignment shops, too, and the charity stores when they were looking for things Susan could sell on eBay. They said Casselrod had no compunction about elbowing a person out of the way to snatch up some nice bargain before you could get at it.

No compunction either about selling the stuff he bought in his fancy antiques store, Gabrielle said. She said he would buy stuff from his neighbors and from the charity shops, put it in his show window, and double the price for the tourists. The locals held out for better prices; they knew how to bargain with him. And now, Susan said, he was selling his purchases on the Web as well.

But the Senior Survival ladies were selling in the same way—only theirs was for a better cause. And after all, if that was the way Richard Casselrod wanted to make his living, it was no one's business. No one had to patronize his store. All three senior ladies watched him as he moved along the tables examining each item, collecting a few nice things that, very likely, they wished they had grabbed up first.

But Casselrod's attention was half on Vivi Traynor, giving her quick, sliding glances, making Dulcie wonder if Vivi was the kind that appealed to Richard Casselrod. She didn't see how could Vivi be attractive to any man, with that grating giggle, and the way she was always sucking on a cherry, her mouth all pursed up.

I am being mean, Dulcie thought, smiling. Charlie said Vivi kept a container of cherries in the freezer, so she could suck on them like little round Popsicles. Even as Dulcie watched, Vivi spit out the pits and dropped a handful of cherry stems on the grass. Casselrod had turned away, moving toward Cora Lee, who knelt sorting through a tangle of toys and small appliances. As she reached for something underneath, Casselrod moved closer.

Cora Lee was still a moment, then stood up holding a white-painted box, a small chest the size of a toaster. The wooden cask was lumpy looking, and the paint was streaked like thick whitewash. The front seemed to be carved with some kind of crude design. Examining it, touching the lid, she glanced up, startled, when she sensed someone watching her.

She stood looking at Casselrod, then turned away quickly, carrying the box, heading for the driveway, where Mr. McLeary sat at a card table, taking in the sale money and making change. She was paying for the chest when Casselrod moved past her up the drive and turned, blocking her way.

Cora Lee accepted her change and started to hurry past him, then everything happened at once, so fast that later, trying to recall the moment, even the cats weren't sure what they had seen.

As Cora Lee started past Casselrod, he shouldered her aside, jerking the box from her hands. Then he swung around, and the box hit her in the shoulder so she stumbled and nearly fell. Casselrod backed away cradling the box, muttering a quick "Sorry." He shoved a bill at Cora Lee as if to pay for what he'd taken, then spun away toward his SUV.

Cora Lee stood looking after him, the bill blowing on the grass at her feet. But Vivi Traynor took off following him, running, swiveling through the crowd and sliding into her black Lincoln, burning rubber as she headed out, on the tail of Casselrod's Mercedes. Joe and Dulcie watched, rigid with interest.

A dozen people crowded around Cora Lee, helping her and looking away after Casselrod, all talking at once. Mavity hurried to her, but Gabrielle didn't move. Her hand was lifted, as if she'd wanted to snatch Casselrod back, but she was very still.

"What was that about?" Joe said, digging his claws into the rough bark. "All over some piece of junk?"

"Apparently Casselrod didn't think so. Nor Cora Lee," Dulcie said. "Does he plan to put that ugly old box in his shop and call it an antique? Make up a history about it the way he does some old kitchen chair and sell it for a bundle?"

Joe looked intently at Dulcie. "Casselrod might boost the price, but he knows his antiques. And why was Vivi Traynor so interested?"

Dulcie flicked her tail. "I don't—" But suddenly, below, something moved in a jumble of broken toys and faded baskets, a dark shape pressing the baskets aside. A mottled black-and-brown shadow coming to life, her dark, plumed tail flipping free, her long fur tangled with leaves. Her round yellow eyes were wide and earnest, gazing up at them.

"Well, Kit," Dulcie whispered. "Come on up here."

"Get up here, Kit," Joe Grey snapped. "Get your tail up here. What are you into, with that innocent look?"

Like an explosion the kit swarmed up the oak's thick trunk and onto Dulcie's branch to nuzzle at her, purring.

"Where have you been?" Dulcie said suspiciously.

"Nowhere," said the kit, her expression secretive.

"You smell of paint. You've been in the theater again."

The kit smiled. Joe and Dulcie exchanged a look, but what could they say? The theater was huge and dark and mysterious—all the things that drew the little tattercoat. Though she was usually there with Cora Lee, and what could happen when Cora Lee was nearby to watch over her?

5

ON THE PATIO OF THE SWISS CAFÉ, ONLY ONE TABLE offered any degree of privacy where it stood in the corner behind a pair of potted trees and a climbing jasmine vine. The restaurant itself defined two sides of the terrace, while a high brick wall offered shelter from the street and side street. Atop the wall concealed within the flowering vine the three cats had joined, in their own way, the ladies of the Senior Survival club. Hidden, they looked down on Mavity and Wilma, Cora Lee and Gabrielle. The ladies had just ordered, and had ordered for Susan, as well. Wilma sat with her back to the wall, cozy in a red sweatshirt, a red scarf tying back her long white hair. She looked up as Susan arrived, with Lamb walking quietly at heel. Susan sat down unsteadily, next to Mavity. Her hands didn't want to be still. She fiddled with her menu and stroked Lamb, who settled under the table leaning his head against her knee. She had called Wilma from her car, as she headed for the restaurant after her long session with Detectives Davis and Garza.

"I filled everyone in," Wilma said. Cora Lee looked at Susan with sympathy, pulling her white stole closer around her shoulders, as if trying to ward off the ugliness of Susan's experience.

Mavity put her arm around Susan. "What a shocking, terrible thing, and how frightening. Do the police have any idea who the man was? But there had to be two men."

Susan shook her head. "If they can find the wounded

38

man, find out what he was looking for . . . I didn't know a break-in could make you feel so helpless."

"As if you aren't safe anymore," Mavity said. "Can't feel safe in your own home." The ladies said all the trite, comforting things, hoping to ease Susan's distress.

Cora Lee laid her hand on Susan's, her slim, dusky fingers still graceful, though knotted from work and age. Her nail polish was the soft, blush red of persimmons, pulling attention away from the darkening veins. "What could they have wanted? No single item we've ever bought would be worth breaking in for and tearing up a house, pulling the shelves from the wall. All our work . . ."

"We'll make it right," Mavity said. "We'll clean up. Could they have thought something was hidden behind the shelves? But it would have to be thin. A painting, maybe? How silly—like some old B movie. Or did they think there was another cupboard built in behind the shelves?"

Beside Mavity, Gabrielle was quiet, looking from one lady to the other. Above, them on the patio wall, the cats listened and wondered. Joe's scowl was deep as he weighed the events of the morning. The kit snuggled close between Joe and Dulcie, her black-and-brown coat a part of the shadows, her attention not on the conversation but on the surrounding tables, where pancakes swam in butter, and sausages and ham laced the breeze with their delicious aroma. It wouldn't take much, Dulcie knew, and the kit would be down there with her feet in someone's breakfast.

But when, pressing against the little tattercoat, Dulcie gave her a warning look, the kit smiled back at her innocently, her round yellow eyes bright and teasing.

Only Wilma seemed aware of the cats—and Lamb, of course. He knew they were there. Entering the patio, he had rolled his eyes up at them as if amused, then had padded obediently under the table, the big poodle far too much of a gentleman to bark at cats.

"After all the trouble we went to," Cora Lee said. "All those lovely shelves—all the hours we spent, putting them together. And our nice work tables broken. Did they get the digital camera?"

"No," Susan said. "It was locked in the file drawer of my desk. I guess they didn't have time to break the lock. They certainly broke everything else. And they didn't take my reflex camera, just dumped a pile of dirt on it. They had the computer on, too. But why? It's so frustrating not knowing what they were after—and maddening not to be able to get into my own house. I want to clean up that mess. All I did was pack a bag and lock up—after I looked things over for Detective Garza, trying to see what might be missing."

"And?" Gabrielle said. "Nothing was missing?"

"Not that I could see. I went over it all as carefully as I could. It made me sick to look at so many of our treasures destroyed. I thought it strange that both detectives came out on the call, but they were very thorough—and they're not finished. I hated leaving everything in that mess."

"If the intruder turns up dead," Wilma suggested, "your house would be the scene of a murder. There's only one chance to collect evidence properly at a murder scene—when it's fresh. You start cleaning up, the whole thing is contaminated."

"How will you clean up?" Cora Lee said. "Do the police do that? I never thought about it. Or do we all pitch in?"

"Detective Garza suggested I call Charlie," Susan said, glancing at Wilma. "He said Charlie's Fix-It,

Clean-It has had training in crime scene cleanup."

Gabrielle looked surprised. "Is that wise?" she said hesitantly. "Should Charlie be doing that—accepting police work, when she and Captain Harper are . . . an item?" She looked at Wilma shyly.

"Charlie's the only one in the village who's had the special training," Wilma said. "No other cleaning outfit has bothered to take those courses."

"Well, I didn't mean to imply . . ." Gabrielle began, embarrassed. "I know Captain Harper wouldn't play favorites. I just . . . I'm sorry. This has been an upsetting morning."

Yes it had, Dulcie thought. But upsetting for all the ladies. Well, Gabrielle was easily stressed. Watching the five women, she wondered whether anyone would guess that Gabrielle, or Cora Lee with her dark beauty, was over sixty. Both could pass for far younger than Wilma or Mavity or Susan, with their silver hair.

But it was more than their hair that made Cora Lee and Gabrielle look maybe ten years younger. *It's the bone structure,* Dulcie thought. *Long, lean bones. Like two Siamese cats, one dark, one light.* And, watching Gabrielle, she wondered what was bothering the tall blonde, who seemed even more uncertain than usual, withdrawn and on edge.

"I hadn't realized before," Susan said, "but of course that man's blood would be considered hazardous. I hope it will come out of my rug and walls, that I don't have to get rid of my nice, hand-braided rug. Though I may have to repaint." She sipped her coffee. "My insurance should pay for the cleanup. I'll call them after breakfast."

"And you have no idea who the man was?" Mavity said, brushing a crumb from her white uniform.

41

"He was lying with his back to me. Detective Garza said I shouldn't discuss it. I just . . . No, I don't know who he was. When Charlie's done with the bad part of the cleanup," she said, "would you . . ."

"Of course we will," Cora Lee said. "We'll get the workroom back in order, make it fresh and new again. And the broken items should be a claim loss."

Susan nodded. "But only for the purchase amount, not for the profit we would have made."

"Not a good morning," Mavity said. "On top of it all, Richard Casselrod stole a wooden chest from Cora Lee."

"He did what?" Susan said softly. "A wooden chest?"

"Snatched it from her, nearly knocked her down, threw her some money, and took off. He hit her with it, really hurt her," Mavity said.

Cora Lee pulled back her stole to reveal a large bruise, ugly against her white sundress. "If Casselrod's looks could kill, I'd be singing with the angels. Those black eyes flashing—as if I was the one who had snatched the box away."

"What did it look like?" Susan said.

"That's what's so strange," Cora Lee said. "Just a crude wooden box with a bad paint job. It didn't look like it was worth fifty cents. I'm not sure why I wanted it. Something about its shape, about the hint of carvings under the paint. It made me think of the stage props— the boxes we made to look like carved Spanish chests, for Elliott Traynor's play."

Susan looked startled. She started to speak, then glanced at the tables around them and seemed to change her mind.

Mavity had no compunction about being overheard. "Vivi Traynor was so interested that she jumped in her

42

car and took off after Casselrod."

Susan sipped her coffee, both hands around the cup, as if trying to get warm. Beneath the table, Lamb whined, and she reached to stroke him.

Mavity said, "That Vivi Traynor is such a snip. She didn't even wave to you, Gabrielle—as if she'd never seen you in her life. After all, you did go to school with Elliott's sister and you did visit them in New York."

"The day I stopped by their apartment, she was only there a few minutes," Gabrielle said. "Elliott fixed coffee for me, but Vivi had an appointment. She probably doesn't remember me. My visit was really a duty call, condolences for his sister's death; she died a year ago. I never met him when she and I were in college. He was nice enough, but I only stayed a little while.

"He's surely very busy," she added, "and preoccupied, if he's finishing up a novel. I must confess I haven't read his books."

"He's quite a wonderful writer," Wilma said. "This last trilogy of novels is set right here, along this part of the California coast. It takes you from the Spanish occupation through the land grant days, the Mexican revolution, and on through to the gold rush. But you've read the play; you know it's based on a segment from the novels."

Gabrielle nodded. "Cora Lee and I read it as soon as we knew we were doing the play here."

"It's such a painful story," Cora Lee said. "And lovely. The music is beautiful."

Days earlier, the cats, slipping into the empty theater, had heard Cora Lee singing one of the numbers, practicing to try out for the lead in *Thorns of Gold*. Dulcie thought the dusky-skinned, dark-eyed woman

43

would make a wonderful Catalina Ortega-Diaz. The play began when Catalina was very young—and onstage Cora Lee had looked young. The way she sang the lonely Spanish laments made Dulcie shiver right down to her claws. And Wilma had read the play to Dulcie and the kit, the three of them tucked up in bed with a warm fire burning in the grate; they agreed that Cora Lee would be wonderful in the part, that the sad story seemed to fit her.

"I don't understand why," Cora Lee said softly, "if Elliott Traynor is working so hard to finish his current novel, and he's being treated for cancer, he would come all the way out to California. Why he didn't stay in New York, not spend the time and energy to make such a move. Even if this play is close to his heart, you'd think . . . Oh, I don't know. It just seems strange." Cora Lee knew well the value of unbroken solitude in which to create.

Gabrielle offered no opinion. She seemed, Dulcie thought, distressed when the ladies talked about the Traynors.

Well, Gabrielle would be seeing them at the theater, as soon as they began to cast the play. She would be doing the costumes. Dulcie supposed whatever friction was between them would sort itself out then.

She knew from Wilma that Gabrielle had already bought the fabric or found costumes from other plays that she would remake. Of course, Catalina's Spanish finery was traditional, the bride's white embroidered gowns, her white and black mantillas, her fans and lace flounces and Roman sashes, as well as the caballeros' bright ruffled silks and sombreros and serapes.

In the village library, while Gabrielle had done her research, making sketches and photocopies, Dulcie had

44

wandered across the library tables near her, and for a while had sat on the table beside Gabrielle's books, looking at the illustrations. The library patrons were used to Dulcie; she prowled the stacks as she pleased. No one paid much attention to her except to pet her and sometimes to bring her little treats.

Often she stayed into the small hours, long after the library closed. Her access to the empty rooms, through her cat door in Wilma's office, was one of the best perks of being Molena Point's official library cat. Even Dulcie's favorite library patrons would never imagine the little cat's midnight literary excursions. They were happy just to enjoy her purring attention during library hours; and the children liked her to curl up with them on the window seat during story hour, while the librarian read to them.

But late at night, in the silent rooms, reading by the faint village light that filtered in through the library windows, Dulcie enjoyed an amazing kind of freedom. She could touch, then, any world she chose, could enter any year or century that appealed to her, could be transported away to far and wonderful places before she returned to the blood-hungry aspect of her nature and went to hunt rats with Joe, on the Molena Point hills.

And though Dulcie had been fascinated with the Spanish costumes for *Thorns of Gold*, imagining the soft silks and velvets, the kit was wild with enthusiasm. The little tattercoat had fallen in love with the play, with the music, with the sets. She would follow Cora Lee into the theater and watch for hours as Cora Lee painted those vivid scenes.

The kit did have a fine imagination, Dulcie thought. Look at the kit's stubborn insistence that she could slip underground through a cave or fissure into a subterranean world that waited to welcome their kind of cat; into a netherworld of green wizard light and granite sky, a country the kit described in such detail that sometimes she frightened Dulcie—but sometimes she had Dulcie dreaming, too, imagining that place as real, that land where speaking cats might have had their beginnings.

"I think we should all be careful for a while," Wilma was saying. "To avoid another break-in, or worse. Susan will be staying with me, but . . . We all live alone. And all of you are seen at the sales. Until we know what this is about, I think we should watch ourselves. Check our locks and windows, look around outside before we go in the house, see if any window is broken or jimmied, that sort of thing."

Wilma didn't mention that she had some defense, where the others did not. Though if they'd thought about it, surely the ladies would guess that a retired U.S. parole officer might keep a firearm at home, might like the security of being armed. Not all Wilma's parolees were far away; several had turned up in Molena Point, some with no love for the woman who had sent them back to prison.

Gabrielle said, "Wilma, you and the captain are good friends. Can't you find out the identity of the man—so we'll know what to watch for?"

"It's too early for the department to know that," Wilma said. "Even if they have a lead, it's too early to share that with a civilian, even with me."

There was a little silence as their waitress brought their breakfasts. Then after some moments, over pancakes and omelettes, the five ladies turned to quietly discussing the kind of comfortable Molena Point house they would like to find, with many bedrooms and baths, a home big enough to accommodate a housekeeper and caregiver when the ladies grew frail—which none of them was, yet—and maybe an extra bedroom or two that could be rented out to pay upkeep and taxes. The women had it all worked out. A private, do-it-yourself retirement home where they would share all expenses and all profits.

Only Wilma remained somewhat removed from their plans. Dulcie's housemate wasn't nearly ready yet for a change in lifestyle. She liked doing her own housework and gardening. She worked out at the gym twice a week and walked two miles a day, intending to hang on as long as she could to her independence. But Wilma said the ladies were to be admired, that too many women couldn't bear to leave their own homes despite better alternatives, that these ladies were making their own options, and she respected that adventuresome turn of mind.

Though Mavity had no choice, Dulcie knew. She'd have to move when the city condemned her house. As for Cora Lee and Gabrielle, with both their husbands gone, they seemed eager to throw in together. And Susan, too, was a widow, living in the two-apartment home she had bought from her daughter just recently when the daughter's job took her to Portland.

The thought of Wilma moving was unsettling to Dulcie. Moving was easier for a human than for a cat. When people changed to a new home, they took all their familiar possessions with them, all the things that gave their daily lives resonance. A cat couldn't take her treasures. A cat's hoard was places, a nook in the garden wall, the shade beneath a favorite bush, a tree branch that suited her exactly, the best mouse runs. All these formed a cat's world, affording her security and comfort, giving her own life structure. A cat's treasures could not be carried with her.

That was why, when humans moved with their cat, the cat wanted to return. The humans took their belongings. The cat was forced to leave hers. That was why, when sensible folk moved to a new home, they kept their cat inside for a month, gave her time to establish new indoor haunts, discover new pleasures, wrap that new world around herself. They didn't let the cat bolt out the door and head straight for the old homestead—a matter of a mile away, or maybe hundreds of miles. Distance didn't matter to a cat, all she wanted was to be among her belongings.

Well, whatever Wilma did in the future, Dulcie thought, the two of them were together. Just as were Joe Grey and Clyde. Besides, she and Joe and the kit had ties to the whole village; their treasured haunts were scattered all over the square mile of Molena Point—and no one ever imagined that Wilma or Clyde would move away from the village.

The kit's own situation was not quite so secure. Her real home was with elderly newlyweds Lucinda and Pedric Greenlaw, but she had moved in with Dulcie and Wilma on an almost permanent basis. Shortly after the Greenlaws were married they had succumbed to travel lust, had begun driving up and down the coast and through Arizona and Nevada and Oregon in their comfortable RV The kit had a special bed in the RV, where she could look out the windows; she should, with her wild enthusiasms, have relished such traveling. But all that driving caused her to throw up, made the little tattercoat as sick as a poisoned hound dog.

"Could there be," Mavity was saying, "a connection between Richard Casselrod's snatching that box and the break-in at Susan's house? So strange . . . two violent, senseless attacks in the same day, at almost the same time, and both to do with buying people's cast-offs."

Joe and Dulcie exchanged a look, Joe's ears flat to his head, the white triangle down his face narrowed in a frown. Of course it was strange. These elderly ladies, who should be safe and cozy in the small village, had twice this morning been senselessly attacked. Whatever was astir put his fur on edge, made his yellow eyes blaze with challenge.

6

THE KITCHEN COUNTER WAS COLD, THE TILE ICY beneath Joe Grey's paws. Beyond the closed shutters, the glass radiated a sharp chill. Turning his back to the night, he watched, beneath the yellow kitchen lights, as Clyde worked at the table laying out the snacks for a poker game. Clyde's muscular frame showed clearly his addiction to the weights and bench press. His dark hair was freshly cut, sporting a thin line of pale skin around his ears. At forty, he might pass for thirty-five, Joe thought, if the lights weren't so bright.

The tray he was arranging was impressive: thin slices of roast beef and turkey, three imported cheeses, and deviled eggs done up fancy with ruffled tops and sprinkles of paprika. No grocery store deli tonight, served up in their paper wrappings. Joe studied his housemate. "Who's coming? How many ladies?"

Clyde laid out slices of imported Tilsit fanning one atop the next. "What ladies? Poker's a man's game."

"Right. And for a couple of guys you're wearing a

new polo shirt and freshly pressed chinos? New Birkenstocks instead of those grungy jogging shoes?" Joe reached to snag a slice of Tilsit from the open wrapper. "Smoked Alaskan salmon instead of sardines? George Jolly's world-class shrimp salad instead of grocery store potato salad? Hey, for Max Harper, you serve from cardboard cartons. So who's coming?"

Clyde fixed a small plate for Joe, heavy on the roast beef. "This is to avoid problems later in the evening." He fixed Joe with a look. "To keep your big feet out of the platter."

"That is so rude. When have I ever touched your fancy buffet—in front of guests? So who's coming?"

"Charlie and Detective Davis are coming, if it's any of your business."

"It's my house, too. Charlie's my friend as well as yours. What's the big deal?"

Charlie Getz was, in fact, Joe's very good friend, one of the four humans who knew his and Dulcie's secret and with whom the cats dared speak. Until recently, Joe had hoped that Clyde and Charlie would marry, but then she got cozy with Max Harper.

Joe had briefly considered Detective Kathleen Ray as a wife for Clyde. It was time Clyde got married; he was getting reclusive and grouchy. And Kathleen was a looker, slim, and quiet, with nice brown eyes and sleek dark hair. But then Kathleen had taken a detective's job in Anchorage, where her grandfather had grown up. She'd packed up and moved practically to the north pole, surprising everyone.

"I miss Detective Ray," he told Clyde, slurping up shrimp salad. "She was a real cat lover. You think she's happy in Alaska?"

"How do you know she's a cat lover? I never saw her

make over you and Dulcie, or even notice you."

"No one said you were super-observant. Kathleen had her moments—a pretty glance, a gentle touch, a little smile."

"Well, aren't you the ladykiller."

"She's happy in Alaska?"

"Harper says she loves it. She sends him e-mail messages every few days telling him how great it is. I think she has talked him into going up there on vacation."

Joe snorted. "Max Harper hasn't taken a vacation from Molena Point PD for as long as I've known him."

"Harper and Charlie. They'll take the cruise, spend a month with Kathleen."

Joe stared at Clyde. "You are so laid back about this. Charlie was your girl. Your girl! I never saw you as serious about anyone. Now Harper takes over, and look at you. Couldn't care less. You actually seem pleased with the idea. What, were you glad to dump Charlie?"

Clyde glared.

"Well, of course, now that Kate Osborne's in the picture . . ."

"Kate is not in the picture, as you put it. We are merely friends."

"I like Kate all right. But I like Charlie, too. I thought you and Charlie might get married."

Clyde stopped dishing up shrimp salad into his best porcelain bowl. "Why do you always go on about my getting married? What earthly business is that of yours? Why do you always have to—"

"Keep in mind," Joe said, "that Kate can't repair the roof or fix the plumbing. Charlie can do those things. I don't even know if Kate can cook."

Clyde wiped the rim of the bowl, licked half the

spoon, then held it out for Joe. "Who I marry is my business. *If* I get married. And in case you're interested, one doesn't marry a woman because she can fix the plumbing."

"You have to admit, it's a nice perk. With the cost of plumbers and carpenters, Charlie's skills shouldn't be sneezed at."

"If I get married, I will pick the woman—without quizzing her on her skills as a handyman and without any help from a cat."

Joe licked shrimp salad from his whiskers. "Your face is getting red. Have you had your blood pressure checked lately?"

"Marriage is serious business."

Joe gave him a hard, yellow-eyed stare. "Has it occurred to you that Charlie Getz knows all about me and Dulcie?"

"So does Kate."

"But Max Harper doesn't."

"So?"

"If Charlie and Harper are as serious as they seem to be, and if they get married, what then?"

"What *what*, then?"

"It's hard to keep a secret when you're married. Every time Harper gets an anonymous phone call from me or Dulcie, he gets edgy. If the tip is something no human could easily know—like when we found that killer's watch way back in that drainage pipe where no human could have seen it, he gets really nervous. If he finds cat hair at the scene of the crime, you can see him wondering. That stuff really upsets him."

"So? What are you getting at?"

"So, how is Charlie going to handle that? Seeing him upset like that, when she knows the truth? Don't you think she'd want to let him in on the facts, so he could stop worrying?"

Clyde turned hot water on the spoon, dropped it in the dishwasher, and turned to look at Joe. "You think that would stop Max Harper from worrying? Charlie tells him that a cat is the phantom snitch? That Clyde Damen's gray tomcat is messing with police business and placing anonymous phone calls? That is going to ease Harper's mind?"

"If she explained it to him, if he knew the truth . . . "

Clyde's look at Joe was incredulous. "That information, if Charlie could prove it to Harper, could make him believe it, could put Harper right over the edge. Drop him right into the funny farm."

"Come on . . ." Joe said, trying to keep his whiskers from twitching. Clyde did rise to the bait.

"Cops are fact-oriented, Joe. Harper couldn't deal with that stuff?" He looked hard at Joe. "Anyway, Charlie has better sense, she knows what that would do to Max."

"Pretty hard to keep her mouth shut when she's crazy in love and sees him suffering, and when she wants to share everything with him."

"Who said she's crazy in love?"

"She would be, if she married him. Don't you think—"

"I think you should mind your own business. I think that would be a nice perk in my life. And for your information, Max Harper is not constantly puzzled, as you seem to believe, about a few anonymous phone calls."

"More than a dozen arrests and convictions," Joe said, "thanks in part to our help. Harper's record of solved crimes has made a big impression on the city council."

"Talk about an overblown ego. You take yourself way too seriously."

"Such a big impression on the city council that the one bad egg on the council tried to ruin Harper's career, set Harper up to be prosecuted for murder. Tried to get him off the force big time—get him sent to prison on a life sentence."

Clyde slid the platters of meat and cheese into the refrigerator, with the bowls of salad, and busied himself arranging crackers.

"Who found young Dillon Thurwell when she was kidnapped—when all the evidence pointed to Harper? Who helped her escape?"

"Harper would likely have found her."

"Right. After she was dead. That woman was going to kill her."

"All right," Clyde said. "I have to admit you and Dulcie saved Harper's skin on that one, and maybe saved Dillon's life. But you two have come to believe that Harper can't solve a crime without you, and I call that really insulting. You two cats think—"

"I never said he can't solve a crime without us. I said we've helped him, that we've offered some positive input—the way any good snitch would do. Why can't you enter into a simple discussion of the facts without getting emotional? Without getting your back up, to use a corny and inappropriate colloquialism!"

Clyde sat down at the table and put his face in his hands, shoving aside the rack of poker chips and two new decks of cards. He didn't say, What did I do to be saddled with this insufferable, ego-driven animal? But it was there, in his silence, in the slump of his shoulders.

"And," Joe said, "when you do marry, you'll be in the same position as Charlie is with Harper. You marry anyone but Kate or Charlie, marry a woman who doesn't know what kind of cat you live with, you try to hide the truth from her, there's going to be trouble. It would never work. I'd have to move out, find another home—or you'd end up telling her about me! Sharing my fate with a total stranger. Compromising and endangering my life, and Dulcie's. Putting us—"

Clyde swung around in his chair, his face decidedly red. "If you don't get out of this house now, and stay out until we're done playing poker and everyone has gone home, I swear I will not only evict you and nail your cat door shut, I will take you to the pound. Shove you in a cat carrier and leave you at the animal shelter. See you locked in a metal cage forever—because no one would want you. No one would adopt such a bad-tempered tomcat."

Joe Grey smiled, leaped to the center of the table, and lifted a gentle white paw to Clyde. "You are becoming very creative. If you even tried such a thing, I would spill it all to Max Harper. I would break out of the pound—no trick for yours truly. I'd go straight to Harper. Sit down face-to-face with him and tell him my entire story. I would lay it all on him, every corroborating fragment of proof, every tip, every detail of past phone calls. Proof that I—I alone, not Dulcie—am his phantom snitch."

He thought Clyde would laugh, but Clyde's brown eyes blazed with anger. "If you ever did such a thing, I swear, Joe, I'd kill you."

Clyde shoved his face close to Joe's. "Do you remember the night at Moreno's Bar, after Janet Jeannot was murdered, when Harper tried to tell me his suspicions about certain cats being involved in the case? About certain mysterious phone calls? And you were eavesdropping under the table? Do you remember how shaken Max was?"

"Come on, Clyde . . ."

Clyde glared. "You so much as whisper to Max Harper, and you're a dead cat. Finished. Comprende?"

"You are so grouchy. You really need to get your life in hand." Joe dropped down to the linoleum, stalked through to the living room, pushed out his cat door, and crept under the front porch. He'd never seen Clyde so irritable.

He really did have to blame Clyde's mood on pretty, blond Kate Osborne. Clyde and Kate were old friends, but now that Clyde had really fallen for her, she'd turned standoffish. Wouldn't come down from San Francisco, hadn't been down for over a month, didn't want Clyde to come up. Something was going on with her. Clyde didn't know what it was, and as a result, he'd been fierce as a goaded possum. Maybe it was Kate's search for her unknown family, maybe she was totally wrapped up in that, didn't want to think of anything else. Though that project, in Joe's opinion, could lead her into more grief than she'd ever wanted.

Looking out through the cracks between the porch boards, he saw Charlie coming down the street, walking the few blocks from her apartment—and looking very pretty, her kinky red hair tied back with a calico ribbon, her blue-and-white striped dress as fresh as new milk. When she had hurried up the steps above his head and gone inside, he slipped out of the musty dark to the porch again and sat down beside his cat door, his face to the plastic flap to listen.

"Hi! Clyde, you there? Am I the first one here? You in the kitchen?"

Her cheery greeting met silence. Joe heard the kitchen

56

door swing. "Hi! There you are. I brought some chips."

No answer.

"What?" Charlie said.

"Can't you knock? Since we're not dating anymore, you could at least—"

"Well, pardon me."

Again, silence.

"Where's Joe?" she said. "You two have a fight?"

A longer silence.

"Well?"

"No, we didn't have a fight!"

"So where did he go to sulk? And you're sulking in here, in the kitchen. Were you fighting about the house again, about selling the house?"

"No, we weren't fighting about selling the house."

Charlie said no more. Joe heard one of them open the refrigerator and pop a couple of beers. Charlie knew how to handle him; Clyde's moods didn't bother her. And she was partly right. The problem about the house did make him cross.

Ever since construction had begun on Molena Point's new, upscale shopping plaza—ever since its two-story, plastered wall had risen at the boundary behind Clyde's backyard, blocking their view of the sunrise and the eastern hills, Clyde had been entertaining offers from realtors. The mall hadn't affected the property values, not in Molena Point, where village lots were so scarce that a buyer would pay half a million for a teardown. And this latest offer to Clyde had topped all the others. It was not from someone wanting a home or vacation cottage, but from a restaurateur planning to open an upscale café—a perfectly understandable plan, in a village where the businesses and cottages were mingled, many shops occupying former residences.

57

The offering realtor said the house would remain, along with the house next door, which the buyer had already purchased. The two buildings would be converted into dining and kitchen space and joined by a patio whose tile paving would run back to the two-story plaster wall, with outdoor tables and umbrellas and potted trees.

Dulcie thought it would be charming. Joe thought there were enough patio restaurants in the village. Clyde vacillated between outright refusal and considering the offer; he couldn't make up his mind. But he was as angry as a maimed wharf rat about his view being destroyed. Joe could understand that. The wall made Joe, too, feel like he was in a cage.

But what if Clyde did sell? Where would they live? The idea of moving upset Joe and seemed nearly as unsettling to Clyde.

Joe thought maybe his own distress came from his kittenhood, from the time when he'd had no real home, just an alley and a few one-night stands, then for a while a stranger with a shabby apartment and a bad disposition—until he met Clyde.

His and Clyde's move down from San Francisco, when he was still a half-grown kitten, had left him nervous for weeks afterward, distraught at losing the only real home he knew. Even Charlie's recent moves had unsettled him, first from her aunt Wilma's and Dulcie's house into an apartment, then into another apartment. Places that he'd liked to visit, gone before he got used to them. And now Mavity Flowers was about to be evicted, closing another door to him—and Mavity's cottage held some rare memories.

It was there that he had spied on the black tomcat and his human partner in crime, Mavity's no-good, thieving brother. It was there that Joe had routed some of the evidence that convicted the killer of Mavity's niece. Besides, though Mavity's cottage was just an old fishing shack, it was all Mavity had—he felt, too sharply, the little woman's distress at her own impending loss.

If all those houses along the bay were destroyed, who knew what the village would do with that land? The city council was still arguing the issue. And now, with Mavity's friends planning to sell their houses too, and buy some big old house where they would rattle around, everything was changing. All these moves and prospective moves made the whole world seem shaky under his paws.

And to top it off, the entire Molena Point Police Department was being renovated, Harper's officers taking up temporary quarters in the courthouse while Harper remodeled the building.

Already Joe missed the big, casual squad room with all its desks and clutter. Now the space was full of lumber and Sheetrock and carpenters with loud hammers and louder power tools. The department that Joe thought of as the heart of the village was going to be totally different. He had no idea whether, with the new design, he'd even be able to get inside. When finally the renovation would be complete and everyone back together again, who knew what the offices would be like? Harper might make the building so secure that no cat could breach the locks to slip in to hide under the first handy desk.

What was he going to do then? It was hard enough for a cat to get police intelligence. Imagining the new setup made him feel like he was walking on a broken tree limb that hung shattered and ready to fall. As if there was nothing secure left in the world, nothing steady that he could count on.

When two cars pulled to the curb in front of the house, he dropped off the porch into the bushes. Watching Detectives Dallas Garza and Juana Davis and Captain Harper thunder up the steps, laughing—likely at some rank cop joke—and bang into the house, Joe felt for an instant incredibly lonely. Quickly he slipped through his cat door, following them inside. Slipping behind the couch, he heard beer cans being popped and the cards shuffled. He listened for sometime, staying out of sight as Clyde preferred, and feeling put upon, but the conversation didn't touch on the break-in at Susan Brittain's house, it was just light banter. He had nearly dozed off when the phone rang.

Clyde answered, then Detective Garza took the phone. It was apparently a personal call, from the tone of Garza's voice. Yes, he was talking to his niece, Ryan, a young woman who was as close to Garza as if she were his own daughter.

"You what? You're kidding!" Garza sounded pleased. But Joe could hear the faint echo of a tight, angry female voice from the other end of the line.

"You're leaving him?"

Ryan was Garza's youngest niece. He had helped raise her and her two sisters after their mother died. Likely Ryan was calling from San Francisco, where she and her husband ran a building construction business— or apparently had run it. Sounded like they were splitting. For an instant Joe sensed what Garza must be feeling, deep parental distress for a young woman who had apparently decided to pull up stakes, chuck everything, and start her life all over again.

The foolish mobility of humanity, Joe thought. *People abandoning families, racing off in every direction—it's*

60

a wonder the world itself doesn't fly apart.

"That's the best news I've had in ages," Garza said, laughing. "Where are you now? You have your key to the cottage?"

Garza listened, then, "Of course I understand. Guess I'd feel the same. But the cottage is there if you want it—when you want some company."

They talked for some time, something about a job Ryan had just finished. Interested, Joe trotted into the kitchen and leaped to the counter. When Garza hung up, he was grinning. He sat down at the table between Clyde and Juana Davis, where Clyde was counting out poker chips.

"She's left him. Packed up and moved out. He's been cheating on her for years. She came on down to the village, she's in the Turtle Motel up on Fifth. Wants some time alone. Wants to look for a house. Sounds like she means to stay."

Joe couldn't remember when he'd seen Garza looking so pleased. Stretching out, he waited to hear how the scenario would develop—and waited as well for the conversation to turn, as it inevitably would, to police business. Did the department have a make on Susan Brittain's burglar? Had they found him? Surely by now they would have a record of his prints. Joe waited patiently to pick up whatever tidbits the officers might toss back and forth over the poker table—until he felt Clyde's gaze on him. Then he closed his eyes and tried for a soft, rhythmic snore—not to fool Clyde, but to keep his relationship with the department as untainted as a sleuthing cat could manage. No point in enraging Clyde furthur, and making Harper edgy; though it was hard to resist the urge to taunt them both.

7

CLYDE PULLED THE SNACK TRAY FROM THE refrigerator and set it on the counter, giving Joe a warning look, his dark eyes threatening dire repercussions if Joe so much as reached a paw into the party food or made a scene in any way. Joe hissed at him in a casual manner and settled more stubbornly down onto the cold tile counter, watching the three officers and Charlie rise to load their plates, then fit them in beside their cards and poker chips and beer cans.

Harper's lined, sun-wrinkled face made him seem years older than Clyde, though they were the same age, had gone all through grammar school together, had rodeoed together when they were in high school. With his lean, tall build, he looked very at home on horseback.

Dallas Garza was built more like Clyde, blocky and solid. He was about the same age as Clyde and Harper, somewhere around forty. His tanned Latino face was square and smooth, his expression closed, his black Latin eyes watchful—a man who exuded a steady and comforting presence. Garza seemed always in control, calm and unruffled. And Joe had learned that Garza was an officer to be trusted—as was Detective Davis, with her dark, steady gaze. Juana Davis was maybe in her early fifties, had been widowed, and had two grown children, both cops.

Charlie was the only fair one at the table, with her bright freckles and brighter hair. She was younger, too, maybe four years out of art school—which she described as her squandered past.

Garza said, "Ryan's been up in San Andreas for a month, designing the addition to a vacation cottage, surveying the land, finalizing the plans. She gets home, another woman's clothes are in her closet, a strange car in her half of the garage.

"She said she wanted to put her pickup in four-wheel drive and run that little red convertible right through the back of the garage. Only thing that stopped her was the legal mess she'd be in—and she didn't want her insurance canceled."

"I'd have killed him," Juana said, with a twisted smile.

Charlie nodded. "A slow and painful death."

"Rupert did her one good turn," Garza said. "The nine years they've been married, she's had a chance to work into the building trade—but only at her insistence. She got him to let her do some designing and to work on the jobs. She's learned the business well, and she has solid carpentry skills."

Garza discarded two cards and watched Juana deal. "In all other ways, Rupert's a real loser. But Ryan's good at what she does, she's made a name for herself as well as for the firm—something Rupert never gave her credit for. She has a nice design style, very original. She wants to get her license in this county, start her own construction firm. She loves the village. When the girls were small, we spent a lot of summers and holidays down here."

From the kitchen counter, Joe watched Garza with interest. He'd seen something of Garza's closeness with Ryan's sister Hanni, who now lived in the village and had her own interior designing firm. But he'd not seen this degree of fatherly pride that Dallas had for Ryan. He knew that, under the guidance of Garza and the

63

girls' father, the three sisters had learned not only to cook and clean house, but to shoot and handle firearms properly, to train the hunting dogs that Garza loved, and to ride a horse—all skills, apparently, that the two law enforcement officers felt would build strong young women. Joe had learned a lot about Garza when he'd moved in with the detective last winter, playing needy kitty.

That was when Garza was first sent down to the village, on loan from San Francisco PD, to investigate the murders for which Max Harper was the prime suspect. When Garza first arrived, Joe and Dulcie both had thought they smelled a rat. They'd been sure that in this prime case of collusion to ruin Harper, Garza was part of the setup. The week that Joe had lived with the detective, he had playing up to Garza as shamelessly as any groveling canine in order to learn Garza's agenda.

He'd ended up not only sharing Garza's supper, and privately accessing Garza's interview tapes and notes, but admiring and respecting the detective. Then later, when the case was closed, Max Harper had thought enough of Garza to ask him to join Molena Point PD. Garza had jumped at the chance to get out of San Francisco for the last five years of his service.

"She'll be taking her maiden name again," Garza said, "R. Flannery. She wants no part of Rupert, except to be paid for her half of the business. Said she doesn't want to see me or her sister for a few days, either, until she gets herself together. That's the way she is. Hardheaded independent."

"Don't know where she got that," Harper said, grinning.

"One thing," Garza said, shuffling the cards. "She drove one of the company trucks down, to haul her stuff. Said the brakes were really soft." He looked at Clyde. "Would you . . . ?"

"First thing in the morning," Clyde said. "Tell her we open at eight."

"Likely she'll be waiting at the door." Garza paused, surveying his cards. "She did say something strange— she asked about Elliott Traynor. Said she'd heard the Traynors were in the village, asked if I'd met them. Said they'd spent a month in San Francisco last fall. Before Traynor got sick, I guess. They flew out from New York, apparently on business. She and Rupert met them through mutual friends."

At mention of the Traynors, Charlie looked quickly down at her cards. Laying her cards facedown, she bent her head to retie the ribbon that bound back her kinky hair, hiding her face, concealing some swift and uncomfortable reaction that made Joe Grey watch her with interest. Was there a look of guilt on her freckled face? But why would Charlie feel guilty about Vivi and Elliott Traynor?

As Clyde dealt a hand of five card draw, Joe's attention remained on Charlie. They played three more hands of stud before Clyde mentioned the break-in at Susan Brittain's. "Have you found the guy yet? Or found his body?"

"Nothing," Harper said. "One set of prints isn't on record."

"That's unusual."

"Very," Garza said. "Information on the other set hasn't come back yet."

Clyde sipped his beer, setting the can on a folded paper napkin. "How did Susan handle the break-in? Was she pretty shaken?"

"Not at all," Garza said. "In fact, very cool. She

65

seems a straightforward woman. She thinks she might know the man. She saw only his back, but when she thought about it awhile, she was certain he looked familiar." He paused, waiting for Clyde to bet. Charlie raised Clyde, and Garza and Davis folded. Harper raised Charlie, winning the pot with three jacks, giving her a superior look that made her laugh.

"So who is he?" Clyde said.

"She thinks he might be an early morning dog walker she's run into, a newcomer to the village, a Lenny Wells. Young man who just moved down from San Francisco. About thirty, six feet, maybe a hundred and seventy, she thought. Light brown hair. She stopped for coffee with him a couple of times when they were walking the dogs, said she told him a little about the village to help him get settled."

Juana Davis dealt the next hand, upping the ante on seven card stud. Clyde showed a pair of aces, but when the hand was finished Davis raked in the pot on three eights. Their poker was never high-powered, with the keen attention and subtleties of a serious professional game, just a friendly excuse to get together. The conversation turned to the remodeling of the police station and how soon the contractor would be finished. "An equation," Harper said, "arrived at by squaring the original four months to completion time."

Joe thought about Susan's break-in, and about the grungy white box that Richard Casselrod had snatched from Cora Lee French. He saw again the shocked, angry look on Cora Lee's face when Casselrod swung the box and hit her, saw her dark eyes blazing with hurt surprise.

He wanted a look at that box, he wanted to know what made it so valuable.

Richard Casselrod's antique shop was in a tight

building, not easy to get into, after hours, even for an expert at break-and-enter. But there was one high, attic window that Joe meant to check out.

He'd as soon not slip in during the day and hide until they closed up. There was something about Richard Casselrod that did not invite close proximity among closed doors and solid walls.

He came to attention when Charlie raised on a pair of sixes, though Juana had three jacks showing. Was Charlie bluffing? Did she have two sixes in the hole? Or was she merely preoccupied? *Wake up, Charlie. Pay attention. What are you thinking about?*

Charlie saw her mistake and watched Juana rake in the pot, her mind uncomfortably on Elliott Traynor. How strange that Garza's niece should know Traynor. And how interesting that the Traynors had so recently been in San Francisco. Maybe that explained the envelopes with San Francisco postmarks that she'd found in Traynor's wastebasket.

When you're cleaning for such interesting tenants, and when they're gone most mornings, it's hard not to snoop. At least it was hard for Charlie, when the snooping involved an author whose work she so greatly admired. The Traynors had been in the village for over two weeks. She cleaned their cottage each morning, did the shopping and the laundry, put the dinner and breakfast dishes in the dishwasher, and sometimes started lunch or something for dinner with Vivi's written instructions. She was at the cottage from eight until twelve, quite often alone because Traynor wrote at night, and they went to the theater some mornings, or out walking. When she did see him, he seemed dour and unresponsive.

Traynor was a wide-shouldered man in his late sixties. Close-cropped salt-and-pepper hair, a nice tan despite his illness, strong-looking square hands that she could imagine handling a sail and jib or a hunting rifle. Friendly green eyes that seemed to analyze and weigh her far too closely. The eyes of a writer, exhibiting a nature intriguing but too intimately curious for comfort. An unusually virile-looking man, considering that he was suffering from some serious sort of cancer—she hadn't asked what kind. Not that it was any of her business. The times when she did see him, he would look her over in that too interested, piercing way, then would turn remote and unsmiling.

Well, she was, after all, only the cleaning woman. And he had to be preoccupied—from his cancer treatments, and working on his new book, and overseeing the production of his play. His medical treatments alone could make him feel too ill to be civil. Very likely it was all he could do to handle his work and find time for the theater; surely there was nothing left over with which to be courteous to some housekeeper.

Except, much of the time, he wasn't civil even to his wife. That relationship, on both their parts, seemed cold and rigid—certainly not in keeping with what Gabrielle and Cora Lee had told Wilma, that at the theater, meeting with the producer and directors, Vivi clung to Elliott so attentively that he could hardly move.

The six envelopes that Charlie had pulled from the trash in Traynor's study—just to have a quick look, out of innocent curiosity, she told herself—had not been wadded up but simply dropped into the leather wastebasket all together. Lifting them out to put them in her trash bag, she had flipped through them, her face warming with embarrassment at the transgression.

68

All were from San Francisco, all but one from antique dealers, maybe answering some research questions about the furniture or artifacts of the period in which his novel was set. At first she thought there were no letters, just the envelopes, all handwritten and sent first class. But then she saw the one letter, tucked under the flap of the last envelope. It was also from the city. Both the letter and the envelope were typewritten, from Harlan Scott of the *San Francisco Chronicle*, a book reviewer whom Charlie usually read. Had Scott written about a review? Did authors have their work reviewed before they finished it? She read quickly.

Dear Elliott,

Good to hear from you and to know you're settled so quickly and back at work. The new book sounds fascinating. You're to be commended for being able to finish writing the novel and oversee production of the play—two very distinct projects— when you're feeling under the weather.

Yes, there are several collectors in the bay area. I'll put together a list, try to get it off to you at the end of the week. All my good thoughts are with you. I hope the casting and rehearsals go well. Hope the treatments are not too uncomfortable. Sounds to me like you're doing very well. Give me a call if you and Vivi want to come up for a talk with these people, or if you simply want to get away for a weekend.

Very best, Harlan.

When she heard the Traynors returning, she had dropped the envelopes and letter hastily into her trash bag. But it was the next day that she faced real

69

temptation, when Traynor's manuscript pages began to appear on his desk, one new chapter each morning, printed out, lying beside the computer.

Alone in Traynor's paneled study with its leaded windows and pale stone fireplace, she had guiltily reached for the first pages, telling herself she wanted just a peek. Because she loved his work. Because she longed to see his work in progress, still forming, see how he accomplished his smooth and exciting prose. The guilt she should normally feel took a weak second place to the artistic hunger that rose in her, a keen fascination at the proximity of this fine writer.

Traynor's study looked the same each morning when she entered, the desk immaculate, no paper left out. The little footstool pushed just so, to the corner of the desk against the bookcase, its loose, tasseled pillow aligned perfectly on top. She thought perhaps he used the pillow to ease his back as he worked. The books he had brought with him from New York were few, and all on California history—a row perhaps two feet long standing neatly on the otherwise empty shelves, beside a stack of photocopied research material. The bookshelf stood at right angles to his desk, close enough to be reached from his chair. It was flanked by a window directly at the end of the desk that looked out on the drive and front garden.

Charlie's aunt Wilma, who was a research assistant at the Molena Point library, had mailed a thick package of machine copies to Traynor nearly a year ago, all research on local California history, much of it family journals collected over the years by priests at the nearby mission, and a history of the mission itself as well as the surrounding land, which had been divided by grants into huge cattle spreads. Because of Wilma's thoroughness in her assistance, Traynor had sent quite a nice, and welcome, donation to the library's book purchasing fund.

Alone in Traynor's study, eagerly picking up the pages, Charlie had thought, *Why am I doing this, why am I so interested? I'm not a writer, I have no professional curiosity.* Her animal drawings were quite demanding enough of her creative skills; there was plenty to learn studying bone structure and doing quick sketches of moving animals. She had no time to divert her attention to a second discipline, no matter how much the beauty of the written word made her want to try. And yet any work of art, in a state of becoming, was fascinating stuff, seeming to her vividly alive. She had begun to read eagerly, glancing out the window in case they might return.

She'd had no idea how Traynor's prose would affect her—no notion of the sudden, perplexed unease that would wash over her.

She had laid the pages down, had stood beside the desk staring out at the empty drive, confused and puzzled, not understanding why he had written this— how he could have written this.

This was not the lyric prose she had so admired from Elliott Traynor; his sentences were awkward and confused. The experience had shocked and saddened her. There was no other explanation than that his illness had affected his work. She had turned away filled almost with a personal loss. And ashamed, too, that she had pried—and she was touched as well with a cold little fear for herself, with a sharp sense of helplessness, that creative skills might so suddenly be diminished.

8

CLYDE WOKE IN THE DARK PREDAWN WHEN HE FELT Joe drop off the far side of the bed. He hadn't slept well, had just managed to drift into sleep, and wasn't happy to be jerked awake again. He'd dreamed of Kate, not pleasant dreams. Why did she insist on staying in San Francisco? Jimmie was safely in prison, he couldn't hurt her now. In the dream, she'd been so—distant. So removed, darkly preoccupied, not at all like the bright, sunny Kate Osborne he knew.

He could feel the warmth at his back where the tomcat, moments before, had been curled up asleep before he thumped softly to the wood floor, apparently trying to be silent. Why all the stealth; what was he up to? Joe's usual departure was a four-star performance, tramping across Clyde's stomach with those big, hard paws, dropping to the floor with all the finesse of a truckload of rocks.

In the near-dark, Clyde watched Joe pad softly around the end of the bed, a shadow sneaking across the Sarouk rug, heading away down the hall.

In a moment he heard Joe's cat door slap, swinging against its metal frame.

Between Joe's unusual behavior and his own unpleasant dreams, Clyde was wide awake. Leaving the warm bed, he stood at the open window, peering out from behind the curtain like some little old lady spying on the neighbors. The sea breeze was cool against his skin. In the faint moonlight that filtered through the blowing oak leaves, he could see Joe fast disappearing up the sidewalk, his gray coat nearly lost among the leafy shadows, only his white paws clearly visible, flashing along with swift determination.

Joe went out every night to hunt rabbits or, if he was obsessed with some police business that was none of *his* business, to peer into windows or slip into people's houses, poking and prying—Clyde had ceased to ask for details. But the tomcat was seldom silent in his nocturnal departures. And it wasn't like there was some big crime under current investigation—nothing but that break-in at Susan Brittain's place. No jewel heist or bank robbery, no murder that they knew of. Well, the damn cat wouldn't leave anything alone. Let someone steal a pencil, Joe was on their case.

Wide awake and angry, he had half a mind to pull on his jeans and shoes and follow Joe. He could see him, almost to Ocean now, hardly visible in the blowing night. Clyde reached for his jeans but didn't pull them on. If he tried to follow, the tomcat would simply take to the roofs and vanish.

His dream of Kate was still vivid; he'd been with her in San Francisco, walking the windy midnight streets. She told him she wasn't coming back to Molena Point ever, that she wouldn't see him again, that they didn't belong together, that he wasn't right for her.

But they had been right for each other, they'd known it long before she left Jimmie, though neither did anything about it. And then suddenly Jimmie was involved in murder and car theft; those days came back to him sharply. A killer loose in the village, hired by Jimmie to murder Kate—an incredible scenario, and the Welshman killer also had personal reasons for stalking Joe Grey and Dulcie.

That was when Clyde first learned that Joe Grey

could speak, and Joe himself first became aware of that alarming talent—as if the shock of seeing a man murdered had thrust Joe from one facet of his existence into a deeper consciousness. That was when Joe's true nature had come to light, and of course Dulcie's hidden abilities as well.

Standing before the open window in his shorts, holding his jeans and a sweatshirt, he wondered how long before Kate *would* get over her fear of being in the village and decide to move back home. He thought of her not as in the dream, but as she really was, imagined her there with him, her golden hair catching the faint moonlight, her eyes loving and kind. Dreaming of Kate, he started when a dark shape leaped to the window, crouching on the sill, pressed against the screen.

In the darkness, Joe's white paws and chest were sharply defined, the white triangle down his nose pinched into a scowl. He looked intently at Clyde, at the jeans and sweatshirt. "What are you doing, Clyde? You weren't going to follow me?"

Clyde looked at him innocently. "Couldn't sleep," Clyde said inadequately.

"You weren't going to sneak out into the night and follow me? Pry into my private business? At three in the morning?"

"Would I do that? That's very insulting. In all the hundreds of times you've gone out looking for trouble, in all the nights I've lain in bed worrying that you'd got yourself killed, have I ever followed you?"

"So why were you putting on your jeans?"

"I wasn't putting them on. I was holding them. And is there any law against putting my pants on, going into my own kitchen, and making a sandwich? I couldn't sleep. All right?"

74

"You never put your pants on when you invade the kitchen in the middle of the night, waking up old Rube and the other cats. Why are you so testy? Why would you want to follow me?"

Clyde glowered. Why did he have to get involved with a tomcat who seemed to know exactly what he was thinking?

"You were dreaming about Kate, calling her name in your sleep. Go on out in the kitchen, Clyde. Drink some hot milk and brandy, maybe that will help you sleep."

Clyde just looked at him.

"You want to know where I'm going," Joe said. "What difference does it make? You can't stop me, and you can't help me. You're getting way too nosy in your advanced years."

"Forty-some is not advanced, as you put it. I had no intention of stopping you. I simply wondered where were you going. Wondered why the secrecy? Why all the silence, slipping out trying not to wake me?"

"For your information, I was being thoughtful. Apparently that concept escapes you. You were obviously having trouble sleeping. You'd dozed off at last, and I didn't want to wake you. Okay?"

"So where are you going? This is some kind of state secret? I know what you do at night, I know about your snooping. Someday, Joe—"

"If it's any of *your* business, Dulcie and I thought we'd wander over to Hidalgo Plaza and check out the shops."

"At three in the morning."

"Why not? We can look in the windows. Dulcie loves to look in shop windows."

"So you're nosing around Casselrod's Antiques, just because he snatched that old chest from Cora Lee. And would this have anything to do with the break-in at Susan Brittain's?"

Joe sighed. "For your edification, antique stores, estate sales, yard sales . . . That's where any cop would start looking for the guy who trashed Susan's place."

"That's so simplistic. Max Harper would laugh his head off."

"Not at all. A cop checks out the obvious first, even if it is simplistic. Take my word. Dallas Garza will be having a good look among the local junk dealers." Joe gave Clyde a toothy smile, twitched a whisker, and was gone as swiftly as he had appeared, swarming up the oak tree to the roof, where he would again head for Ocean Avenue. Clyde imagined Dulcie waiting for him there among the trees of Ocean's wide, grassy median, imagined the two galloping up the median to disappear in the direction of the long, wild park that bordered Molena Point on the southeast.

At the mouth of the park stood the cluster of converted buildings that made up Hidalgo Plaza, a collection of steep-roofed houses and old barns remodeled into a complex of antique and craft shops, boutiques, and art galleries. The largest structure among them, the old Hidalgo mansion, was now Molena Point Little Theater. Above many of the shops were offices and small businesses that didn't need the exposure of a storefront. Casselrod's Antiques occupied the entire two floors of its building, with wide showroom windows facing the brick walk.

Up on the roof, on the tilting peak, the two cats padded along the sharp hip. Where the peak ended, they dropped down to the tiny false balcony that protruded

76

from the featureless wall three stories above the ground.

Rearing up on the four-inch protrusion, Joe pawed at the glass, shaking and forcing the frail old casement. Because the window opened in a sheer wall with only the fake four-inch balcony, it had never presented a security problem, and no one had bothered to lock it. The casement gave, and Joe and Dulcie slipped inside.

Padding through the dark attic beneath stacked chairs and tables, between ancient trunks and antique dressers and cartons of bric-a-brac, their paws stirring through rivers of dust, they were searching for a way down to the shop below when they saw, against the far attic window, a figure poised, back-lighted from the street below. Though they had been silent, and hadn't spoken, she was surely watching them.

Scenting out, they couldn't smell anything remotely human. Warily, they crept closer.

"A mannequin!" Dulcie breathed.

"Buckram and wire," Joe said, disgusted. Sniffing at the construction then brushing past the flimsy form, he headed for the stairs.

The second floor of Casselrod's Antiques was not only cleaner and smelled better but was handsomely arranged, with small groups of ornate furniture displayed on fine Oriental rugs, against nice paintings and antique screens.

"Just like the architectural magazines," Dulcie said, lifting a paw to stroke the soft patina of a fine cherry dresser, patting at the clustered grapes that had been wrought by a master carver.

Trunks and small chests stood on the floor among the furniture or on various tables. "Mostly Chinese," Dulcie said. Certainly they were not roughly made, like the chest from the McLeary yard sale. Some were no bigger than a little birdhouse, some large enough to conceal a German shepherd. The cats prowled every dark corner and open shelf but did not find the chest they were looking for.

Descending the last flight to the main floor, they faced a wide bank of windows where beyond the glass shone the street lights of the plaza, and the softly lit windows of other shops. Here on the main floor, they could smell the perfume of Richard Casselrod's assistant, a distinctive and clinging scent, in one of the upholstered chairs where Fern Barth had apparently sat. Joe sniffed at the too sweet perfume and made a flehmen face, lifting his lip in disdain. "Does she buy that stuff by the quart? Smells like dimestore jelly beans."

"Maybe it's something very expensive, to appeal to the opposite sex."

"I bet it has the men flocking."

Dulcie backed away from the smell, leaped to the shelves, and prowled carefully along them, skirting among delicate Dresden figures and porcelain dinnerware. To her right, a table was covered with boxes of silver flatware and stacks of lace and linens. Amazing how much care, how much time and art went into the accessories for human lives. "No matter how much we dislike Richard Casselrod," she said softly, "you have to admit, he buys lovely things."

But Joe had vanished. No shadow moved, not a sound. She mewed softly.

Nothing.

Leaping to the top of a drop-front desk, she yowled.

"In here," he hissed from beyond an open door.

Dropping to the floor, trotting under the chairs and between table legs, she paused at the door to a small, fusty office that was nearly filled with a rolltop desk. "In here?"

No answer. Moving on, she slipped into a large workroom that smelled of paint, and raw wood, wax and varnish. The floor was scattered with sawdust and with curls of wood trimmings that tickled her paws. Joe stood atop a worktable, poised rigid with interest. She leaped up.

High above them through a small window set among the rafters, faint light seeped in from the street, seeming in the dusty air to filter all to one place, onto seven white slabs of painted, carved wood that lay among a collection of hammers and screwdrivers.

Two sides, two ends, and the lid of the chest lay beside two planks that had made up the base. These appeared to fit together like two slices of bread for a sandwich, each slice hollowed out in the center to form a shallow dish. When joined by their neatly carved wooden dovetails, the base of the chest would have a hiding place.

Joe sniffed at the planks. "Smells like jelly beans."

"I smell Casselrod, too," Dulcie said. "That tweedy, musty scent. So what was hidden in here? Or did they take it all apart and find nothing? What were they looking for?"

Where the joints of the little trunk had been left unpainted, the old, seasoned oak shone deep and rich. The four sides and top had been carved in geometric patterns, with a circular design in the center. The paint over the carving was thick and uneven, filling up some of the indentations. "The circle is a rosette," Dulcie said. "It's a . . ." she stared at Joe. "Oh, my."

"What?"

"It's a Spanish motif. I've seen it on pictures of
79

Spanish furniture."

"So?"

"Like the old Spanish chests in Elliott Traynor's play, that Catalina's lover carved and gave to her, where she kept some of the letters she wrote to him, that she never sent. Could *this* be one of those? Is that why Casselrod was so interested—why he snatched it from Cora Lee?" Her green eyes widened. "The research that Wilma collected for Elliott Traynor said that likely the old casks had been lost, broken or rotted or burned in the fire that destroyed the rancho some years after Catalina died."

Joe nosed at the rough white slabs. "This stuff doesn't look all that valuable."

But Dulcie was fascinated, tingling with a resonance that made her whiskers twitch. She wasn't sure what to call the feeling, but the sensation made her purr boldly, the same as when she had a rat by the scruff of the neck, ready to dispatch it.

Was this the key to the events of the last few days? Was the answer right there in Elliott Traynor's play? Had some of the letters survived that Catalina wrote to her lover? Dulcie was wild with excitement—but Joe was still thinking it over.

"Why now?" he said. "Why would Casselrod and the men who broke into Susan's suddenly be so interested?"

"Because now that the play is about to be produced, everyone has a script. All of a sudden, more people know about the letters."

Joe wasn't convinced but he helped her search for some old, frail letter written in Spanish, trying the desks and file cabinets and the rolltop desk which looked like a good place to hide valuables. All its drawers were locked with heavy, old-fashioned brass locks that wouldn't budge.

And later, when Dulcie asked Wilma's opinion, Wilma said, "I've always supposed the letters didn't survive. Or maybe that some collector had them—tucked away. I've never given them much thought." She looked at Dulcie as doubtfully as Joe Grey had done, as if Dulcie was way off base on this one.

But then Joe and Dulcie caught Charlie snooping through Elliott Traynor's desk, something they'd never dreamed that Charlie would do. Spying was a cat's prerogative, but there was Charlie brazenly prying, shocking the cats with her nosiness and delighting them—and soon, both Charlie and Ryan Flannery would add tinder to the fires of their sharp curiosity.

9

IN THE VELVET EVENING, MEXICAN MUSIC BEAT brassy and sweet, and the aroma of chilies and roasted meats floated on the cool air, enticing Joe Grey and Dulcie as they trotted along behind their human friends. Licking their whiskers at the good smells, the two cats tried not to draw attention to themselves. But the kit raced boldly ahead, brushing past Charlie's ankles and between Max Harper's feet with no thought to keeping a low profile. Charlie glanced down at her once, grinning, and reached down to stroke her. Walking between Max Harper and Clyde, Charlie moved together with Harper as if their thoughts, their very spirits were in perfect sync.

Lovers, Dulcie thought, watching them. Or soon to be lovers. You could always tell, in the beginning. And that made her feel sad for Clyde, made her wish Clyde and

Kate would work out their differences, wish that Kate would come home, that she would get serious about Clyde and move back to the village. Clyde seemed so— unfinished, Dulcie thought. She knew, with typical female logic, that it was time Clyde Damen got married.

Though apparently Joe didn't think so. Why must he always know her thoughts? Beside her, he flicked a whisker with annoyance, his yellow eyes burning, his look saying clearly, *Leave it alone, Dulcie. Leave Clyde alone, quit matchmaking.* Joe said when she was matchmaking, her tail flicked in a certain way. Well, he wasn't any help, he did nothing to nudge Clyde along. For all of Joe Grey's input, Clyde could stay a bachelor forever.

Only, sometimes she did catch an irritated and speculative look in Joe's eyes that made her wonder what he and Clyde talked about, in private. Made her wonder if, alone with Clyde, Joe hassled him to get married more than she imagined. Maybe, she thought, amused, Joe didn't want her to catch him matchmaking.

When Clyde and Charlie and Harper entered the patio of Lupe's Playa, moving in through the wrought iron gate, the kit barged in right between their feet—until Dulcie snaked out a swift paw and snatched her back, hissing at her and then purring and licking her ear.

Chastened, the kit followed Dulcie and Joe away from the entry and around behind the restaurant and up a bougainvillea vine to the top of the high patio wall. Padding along above the diners' heads, the three cats slipped into a mass of purple blossoms where they were well concealed yet had a fine view of Lupe's Playa. Below them, at Harper's usual table, Detective Garza and his slim, dark-haired niece were already seated.

The patio was softly lighted by colored oil lamps that

hung from the branches of three giant oak trees around which the tables were clustered. From the eaves of the building hung bright piñatas and Mexican flags. The restaurant itself, with its bright dining rooms, flanked two sides of the terrace, the lighted windows revealing more crowded tables and happy, laughing diners. Lupe's Playa was the pièce de résistance for fine Mexican food, a four-star winner, Harper and Clyde said. Both men were authorities, their appraisal of Mexican cuisine a serious avocation.

In their rodeo days, Max Harper and Clyde had frequented every good Mexican café between Portland and San Diego, and inland to the Nevada border. Both could describe in detail the specific virtues of an excellent chili relleño or an enchilada ranchero; both would turn up their noses at ground beef as a filling; both could name the painstaking steps in the proper preparation of tamales, a process that, when correctly done, took three days, from the soaking and roasting of the corn to the drying of the husks and the final rolling of the tamales.

Garza and his niece sat with their backs to the wall, unaware of the three cats hidden in the vines above them. The cats' view of Ryan was the top of her head, her dark curly hair tousled and windblown. She was dressed in jeans and a pale blue T-shirt with no cutesy logos emblazoned on it. Was she reading Garza off, or only laying out her troubles? Whichever, this lady had a hot temper.

"This is not a simple quarrel! I'm not going back to him. I'm not staying with a man I don't trust or respect." She shifted in her chair, looking at Dallas more directly, her green eyes blazing beneath thick black lashes.

Garza was grinning. "Don't lay your anger on me—I couldn't be happier. You should have done this years ago."

"I have an appointment tomorrow morning with the attorney Max Harper recommended. Thanks for talking to him." She sipped her beer. "I want to get the divorce started, get my contractor's license—and my half of the value of the business. In a few months, I'll be running my new company. R. Flannery Construction." She laid her hand on his. "I want to get into a place of my own, lick my wounds alone. Does that disappoint you?"

"Of course it doesn't. You're in the village, we can have dinner, run the dogs when I bring them down—go hunting this fall without Rupert pitching a fit." He patted her hand. "Just glad to have you near, honey. Glad to see you free of him."

"An apartment with good storage space," Ryan said. "Have to buy all new equipment, power tools, ladders, wheelbarrows, you name it. Have to do some advertising—to say nothing of hiring. Besides the job in San Anselmo, I have a couple of other nibbles, contacts from San Francisco. One of our—of Rupert's—clients wants me to build a small vacation cottage down here. They bought a lot last year, a teardown."

"So you're not only going to fight Rupert for your half of the business, you're going to steal the firm's clients."

"I don't consider it stealing, if they come to me. None of them was happy with Rupert, with his attitude."

"I have to say, you came away armed. Armed for what, time will tell."

"Don't be a cop, Dallas. I'll work it out."

Garza stood up as Clyde and Charlie and Harper approached. Harper pulled out a chair for Charlie; but as

84

the three were seated, Joe nudged Dulcie. She followed his gaze across the patio, where Vivi and Elliott Traynor had just appeared, waiting for a table.

Vivi looked incredibly small and thin next to Elliott, who seemed twice her size. He was a handsome man, with well-styled silver hair, dressed in a suede leather sport coat and pale slacks, a man who looked used to living well. Vivi, in her black tights and black sweater and wildly frizzy hair, looked like something he might have picked up south of town.

Glancing around the patio, Vivi began to fidget as if she should not have to wait to be seated. When she spotted their table she did a comic double take, turned her back to the party, and grabbed Elliott's arm, dragging him toward the door. Looking surprised, Traynor followed her. When the maître d' turned back to them, they were gone.

Ryan sat very still, staring after them. "Why did they turn away? She spotted us, and spun around like she'd been scalded."

"I told you the Traynors were here," Garza said. "She was looking straight at you." He studied his niece. "Something happen in San Francisco? I thought you hardly knew them, that you'd met them only once. Some business dinner?"

"Rupert and I had dinner with them one evening, with friends. Then Rupert insisted we take them out. We did, but I didn't especially enjoy it. Though I can't think of anything that would make them avoid me."

"Unless . . . " Ryan colored. "Unless she and Rupert . . . "

Garza's expression didn't change.

"Dinner was—well, both evenings were pleasant enough, really. But Rupert was fidgety and rude because

85

he had to listen to details about Elliott's play. He thought Elliott was totally egocentric. I didn't think so, I liked him, he's a charming man. He'd been making arrangements with Molena Point Players, someone down here was doing the music and lyrics. Mark King?"

"Yes," Charlie said. "Mark King."

"He talked about his historical trilogy, too," Ryan said. "It was interesting. But Rupert . . . Well," she said slowly, "Rupert did spend a good deal of time talking with Vivi." She went a shade paler, lowering her gaze.

Charlie looked across at Ryan. "Elliott Traynor's play—isn't it based on the same historical material as his last three novels?" Under the table, Charlie and Harper were holding hands. Only the cats could see them, from the angle of the wall. The kit's tail twitched with merriment.

"Yes," Ryan said. "He seems totally caught up in early California history. But the material of the novels is different. The play centers around Catalina Ortega-Diaz and her love story."

"My aunt Wilma supplied some of the research for the books," Charlie said, "as well as for the play, from the library's local history collection and from the records kept at the mission."

"I haven't read the trilogy," Ryan said. "But Traynor told us the true story of the play. Catalina was the daughter of a wealthy Spanish ranchero—this would be somewhere in the eighteen fifties, when the rancheros began to mortgage parcels of their land to buy luxuries—silks, crystal, golden goblets brought over by ship from Europe. Apparently they and their families lived pretty high, enjoyed life day to day and really didn't take the mortgages seriously. Didn't think the notes would ever be called in.

"The heart of the play is the effect of this on Catalina's life. When the notes were foreclosed and the merchants started taking over the land, some of the rancheros went bankrupt, Catalina's father included. Well, I didn't mean to lay out the whole story."

"Go on," Charlie said. "Don't leave us hanging."

Ryan smiled. "Along comes a wealthy American named Stanton, offering to pay off Ortega-Diaz's debts in exchange for his land—and for Catalina's hand. Keep the ranch in the family. He promised Diaz that he could stay there in his own home and live well. It was the answer to the ranchero's prayer.

"But Catalina was in love with someone else," Ryan said. "When she refused to marry Stanton, her father locked her in her room, fed her on bread and water. According to Traynor, she finally gave in. Though she married Stanton and bore his children and made a respectable life, she wrote letters to her lost love until she died.

"No one knows how many of the letters she sent. According to Traynor, she hid many of them in her chambers—rather like a secret journal. The way Traynor described it, the whole thrust of the play is on the letters between Catalina and Marcos Romero—her songs are the letters. Traynor tells the story so beautifully. I was fascinated. But Vivi seemed annoyed that he talked so much about the play; she seemed as bored as Rupert."

Charlie laughed. "I know how she is. I work for them, I do their cleaning. Vivi can be . . . off-putting."

"I liked Elliott," Ryan said. "He's a fiery man, but he seemed kind. I think he could be kind—without Vivi."

From atop the brick wall, Dulcie watched the two women, thinking that they hit it off very well. They seemed about the same age, and certainly they agreed about Vivi—but then, who wouldn't?

When the waiter came with their menus, the conversation died. From the wall, the three cats peered over, considering the selections and what they might be able to cadge. That was when Clyde spotted them, when the kit thrust her nose out to see better. Everyone looked; no one laughed. Detective Garza seemed to find their presence amusing. "That gray tomcat gets around, Damen. I never saw a cat quite so—with so much presence. He's almost like a dog."

The tomcat thought of several things he'd like to tell Detective Garza, none of them polite.

Clyde shifted his chair so his back was to the cats, disclaiming all responsibility for their presence; but he included in his order a selection of their favorites on a paper plate: chicken fajitas with jack cheese and sour cream. The egg-and-batter portion of a chili relleño, with mild sauce. And a cup of flan, for the kit. Ryan appeared as entertained as Garza; she kept glancing up at the three cats, as if watching for further developments.

When the orders came and Clyde placed the paper plate on the wall, the cats feasted, Joe and Dulcie eating in silence and neatly licking their whiskers, the kit guzzling loudly and enthusiastically, smearing flan from her whiskers to her ears. She received amused glances from several tables.

The village was used to dogs in their restaurant patios, but companion cats were another matter, though most of the villagers knew Clyde Damen's odd preference for the gray tomcat. This was a community of writers and artists and of people rich enough or confident enough to be as eccentric as they liked—if

Damen wanted to bring his cats to dinner, that was fine.

But Dallas was asking Charlie about the apartment she had for rent. "Max told me it was a duplex?"

"Yes, both sides of a duplex." She looked at Ryan. "One is a studio, double garage underneath. The other has one bedroom, same garage arrangement."

"I'd like to see the studio," Ryan said. "Would you mind my keeping construction equipment there?"

"Not at all. It's a perfect arrangement. After dinner, you want to take a look?"

"Love to."

"So would I," said Clyde. "I haven't seen it since you painted and fixed it up."

"We're not finished with the larger one," Charlie said, watching him with interest. "Mavity's helping me. The studio side is done."

"I'd like to see the one-bedroom," Clyde said. "We're—I'm thinking of taking that offer for the house, since they built the wall of China behind me."

Joe and Dulcie exchanged a look.

"What about your own apartment building?" Charlie said.

"Those are all one-year leases, Charlie, with options to renew. You were there when I rented those units, you were still working on the outside of the building."

Charlie tried to look at him seriously, but the cats saw a sly grin creep across her freckled face, as if she could read Clyde too well. Her look seemed a mixture of jealousy, levity, and honest pleasure and relief.

How complicated humans were, Dulcie thought. A she-cat would either turn away uninterested, or would leap on her rival spitting and clawing.

But Charlie had already abandoned Clyde, he was a free agent. Dulcie watched the exchange of looks between Charlie and Harper. Charlie's leg was pressed against his under the table. Clyde didn't seem to notice, his full attention was on Ryan. He rose with her as dinner ended and as Harper and Garza headed back to the station. He escorted her out as if she were his date, handing her into his antique yellow roadster to ride the few blocks to the duplex. The kit crouched, meaning to leap down and follow, but Dulcie snatched her back.

"Let them go, Kit. We don't need to act all that eager for a car ride. No need to put too many questions in people's heads." She looked after Clyde's convertible. "Ryan Flannery is a looker. I don't think Kate will like this."

"Serve her right," Joe said, wondering how this would play out. Ryan was a beauty, all right, and apparently full of fight and determination. She seemed, in fact, the kind of human woman he most admired. Well, but so was Charlie. Determined and feisty.

But the woman he was really curious about, who sent Joe leaping from the wall and snaking away up the street between pedestrians' legs, was Vivi Traynor. Why had she practically run from the restaurant to avoid either Detective Garza or his niece Ryan Flannery?

Heading across the darkening village dodging tourists' shoes, the three cats' eyes caught light from shop windows and from passing cars. The sky above them was heavy with cloud behind the black silhouettes of oak and pine trees. Above the cats, a little bat darted over the treetops, squeaking its high-pitched sonar. Dulcie, hurrying along beside Joe, puzzled over Vivi Traynor's hasty retreat but also kept thinking about Traynor's play and about the research that Wilma had done for him.

Wilma had read her some of the research that came from the mission archives, before she sent it to Traynor. Apparently one of the priests knew about Catalina's letters and wrote about them in his journal. The Ortega-Diaz ranch wasn't far from the mission. "That priest wrote that Catalina made little paintings on the letters—of the ranch, of branding, whatever they do with cattle. How strange," she said, "the way humans collect and record history."

"How else would they do it?" Joe said sensibly.

"I don't know. All the letters and journals and all kinds of old records woven together to make a pattern of the past. To a human, that may seem dull. I think it's like making magic, to be able to bring the dead past alive."

Joe stared at her. "You're talking just like the kit," he said rudely.

Hurt, she glanced back at the kit, who had stopped to paw at a snail. "Sometimes," Dulcie said, "I feel like the kit." And she turned away from Joe.

But he pressed against her, licking her ear. "That's why I love you," he said softly. "Because you see not only the rat to hunt but also the flowers where it's crouched."

She looked at him, her eyes wide, then gave him a nuzzling purr. Sometimes this tomcat wasn't so rough and uncaring. Sometimes he truly surprised her. And in a little while, she said, "Hundred-and-fifty-year-old letters from California history with sketches of the period should be worth a bundle, Joe. Maybe Traynor's looking for them himself."

"Traynor or Vivi? It was Vivi who followed Casselrod when he snatched the white chest."

"If Traynor wants the letters, why would he put them

in the play so everyone would know about them? So other people would start looking?"

"Maybe he planned to have found them already before the time the play was produced." Joe leaped to the top of a fence and down the other side. He watched Dulcie and the kit drop down beside him. "If Elliott and Vivi are still having dinner somewhere, and if we're fast, we can be inside their cottage before they ever get home." Joe's yellow eyes blazed. "I want to know more about Vivi, about both the Traynors."

10

TROTTING SINGLE FILE ALONG A TWISTED OAK branch, the three cats crossed above Elliot Traynor's roof to the high clerestory windows that looked down into the living room. Within the house, no lights burned. The Traynor's black Lincoln was not in the drive where they usually parked. Peering down through the glass, the cats could see the stone fireplace and a pale leather couch and love seat, set on a richly patterned area rug. The handsomely designed room was now strewn with items of clothing as if Vivi had wandered through undressing as she went. Joe was pawing at the sliding panels trying to open one, when car lights swept the garden. As the Lincoln turned into the drive, the cats closed their eyes so not to catch the glow like a row of miniature spotlights mounted among the shingles.

Vivi got out of the driver's side carrying a large paper bag in both hands. The cats could smell enchiladas. Elliott followed her in through the back door, and light came on in the kitchen, reflecting across the drive and illuminating the flowering shrubs, burnishing their leaves like polished copper.

Soon the cats could hear water running in the kitchen, then a metallic clatter as if silverware was being taken from the drawer. They imagined Elliott and Vivi sitting down to Styrofoam containers heaped with enchiladas and tamales. Maybe, when the cats saw them hurry out of Lupe's, they told the waiter that they'd changed their minds and that they wanted take-out, then had waited outside for their order like any ordinary villager, lurking beyond the patio wall where they wouldn't be seen.

When the clerestory windows wouldn't open, Dulcie dropped from the roof and headed for the back door to see if it might be ajar, though she didn't relish slipping into the house that close to Vivi. Trotting through the dark garden toward the back porch, she brushed through tall stands of daisies and overgrown clumps of daylilies and yellow-flowering euryops bushes, collecting their scents on her coat. Above her, up the stone walls of the cottage, the many-paned windows remained dark, there was only that light at the back, in the small bay window that extended out from the kitchen. The spicy smell of Mexican food filled her nostrils, so strong she could taste it. She heard Vivi giggle somewhere inside, that high, irritating laugh that set Dulcie's fur on edge. Elliott said something that Dulcie couldn't make out, and Vivi snapped angrily at him, her shout coming clearly enough.

"She was with two cops. Those guys were cops. That tall skinny one is the chief. What did you expect me to do?"

Elliott's muttered reply wasn't clear. It sounded like, ". . . other one . . . didn't see the . . . mumble mumble . . ."

"Well, she would remember!" Vivi said. "One wrong word in front of the law, one little wiggle . . . If you run into her, you be careful. You're way too casual about this."

Again his response was too low to be heard, sullen and angry. Why didn't he yell at her? He was way too casual about what? Had Vivi had an affair with Ryan's husband, the way Ryan thought? And Vivi didn't want to confront Ryan? But if Elliott knew about that, didn't he care? How strange humans were, Dulcie thought. Joe would have killed another tomcat who touched her.

He had wanted to kill that black tom, Azrael. Had tried to kill him. Though Dulcie hadn't really looked at another tomcat since she met Joe, there had been that one weak moment when Azrael came on to her, she remembered ashamedly. When the dark voodoo cat ignited a frightened purr—until she angrily rejected the philandering thief.

They were still snapping at each other as Vivi's high heels clicked across the room toward the back door. Dulcie backed into the bushes as the door opened and light spilled out. She could never get over the feeling that people would know she was eavesdropping; she always wanted to hide.

But how could anyone know? So Vivi saw a cat in the garden. What was she going to do, throw the garbage can at her?

Knowing Vivi, she might. Vivi dropped a bag of trash into the garbage can. She stood a few moments in the cool night as if trying to control her temper, then turned back inside, where Elliott had switched on the TV, and the canned voices of a late newscast filled the kitchen.

Racing back through the quiet dark of the garden, Dulcie let the human sounds fade behind her, let the garden smells fill her nose, and the damp earth ooze cool beneath her paws. Brushing through the scented leaves of geranium and lavender, in the deepening evening chill, she raced up the oak tree again. From somewhere high above her came the scream of a screech owl crying his hunting call—hunting in the wind, diving among the pines and oaks. Catching arboreal mice? she thought, amused. Or snatching up tree-climbing crickets?

Feeling lonely suddenly, she fled to Joe. She and Joe were launched on their own kind of hunt, the game far larger and more dangerous than anything that little owl could trap. And, thinking of what they might find, she was suddenly afraid.

Storming up through the thick foliage of the oak tree, darkness seemed to crush in around her. Racing along the branch with clinging claws, she nudged Joe with her nose, sniffing in his scent, rubbing her face against his sleek, silken fur. But after a moment, she asked, "Where's the kit?"

Joe smiled and glanced above them. She followed his gaze to where the kit clung nearly at the top of the oak among the smallest branches, a dark lump, her long, fluffy tail hanging down like a pendulum, the tip of it twitching in that slow rhythm that indicated some prankish desire or some other, equally busy mental process.

"Vivi and Elliott were arguing," Dulcie told Joe. "Talking about Ryan. Vivi said, 'She would remember. And she was with two cops—those guys were cops.' Then, 'That tall skinny one is the chief. What did you expect me to do?' "

Joe listened, saying nothing.

"Elliott muttered something like,' . . . other one . . .

95

didn't see . . .' That's all I could make out. She told him to be careful, that he was way too casual. Then she closed the door tight. And no windows are open."

Somewhere near, a barn owl hooted, deep and frightening, and the kit came backing down the tree fast, to snuggle between them. Joe peered in again through the high window. "Strange, what a bad feeling I have about this."

"So do I," she said. "Likely it's Vivi, she'd make anyone uneasy. Wilma calls her a name I won't repeat," she said, glancing at the kit.

"What name?" asked the kit.

No one answered her. Joe worked at the window again, clawing and pulling, then backed down the tree to the garden and went to circle the house, a gray streak in the darkness leaping up at each window, scrabbling and pawing. Dulcie followed him down to try the vents in the foundation. She was clawing at a grid when suddenly from above, lights poured down on them. They fled into the bushes, hunching down in the leaves, looking up through the little twiggy branches at the one window, halfway along the house, that shone brightly.

No figure moved against the glass, no one looked out. They could see beyond the curtains a tall chest of drawers with a small mirror standing on top, light reflecting from it.

Lights blazed on in a second room, at the front where the draperies were drawn, then a smaller window in between burned brightly. They heard water running, but then at last the bathroom light went out and the back bedroom darkened except for the glow of a TV.

In the illuminated front room, a shadow moved behind the draperies, thrown tall by the lamp, and then sat down. In a few minutes they heard the soft click,

click of computer keys.

"So Vivi's gone to bed to watch TV," Dulcie said. "And Elliott's at work on the book."

Moving out from beneath the bush, Joe looked up at the vents of the attic.

"Wait for me," he whispered. "Watch the window." And he was gone up the rose trellis, his white paws flashing as he skillfully avoided the thorns. She watched nervously from the bushes, wishing she didn't feel so edgy. In a moment she heard him scratching and tearing at the wall, rustling within the foliage. She had never seen Joe so interested, when no serious crime had been committed. Usually he reserved his predatory sleuthing for some major transgression, but tonight he was keen to break and enter, hot on the trail—of what? Oh, Vivi and Elliott did put him off, did make him uneasy. Above her, Joe snatched and clawed at the vent as he swung from the trellis anchored only by his hind paws, fighting to get inside, following his instincts.

Max Harper, she thought, would never move on cop sense alone, on some itchy feeling, without due cause. Whatever problems the Traynors had, such as their avoidance of Ryan Flannery, and Vivi's nervousness around police, didn't necessarily point to criminal activity. And yet . . .

She wondered if they could be dealing drugs. She didn't like to think that about someone like Elliott Traynor. Were his medical bills so high that he was desperate, hard up for cash even if he was a famous writer? Cancer treatment must be very expensive. Maybe writers didn't have medical insurance. Certainly drugs were easy to sell. On the streets of New York and San Francisco there would be plenty of buyers eager to hand over their money.

But she was letting her imagination go wild. And how was Garza's niece involved? Did Ryan know more about the Traynors than she was saying—more than she wanted to tell her uncle?

"I could go to the door," the kit said. "Scratch at the door."

"Do what, Kit?" Dulcie stared at her, then looked up to where Joe had his claws hooked in the vent, stubbornly pulling.

"I could play lost kitty like Joe did at Detective Garza's house, when he moved in to spy. Like you did with that old lady, after Janet Jeannot was killed. You lived with that old woman for a week, and look how much you found out! I could—"

The vent came loose and fell, as Joe leaped clear. It clattered loudly to the brick walk—and Elliott's typing stopped. Dulcie and the kit froze, ready to run. Above them, Joe disappeared into the attic.

In a moment the typing started again. The kit, fascinated with her idea, went on as if she'd never been interrupted. "I could make nice to Elliott Traynor and Vivi and get them to feed me and make a bed for me and I would purr for them, and when they went to sleep I would open the door for you, catch the knob in my paws, and swing and hold tight—I can do that. I could—"

"Hush, Kit, you're making me crazy. You mustn't do any of that. Be still." She could hear sounds from the front of the garden. Someone was coming. She pulled the kit deeper under the hydrangea bush. Crouching among the leaves and branches, they listened.

Was it a person approaching in the dark? More likely a dog, Dulcie thought. The brushing noise was too low to the ground for a human. The kit, very still now, pressed close to her as something came lumbering in their direction, waddling back and forth on all fours.

This was no dog. Dulcie could feel the kit's heart pounding against her. She could see the beast's stripes now, his black beady eyes, could see the mask across his face. He was bigger than a bulldog and seemed twice as broad, and behind him came four smaller raccoons looking out from behind identical masks, swinging along predatory and bold on their dainty black paws. Five lethal fighting machines. Dulcie and the kit didn't breathe.

The raccoons lurched past not ten feet from them, their raised noses sucking in the lingering smell of enchiladas. Maybe that garlicky confection of meat and chilies and cilantro would hide the smell of cat. Lurching toward the back of the house and the garbage cans, they were soon scrabbling on metal and chittering impatiently, pawing to get the lids off. A lid dropped into the bushes. The can fell, breaking leafy twigs and immediately the raccoons were into it, scrabbling and fighting.

Dulcie led the kit back up the trellis, the kit's long fine fur catching in the thorns with little ripping sounds.

"We're safe now," the kit whispered, edging toward the hole that Joe Grey had opened to the dark attic.

"Hush!" Dulcie said. "They can climb, too. Get yourself inside!" Below them, the sounds of bickering and of claws tearing at Styrofoam gave her the shivers. She imagined the animals devouring enchilada-flavored Styrofoam as if it were candy. But when they finished with the garbage, what would they do next?

Following the kit into the dusty, mouse-scent dark of the attic, she mewed softly for Joe Grey. There was no answer, no movement among the shadows. She heard, from the yard below, the sounds of the raccoons change from gorging garbage to little chirps of curiosity, then heard the beasts coming back, shouldering through the bushes toward the trellis that she and the kit had climbed. Beside her, the kit peered down. "What are they doing? Why . . .?"

"Be still! They'll climb up here quick as squirrels!" She looked hard at the kit, whose tail was twitching with that devilish, looking-for-trouble rhythm.

"Didn't you ever have to battle raccoons, Kit, when you lived with that traveling band of cats? They're as dangerous as coyotes or bobcats."

"The big cats fought them. I was too little. I always hid. But I'm big now, and you and Joe are big. They wouldn't—"

"Oh wouldn't they?" She turned blazing eyes on the kit. "Have you never seen a cat torn apart by raccoons? Like you would tear apart a little mouse!"

The kit's eyes grew round. She dropped her tail, dropped her ears flat to her head, and backed away from the vent into the deeper shadows of the attic. And Dulcie began to search for something heavy they could push against the vent hole.

11

IN THE BLACK ATTIC DULCIE RACED AMONG HULKING furniture, clawing at cartons, searching for a box that she could move, could shove against the hole to block the raccoons' entrance. In the little square of moonlit sky that marked the vent hole, a black shape loomed, and another was coming fast up the trellis. Her nose was filled with the smells of mildew and dust and ancient mouse droppings, as if all the house dirt of generations had been sucked upward into this dank space. Searching, pulling at heavy boxes, she watched the lead raccoon forcing himself through the little vent, could hear the others behind him pushing up the trellis following the scent of cat.

They daren't shout; the Traynors would hear them—she wondered if Elliott heard the raccoons scrabbling up the wall of the house. She attacked another box, straining with claws and teeth to drag it toward the opening. Where was Joe? Cats weren't built to move heavy loads. If she got a grip with her claws and pulled, she pulled her own back feet out from under herself. When she tried pushing with her shoulder, the box might as well be nailed to the floor. Straining, lying on her back, pulling, she mewled when the box gave suddenly, was shoved so hard it nearly ran her over. She rolled away as it rammed against the wall.

"Push, Dulcie. Push now!" Joe hissed. In the darkness behind the box, his white face and chest gleamed. But as they fought the carton toward the opening, the beast pushed through, forcing the box back in their faces. He was a huge animal; he seemed to fill the attic.

"Run, Kit. Run." The three cats flew through the dark, dodging between the legs of stacked furniture.

"Here," Joe hissed. "Down through the crawl door." He shouldered the kit toward a thick slab of plywood lying askew on the rough flooring, a crack of blackness showing at its edge.

"This?" Dulcie said. "We have to move this?" She pawed uselessly at the slab.

"All together. Hook your claws in the edge."

They hooked into the rough splintery plywood and pulled, lunging backward. The slab moved, and moved again. Behind them, the beasts came swaying and lumbering. Pulling again, they jerked the cover aside far enough to free a six-inch hole. As the masked bandit lunged at them, Joe shoved the kit, and they dropped through into blackness.

They landed on hard linoleum, in a little room walled by shelves that smelled of raisins, brown sugar, cereal. Above them in the hole, a masked face peered down, and another. Trapped in the pantry, they watched the raccoons turn, preparing to back down, watched the first one reach a hind foot to grip the nearest shelf.

Leaping, Joe pawed at the pantry door swinging on the knob and turning it. The door flew open, they were through.

"Get your tail through, Kit."

She flicked her fluffy tail away, and Joe flung himself against the door again, slamming it closed.

They heard the raccoons drop, then a terrible thudding racket as they fought among themselves, scrabbling at the door to force it open. The cats fled, searching the kitchen for a place to hide, listening to the latch rattle as if any minute it would give.

The animals charged the door for some moments, then began, apparently, to vent their rage and hunger on the pantry shelves. Cans and boxes fell clattering, cardboard was torn and ripped to the sounds of munching and slurping—five voracious eating machines heralding their entry into Elliot Traynor's cottage, announcing their arrival with enough noise to wake the village.

The Traynor kitchen, even without lights, was a bright room, its cabinets and tile floor creamy pale, its wide bay window over the sink offering a vista of starlight above the massed houseplants. But its pristine

102

counters afforded no shelter. When a door banged, down the hall, the cats fled behind the refrigerator.

Elliott Traynor came running, Vivi close behind him. Peering out, the cats watched the Traynors pause, staring at the closed pantry door where, within, the raccoons were knocking down cans and thudding against the walls. Elliott was dressed in a velvet robe, pajamas, and slippers—and carrying a black automatic. Crouched behind the refrigerator, Dulcie and the kit hunched close to Joe.

Moving to the pantry, Elliott paused for a long minute, listening. When he jerked the door open, Vivi screamed. Two shots rang. At the booming explosion, the cats scorched down the hall, into the living room and underneath the couch.

"He shot them," Dulcie whispered, shocked. As terrified as she'd been of the raccoons, she was appalled that Traynor had killed them. Crouching in the black dusty dark beneath the couch, she pressed against Joe, shivering. "He might have shot us."

"Shhh." Joe's warning hiss was cut off by Vivi's high, nervous giggle.

"My God! Why did you have to shoot them! Look at the mess you made. What on earth are they, what kind of animal would . . . ?" She giggled again. "Oh, it's gory. What are we going to do?"

"Raccoons," Traynor snapped. "Get some garbage bags."

"You had to load with soft-nose."

"Be glad I did. Bullet could go right through these walls, who knows where. Then there'd be hell to pay. Get me the damn bags. Hope to hell the neighbors thought it was a backfire."

"How did they get in?"

Silence—as if Traynor might be pointing above them, to the crawl hole.

"Well, how did they get in there?"

"How the hell do I know? There are vents in an attic. Get the damn bags."

"You don't need to snap at me."

"I'll snap if I want. And look in the garage for a ladder."

Beneath the couch, Dulcie said, "Maybe our uneasy feeling wasn't so silly. Why would Traynor have a gun?"

"I don't know, Dulcie. Maybe he carries it when he's traveling. Clyde carries a gun in the car when—"

"The Traynors flew out. People aren't supposed to carry guns on planes."

"They can, if they check their bag. And lock it. Unload the gun and declare it. Get a special tag—"

The back door banged. Elliott snapped, "Hold the damn bag open!"

"I don't want to do this! Leave that for the cleaning woman—keep it away from me. This makes me sick."

"Shut up and hold the bag!"

They listened to sounds of scraping, laced with plenty of swearing. Pretty soon they heard the back door open again, then the clanging of metal from the backyard as if Elliott had righted the garbage can that the raccoons had earlier turned over. The idea of a dead animal, even a raccoon, stuffed into a garbage can sickened the cats. They heard Traynor secure the lid and pound it down, as if with an angry fist.

"How many did he kill?" Dulcie said. "There were only two shots. Why didn't we hear the others running away across the attic?"

"Maybe two for one," Joe said coldly. "I hope he

104

closed the door tight."

The kit began to wriggle. Joe scowled at her.

"Curl up, Kit. Close your eyes. We can't leave with them fussing around in the kitchen."

"Come here, Kit," Dulcie said, nudging her. She licked the kit's face and ears, washing her gently until the kit stretched out and dozed off. Dulcie didn't mean to sleep, but she woke later with the kit curled against her and Joe Grey gone.

Listening, she heard not the faintest noise in the house. Leaving the sleeping kit, she crept out from behind the couch and followed Joe's scent down the hall.

No light burned beneath the bedroom door. She could hear Vivi and Elliott breathing, in two separate rhythms. Their human sleep-smell was sour. Beyond the bedroom, Elliott's study was dark, the door pulled nearly closed. Pressing it open, she padded in.

Against the pale color of the drawn draperies, where a thin wash of moonlight brightened the window, Joe sat atop Elliott Traynor's desk, his silhouette black, his white markings gleaming, his ears pricked sharply—he was as still as a sphinx, watching her. The illuminated clock on the desk said 1:30. She leaped up beside him.

A heavy brown folder lay at his feet, from which he had pawed out a thick sheaf of papers, scattering them across the blotter. There was barely enough light to read, even for a cat. She looked at the pages, frowning.

"Traynor's research," he said softly. "Take a look at this. A San Francisco museum owns some of Catalina's letters, which they have translated—pretty impassioned letters," he said, grinning. "She was mad as hell when her father made her marry the American. And look at this."

With a deft claw he pulled out several pages revealing a paper tucked between them, an auction house notice offering two letters written by Catalina Ortega-Diaz, the bidding for each to start at ten thousand dollars. A handwritten notation at the bottom indicated that one had sold for twelve thousand, one for fourteen. Clipped to the notice was a printed statement listing the two items, and making payment to Vivi Traynor.

In the gloom, Joe Grey's eyes were as black as obsidian. "Did someone say there's been no crime? Famous author or not, this is most interesting. There's money here, Dulcie—how many letters did she write over her lifetime? How many did she never send?

"Catalina had seven carved chests that Marcos made for her. Was that white cask one of them? And did they all have secret compartments? Even so, how did she keep her husband from finding them?

"The research said they had separate chambers— bedrooms—where the chests were hidden."

Dulcie looked at the date on the auction notice. "Only a few weeks since these letters were sold. Then Susan Brittain's house is broken into, and the burglar is attacked. Did those men think she had one of the chests? And the same morning, Casselrod snatches the white one."

"Add to that," Joe said, "that Elliott carries a gun and that Vivi and Elliott are afraid of the cops and apparently of Garza's niece." He looked intently at Dulcie, his yellow eyes gleaming with a hot predatory flame—with the same resolve that he had reserved, in the past, for thieves and killers.

"He's a famous author," Dulcie said softly. "He's . . . Well, I don't know. To accuse a man like that . . ." Looking around the study, looking at the papers that Joe was neatly pawing together, she shivered. "Prying into Elliott Traynor's business makes me nervous."

"Come on," he said, pawing the envelope open and pushing the papers in. "Get the kit, let's get out of here. I need fresh air, away from these people." Quickly he pushed beneath the draperies and slid the window lock. He had the glass open when Dulcie returned with the yawning kit. And they left the Traynor's with far more silence than they had entered, softly sliding the window closed behind them, as they dropped down among the bushes.

But Joe Grey was back inside the cottage again by the time Charlie got to work. He had watched from the oak tree as Vivi and Elliott left the house, had come in through the window, returning to Elliot's study, his curiosity not nearly satisfied.

He had no idea what else he would find—and no idea that he would catch Charlie snooping, exactly as he and Dulcie had done, hiding her prying with energetic bouts of vacuuming and dusting.

12

WHETHER YOU'RE A COP WITH A SEARCH WARRANT or the weekly cleaning person come to scour the bathrooms and vacuum the rugs, if you peek through someone's private papers you can stir matters you might wish you'd let lie. The more bizarre the results of such prying, the more compelled one may feel to keep searching, to see what else might come to light.

Charlie Getz had no idea, when she let herself into the Traynor cottage at nine on Monday morning, of the bloody mess she'd have to clean up or of what she would find later in Elliott Traynor's study.

The cottage the Traynors had rented was one of the most charming in the village, with its pale stone exterior and winding brick walk through a lush and tastefully planted garden. The high roof, above tall clerestory windows, was sheltered by an ancient oak. The front porch was laid with pale stone. The hand-carved front door opened into a handsome foyer brightened by a skylight and by a floor of cream-toned Mexican tiles. From the high-ceilinged living room to the tile-floored kitchen, the interior was filled with light.

The furnishings were casual and well designed, the copies of antique Persian rugs well made and rich in color, every detail planned for a tasteful but durable upscale rental. The owners had only recently refurnished, storing their antique pieces in the insulated attic among chests of outgrown children's toys and personal mementos.

Unloading her grocery bag, Charlie rinsed the salad greens and the pound of Bing cherries she had bought for Vivi, put the cherries into a flat plastic container, and slipped them in the freezer—frozen cherries for Vivi to suck on during the day, a childish habit that seemed to Charlie to have weird sexual connotations.

Moving into the living room, she watered the plants with a specially prepared plant food that was kept in a gallon plastic bottle under the wet bar. It was when she returned to the bright kitchen to get the vacuum from the cleaning closet next to the pantry, that she smelled something sour and metallic, a vile stink like spoiling meat, seeping out around the pantry door. Had some food gone bad, or a can of something exploded?

That didn't seem likely. She had stocked the shelves herself, only three weeks before, with freshly purchased

108

staples, following instructions from the rental agent. Reaching for the doorknob, she hesitated, filled with a strange apprehension.

Slowly she pulled the pantry door open—and slammed it closed again, trying to catch her breath.

Her first thought was that some kind of meat had been butchered in there and been flung around, then left lying in globs on the floor. Who would do such a thing? And there were hanks of hair on it, pieces of fur.

Dark fur, mixed with gore and blood.

Fur mottled like . . .

Terrified, ripping open the door again, she expected to see tortoiseshell fur mottled black and brown. Those cats roamed everywhere, they were likely to slip into anyone's house. But who would . . . ?

Oh, not the kit. Please, not the kit.

Having flung open the door, she forced herself to look carefully.

Relief flooded her. This wasn't the kit's tortoiseshell fur, nor Dulcie's tabby-striped coat. This fur was coarse and rough—black and gray, not brown.

Raccoons?

Raisins and crackers were mixed with the blood. From the shelves, the contents of burst cans of corn and fruit salad dripped down. Raccoons couldn't do that—the cans had been blown open by some tremendous force.

She turned away, her breakfast wanting to come up. What kind of horrible prank was this? What sick joke? She stood holding her hand to her mouth, trying to mask the smell, trying to keep from heaving. Trying to construct a plausible scenario.

Chill air touched her from above, a cold draft. Looking up at the pantry ceiling, she saw the access

109

door had been tampered with, the plywood cover apparently pulled aside, then pushed crookedly back again into place, its unpainted parts marking its altered position. Would raccoons be able to pull aside an attic door, would they know how to do that?

Certainly raccoons had broken into several village houses that were supposedly vermin proof. She remembered when a dozen of the beasts got into the Carvers' house through the attic and down into an upstairs bedroom, terrifying old Mrs. Carver nearly to apoplexy. And that wasn't the only bizarre tale of the damage raccoons could do. When two of them got into the high school by shoving aside an acoustical tile, they took over the principal's office and quite effectively rearranged his filing system before they could be evicted. As she stood studying the bloody mess, trying not to be sick, she realized she was looking, among a pattern of dark splatters, at a ragged hole in the sheetrock.

A bullet hole? Was that what happened, had these animals been shot? She thought the bullet would have to have been a hollow-point, to tear the beasts up like that and to make that huge ragged hole in the wall.

She imagined the animals breaking in, making a racket as they attacked the food, then Elliott flinging open the door and shooting them. Afterward, he must have pushed the plywood back over the ceiling opening, maybe thinking that more of the beasts were up there.

Couldn't he have thought of some other approach than killing them? The police carried animal nets for this kind of emergency. Or the police would have called a specialist. There were several services in the area that had humane traps to deal with such cases. She felt rage that he had called no one, that he had shot them. And then, to top it off, he had left the mess for her to clean up.

Swallowing back her anger, she fetched rubber gloves from her tote bag, and put on one of the surgical masks she carried for use when she didn't want to breathe caustic fumes. Tying a dish-towel over her hair, she cursed the Traynors. She was a cleaning professional, not a dead body disposal service. Not in this situation. This wasn't the aftermath of police business, to which she had been summoned. She felt like walking out, telling them to clean up their own mayhem.

With a roll of paper towels and a dustpan to use as a scoop and several heavy garbage bags, she cleared out the spilled food and scrubbed away the blood where it had splattered on the walls and shelves. She dumped the undamaged cans in a bucket of hot, soapy water and scrubbed each one. As she cleaned, she found three other holes. From one, she dug out a soft-nosed bullet smashed like a mushroom. The other was too deeply embedded. When she had finished scrubbing and disinfecting and carried the bags out to the garbage, she saw that her work wasn't finished.

The yard around the back door was covered with garbage—empty cans, soiled wrapping paper, all kinds of household refuse. Strange that the garbage can itself was upright, with the lid secured.

After pitching the scattered garbage piece by piece into a fresh plastic bag, she opened the tall can and saw that two bags were already there, heavy with something, and smelling of gore; and she felt disgust all over again. Traynor had put the bodies here. That sickened her. Couldn't he have given them a decent burial? This was going to be her last day working for Elliott Traynor. It took a really colossal nerve to leave such a mess, not

111

only in the pantry but in the yard, not even to pick up the garbage, no matter how famous he was.

When she'd finished cleaning, she threw her mask and hair cover and gloves into the garbage, fetched a clean uniform and shoes from her van, and, in the Traynor's guest bath, washed her face and hands and arms, washed every exposed part of herself, dropping her soiled garments and shoes in a plastic bag to be discarded. She'd bill Traynor for replacements. Cleaning up after a murder didn't hold a candle to this.

Returning to the kitchen to fetch the vacuum, the thought struck her that not only raccoons but a man could have been shot in there.

How silly. Did she always have to imagine more than was possible?

And yet . . .

If there had been a man, she thought, panicked, she had destroyed the evidence.

Hurrying out to the garbage can, she hauled out the plastic bags she had filled and opened the two at the bottom.

Raccoons. Badly mangled. Surely that accounted for the blood and gore.

Tying up the bags again and stuffing everything back on top, she closed the lid tightly and went inside to scrub herself all over again—and to call the police department. Her feelings about Elliott Traynor, which had before today deteriorated from admiration to puzzled unease, had turned to disgust.

She supposed she was too inclined to see her heroes as giants above reproach. She expected Elliott Traynor to be without any possible fault.

Though she didn't suppose that it was illegal to shoot raccoons, under the circumstances, she thought she

112

ought to tell Max of the incident, thought there might be some reason that he would need to know this. When she'd placed the call, the dispatcher told her Captain Harper was in court. She left a message for him to call her, she didn't want to tell the dispatcher why. She felt tired, enervated. Felt used and unnaturally defenseless— not her usual state of mind.

She wanted to see Max and feel the strength of him holding her, wanted to hear some wisecrack, some wry, comment about murdered raccoons, some twisted cop humor that would make her laugh.

But then when she went to dust the dining room and mop its tile floor, she found Traynor's note. It lay on the table beside a hundred-dollar bill.

Ms. Getz:

Raccoons got in the pantry. No time to call anyone. I shot them with a target pistol. Sorry for the mess. Here's an extra hundred. Appreciate if you don't mention this. Embarrassing scene I'd not want talked about.

Not a graceful communication. Short and abrupt. Well, what did she want, a eulogy to dead raccoons? She felt inclined to leave his hundred-dollar bill. Surely Traynor had intended this as a bribe.

But she had more than earned the hundred, cleaning up his mess. If she didn't take it now, she'd be billing him for the extra work. Likely the money was intended as both payment and bribe.

She called it earned, slipped it in her pocket, and got on with the vacuuming. She did the living room and front bedroom, emptying the wastebaskets with distaste, where Vivi's cherry seeds stuck to the plastic liners.

113

Only when she started on Traynor's study did she slow her pace.

When she wheeled the vacuum into Traynor's study, it was as neat and tidy as ever. Nothing on the desk but his computer and the freshly printed chapter he had written the night before. He always left the new chapter on the desk, possibly to go over the next day when he and Vivi returned from their walk or from the theater. They went often to approve the sets that Cora Lee was painting, then had breakfast out.

Tryouts were tonight. Charlie supposed that when rehearsals began they'd be at the theater for longer periods. It seemed a rigorous routine for someone being treated for cancer. Traynor had told her, when they first arrived and were discussing her work routine, that he worked late into the night. He said that was when the juices flowed. She remembered the amused look in his eyes, some private joke—or maybe his faint smile was simply juvenile humor at the off-color connotation. A strange man. He still interested her, despite her anger this morning.

He was far more stern in real life than he looked in the promotion picture on his book jackets. Long before this morning, Traynor had made her uncomfortable. He seemed to analyze and weigh a person far too closely— maybe a writer's penetrating observation, she supposed, as he tried to see beneath the surface.

Did she, when she was sketching an animal, stare like that at her subject? Did she make her animals uncomfortable? With Joe and Dulcie, she'd seen them both wince when she was drawing there. And despite the kit's bright disposition, several times when she'd looked too hard at the kit, she'd gotten a hiss in return or a striking paw that surprised her and made her draw

114

back.

Who knew what an animal felt when you stared at them? In the animal world, a stare meant the threat of attack. One was supposed to stare at a mountain lion, to keep him from attacking first—to show superiority. But one was not, while hunting, supposed to look a deer or rabbit in the eye, that only alerted them.

Joe and Dulcie and the kit were sentient cats, not instinct-driven wild beasts. Most of the time, logic drove those three—but a logic overlying the same deep feline nature as any ordinary kitty—they weren't any less cat, they were simply more than cat.

Vacuuming beneath the fine walnut desk and along beside the walnut bookshelves, she reached to try the desk drawers and file drawers. As usual, they were locked. Hesitantly she reached for the new pages of Traynor's book that lay before her.

All week she had been sneaking looks at Traynor's manuscript. Last Friday, reading his earlier pages, she had been shocked and deeply upset. She'd been so excited to have a look at his work, had told herself that after all, it was written for public consumption, and it was right there on the desk; she only wanted to see how he developed his prose, from the beginning. In school she had been interested in writing fiction—though far more fascinated, always, with drawing, with the visual images she wanted to create. But Traynor had always been a favorite; she had loved reading some of his passages over and over, simply for their poetry.

She'd heard him tell someone on the phone that this new book was set in Marin County, above San Francisco, at the turn of the century. She liked the title, *Twilight Silver*. She had stood with the vacuum paused and roaring, reading the neatly printed pages.

They'd been dreadful. The words stumbled, the paragraphs didn't make sense. She had started again, thinking her lack of comprehension was her fault. She had skipped ahead several pages, but had found no improvement. She'd decided this must be a first draft, a rough beginning. Surely a writer was allowed a flawed first draft.

But why print it out so neatly? Why bother, until it was the way he wanted it—why print out these garbled pages, this lack of clarity with not a hint of his lucid style?

Being an artist herself, with a duly accredited degree—for whatever that was worth, she thought wryly—she felt that she had some sense of how a work of art, a drawing or manuscript, grew to fruition. But those pages, despite the promise of an exciting plot, had been so clumsy they embarrassed her.

Had the illness done this to Traynor? Was it slowly taking his mind as well as his body? The thought deeply distressed her.

Well, she didn't know much about how writers worked. Maybe from this draft he would construct the smooth prose that she so loved. Still, she'd thought that writers edited on screen, didn't print until they felt they had something of value. But maybe not. Surely they didn't all work the same.

That morning, aligning the pages as she had found them, she had felt a deep disappointment, almost a loss.

But now, this morning, maybe these pages would be better. Watching the driveway through the study window, she picked up the current chapter. She read hopefully, but only for a moment. His words were just as inept, just as off-putting. She read two pages, then tried again, but it was no better. She stopped when she heard a car pulling in, and laid the chapter on the desk.

But the car appeared in the next drive, parking before the house next door. Aligning the pages, she glanced up into the bookshelves—and caught her breath.

Joe Grey stepped out from behind the row of books, his yellow eyes wide with amusement. "I'm surprised at you, Charlie. I didn't dream you'd take the Traynor's money as a trustworthy professional, then pry into their personal business."

"What are you doing here? What are you up to?"

Joe smiled. "Does he always lock the drawers?"

Charlie grinned. "Why would you snoop on the Traynors?"

The tomcat shrugged, a tilt of his handsome head, a twitch of his muscled gray shoulders.

"Where's Dulcie? And what," she said, fixing Joe with a deep scowl, "did you have to do with that mess in the pantry?"

"You think I shot those beasts? That I've learned to use a pistol? Come on, Charlie."

"What did you have to do with those raccoons getting in the house?"

His gaze was innocent.

"Besides the raccoons—besides that gruesome mess that I had to clean up, what are you up to? There's not enough crime in the village? You've been reduced to idle snooping?"

"And what about you?" He lifted a white-tipped gray paw. "You sound so much like Clyde it's scary. No wonder you stopped dating him—before you turned into his clone."

"That is really very rude." She reached up to stroke Joe's gleaming gray shoulder. "Come on down. Were you looking for Traynor's research about Catalina's letters?"

Joe twitched an ear.

"I saw how interested you were, that night at Lupe's Playa. So, did you find it?"

He smiled. "It was right here in this stack. I pulled it behind the books, to read it while you vacuumed—while you snooped."

"And?"

"Catalina's letters to Marcos Romano are worth something. Two of them sold recently at Butterfield's for over ten thousand apiece."

"You're kidding me."

He pawed the sheaf of research from behind the books. "Between pages six and seven."

The auction notice lay there with Traynor's receipt. Joe showed her the notation at the bottom.

She raised her eyes to his, their faces on a level. "How many letters were there? How many did she write?"

"I don't know, Charlie. Maybe no one knows."

"If they're that valuable, why did he write a play about them—or why is he letting it be produced? Already, apparently, people are looking for them."

"Maybe he couldn't resist. Maybe, despite the wisdom of keeping them secret, the letters kept bugging him. The way you get bugged, wanting to draw something. The way you stare at a person, your fingers itching for a piece of charcoal."

"Aren't you perceptive this morning."

"My dear Charlie, cats invented perceptive. If some of Catalina's lost letters are still out there, and if Traynor thinks he can find them, maybe he figured he'd come on out to the coast and search for them while the play was still in rehearsal, before anyone saw the play,

118

before anyone else thought of looking for them."

"But . . ."

"Maybe it was thinking and thinking of the letters that made him write the play in the first place. But now he's sick and dying, he's in a hurry. He wants the letters now. Once he's dead, he won't care who finds them."

He looked at her steadily, his yellow eyes wide and appraising. "What do you think of his work in progress?"

Charlie only looked at him.

"I'm no literary critic," Joe said. "But in my humble feline opinion, that stuff stinks."

Charlie laughed. She stepped to the window, to check the street, then sat down in Elliott's padded swivel chair.

Dropping down from the bookshelf to the desk, Joe patted the new chapter. "Right now, there are more questions about the Traynors than answers. Why did Vivi want to avoid Ryan Flannery? And why did she come in here early this morning and print the pages?" Joe shrugged. "Maybe he didn't feel like it last night after all the excitement. Makes you wonder how he does feel, despite what she tells people about how well he's doing with the treatments."

"She printed out his work this morning?"

"She did. And don't you wonder," Joe said, "why he packs a gun? Why he brought a gun out here from New York? He must not have declared it, must have hidden it in his luggage, with New York so strict about gun ownership."

Charlie sat frowning. "For a rotten-tempered tomcat, you come up with some interesting questions. What . . . Here they come."

As the Traynors' car turned in, Charlie snatched Joe

119

from the desk, tucking him under her arm like a bag of flour, forcing an indignant snarl from the tomcat.

"Shut up, Joe. Hold still." Lifting the vacuum with her other hand, she watched the car pass the window, heading for the back.

"Wait," Joe hissed. "The research. Put it in the stack, on the bottom."

She dropped both Joe and the vacuum, hid the research, and they headed fast for the front door. "Where's Dulcie?" she whispered. "Where's the kit?"

Dulcie and the kit flew out past her as she jerked the door open. Picking up the doormat, Charlie stepped down into the yard to shake it. Already the three cats were gone, vanished among the bushes.

13

THE TALL TUDOR MANSION THAT HOUSED MOLENA Point Little Theater thrust above the smaller cottages like a solemn matriarch, its old shingles gray with time. But its high windows shone clean, reflecting the midmorning sky in a deep, clear azure. Sixty years earlier, the residence had been headquarters for Hidalgo Farms, an upscale cattle and sheep operation. When, in the seventies, the outbuildings and carriage house and barns had been turned into Hidalgo Plaza, wide paseos and promenades had been added, brick-paved, and roofed with trellises to join one building to the next.

The house itself had been gutted, its inner walls torn out and replaced by heavy beams, to form the vast and high-ceilinged theater. The stage occupied what had once been the large parlor. The old formal dining room and morning room and study, now flowing together, were fitted with comfortable rows of theater seats upholstered in mauve velvet.

Three large ground-level bedrooms had become the cluttered backstage with its dressing rooms, two small baths, and the vast costume room. Other workrooms and the prop room had taken over the kitchen and butler's pantry and carriage house.

The upstairs bedrooms supplied office space and a balcony looking down on the audience, a long, narrow gallery that accommodated the control panel for the house lights and stage lighting, an area strung so densely with conduit and thick wires that it looked like a den for families of sociably oriented boa constrictors. The balcony was separated from the raftered ceiling space beyond, which yawned over the rows of seating, by a three-foot-high plastered rail. Beyond the balcony, beams and rafters stretched away in an open grid on which were hung banks of lights. The timbers, jutting across empty space, provided to the surefooted and arboreally inclined a fine series of catwalks above the heads of the audience.

Though it was midmorning, barely 10:00 A.M., the vast and empty theater was as dark as night, a sepulchral world woven of flattened shadows and inky and indecipherable vistas. No window opened into this part of the theater. The outer walls of the old mansion, where tall panes of glass had once lighted the living areas, were now blocked by inner barriers. The ten-foot space between these walls was broken into small offices, and storage and work rooms, all cheerfully brightened by those antique panels of mullioned glass. A sunny morning without, but the theater within so dark that only a cat could see her way. On a ten-by-twelve beam above the stage, the kit prowled impatiently, an agile tightrope walker, a swift black-and-brown smear of shadow within shadows, a small phantom personage alone in the empty building, waiting for Cora Lee to appear for work dressed in her painter's smock.

Usually Cora Lee arrived at the theater much earlier, unlocking the back door from the parking lot and turning on the lights so the stage shown cheerfully around her as she painted the sets for *Thorns of Gold*. This morning, the kit had waited a long time. She had been here from first light, impatient and hungry. Cora Lee always brought a snack to share with her. She waited, dreaming of far worlds peopled by cats like her and Dulcie and Joe Grey, worlds she half invented, and half knew from the tales of elder cats and from the old Celtic myths. But now, as morning wore on, even those stories paled. Her patience frayed at last. Painfully lonely in the empty silence, she gave up on Cora Lee.

Leaping down to the top of an open stepladder and then to the stage, and across the stage and down to the carpeted aisles before the seats, she went to explore the rest of the theater. Trotting into the outer rooms where the windows let in light, she made her way toward the prop room. She knew the theater office; she had walked on all the desks there, across stacks of playbills and papers, had rooted in the wastebaskets, prowled the cluttered shelves, and snatched cookies from a desk drawer. In the wardrobe room, she had wandered dreaming beneath the rows of hanging costumes, sniffing the old smells of lace and satin and leather and the metallic scent of tarnished necklaces. She had patted her paw carelessly into a jar of greasepaint that had been left open, then had printed her paw marks along the hall floors. She had, upstairs on the balcony, tapped at

122

dozens of light switches on the control panel, an exercise that, if the main switch had been on, would have created a wonderland of flashing lights in the theater below. She had tasted the powdered cream in an open jar in the cluttered coffee room and had stuck her nose in the sugar bowl. But best of all she had wandered through the prop room exploring an amazing array of surprises.

It was there she headed now, purring to herself. She had no notion that she was not alone, she heard no sound but her own purring. Only when she stopped purring to nibble at an itch on her shoulder did she pause, suddenly wary.

She'd heard nothing, really. But she thought the air stirred differently, the spaces around her disturbed in some way, as if something was moving unheard and unseen through the theater's dark reaches.

It was not Joe Grey or Dulcie. They would have mewed a tiny sound asking if she was there, a faint murmur inaudible to human ears. And when they drew close, she would have smelled their scent. Now she smelled nothing different at all among the rich medley of theater scents. What was here in the dark with her that she couldn't see? Few humans could be so quiet. And why would a human come into the theater and not put on a light?

Did she smell Gabrielle's lavender scent? The tall blond lady was, after all, the wardrobe mistress; she came and went quite a lot.

Or perhaps she caught a whiff of candy? But, trying to identify the smell, her nose was too filled with the harsh aromas of dust and paint, of turpentine, floor wax, and the body smells of humans. She stood sniffing, more curious than wary, trying to understand the mysterious movement she could detect among the black and angled shadows.

She had heard no door close. Had someone been in here all along, even before she herself came through the narrow attic window beneath the big duct pipes and black ropes of electrical cords? Before she squeezed down through the hole from the attic, past the round silver heat duct, and dropped to the balcony among the huge snakes of wire that always gave her the shivers?

Well, whatever was in here, she was safe. No human would see her in the darkness, and anyway, she could dodge any human.

Happily she padded on again toward the prop room, to play her solitary games among that richness of crazy human possessions that no yard or garage sale could match, among the baby crib and beer signs and bicycles, the wrought iron gates and painted china bowls and metal shields and stuffed horse's head and the front end of an ancient car. Everything in the world was there— beaded floor lamps, rocking chair, ten green glass bottles each as big as a doghouse, a set of elk horns, pieces of machinery so strange that not even Joe Grey, who had named these things for her, could identify them. The saddest objects were a ship's lantern and anchor smelling of dust and not of the sea, as if these nautical wonders had forgotten where they belonged.

The game was to see if she could roll and walk and tag among the shelves without knocking anything off. When she tired of that she liked to lie on the pink satin fainting couch that stood wedged between the unicycle and a woodstove with a red paper fire burning in it—not warm, but pretty to look at. She liked to nap on the pink couch imagining what the play would be like all in costume and Cora Lee singing under the lights, and she,

Kit, lying on a rafter above the stage, enjoying the best seat in the house. But now, crouched beside the horse's moldering head, she heard a footstep.

Well, a footstep was better than hearing nothing when she knew someone was there. As the door swung open, the kit slid beneath the old car, tucking her long, fluffy tail under too.

A light blazed, a harsh flashlight beam striking the shelves and moving along them, stopping now and then, a great eye of light searching and peering.

The woman who held the light was small and thin, dressed in dark tights, her black hair pulled back under a cap. Vivi Traynor smelled of cherries. Her full attention was on the crowded shelves, her movements as wary as a thieving dog's.

But what would the theater's junk room offer that a famous author's wife couldn't buy? Whatever she was looking for, it wasn't small; she wasn't poking into the narrow niches. The kit thought of the white chest that man, Casselrod, had snatched and that Vivi wanted badly enough to follow him—but that chest was in his store, already torn apart.

Working her way along the shelves, pushing and pulling and rearranging, Vivi turned at last to fetch the dusty ladder from the corner. Climbing to investigate the topmost shelves, again she moved only large items. She investigated a closed cardboard box, a leather suitcase, a lidded roasting pan big enough to cook a St. Bernard. Vivi opened each, looking in, then closed it again and shoved it back. When she had finished with pulling things apart, looking in and under, and didn't find what she wanted, she gave a huff of anger, backed down leaving the ladder standing open, and went out again.

The kit followed her, slipping through the door before she closed it, silent and unseen, then padding along behind. She had never seen a human who could be so quiet.

She had never seen a human she disliked in quite this way. When the raccoons were shot and that smell filled the house, she had blamed that all on Vivi. If Vivi Traynor had been a black lizard the kit would have chomped her, and spit her out dead, then chewed leaves to get the taste out. Following Vivi through the theater, she slipped ahead, stopping under the front row of seats, peering out at the darkly clad woman.

Vivi passed by, inches from her, moving silently to the exit door. There was not a creak when she opened and closed it, and then she was gone, no squall of hinge or snap of the latch. The kit made a flehmening face of disgust. What had she been after? Another chest like the white one? Were there letters worth a lot of money, like Joe Grey said? She hoped, if there were such letters, that Vivi Traynor wouldn't find them. Or Richard Casselrod either. She hoped her own friends would find them and sell them for a lot of money and buy a nice big house with a nice cozy kitchen and room for a cat to visit. She would like a little bed in a sunny window or by a fireplace. Meantime, she wanted to know what Vivi Traynor was up to with her snooping and prying, and she wished that Cora Lee was there close to her because she suddenly felt very lonely. Her paws were cold with fear.

14

RACING UP AND DOWN THE EMPTY BEACH IN THE early dawn, the dog searched frantically for his master, his black-spotted white body sharply defined against gray sky and sea. He stopped to stare at anything moving, a wave, the shadows of a wheeling gull, then plunged on again, racing so fast that his polka dot markings smeared to lines across his snowy coat. His expression was urgent and confused. From a block away, Wilma Getz saw him, where she was walking her usual two miles down the shore. She stopped, watching his frantic seeking.

She could still taste her morning coffee, its flavor mixed now with the smell of the sea. She had pulled on a red sweatshirt over her jeans, against the chill; she wore a red wool cap to keep her ears warm, her long white hair hanging down her back, bound with a silver clip. The time was barely six. She had parted from Susan in the village, after they had walked down from Wilma's house together. Susan and Lamb had turned up the shore to the north for the big poodle's run, where Lamb liked the outcropping rocks and the tide pools in which to pad a hesitant paw.

Wilma stood very still, watching the dalmatian. When the dog spied her, he came racing, so glad to see a human in this empty world. She knelt, fending off his excited licking, and took hold of his collar. Had he strayed from some tourist, a dog who didn't know the area, didn't remember how to get back to an unfamiliar motel? But she already suspected who he belonged to. Trying to hold him still, she searched for a tag or a metal plate on his collar. There were not many dalmatians in the village, and this dog was not one she knew.

The leather collar was old and curled and wet from the sea. There was no identification of any kind to tell her the dog's name or the name or phone number of his owner. He was a young animal, and so thin she could see every rib. He pushed against her, panting and slurping as if she was his last hope.

"Do you belong to the mysterious walker? To Susan's young friend? To Lenny Wells?" The dog shivered and licked at her. She looked up and down the beach. "Do you belong to the man who broke into Susan's house?"

Why would someone abandon such a nice dog? Could the young man have died from his head wound? Perhaps passed out in the bushes after he escaped Susan's, never waking again from a severe concussion? She imagined him slowly making his way to the shore with the dog beside him, trying to get away from the police, perhaps not realizing how badly he was hurt. Where had the dog been while he broke into Susan's? Why hadn't the police seen him when they searched the neighborhood? If Lenny had died on the beach, had the dog, when he could not rouse his master, run away confused and kept running?

But that was two days ago. Someone would have found the body by now. The beach was full of people once the sun came out, kids playing in and out among the greenbelt that met the sand. Why hadn't someone taken charge of the dog, and called the police or the animal shelter?

Turning back toward home with the dalmatian clinging close to her, she walked him through the village to meet Susan. He didn't try to leave her, but pressed against her

128

leg as if in terror that she would abandon him. He had to be starved. She had turned into the village market to buy dog food when she saw Susan ahead, on the far side of Ocean, her multicolored sweater and red scarf bright against the pale stucco shops. Drawing near, Wilma held on to the dalmatian's collar. The minute he saw Lamb he lunged and squirmed, trying to race to the big poodle, leaping and dancing like a puppy so it was all she could do to hold him.

"Same dog?" she called to Susan when they were still half a block apart.

Susan nodded, holding Lamb on a short lead. "Same dog. Where did you find him?" She hurried to them and knelt to inspect the dog, looking at his collar. "Same three long overlapped spots on his left ear. Same thin face and frightened expression. Jobe, Lenny called him." She looked along the street as if Lenny might suddenly appear, then looked up at Wilma. "He wasn't with anyone? You didn't see Lenny?"

"No, no one on the beach. He was frantic, running, doubling back and forth. I couldn't leave him there, even if I'd wanted to. He's clung to me like glue. Do you think Lenny was the man in your breakfast room?"

"I keep wondering. I saw only the back of the man's head, but he was like Lenny. Same color hair, same general build. Lenny always wore—wears a cap, usually with his collar turned up." Susan hugged the dalmatian, drawing a disapproving glare from Lamb. "This poor dog. Has he been wandering for two days, trying to find his master?"

"Harper will want to know about him."

Susan nodded. "Is it all right to bring him to your house? We can put him in the garage. I brought plenty of food for Lamb. Or we could put him on a long line in the drive, leave the garage door open, make him a bed inside."

Wilma was glad she had finished her garage enclosing the carport. It had come in handy. Her English-style cottage had no backyard at all, only a narrow stone walk between the house and the hill behind that rose in a steep, unfenced wilderness. "Of course it's all right." Certainly Susan respected her front flower garden as off-limits to canine romping and digging. Lamb was always a gentleman, although it hadn't been easy for him having no fenced yard to run in.

"Oh," Susan said, watching the two dogs play, "Lamb does like him. But we can't have them together in the house, not romping like that."

"He'll settle down when he's eaten," Wilma said.

Susan snapped Lamb's leash on the dalmatian, handed it to Wilma, and commanded Lamb to heel. Heading home to Wilma's, they soon turned up the stone walk through her deep garden, the air cool and still beneath the giant oaks. The pale stone cottage, with its steep slate roof, mullioned windows, and stone chimney, sat against the hill behind as if civilization ended at its back door, the well-maintained house with its carefully tended flowers an abrupt contrast to the hill's wild tangles. They took the dogs inside through the back door, which opened to the street at the opposite end of the house from the front door, and into the kitchen. Susan fed both dogs while Wilma heated the skillet and laid strips of bacon in it. She had already made the pancake batter. Balancing the cordless phone in the crook of her shoulder as she cooked, she called Max Harper at home before he left for the station. The phone rang five times.

"Did I wake you?"

"I'm in the stable feeding the horses. Had a loaded pitchfork in my hands. This a social call?"

"We—Susan and I—have the dalmatian that belonged . . ."

"Have you? Hang on to him, I'll be down in twenty minutes. Sure it's the same dog?"

"Susan says so. He was running the beach, lost."

"Did you look around? See anyone?"

"I scanned the beach. Didn't beat the bushes. He acted like he'd been left."

"Be right down. No, I haven't had breakfast," he said to her unasked question.

Wilma hung up, laughing, made fresh coffee, and put more bacon in the skillet.

When Harper arrived, Lamb greeted him with dignity. But the dalmatian was all over him, whining and leaning against him. Harper looked him over, feeling him for wounds, looking at the pads of his feet. Removing his collar, he examined it. He looked in the dog's eyes, his ears, his mouth—wanting to know the dog was all right, Wilma thought, simply because he was that kind of man. But, as a cop, wanting to find anything unusual about the lost animal.

Apparently he found nothing of note. Buckling the collar on again, he gave the dog a pat. The dalmatian lay down by the door, full of breakfast and attention, sighing deeply.

Harper sat at the table between Wilma and Susan, looking with appreciation at the tall stack of pancakes on his plate, and the eight slices of bacon. Max Harper still ate like the wild young bull rider he'd been at eighteen; and he weighed about the same. Clyde claimed Harper took in enough groceries for three men.

131

Everyone had said he'd gain weight when he quit smoking, but he hadn't.

"We have no line on a Lenny White," he told Susan. "No one by that name or fitting that description was treated in the hospital emergency room. We do have a response on the other set of fingerprints—which could belong either to the victim, or to whoever attacked him."

Susan stopped eating, watching Harper.

"There was a fair set of prints on the computer. None on the hammer we picked up, though it appears to be the weapon. Traces of blood and flesh embedded in the creases of the metal. The prints belong to a man named Augor Prey. Does that name mean anything?"

"No." Susan shook her head.

"We'll have a picture later today. Prey's father is a professor of history at Cal, Berkeley. Dr. Kenneth Prey. He taught at Davis while the son was in grammar school. Augor's description fits your dog-walking friend. Thirty-four, slim, about six feet, brown hair, hazel eyes."

Susan nodded uneasily. "If that is Lenny, he gave me a false name. And it's strange. He said he'd moved out from New York, but he didn't sound like the New Yorkers I know."

"Prey seems to have spent his adult years bumming around up and down the coast, working here and there. Never been in real trouble. A few minor arrests, fighting, tearing up a beer tavern, petty theft. No record of burglaries. He ran an antique shop in Salinas for eight months, and worked in a San Francisco book store. He's been living in a cheap room in Half Moon Bay, some-times works in an antiques shop up there. He's also worked here in Molena Point, for Richard Casselrod,

132

when Casselrod or Fern has taken time off. When he does that, he sleeps at the shop. Casselrod said he hasn't needed extra help recently, hasn't seen Prey for six months.

"If Augor Prey is your Lenny White," Harper said, "it's possible he may have been staying somewhere else in the village. We've found no motel registration in either his name or for Lenny White."

"You've been very thorough," Susan said, "considering that we don't know whether this was a murder or an assault, considering the only charges I could make were for breaking and entering, and vandalism—not for theft."

"It could turn into murder," Harper reminded her. "Meanwhile, the detectives have been over your place again. They have everything they're going to get, pictures, prints, blood. You can go ahead and get someone in to clean up, get your life back in order."

Susan smiled. "I'll call Charlie this morning."

"Please let us know if you find anything missing when you get back home. You still have no idea what they might have been after?"

"No. The only thing I've bought recently that wasn't in the house was the carved chest I called you about. That was in my trunk."

"I'd like to see it."

Taking her keys from her pocket, Susan stepped out to the drive. In a moment, they heard her car trunk slam. She returned carrying a small wooden chest, perhaps eighteen inches long, its lid shaped like a peak, with the top cut off to form a three-sided slab. She set it on the table before the police captain.

"There's an old chest like that in the mission museum," Harper said. "Only much larger—made to use as a saddle rack. Just fits a stock saddle."

The sides and lid of the chest were roughly carved with geometric patterns and simple medallions. The wood was oak, apparently unfinished, darkened by age. One end had split through the carvings. The inside of the box was so rough they could see the chisel marks.

"You said you bought this at the Barmeir estate sale?" Harper asked.

"Yes. I got there before seven that morning, took a number, came back at ten to wait my turn. It was mobbed; the estate sales always are. When I saw this little chest on a table in the den, I just—well I grabbed it up and bought it and got out of there. Didn't even look at anything else."

"Why?" Harper asked, watching her.

"Because of the play. Elliott Traynor's play. Do you know the story?"

Harper nodded.

Susan looked at Harper. "Catalina died on the Stanton Ranch, just a few miles from here. Apparently no one knows what happened to the chests."

"You bought this after you met Augor Prey?"

"Yes."

"Did you ever mention it to him?"

"I—yes, I did. We talked about the yard sales, and about our plans for Senior Survival, about our buying and selling on the Web. I'm afraid I did tell him about the chest."

"How long was this before the break-in? You discussed these matters only once or several times?"

"Only once. Just . . . just a few days before the break-in." She lowered her gaze. "I told a lot to a stranger. Though most of our conversation," she went on defensively, "concerned my suggestions for him to meet

134

people in the village, meet some younger folks."

Wilma said, "Didn't it seem strange to you that he would need help meeting people? Everyone's friendly, and there's more to do here than a person could handle in ten lifetimes with plays, concerts, classes."

Susan nodded. "I put it down to shyness."

"Did he know where you lived?" Harper asked.

"Yes," she said, embarrassed. "He never came to the house, but I told him where it was, while talking about the weather, about how much wind we get. So foolish of me."

Wilma rose to pour coffee, glancing out her kitchen window. "There's Mavity." She went to open the back door, calling out as Mavity turned up through the garden. "We're in the kitchen. Where's your VW? Don't tell me you're having car trouble?"

Mavity laughed. "That old bug wouldn't dare. I'm parked up the street to clean at the Rileys'. They like me early, but . . . Well, I saw the captain's pickup truck . . ." She glanced shyly at Harper. "Wondered if anything was wrong, if anything else has happened . . ."

Wilma poured coffee for her. "Have you had breakfast?"

"Oh, yes. But coffee would taste good. Yours always tastes better than mine." She sat down, smiling at Susan. "It's pretty early, even for the Rileys. Guess I get restless staying home anymore, thinking about the city tearing down my house. Seems like I can't feel cozy, knowing it will be gone soon. I just wish the city would make up its mind. If they decide to condemn, then get on with it." Mavity's uniform this morning was the ubiquitous white, with pale blue piping at the seams, likely a top-of-the-line model that had seen its share of launderings.

Wilma laid her hand over Mavity's. "You know my guest room's yours as long as you want."

"And my house, too," Susan said. "I'll be going home today, to get that mess cleaned up. And who knows how soon we might find a big place that's just right for all of us."

Mavity nodded, looking both uncertain and hopeful. She reached out to touch the oak chest. "This is old. Look at that crack, and how dark the wood is. It's sort of like those wood carvings my brother, Greeley, sends me sometimes from Panama."

"I got it at the Barmeir sale. I had it in the trunk of my car the morning that man broke in."

"It's nicer than that white chest Richard Casselrod made such a scene over—stole it, is what he did. No other word for it. Jerked it right out of Cora Lee's hands, even if he did throw down some money."

Harper rose, calling the dalmatian to him. "I'll take him up to Dr. Firetti to board. Firetti owes me a favor."

"I . . ." Susan began. "He and Lamb get along very well. If you don't find Lenny . . ."

Harper nodded. "That would be fine. But right now, it isn't wise for you to keep him. You don't want Lenny White coming around, using the dog as an excuse. In fact," Harper said, "I'm not keen on you going back home alone."

"I'll be fine with Lamb. If Lamb had been home that morning, those men wouldn't have gotten in."

Harper didn't reply. He rose and left, taking the spotted dog with him. Wilma stood at the window, watching the dalmatian leap up into the cab of Harper's Chevy pickup. And Susan sat looking silently at Wilma and Mavity, realizing suddenly how very much she did not want to be home alone, did not want to go to sleep at night wondering if someone would break a window and come in—except of course Lamb would bark and wake her.

But she grinned at Mavity's wrinkled frown of concern. "A poodle's no sissy, Mavity. Those teeth could take your arm off."

Though in truth, it was Lamb she worried about. Worried that someone would hit him with a heavy weapon or shoot him, leaving both of them defenseless.

15

DRIVING UP OCEAN, WITH THE DALMATION IN THE seat beside him, Max Harper's mind remained on Susan Brittain. An extra patrol around her place wouldn't hurt, as long as he had the manpower. Turning off Ocean beside Beckwhite Automotive, he glanced toward the east wing of the handsome Mediterranean building where Clyde Damen's large, sprawling repair shop was housed, with its separate body and paint shops, its storage sheds and parking space, and Clyde's private workshop where he restored antique cars. He could see into the main shop, but he didn't see Clyde. The low morning sun brightened the red tile roof of the complex and picked out the brilliant colors of the Icelandic poppies that bloomed before the dealership's show windows. The bright colors made him think of his dead wife, of the garden Millie had loved.

Through the shaded glass of the showroom, he could see a dark green Rolls-Royce gleaming, and two new Jaguars, one bright red. He wondered how it would be to have that kind of money.

Grinning, he stroked the spotted dog. "I wouldn't spend it on cars," he told the dalmatian. "Spend it on horses, and maybe dogs, too—and on Charlie," he said. And maybe that was all right. Millie had told him more than once that she wouldn't want him to be alone. Until now he'd been content enough, cherishing only her memory.

Dr. Firetti's home and hospital were just beyond Beckwhite's, on a residential side street. His facility was a complex of three small, frame cottages that had been built back in the thirties, and were now joined by high patio walls to make an entry and secure dog runs. Harper sat in his truck a moment before going in.

"I guess," he told the dog, "when this blows over, if no one's claimed you, Susan would give you a fine home." He ruffled the dog's ears. "Companion for Lamb. I bet you'd like that."

Susan Brittain had had enough trouble with that wreck that had put her in the retirement home, that had left her so crippled her daughter wasn't sure she'd walk again. But walk she did, got herself up out of the wheelchair, surely with the help of the poodle for moral support. And now this mess at her place, which he hoped wasn't going to escalate into something worse. Seemed to him that a woman living alone ought to have better security. He had some thoughts on the matter, but his ideas weren't popular.

This break-in had him uneasy; there were too many vague connections. But that's what investigating was about. What was the matter with him? Was he getting old, losing his edge? Fetching a halter rope from the back of the truck, he snapped it on the dalmatian's collar and led the dog into the waiting room.

The ten-by-ten foyer was furnished with a green

138

tweed carpet, green leather couch and love seat, and a couple of wooden chairs. A small old lady sat on the love seat, clutching a cardboard cat carrier on her lap. As Harper entered, a low hiss filled the room, sending the dalmatian bolting away from the carrier, toward the door. The receptionist nodded to Harper, spoke into the intercom, and in a moment motioned Harper on back to Firetti's office.

Firetti was a small man with a smooth round face, pale hair thinning on top, and rimless glasses. When he examined a large dog, as he prepared to do now, he put on safety glasses. He'd been hit in the face more than once by a lunging animal. Changing glasses, he lifted the dalmatian to the table, though Harper hadn't suggested an examination.

"Just a quick look-over. What's the problem?"

"Can you keep him out of sight for a while? One of those back kennels? If you get anyone in here inquiring, let me know at once. Or if it's a phone call, get whatever information you can. Say you'll keep a lookout, and call them."

Firetti nodded, smiling as if pleased to be a part of police business. He ran his hands down the dog, stroked him, checked mouth and teeth and ears, took his temperature, listened to his heart, then set him down off the table. He didn't ask questions, just nodded to Harper, and led the dog away to the isolation wing. Harper was back at the department in time for court, acting as a witness on a drunk driving case that he hoped would net the defendant the maximum sentence.

He was out of court again by 10:50, heading down the hall to the department, wishing the remodeling was finished, wondering if things would ever be back to normal. Why did any kind of building project take four

139

times as long as the contractor promised? Half his officers were in temporary quarters scattered all over the courthouse. The other half were doing their desk work among bare stud walls, stacks of two-by-fours, sawhorses and piles of sawdust and screaming power tools, and no kind of security. He wondered why he'd started this project.

Though, to give the contractor credit, his carpenters were as quiet as they could be, they didn't shout, didn't talk on the job except when their work demanded a few words—no long-winded bouts of sports talk and male gossip that most carpenters indulged in while they hammered away.

When he checked with the dispatcher, two calls got his attention.

At 9:15, the neighbor living next door to Elliott Traynor had called to report gunfire the night before. A Lillian Sanders. She said she couldn't call until her husband went to work because he had considered the noise backfire and said she shouldn't bother the police, that she would only make a fool of herself. Checking back over last night's calls he found four reports of possible gunfire, though it could have been only backfire. An officer had patrolled the area for some time, with no indication of trouble.

At 9:40, Charlie had called for him but wouldn't leave a message. That wasn't like Charlie. The number she gave was Elliott Traynors'. She told the dispatcher she'd be there until noon.

Leaving the station, he headed for the Traynors'. Why anyone needed their house cleaned every day was beyond his comprehension. The Traynors didn't even have children or pets to mess things up.

But Charlie did the shopping as well, and some meal

140

preparation, so she functioned more as a housekeeper than a cleaning service. He wondered, if he and Charlie got married, if she'd want to keep the business or sell it. They hadn't really discussed marriage. He just kept thinking that way.

Never thought he'd want to marry again. Sometimes it seemed like he'd betray Millie if he married Charlie. But other times, he thought Millie would approve. Thought if she could speak to him she'd tell him she liked Charlie, that he was a damn fool to feel guilty. Thought she'd tell him to get on with what was left of his life.

As for Charlie's Fix-It, Clean-It business, maybe she'd just hire more help. She'd worked hard building the service, had turned it into a first-class operation in just a couple of years. It would be a shame to let it go. But her real work was her animal drawings, that was where he'd like to see her spend her energy. Her work was very fine, and that was not only his opinion.

She'd tried commercial art, after getting her degree, and had left the field totally discouraged. She had no patience working for others. Maybe that's why they got along so well. She'd been feeling desperate, just about at rock bottom when she left San Francisco and moved down to Molena Point, living with her aunt Wilma and starting Charlie's Fix-It, Clean-It.

Then a local gallery had seen her animal drawings. This was the only artwork she truly loved doing. They'd liked her work enough to give her a show and represent her, and she was making a name for herself. She had a feel for animals, she knew anatomy, and she truly captured each personality. She'd done two of his horses, large framed portraits that he treasured. And Clyde's and Wilma's cats—Charlie made them look so

141

intelligent they almost scared him. That was the only time he'd seen her digress from an animal's true character. He didn't know why, when she drew those three cats, she gave them more intelligence and awareness than even the brightest animal could command. Maybe she didn't realize how bright she made them look.

Or maybe she did that to please Wilma, and to stroke Clyde's ego. Clyde did love the gray tomcat, Harper thought with amusement. He'd never thought, when they were young kids bronc-riding and raising hell, that Clyde would end up with a houseful of cats. Clyde had three cats besides the gray tom, though you hardly noticed them much; they seemed to drape themselves around the house minding their own business. It was the gray cat that seemed to be always in your face.

Arriving at the Traynors', he found that Charlie had already gone, apparently earlier than she had expected. He sat in his truck for a few moments, studying the cottage, then called Charlie on his cell phone. He'd like to question the Traynors, to ask if they'd heard gunshots, but he had no real reason to do that. Charlie answered on the second ring.

"You free for lunch?"

"Yes. I meant to stay there until noon, but I was so ticked. When they got home early I knew I'd better get out or I'd blow at them."

"You want to tell me now?"

"No. Shall I order some deli?"

"Yes. I'll meet you in front of Dolly's."

When he arrived at the deli, Charlie had just picked up their lunch. She left her van at the curb, and they drove down the coast to the state park. Cruising in through the security gate and slowly through the cypress woods to the ocean, they parked where they could enjoy the waves crashing high against the jagged rocks. Charlie was pale, her freckles dark, the way she looked after a flash of anger or disappointment. She had ordered crab sandwiches, coleslaw and nonalcoholic beer.

He opened two bottles of O'Doul's. "A neighbor of the Traynors thought she heard gunfire last night. Thought it might have been from their place."

"You talked to them?"

"I had no real reason to. Several calls were logged in last night, and an officer did an area check. He found nothing. Most of those reports turn out to be backfire." He looked at Charlie, waiting.

"There was gunfire. It was so . . . Traynor left me a hundred dollars for cleaning up the mess he made."

Harper let her tease him along, amused at her anger.

"Raccoons, Max. In the pantry. They got in from the attic. They must have made a racket—tore everything up. He shot them, right there in the pantry. He made a terrible mess, blood and gore mixed with all the food they had spilled."

She didn't know whether he was going to laugh or continue to sit there watching her. "Traynor shot them, and put the two bodies in the garbage. Left that mess for me to clean up, along with all the garbage strewn across the yard."

She saw a grin start at the corner of his mouth, a wry smile that made her want to smack him, then want to laugh, herself. "There was a loose vent into the attic. I got a ladder, nailed it back in place. The raccoons had worked the plywood cover off the crawl hole. Traynor left me a note and a hundred-dollar bill. Said he shot them with a target pistol—didn't want me to tell anyone."

The lines that mapped his lean, tanned face deepened with interest.

"It's a big pantry, a walk-in. Took me half the morning. I didn't do much else; I'll make up for it tomorrow. He got home as I was leaving, said he thought it was a burglar in there, that he got the pistol, jerked the door open, saw these huge raccoons tearing up boxes of food. Said they snarled at him and scared him, and he didn't know what else to do but shoot them. Said he was really afraid of them."

"A lot of explanation."

"Why would he not want me to tell anyone? Not want me to tell you? Because he has a gun?"

"It's not illegal to have a gun if he stores it properly and if he's not a felon. If he keeps it locked up in the house, it's not my business."

He looked deeply at Charlie. "You might want to watch yourself around Traynor, until we know what that's about. He has to have a hot temper, to blow away two innocent animals when he could have called the dispatcher and gotten some help."

"It's hard for me to think of him as being crosswise with the law. Though I do have other questions about him."

"Oh? Like what?"

"Umm—about his writing."

"About his writing?" Harper leaned back, watching the breakers crash against the rocks sending up white showers of spray. The smell of brine was sharp through the open window.

"I read part of his manuscript that he left lying on the desk."

He looked at her, raising an eyebrow.

144

She ignored his silent sarcasm. This was nothing she wanted to joke about. "It's crude, Max. Clumsy. I don't understand. Traynor's a beautiful writer."

"I didn't know you were a literary critic. Or that you were so nosy."

"Call it hero worship," she said lightly. "But this has truly upset me—a real let-down."

He began to peel the label from his beer, rolling it into a little ball. "It's a let-down because his writing is bad. Because you admired his work. You're disappointed in the man you thought of as perfect."

"Maybe." She sipped her beer, staring out at the sea, eased by its endless and constant rhythm. "Somehow the Traynors make me uneasy. They aren't what I expected. I guess I thought Vivi, too, would be different. That she would be gentler, wise and capable and supportive. My idea of an author's wife," she said, laughing. But then, watching Max, she frowned. "You—the police have no reason to be interested in Traynor?"

"Not at all. Not at the moment."

She watched him, then changed the subject. "I'm keeping the hundred dollars. I earned it. Tucking it away for a special occasion."

"Like what? A bottle of champagne for our wedding?"

He shocked himself. Shocked them both. Charlie's eyes widened. Beneath her freckles, she blushed.

He said, "Maybe a wedding and champagne on shipboard, on our way to Alaska?"

"Now I know you're putting me on. You haven't been away from the department since you joined the force."

"Not true. Been to Quantico twice for FBI training.

145

And more conferences on police administration than I want to remember."

"Well, bully for you."

He grinned. "A lot of vacation time to use up. I figure a month's cruise, this fall, before the weather turns."

Her response was so enthusiastic that she startled Harper. The moment amazed them both. It was a while before they opened their sandwiches and the containers of coleslaw and popped another beer. She tried to get hold of herself, but she couldn't. When she started to laugh, she couldn't stop. She leaned against him, laughing.

"So what's the joke?"

She knew her face had gone red. "Just . . . just excitement," she lied. "I . . ." She looked up at him. "Just happy!" But what she'd thought of suddenly was about telling Dulcie and Joe Grey. Thinking how happy the cats would be—and then that knowledge sobered her.

That was a hard call; no matter how close she and Max might be for the rest of their lives, there was one secret she could never tell him. One part of her life that she could never share.

16

SPOTLIGHTS ILLUMINATED CENTER STAGE. THE house lights were dark, the rows of seats marching away empty into the hollow blackness of the theater. Only a few front seats were occupied where Elliott and Vivi Traynor, director Samuel Ladler, and music director Mark King sat together softly talking, and occasionally rattling a script. Elliott had hunched down in his wrinkled corduroy sport coat as if perhaps he felt unwell. On the far side of the theater near the exit door, a dozen actors had taken a block of seats, whispering among themselves, waiting for their callback auditions for *Thorns of Gold*. Above the house among the rafters, where night clung against the high ceiling, crouched an attentive feline audience of three: two pairs of yellow eyes, one pair of green, catching glances of soft light. No human, below, bothered to look up, to find those tiny spotlights.

"But where's Cora Lee?" Dulcie said softly, peering down at the waiting actors.

"Still backstage," said the kit. "Painting sets like she doesn't care at all about the part."

Of the seven women who had read and sung for the part of Catalina during yesterday's tryouts, Cora Lee was one of two callbacks. Director Ladler felt so pressed for time that he had notified the actors last night before they left the theater, had stood on the patio with the little group gathered around him and read out the names of the callbacks. Then he had quickly turned back inside before anyone could challenge his decisions. No director liked that part of the casting; no one enjoyed seeing the disappointment of those who were turned away.

Below the cats, Vivi leaned over to Elliott, whispering something, then giggling. She leaned forward in her chair, looking down the several seats to question Sam Ladler and to give him orders. Elliott hardly paid attention. Surely he wasn't feeling well, Dulcie thought. Maybe the decisions that should be his had suddenly fallen on Vivi's shoulders and she was nervous about that.

Director Sam Ladler was a lean, tanned man with

thinning hair that heightened his forehead into a deep widow's peak. He looked like he ran or played tennis. He was dressed this morning in old jeans and a limp sweatshirt. He was a terse man, Wilma had said, with a dry humor. Wilma said that he and his casts had created outstanding theater for Molena Point. He sat between Traynor and Mark King, the two directors having managed to put Vivi down at the far end of the row.

Mark King was smoothly pudgy, a young man who seemed to have turned middle-aged before his time. He was short, maybe five-four, with straight, faded brown hair down to his shoulders and rimless half-glasses that he kept wiping as if he found it impossible to remove the smudges. He wore wrinkled chinos and a T-shirt with palm trees printed across it. He rose as Ladler called for Catalina and moved up onto the stage, to the piano.

"We'll have Fern Barth," Ladler said, looking down at the little group of actors. Fern was Richard Casselrod's assistant at the antiques shop, a pale, spiritless woman, in Dulcie's opinion, whose singing during tryouts had sounded as if she was practicing for second line in the choir box, hitting the notes okay, but with no more feeling than a china doll. As Fern stepped up on stage, a whiff of her perfume rose to the cats as sweet as cake icing.

"Why," Dulcie whispered, "was this woman called back?"

Joe Grey shrugged, yawning. "Doesn't stand a chance."

"I hope not," Dulcie said uneasily. And her dismay was sharp when Fern had finished, and Vivi smiled and nodded at Sam Ladler. Elliott came to life long enough to give Fern a friendly wink. Sam Ladler looked over at them blankly and called Cora Lee.

Cora Lee came out from the wings rolling down the sleeves of her smock and wiping paint from her face. Moving to center stage, she turned to the piano, smiled at Mark King, then stood quietly looking out at the rows of empty seats, collected and composed.

"Read from where she refuses to marry Stanton," Ladler said. "Then where she's locked in her room, and that first number."

Cora Lee read her lines with cold anger as Catalina was led away to her prison. Watching her, the cats forgot her stained smock and the green smear down her cheek. She stood and moved with the grace and dignity of generations of Spanish queens.

But when Catalina faced the audience from behind her locked door, her movements were restricted and disheartened, her song holding all the misery of imprisonment and of love denied.

"One more number," Ladler said. "Let's hear her plea."

As Catalina begged for rescue, her audience on the rafters above was very still. The kit mewled softly, and Dulcie felt her own heart twist. This was not Cora Lee French, the gentle waitress with gray in her hair; this was a young girl frightened and alone, her pain wrenching their very cat souls. When the number ended, there was not a sound in the theater. Cora Lee bowed slightly to Samuel Ladler and to King, but did not move from the stage. The ghosts from the past that she had summoned clung around her, lingering in the shadows.

"Thank you," Ladler said softly, and watched Cora Lee move offstage. But as she stepped down to sit with the other actors, again Vivi leaned to speak to Ladler, shaking her head. Her whisper rose clearly to the cats.

"Too bad, Sam. She's just not right for the part—that gray hair, for one thing. Really too bad, but the part calls for a younger woman.

"And," Vivi said, "to be honest, Elliott doesn't care for overacting." She gave Ladler a bright smile. "Well, Fern is perfect for the part. We're fortunate to have her. So sweet—just the way a young girl would sing, with a broken heart."

Sam Ladler sat looking at Vivi, very still and rigid. He rose, turning to Elliot. "Shall we step out to the lobby to discuss this?"

"There's no need," Vivi said. "We love Fern's performance. Elliott loves her. She's perfect." Beside her, Elliott nodded.

Sam continued to look at Elliott. "I don't discuss the tryouts in front of the actors. Would you like to continue this in private?"

Vivi said, "You notified the others right away, before they left the theater."

"Fern's the one," Elliott said. "No question."

Sam looked across to the waiting actors. "Go home. We'll call you in the morning."

"No!" Vivi snapped. "Let them stay. You know we're short on time." She looked hard at Ladler. "Have you forgotten, conveniently, that Elliott's permission to produce is subject to his approval of the cast?"

Ladler nodded to the small group and they settled back, dropping their jackets and scripts again on empty seats. "Fern, if you and Cora Lee would like to go out to the lobby and get a Coke, we'll call you in a few moments."

Cora Lee slipped away backstage. Fern took a seat beside Vivi, looking defiantly at Ladler. The cats watched the little drama, fascinated. They felt terrible

150

for Cora Lee. The kit's tail lashed so hard that Dulcie put a paw on it. "Stop it, Kit. Before someone looks up here."

Ladler looked Fern over. "All right, if you want to hear this." He turned his back on her, facing Elliott. "Fern's not right for the part. She can't hold a candle to Cora Lee. Not right physically or emotionally. Her singing does not do justice to the songs, or to your play."

"I have to disagree," Elliott said. "Fern has the part, or there is no play."

"They're not in the same league," Sam snapped, the color coming up in his lean face. "Cora Lee is Catalina. We couldn't have a better fit. What is it you're seeing here? Do you want to try to explain?"

"Fern's completely right for the part," Traynor repeated, glancing at Vivi. "I'm the writer. I know what I—"

Mark King, stepping to the edge of the stage, stood looking down at Traynor. "There's nothing right about her. Fern, you really ought to leave, and not have to hear this. But I have to agree that Cora Lee is perfect."

"That is so shallow and wrong," Vivi snapped, her look nudging Elliott.

"I'm sorry," Elliott said stiffly. "It's my play. Fern Barth has the part or you can stop production."

Ladler looked them both over. "Cora Lee French has the part or I don't direct the play."

Elliott rose, staring at him.

Ladler stiffened almost as if he would hit Elliott. High above them, the three cats looked down from the shadows ready for a good brawl, even if Elliott was to be considered an invalid.

Ladler looked at Elliott a long time, then turned away.

151

"Stuff the play." He dropped the script on the floor and moved on down to the little group of fascinated actors. "Go home. The play is canceled. You'll have to wait for this one until Mr. Traynor finds another theater."

Vivi rose, snatching up her jacket, but Elliott pushed her into a seat, glaring at her, and moved after Ladler. "Wait, Sam."

Ladler turned, scowling. Quickly Elliott took his arm and walked him outside through the exit door. From the stage, Mark King stood watching them, his round, bespectacled face pale with anger, then he moved away toward the dressing rooms, where Cora Lee had disappeared.

Elliott and Ladler were gone for some time. Fern sat quietly beside Vivi, both staring straight ahead, never glancing toward the other actors. No one spoke, the atmosphere in the theater had swung from the poignancy of Catalina's lament to conflict as brittle as shattered glass. Above in the darkness the kit rose and padded along the rafter heading backstage, looking for Cora Lee.

When Elliott and Sam Ladler returned, Elliott was smiling amiably, Ladler stone-faced. He paused stiffly before Fern.

"The part is yours. Cora Lee will understudy." He turned away to the waiting actors and sat down among them.

In a few moments, Cora Lee and King came out from backstage. Cora Lee looked at Ladler for a long moment. He said, "Will you understudy?"

"I suppose I will," she said, her face closed and expressionless. As she turned away again, the cats could see the kit behind her, lurking in the shadows.

"What did Traynor offer him?" Joe said. "And why?

152

What does Fern have that Traynor needs? Or what does she have on Traynor?"

Ladler rose from the group of actors. "Let's get on with it. I want readers for Marcos. We'll get through tryouts tonight. Rehearsals will start Wednesday."

Joe and Dulcie were too disappointed to listen to further readings; they didn't care who got the part of Marcos. The dark, good-looking young Latino man would likely have it. Or maybe the pale-haired surfer, who had a good voice, too, but would certainly have to resort to dark makeup and black hair dye. Probably it wouldn't matter to Cora Lee who got the male lead. Dulcie could imagine her backstage, dealing with her disappointment, maybe with the kit snuggling up close, trying to cheer her. Why had Elliott Traynor gone along with this? It had certainly been Vivi who pushed for it. Neither Joe nor Dulcie had any answers. Among the rafters, they dozed until tryouts ended. As the players rose to leave, they heard Vivi arrange quietly to meet Fern at Binnie's Italian.

Beating it out of the theater, the two cats headed for Binnie's, galloping across the dark roofs beneath a skittering wind. Watching the street below, they saw the Traynors' black Lincoln pass them, and when they dropped down to a low overhang, then to the sidewalk around the corner from Binnie's, the Lincoln was parked at the curb. Elliott and Vivi were still in the car, arguing.

Crouching by the rear tire, the cats listened, trying not to sneeze at the stink of hot rubber and exhaust fumes.

". . . know damn well you went too far," Elliott was saying. "Don't you think that looked—"

"What was I supposed to do? That was the deal, that Fern get the part. And you were going to cave!"

153

"This Cora Lee French was good, Vivi. How do you think this looks, when we—?"

"Good has nothing to do with it! Looks have nothing to do with it. What the hell are you thinking!"

"I'm thinking that if you keep this up, you'll blow it. Ladler will back out. And don't you think people will start asking questions?"

"Sam Ladler knew it was part of the deal. Fern has the part, or there's no money on the side. What made him defy you like that? How did you straighten him out?"

"I upped the ante. It isn't every day a little theater director sees that kind of money."

"And he didn't ask questions?"

"What's he going to ask? He knows not to ask. We've been through this. I said he'd get twice what you offered."

"You what? Didn't you think—"

"Twice what you offered. You don't have a choice, Vivi. So shut up. Right now, I'm in the driver's seat."

17

THE TWO CATS WATCHED FERN'S TOYOTA PULL UP IN front of Binnie's Italian. Vivi and Elliott were still sitting in their black Lincoln, snapping at each other. When Fern parked in front of them Vivi got out and hurried into the restaurant with her, slamming the glass door nearly in Elliott's face. Catching the door, he swung in behind them and eased it closed.

On the warm concrete beneath the newspaper rack, Joe and Dulcie crouched looking up through the restaurant window where Vivi and Fern and Elliott were settling into a booth. Vivi glanced out blankly to where the cats were idly washing their paws, the cats of less interest to her than the metal newsstand. Dulcie loved spying on someone when she was in plain sight. Through the thin glass they could hear every word.

The waitress on duty was Binnie's niece, a slight, shy Italian girl who didn't look old enough to have a work permit. Certainly she was too young to serve liquor. When Vivi ordered a bottle of Chablis, Binnie himself hurried out with it, uncorking the bottle across his white-aproned, ample belly, his jowled face rosy from the kitchen. Binnie did enjoy going through the little tasting ritual. Elliott handled Binnie's ceremony with abject boredom. Binnie poured in silence, smiled hesitantly at Vivi, and when his smile was not returned, he retreated quietly to his kitchen.

"Here's to it," Vivi said, lifting her glass. "So far, very smooth. Even Ladler wasn't much of a problem."

"It's a wonderful part," Fern gushed. "I'll do well by it, you'll see." She patted Elliott's hand. "I'm going to be great in this part; it's going to make my career." Fern was, apparently, not the brightest young woman. The cats sat through interminable small talk, licking their whiskers when the pizza was served. Vivi and Elliott ate in silence, letting Fern ramble, a tedious monologue that left Joe and Dulcie yawning. They were ready to cut out and go hunt rats when Clyde and Ryan Flannery came around the corner, walking arm in arm, softly laughing.

Clyde didn't see the cats slip deeper under the newsstand, he was totally involved with Ryan. "So that's the rest of the shop. That's what we do, master mechanics to Molena Point's wheels."

"All those beautiful Mercedeses, Jags, and BMWs parked in your garage, to say nothing of that silver

Rolls. It's a great shop, Clyde. I'm awed by the state-of-the-art electronic equipment—a far cry from my cordless drill and electric saw." As the couple passed the window, Vivi's eyes widened. She nudged Elliott so sharply he spilled his wine.

"You really find that stuff interesting?" Clyde said, holding the door for Ryan. Before he could close it, the cats slipped through behind him. He scowled down at them, surprised and annoyed, but said nothing.

"If I hadn't ended up as a building contractor," Ryan said, "I might be a mechanic. I seriously thought about it at one time."

Elliott had risen and was heading toward the men's room, behind a partition that also led to the kitchen. Ryan looked after him, glanced at Vivi, and turned away, moving beside Clyde to a table in the far corner. Clyde looked toward the kitchen, waving to Binnie, and they slid into the booth. "You'd like being a mechanic? Working with a bunch of guys? They can get pretty rank."

"I do work with a bunch of guys," she said, laughing. "They're okay if you set some ground rules. But, I don't know, there's something restful about putting things together, about figuring out the little mechanical glitches, solving the problems and making them right. Makes me feel safe, somehow, in a chaotic world. Does that make any sense?"

"Quite a lot of sense."

Under the table, the cats settled down next to Clyde's shoes, looking around his pant cuffs to where the Traynors sat. The carpet smelled clean and was of good quality, not like some restaurants where the rug stank of ancient French fries. Elliot had not returned. At the Traynor table, Vivi was pale and agitated, gulping her

156

wine. Fern only looked perplexed, her round face and short golden hair catching light from a stained glass corner fixture. Binnie had recently redecorated, abandoning the simple red checkered tablecloth and candle-in-a-bottle motif, with which the village had long been familiar, for bright abstract murals covering the walls and tabletops, splashes of primary color illuminated by the colored glass fixtures. The effect was cozy and inviting. But then, any place that smelled as rich with tomato sauce and garlic and herbs as Binnie's had to be inviting. As the cats watched Vivi nervously wolf her dinner, Ryan bent down to look under the table.

"Hi, cats. You having pizza?" They smiled at her and purred, and Dulcie rose to rub against her extended hand. She scratched Dulcie's ear, looking pleased with the greeting. Her face was flushed from the chill outdoor air, her dark hair tangled in a mass of short, unruly curls. In a moment she sat up again. "They're charming, Clyde. As responsive as any dogs."

"I suppose they can be charming," Clyde said. "When it suits them."

"But pizza, and Mexican food? Doesn't that stuff upset them? What does the vet say?" She was wearing faded jeans, and brown leather sandals that smelled of saddle soap. Her ankles were nicely tanned. Joe sniffed at her toes until Dulcie hissed at him, laying back her ears. "You don't need to smell her feet!"

Clyde said, "The food doesn't bother them; they seem to have cast-iron stomachs." He looked under. "What do you want on your pizza? Cheese, hamburger, and anchovy?"

Joe Grey purred, thinking, *Heavy on the anchovies and plenty of mozzarella.*

"Where's the third cat?" Ryan asked. "The little dark one? Doesn't she belong to Wilma Getz? Wilma worked with my dad, years ago before she retired, in the San Francisco probation office. The dark cat—what's that color called?"

"Tortoiseshell," Clyde said. "She's been hanging around the theater lately. She likes to prowl the rafters."

Ryan laughed. "Theatrical aspirations? But when the cats are out on the village streets at night, don't you worry about them?"

"They're careful about traffic. And all three are pretty resourceful."

"My family has never had cats, only dogs. I had no idea cats would—well, these two follow you, don't they? And they mind you."

"Sometimes," Clyde said. "If they're in a cooperative mood."

"When my sisters and I were young, and we came, down to the village for weekends, we always brought the dogs. Dallas was raising pointers then. We'd each get to bring our favorite pup, we ran them on the beach, took them in the outdoor cafés. It was great fun, everyone made a fuss over them—we were very popular. I've always loved the village. I'm going to love calling it home. San Francisco, under the right circumstances, is wonderful, but I think my nesting place is here."

"And you liked Charlie's apartment—the duplex?"

"It's perfect. One big room, and I love the high ceiling. Charlie says we can put in a wood-burning stove if I like. And that wonderful garage, that's the space I really need. She told me she bought the place for a song."

"In village numbers, yes. It was pretty run down. Will

you need furniture?"

"I don't need much. Right now, I just want the necessities."

"Which are?"

"Drafting table. Bed. Breakfast table and a couple of chairs. Desk for my computer."

"Your taste may be too simple for the Iselman estate sale, but it wouldn't hurt to look."

"Which is when?"

"Saturday morning. You go around seven, take a number, go back at ten to be called. They let people in a few at a time."

"Want to come?"

"Sure. We'll get our numbers, go have breakfast, and walk the beach."

The cats looked at each other, amused. Clyde never did waste time. When the pizza was served, they could hear Clyde cutting their share into bite-sized pieces, could hear him blowing on it to cool before he set it on the floor. Across the restaurant, Vivi and Fern were still alone; Elliott had not returned. Vivi was paying the bill. In a moment she rose, said something to Fern, dropped a tip on the table, and was gone, leaving Fern to finish her dinner alone.

"She sure didn't want any part of me," Ryan said softly. "Elliott can't still be in the men's room."

"I think that slamming kitchen door might have been Elliott leaving," Clyde said.

"Maybe Vivi and my womanizing husband did get together last fall. But why would Elliott avoid me? I can understand Vivi staying away—though at this point, I couldn't care less. But why Elliott? He and I are the wronged parties."

From beneath the table, the cats watched through the

159

far window as Vivi hurried around the corner to her car. They heard her gun the engine and the Lincoln roared away, apparently leaving Elliott to walk home.

The cats looked at each other with amusement. What a tangle humans could devise. No group of cats ever made such a muddle of their personal affairs. Vivi and Elliott's behavior not only entertained Joe and Dulcie but left them puzzled and unsettled. As if they'd followed a rabbit scent that led nowhere; that ended abruptly with no rabbit hole, and no rabbit.

They would be far more concerned, however, when the night ended; when dawn broke and they confronted a dead body, a bloody scene of battle, and one very distraught tortoiseshell kit.

18

REHEARSAL WAS OVER. EVERYONE BUT CORA LEE had left the theater. Mark King had closed the piano and departed reluctantly, worrying about Cora Lee, standing backstage holding her hands, his round face flushed with anger and concern.

"I'll be fine, Mark. I just want to sit here for a few minutes alone, in the quiet theater. Guess this part meant more to me than I thought," she said, laughing.

"There's nothing I can say about this. It's incredible. I'm hoping something will happen to change Traynor's mind," he said darkly, then turned and moved away through the dressing rooms.

The kit heard the back door slam. When Cora Lee sat down on a folding chair near the piano, the little tortoiseshell came out from the shadows and crawled up into her lap. Around them, the empty theater seemed to echo with the spirits that had been summoned from the past—and with the tensions, with the inexplicable trade-off for which Mark King and Cora Lee had no answers. The kit reached a paw, touching Cora Lee's cheek.

"All right," she told the kit. "Let someone else play Catalina. But does it have to be Fern Barth! Fern will destroy Catalina. I do love the story, I love the songs, Kit. I feel so close to Catalina—I don't want her story made ugly and common."

She hugged the kit close. "Maybe after Traynor's dead," she said coldly, "if he is indeed dying, there'll be a real performance somewhere of *Thorns of Gold*. But not for me, Kit. It will be too late for me.

"I'm sixty-four years old. I keep myself in shape, but there's a limit. Maybe Vivi Traynor's right, maybe I'm already too old."

Cora Lee wondered—was it possible that, for some reason she didn't understand, Vivi didn't want this play produced? She looked around the empty theater. "There are ghosts here, Kit. All the ghosts of plays past, people who have been brought alive here. Did you know that?"

The kit knew. She climbed to Cora Lee's shoulder, nosing at her cheek.

"Emotions so powerful, Kit, that they're part of the old walls, even part of the plywood sets that we cut up and use over and over until there's nothing left but chips. All those lives are here. And now, is Fern's saccharine version of Catalina going to join them?"

She rose abruptly, settling the kit more securely on her shoulder. "Well, I can't help it. I can't make anything different, I can't unmake whatever twisted motives Vivi and Elliott Traynor follow." She cuddled the little cat close. "It isn't losing the part that makes me cry, Kit. I cry from anger, always have. Anger at

161

unfairness, at human coldness. Why would Elliott Traynor butcher his own play?

"When I was little, Kit, in second grade, we had a teacher who baited us unmercifully. Prodded us, bore down on us, accused us of things we didn't do, ridiculed and beat us down until she made me cry out of pure rage."

Cora Lee looked down into the kit's round yellow eyes. "I've always been like that. I'm irate when I feel helpless, when I feel used." She touched the kit's nose with her nose. "Can you understand, Kit, how it is to cry with anger when you feel helpless?"

The kit understood. She knew exactly how that felt. The smallest cat in the band of roving cats she'd traveled with, she'd been the butt of them all, two dozen big, cruel felines who delighted in tormenting her, who abandoned her in alleys, who drove her away from whatever food they found to fight over. She knew how helplessness felt. But she couldn't tell Cora Lee that.

"On the streets, in New Orleans, when bigger kids ganged up and hit us and wouldn't let us go, and no grown-up would help us, that made me cry—with pure temper, because no big person would help us." Cora Lee laughed. "I got so mad sometimes that I broke things. Threw china at the wall. That wasn't civilized, but no one took the time to teach us about being civil. Throwing china was the only way I knew to drive away the demons and make me feel better."

The kit shivered. The look in Cora Lee's black eyes was so deep it was like falling into bottomless chasms.

"You make me feel better, Kit. You're good company. You listen and don't try to destroy me. Could I take you home with me tonight? It's just at the other end of the building. I don't like to leave you alone in the

162

theater, and I won't turn you out in the dark. Would Wilma mind?" She looked at the kit, puzzled. "What makes you come here, Kit? What draws you here?"

The kit purred and kneaded her mottled black-and-brown paws gently into Cora Lee's shoulder, careful to keep her claws tucked in.

Cuddling the kit, Cora Lee went backstage to the wall phone beside the dressing rooms, and in the soft light, she dialed Wilma's number. The kit lay her face against Cora Lee's cheek to listen, feeling deliciously secretive and smug, her fluffy tail twitching with pleasure.

"Your tattercoat kit is here, Wilma. In the theater."

"I'm not surprised," Wilma said, laughing. "Shall I come get her?"

"She's been here since early in the tryouts. Could I keep her overnight? She's . . . we're friends. I have cold roast chicken and milk custard, if you think that would agree with her."

The kit smiled and snuggled down with contentment.

"Those delicacies are certainly allowed," Wilma said. "You'd better have your share first, or she'll eat it all. How did tryouts go?"

"Could we talk about that tomorrow? I . . . didn't get the part."

"I don't believe that."

"I . . ." Cora Lee's voice trembled.

"Tomorrow," Wilma said. "Take the kit home. Are you all right?"

"I'm fine. Just need some rest. I'm going to feed the kit and myself, have a hot bath, and get into bed. I'll bring her home in the morning."

"Have another towel handy. She likes to dabble her paws in the tub. Give her something that floats, and she'll have the whole bathroom soaked, splashing at it."

163

Cora Lee laughed. The kit didn't see anything funny. Hanging up, Cora Lee carried the kit over her shoulder as she turned out the last light and then locked the back door behind her. Heading past several closed shops with their softly lit windows, a dress shop, a toy store, a knitting studio, she turned up a lighted stair tucked between two parts of the building. Climbing two flights, with the kit snuggling against her chin, she moved along an open balcony overlooking the street. Unlocking the third door, she switched on a lamp and shut the door tightly behind her. She set the kit down on a creamy leather sofa so soft that the kit rolled and rubbed her face into the pillows.

The room was done all in almond and white and café au lait—ice cream colors, the kit thought. She liked that; this room made her purr. Cora Lee opened a tall, whitewashed music center, and put on a CD of soft jazz. She gave the kit a little smile, as if maybe she had come to some kind of decision. The kit couldn't ask to share her secret.

The small kitchen had a creamy tile floor and white cabinets. Cora Lee fixed a plate for each of them, poured a glass of wine for herself, and carried their tray into the living room, putting the kit's plate on the hearth and her own dinner on the coffee table.

Cora Lee ate slowly, relaxing in the music she loved and in the company of the little cat. It was nice to have a special animal to share her supper, it had been some years since she'd had a pet, since she'd put her dear old spaniel to sleep. She still missed him. She'd depended on him a lot when she was newly widowed, in those months just after Robert died.

Robert was killed on their thirtieth anniversary in a

plane accident, on his way to meet her for a week in the Sierras as an anniversary present. She had never felt quite whole since. But she had not felt, until recently, the true fear of being alone as she grew older, fear of the approaching years when she might be ill and need assistance, and had no one to help her, no family. That sense of helplessness had made her take a hard look at her life.

Was their Senior Survival plan going to work? Was this going to be a practical solution for all of them?

"It sure beats paying five thousand dollars a month, Kit, in a retirement home. I couldn't do that. All of us have too much money to go on welfare, and too little to pay those kinds of prices. We're caught in the middle, Kit."

She thought that, with the right legal setup, they could make something better for themselves. Watching the kit lapping up custard, she wished the little cat could understand what she was saying, she seemed such a sympathetic little soul. Rising, she went to the kitchen to dish up more custard, hoping she wouldn't make the kit sick. Wilma was right, this little cat ate like a St. Bernard.

Returning, she refilled her wineglass and turned down the lamp. Could four or five women living together really get along? Was that going to work; would they make the necessary decisions without bickering? If they could hire someone to cook and clean and care for them when they were older, would they find someone they could trust? But they were civil people. And they had three trustees picked out to handle many of the problems.

When the kit had licked up the last of the custard, Cora Lee took their dishes to the kitchen, washed them

165

in hot soapy water, and put them in the drain. "Come on, Kit. I'm bushed."

She ran a hot bath, found a sponge to float for the kit, and spent more time laughing than relaxing. She mopped up the water afterward with four big towels, wondering where this little cat had sprung from, who was so different and amusing. They were in bed by midnight, snuggled together.

As Cora Lee's breathing slowed toward sleep, the kit lay looking around her at the carved, whitewashed bedroom furniture, at the sheer white curtains blowing across the open window. Even the paintings on the walls were cream toned. What a pity that Cora Lee would have to leave this apartment when the ladies all moved in together. These bright rooms with their café au lait carpet soft under her paws, and the jazz music and cold chicken and custard, this was a lovely place to live. The kit liked it all so much, that she couldn't stop purring. And, purring, she drifted off into dreams.

But in her dreams she was standing on a strange sidewalk, in a strange part of the village and there was blood on the concrete along with broken glass. Afraid, she woke mewling and pressing tightly against Cora Lee.

But it was a dream, only a nightmare like when she was small and the big cats made her sleep alone in the cold behind the garbage cans and she had bad, bad dreams.

Only then there had been no one to hold her. Now there was someone safe, and she burrowed closer under Cora Lee's chin, safe with Cora Lee, and warm.

19

FOG SOFTENED THE LINES OF THE LONG, TWO-STORY building, the milky dawn seeming almost to have absorbed its pale walls. The structure was, in fact, two buildings, with a narrow walkway between. The first floors housed various small businesses, including a cell phone repair shop, and an upholsterer. Offices and apartments occupied the second floor. Of the seven cars parked diagonally at the curb before the Pumpkin Coach Charity Shop, four were frosted with water drops as if they had stood there all night. Cora Lee French's green '92 Chevy was dry and faintly dusty, and the engine and hood were still warm. The driver's door stood open, the keys in the ignition. Cora Lee's purse lay on the seat.

The Pumpkin Coach was a favorite village institution, staffed by volunteers who arranged and sold the used books and furniture and clothes that were donated, the paintings and tableware and office equipment and children's toys and every kind of bric-a-brac from Chinese cloisonné and old pewter to Mexican glassware, all gifts from upscale Molena Point households that were moving or changing decor. The shop's annual income, more than $200,000, was given in total to Molena Point charities—the boys and girls clubs, the Scouts, County Animal Shelter, Meals for the Elderly, and over two dozen other like organizations. At peak hours the Pumpkin Coach was so busy that visitors found it hard to snag a parking place in the large lot. Now, at 6:00 A.M., the shop, of course, was closed.

Cora Lee's car was not reflected in the large front

window of the Pumpkin Coach, though it stood not ten feet from it, just across the sidewalk. None of the cars was mirrored there, nor were the trees that edged the parking lot, or the houses and shops across the street. The window could reflect nothing; its plate glass lay shattered across the paving, its jagged shards reflecting only the milky sky. Sharp pieces of broken glass stuck up from the window frame like knife blades.

The shop's window was done up each Monday night with particularly appealing items, usually arranged on some theme. On Tuesday, viewers could enjoy the display, read the price list, and make their selections. They would return on Wednesday morning to hand over their cash and record their names on the "sold" list, often having to stand in line for the privilege. They would pick up their merchandise the following week, after the window was changed. Though the shop didn't open until 10:00, the first arrivals might be there before 7:00, bringing their camp chairs, intent on being first in line.

The Pumpkin Coach was a mecca for the ladies of the Senior Survival club. They tried to rotate their visits so one or the other dropped by several times a day as new donations were put out. Usually Cora Lee took the Tuesday morning run to check out the contents of the new window display. This morning was the same as usual; she had stopped to check the window on her way to take the kit home—and had looked on the scene startled.

Within the display, broken glass sparkled across the small and handsome caned writing desk that held center stage and across the embroidered table cover tossed casually over one end. There was nothing on the desk, but three indentations had been left in the folded cover.

Behind the desk hung five paintings and seven carved toys, all skewed aside where the backdrop had been pulled awry, revealing the dark shop behind.

At the foot of the desk Fern Barth lay unmoving, the wounds in her chest and shoulder bleeding into the spills of shattered glass, her blond hair flecked with glass, her fingers clutching a fragment of old, faded ribbon. Cora Lee stood looking, feeling cold, her hands shaking, and for a long moment she didn't know what to do.

Joe Grey and Dulcie got their first look at the morning paper as they returned from a midnight hunt. The *Molena Point Gazette* lay folded on a driveway, the front page partially visible. Hastily they pawed the paper open, crouching over the picture.

The Pumpkin Coach was enjoying extra publicity; the shop's display was featured prominently, its window nearly filling the space above the fold—a picture that, if they were right, was going to cause plenty of activity in the village, and not all of it welcome.

Since midnight they had stalked rats beneath the low, dense foliage of a dwarf juniper forest. The decorative conifers covered a residential hillside, a mass of three-foot high bushes so thick-growing that even in the silver dawn the world beneath had been without light, its prickly tangle of interlaced branches stretching away in pure blackness. The warm, sandy earth beneath was riddled with rat holes—a hunting preserve for the small and quick.

Their breakfast catch had consisted of two fat rats and a small rabbit. They could have killed many more, but they couldn't eat any more. Leaving the bony parts and the skin and fur, they had spent leisurely moments washing their paws and whiskers, then wound their way out of the dark jungle, their eyes shuttered and their ears back to avoid the tiny, prickly twigs. They came out onto the concrete drive just below a two-story house whose shades were still drawn. The cats' coats smelled sharply of juniper, and their mouths were filled with the rusty aftertaste of rat. It was as they padded down the damp concrete drive toward the street below that the morning paper caught their attention.

Thanks to the cheaper production costs of modern technology, the photo was in full color. It showed three carved wooden chests sitting on an embroidered table cover atop a small writing desk in the shop window. Joe pawed the paper open to the article, his dark gray ears sharp forward, his yellow eyes keen with interest. He glanced up once at the windows of the house but saw no one, and heard no sound. Flattening the pages with quick paws, they crowded together side by side to read. Any neighbor peering out would suppose the kitties had found a mealy bug or some such innocuous creature in the damp folds of newsprint and were about to eat or torment it. The article held their full attention.

ISELMAN ART COLLECTION UNDER BLOCK

Dorothy Iselman, widow of village benefactor James Iselman, has put the couple's multimillion-dollar art collection up for sale, retaining only a few favorite items. The oils and watercolors by famous eighteenth-century artists will be auctioned at Butterfield's in San Francisco in mid-July. Less valuable pieces, such as the African and Mexican folk art that Iselman enjoyed owning, have been sold to several local galleries and collectors. Several nineteenth-century wooden toys and primitive, carved chests have been donated to the Pumpkin Coach, a special offering for its charity sales. These can be seen in a handsome, display installed last night in the shop's front window.

"What do they mean by primitive?" Joe said.

"Rough, bold. Not all refined and polished," Dulcie said knowledgeably. Her green eyes widened. "Don't they look Spanish? Could these be three of the Ortega-Diaz chests? Sitting in the Iselman house for how many years?"

"Not likely. Wouldn't Casselrod have known about them, tried to buy them?"

"Maybe he did try, we don't know. And did the Iselmans know about the letters? Would they have thought to look for some hidden compartment, like the white chest had?"

The cats looked at each other and took off down the drive heading for the Pumpkin Coach. Galloping through the fog across the empty residential streets, brushing through flowerbeds and trampling a delicate stand of Icelandic poppies, racing through patios and gardens, they had nearly reached the two long buildings standing end to end that housed the charity shop when a pale car pulled out of the street behind, coming straight for them. Dodging across the sidewalk into a recessed entry, they crouched against the door of a tile shop. Joe got one good glimpse of the license.

"Got the first four digits. 2ZJZ. A tan Infinity."

They stood looking after the vanished driver, then raced down the narrow brick walk between the two buildings, approaching the front of the charity shop. Somewhere in the village, a siren screamed, not uncommon in the early morning hours. Galloping past

171

parked cars whose metal bodies exuded chill, they passed a car still warm, a green Chevy with the driver's door open.

"Cora Lee's car?" Dulcie said.

Joe glanced in, catching Cora Lee's scent, wondering why she had left the door open, and where she was. Skirting the glass that glinted across the sidewalk, warily he approached the shop window.

They could smell blood, and the sweet scent of candy. Circling around the glass, the cats reared up to look.

Fern Barth lay in the window, the blood from her wounds turning dark. Joe, leaping up over the jagged teeth of glass that protruded from the sill, stepping carefully around the blood and debris, put his nose to hers.

She wasn't breathing but she was faintly warm. He was backing away when sirens came screaming and a squad car and an emergency vehicle careened around the corner. Joe sailed out of the window over the ragged glass and behind the potted plants that stood before the shop. The cats were never able to shake their need to hide—and maybe for good reason. Max Harper wasn't unaware of cats showing up at a scene, of cat hairs clinging to evidence, of paw prints where they should not have been.

An officer swung out of the car, gun drawn, scanning the area, leaving his partner behind the wheel. From the ambulance, two medics stepped up into the shop window as if they knew exactly where to go. As the officer on foot checked the parked cars, the police unit took off toward the back street, apparently to circle the building. The officer on foot approached the green Chevy. Looking inside, he didn't touch anything. He checked the backseat, but didn't close the door. As he checked out the other cars, Joe and Dulcie slipped through the shadows to the bushes that lined the walk between the buildings. There, Joe tried to pull glass from his paws, dragging his pads across the small branches to dislodge clinging shards, then plucking some out with his teeth, spitting glass into the dirt, his ears back with annoyance.

The officer on foot had left the cars and moved up into the window, they heard him walk on back inside the shop. The minute he was gone, Joe sped for the Chevy and leaped into the seat.

He sniffed at Cora Lee's purse, but when he smelled the dash and the cell phone, he shook his head with disbelief. Dropping out again, he returned to the bushes, to Dulcie.

"The kit's scent is all over the phone."

"The kit made the emergency call?"

"Apparently. She's watched us enough times."

"So where is she? She stayed with Cora Lee last night. Where is Cora Lee? Oh, she's not in the shop! Lying hurt in there! But what happened?" Dulcie peered out toward the shattered display window, then turned to look at Joe, her eyes wide. "Or did she . . . ? Oh, but Cora Lee wouldn't. . ."

Joe just looked at her.

"She was really hurt when she lost the part," Dulcie whispered. "Angry at Traynor, at Vivi, at Sam Ladler— she must have hated Fern. But she wouldn't . . ."

Joe was busy sniffing the bushes. "Cora Lee brushed by here. So did the kit. Come on."

They followed the scents of woman and cat up the brick walk and around to the street behind the Pumpkin Coach, where the shop's back door opened. The empty street smelled of car exhaust. They didn't see the officer

173

on foot, nor was the squad car in sight. As they approached the small, blind utility alley just beyond the Pumpkin Coach, the scents they followed deepened. They could see nothing in the short dead-end alley but a heap of wadded white paper down at the end piled between the trash cans.

But something else was there, besides paper. They glimpsed dark hair among the white, and a tan arm. Then they saw the kit crouched over the figure, pawing at her, trying to wake her.

Cora Lee lay among the rubble, her white dress twisted, her face grayish and sick. When the kit saw Joe and Dulcie she bolted into them mewling.

"She's dead. Oh, she's not dead! Oh, help her!"

Sirens screamed again as another squad car roared through the side streets. Pushing the kit away, Joe nosed at Cora Lee trying to detect breathing. Yes, a faint, warm breath, though her skin was chilled.

"She's alive, Kit. We need the medics, the cops. But you called—"

"From Cora Lee's car phone like you showed me. I told them there was a dead woman in the window."

"You told them Cora Lee was here?"

"She wasn't—I didn't know she was here. Just that Fern woman in the window."

"Stay with her, Kit. Stay until we—"

But Dulcie had already raced away, headed for Cora Lee's car and cell phone.

20

THE AMBULANCE HAD GONE, TAKING CORA LEE TO the hospital bundled onto a stretcher, tucked up under a blanket. Dulcie imagined her in surgery surrounded by doctors and nurses working over her. Stubbornly she imagined Cora Lee awake again, sitting up in a white hospital bed with flowers and get-well cards around her. And, crouched in the shadows of the alley, cuddling the kit close, she tried to stop the little tattercoat's frightened shivering. Licking the kit's ear, Dulcie purred against her, whispering, "It's all right. She'll be all right, Kit." But they couldn't be certain of that.

"She ran from that man," the kit said. "He chased her, he must have hit her. When I found her here she was so cold, then sweating, and then cold again. She looked at me and cried, 'Don't!' and tried to get up and then she twisted, and cried out, then fainted." The kit looked wildly at Dulcie. "All those terrible tubes hanging when they put her in the ambulance. What did they do to her?"

"The tubes could save her life, Kit. The medics will do all they can, and we must be patient." But Dulcie didn't feel patient.

The kit's dark mottled fur stuck up in frantic wisps, and her yellow eyes were as round as moons. "She was taking me home to Wilma's, she. . ."

"I know, Kit. I was there when she called Wilma. She said she'd stop here to look in the shop window at the new display. She'll be all right, Kit. She'll be fine. Did you have a nice evening?"

"Oh, yes. Custard and chicken and music and such a pretty house and a nice creamy blanket on her bed, but I had a bad dream and then this morning it came true. When we got here the window was all broken, and I could see someone lying in there. Cora Lee rushed to look, she was so upset and wanting to help that she left the car door open, didn't think about a cat running away. But I didn't run, I jumped on the dash and watched her through the window. She looked in at the dead woman, then she whirled around toward the car like she meant to call the police, but there was a little white packet nearly under her feet, like papers. She snatched it up, hardly stopping."

"What papers, Kit?"

"I don't know, papers tied in a ribbon, and she was almost to the car when a man burst out of the window and hit her and grabbed at them. She kicked him and hit him and twisted away and ran. She still had the little packet. Ran around the side of the building. I remembered about the phone and punched the numbers like I saw you and Joe do, and told them about the woman in the window.

"He chased her, and I followed them. I was so scared and I wanted to claw him. He chased her into the alley and hit her hard. When she fell he grabbed the papers and ran. Left her there all huddled up clutching her middle. I heard a car roar away. She tried to crawl but she was hurt too bad and I didn't know what to do. She looked at me like she didn't see me right, like she didn't know what I was. I licked and licked her face and was going to go talk in the phone again, but she was so hot and then cold and then I heard the siren, and then you came."

"Kit, what did the papers look like?" Dulcie said.

"Folded up and tied with an old faded ribbon. Old brownish paper like if it's been in the trash a long time."

"What did the man look like?" Dulcie glanced around for Joe but didn't see him.

"Just a man. I don't know. Tan clothes. Tall, sort of thin, running away."

"What color hair? Would you know him? Recognize his smell?"

"I don't know. Maybe." The kit looked crestfallen, her head down, her ears back to her head. "I'm not sure. Maybe I would." She began to sniff around the alley. But the medics and police had been there; the smells were all mixed up.

"Come here, Kit," Dulcie said. "It will be all right, we'll find him." But her mind was on Joe Grey, uneasy because Joe had vanished.

Was he back there among the officers? Had he followed them into the shop through the broken window? Armed officers going in after a killer would be alert to any smallest movement. The faintest disturbance among the shelves and furniture, and their guns would be on him.

But she was being foolish. Police officers didn't fire blind—not like some untrained deer hunter shooting at a sound in the brush.

Yet still she worried, pacing the alley, afraid Joe would do something foolish, something macho and foolish.

Within the shop, Joe looked far from macho. Crouched under a rack of women's dresses with a lacy hem dragging over his ears, he peered out from between swaths of silk and velvet, watching Dallas Garza clear the premises. The resale store was so

177

crowded with racks and shelves and overflowing boxes that he felt like he was back among the heaped refuse of some San Francisco alley—except these cast-offs were a far cry from the junk he'd encountered in the city; that trash had been so tacky that even the homeless didn't want it. This shop had some nicer cookware than Clyde's kitchen, some handsome lamps, and typewriters and even a microwave oven. In the center of the room between the clothes racks stood a child's desk, a faded easy chair, a pink crib, three dining chairs, and a sign proclaiming that all mechanical items were in working order.

Slipping along beneath the ladies' hems, flinching as clothes slithered down his back, he followed Detective Garza. Garza was taking his time, photographing and making carefully recorded notes in a small black notebook.

Pausing under a rack of men's pants and shirts, Joe followed Garza through an archway, creeping belly-to-carpet among the shadows, into the back room—into chaos. A bookshelf lay toppled, its books scattered open across a cascade of phonograph records and broken china. An accordion lay crushed beneath an overturned table, among a spill of mismatched shoes. And there were splatters of blood, the smell of human blood.

Beneath the fallen books and records, he saw a small, carved chest. A second chest lay half hidden by a scatter of baby clothes. Both looked old, dark, and roughly made, very much like those in the newspaper picture. Watching Garza photograph the scene, Joe slipped behind an upended suitcase for a better look. He wondered if Garza had seen the morning paper, if he was aware of the wooden casks. One was the size of a small bread box, incised with primitive birds and painted in soft greens and blues. The other was half that big, carved with flowers and stained in red and green. The pieces of a third box lay beneath it, smashed and split, with the lid torn off. Joe studied the scene of what must have been a violent fight, and sniffed the tangle of smells.

He had, following Garza in through the front door, reared up to look into the window at Fern's body where she lay waiting for the coroner. The two bullet holes, one through her chest, one through her throat, were both small and neat. As the detective turned away, Joe had nipped into the window for a better look.

The bullet holes were larger in front, raggedly splattering blood and flesh, as if she'd been shot in the back. Certainly she had been shot at close range. He couldn't see her back, to know if there were powder marks. The unpleasant smells of death mixed sickly with Fern's perfume.

But here in the back room, Fern's perfume came sharper, clinging among the broken furniture.

Had she fought with her killer here? Had she been shot here, from behind, then dragged into the broken window? Or had she managed to crawl there before she died? Or had she run, and gotten as far as the window? He watched Garza photographing, taking advantage of every angle, capturing every smallest detail. Was it Fern who broke the window to get at the chests or did her killer show up first and shatter the glass? If Fern broke in, why would she bring the casks in here? Maybe she was followed, maybe she ran back here to get away.

Too many possible scenarios. He wanted to hear the kit's story. And he wanted to know more of what Garza and Davis found before he tried to fit the pieces together.

The fur flew in both directions. Joe's clandestine method of investigation, even with the advantage of his highly superior scent detection, his finer night vision, and his acumen at breaking and entering, was seldom adequate alone, without input from the police. A cat sleuth, picking up what the cops missed, was still deeply dependent on the findings of the crime lab.

Face it, Joe thought, he and Dulcie and the cops were a team—even if MPPD knew nothing of the arrangement. What a cat laugh, Joe thought, stretching out under an antique baby carriage, watching Garza bag evidence. The department had no notion that it was the cooperation of cat and human that had made them one of the finest detecting machines in the state, had put them right up there in the top percentage of cases solved.

Garza had photographed the area where the three chests lay, and was now bagging them, taking great care, placing each piece of the broken cask in a separate evidence bag. One thing was sure. If the fight in the back room was between Fern and the man who hit Cora Lee, if Fern had held her own long enough to create this amount of damage and chaos, Fern was stronger than she looked.

But she would be strong, Joe thought. Working for Richard Casselrod in the antiques shop, she not only kept the books but helped with the displays and moved heavy pieces of furniture. Though a lot of that skill was in the balance, in little tricks like moving a heavy dresser across smooth floors on an upside-down throw rug, sliding it along as he'd seen Wilma do when she rearranged her furniture.

Say the unknown man broke the glass and grabbed

the chests, but saw Fern approaching. He ran into the shop. Fern followed him, tried to take the chests, and there was a fight. One of them fell, breaking the one chest. The guy pulled a gun, Fern ran, and he shot her.

Too soon to speculate. So far, his ideas were no more than a forensic shell game—Clyde would say Joe was playing Monday morning football. Yet he couldn't leave it alone; something kept nudging him. He was missing something, some fact right in front of his nose, some small bit of evidence that, apparently, even Dallas Garza hadn't found.

He sure didn't want to think that Cora Lee was involved in this. And so far, he'd found no scent of her within the shop, or in the window.

One thing was certain. When the ladies of the Senior Survival club had gotten interested in the old chests, they had fallen into more than they bargained for. Someone intent on making a bundle from the Ortega-Diaz letters had become a real threat to the ladies' innocent pursuit.

Creeping close on Garza's heels among the clutter, Joe sniffed every object, trying to sort out the smells. It wasn't easy, with recurring whiffs of Fern's gumdrop perfume mixed with the aroma of old books and old clothes and shoes, with a regular soup of ancient stinks. Yet he did find one scent worth sorting out, a hint hardly detectable over Fern's perfume. Padding closer to a heap of clothes, he fixed on a tiny bit of refuse barely visible beneath a wrinkled scarf.

He was looking at telling evidence, at a missing piece of the puzzle.

He reached out a paw, but didn't touch. He shoved the scarf away, so the cherry pit was in plain sight. He was crouched, looking, when Garza turned.

181

Backing into cover, Joe remained frozen behind a rack of dresses. Garza stared in his direction and stood watching for further movement, his square, tanned face immobile, his dark eyes watchful, his hand on his gun.

When the detective moved suddenly, rolling the clothes rack aside, Joe moved along with the rack, staying under the clothes, his nose inches from Garza's black shoes.

When Garza found no one behind the rack he circled it, and investigated two more racks that stood against the wall before he decided he was alone.

But he had seen the cherry pit. He stood looking, then knelt and scooped it into an evidence bag.

Smiling, with a twitch of whiskers, Joe Grey fled the scene, fading among the shadows to the front door, pawing it open where an officer had left it ajar. Racing up the sidewalk and around the corner to find Dulcie and the kit, the last bit of evidence burned in his brain, Vivi's forgotten little cherry seed, sucked clean.

21

"THIS ISN'T GOING TO WORK," JOE SAID, LOOKING UP at the new, locked front door of the police station.

"Of course it will work." Dulcie backed deeper into the bushes, away from the sidewalk and the scudding wind that dragged leaves along the pavement past their noses. They were quiet a moment, warm against each other, watching the pub door, half a block down, waiting for Max Harper. Every time the door opened, the wind carried to them the heady scent of beer and hot pastrami.

When Harper emerged at last, returning from an early

dinner, Dulcie slipped from the bushes into the shadow behind the twin urns of potted geraniums that flanked the door. When he entered the station she padded in directly behind his heels, as silent and intent as a stalking tiger.

Joe moved close to her and they slipped behind the front desk, across from the dispatcher's counter. Above them, the new front window was just beginning to darken, the spring sky streaked with swiftly blowing clouds. As Harper headed down the hall to his office, Dulcie slipped out again and approached the dispatcher's open cubicle. Padding in under the counter, looking up at the dispatcher, she mewed softly.

The evening dispatcher was a middle-aged woman with blond curly hair and a thick stomach that pulled her uniform into horizontal wrinkles. She occupied a nine-by-nine room with open counters on three sides, loaded with electronic equipment. When she saw Dulcie, she glanced across the entry and down the hall to make sure no uninvited human had entered with the cat.

"Will you look at this. Where did you come from, you pretty thing? Did you follow the captain in here? Oh, aren't you sweet!" She knelt to pet Dulcie, her curly blond hair brassy in the overhead light. Maybe the little chirping noise she made was the way she talked to her own cats. She was new to the station, working the four-to-twelve watch. Her name tag said Officer Mabel Farthy. Opening a drawer under the counter, she produced a ham sandwich from a crackling paper bag.

"Come on up on the counter, kitty. Want a little bite? Come on up here."

Dulcie leaped onto the counter, smiled sweetly, and accepted the offering, gobbling the ham but daintily spitting out the bread. At least the woman didn't use

183

mustard. Mabel stood stroking and talking to Dulcie until an emergency call pulled her away. When she turned to handle the radio, Dulcie walked along the counter to where she could see Joe peering out from behind the information desk. He couldn't see down the hall but she could.

The coast was clear, not an officer in sight. She flicked her tail, and Joe streaked down the hall toward the offices.

Light spilled from two rooms. The one at the far end was where Harper had disappeared. When Joe vanished into the first room, Dulcie turned to study the communications layout.

This setup had far more space than the old communications desk, and Harper had purchased more and fancier equipment. The three new computers and three radios were indeed impressive. Mabel answered two more calls, sending her squad cars out, then took advantage of a lull in the action to offer Dulcie another morsel of ham, petting and talking to her. Oh, Dulcie thought, fate did smile upon the righteous feline. This woman was a pushover.

Dulcie remained on the counter for some time, shamelessly purring and rubbing her face against Mabel's stroking hand, cementing their relationship. With the increased security in the remodeled department, Mabel and the two other dispatchers were going to be key players.

She just hoped one of the three didn't turn out to be ailurophobic. Smiling up at Mabel, she purred a song of delight that left the officer beaming, and left Dulcie feeling that she could tame the most timorous cat hater. All she and Joe had to do was hang around the department and make cute, and they'd soon be regulars.

Maybe they could even become department mascots, and she could turn her gig as official library cat over to the kit for a while.

This morning, when Cora Lee was taken straight from the Emergency Room into surgery, the kit had been a basket case, pacing and worrying until Wilma, in desperation, took the kit to work with her at the library. The kit had seemed to like that. Cora Lee was out of surgery by noon, minus her spleen, which Wilma said was not critical. Otherwise, Wilma said, she was doing well. Wilma had promised the kit that, if she behaved, she'd smuggle her in when Cora Lee was ready for visitors.

A cat in a briefcase? Or maybe concealed in a pot of fake flowers? Smiling, Dulcie pictured a gift box fitted out with a little door and perforated with air holes.

Following Max Harper's scent down the hall, Joe tried to get the lay of the new design. The remodeling wasn't yet finished, but most of the drywall was up and plastered, and ready to paint. The new bulletproof windows were in place, as well as bulletproof glass between the offices. He missed the huge squad room crowded with desks, with all the officers doing their paperwork and taking their phone calls in communal chaos. Now that Harper and the two detectives had private offices, Joe's own life would be more difficult.

Dallas Garza sat at the desk in the first lighted office, deep in paperwork. But the instant Joe peered cautiously in around the door, Garza glanced up, suddenly all attention. "What the hell?"

Joe stepped out into plain sight, his paws sweating, telling himself to stay cool.

Garza laughed. "How the hell did you get in here?" He held out his hand to Joe. Annoyed, Joe approached him and rubbed his face against Garza's fingers. This was so demeaning, to have to ingratiate himself—but then, he did like Garza. It wasn't as if he was playing up to some stuffed-suit type.

"You trying to adopt me, cat? You move into my house, and now here you are in the station. What happened to our beefed-up security? You must really want to be a cop's cat."

Joe! The name is Joe!

Garza rubbed Joe's ears the way he would a dog's, gave him a pat on the butt, and turned back to his reports. Casually Joe trotted away, hoping the detective wouldn't think to mention the incident to Max Harper. Harper would not be so forgiving. He soon found the report-writing room with its six computers, each in a private carrel, with bulletproof glass between. He found the coffee room, and had a little snack of someone's leftover doughnut. But it was the small, padded interrogation room that really interested him.

The cubicle was just big enough for a little table and two chairs. A TV camera was mounted high in one corner. It would be connected to screens in other parts of the building, maybe in the communications room, Joe thought, and in Garza's and Harper's offices, areas where an enterprising cat might, with a cavalier smile and purr, pick up all manner of police intelligence.

The door to the basement was kept closed. He knew that the disaster center down there had been upgraded with state-of-the-art communications equipment, a large supply of emergency food and water, six narrow bunk beds lining one wall, and improved bathing facilities. Harper had described with some pride this brains of

186

rescue operations, to be used in case of flood, earthquake, riot, or war.

Max Harper had created a new and improved crime-fighting plant with all the bells and whistles—efficient, but not cat friendly. Maybe Dulcie was right; maybe feline PR was the best antidote to all this upscale security.

Times change, Joe thought. *Everything today hinges on good PR. Whether you're a writer like Elliott Traynor or just an everyday cat sleuth, face it, networking's become important.* He guessed he could go along with the program, could put forth a little in-your-face chutzpah. If Dulcie could play lonesome kitty, so could he.

He didn't care to see the updated basement firing range; he'd rather just imagine the cavernous room from seeing similar ones on TV. He didn't like the smell of gunpowder. That stink brought back a couple of decidedly unpleasant moments in his career.

Harper had described very graphically to Clyde how the firing booths had been improved, with thicker barriers between them, and more sophisticated targets; with moving figures electrically operated and enough sound effects and flashing lights to unnerve any shooter. Joe was headed back toward the dispatcher, slipping past Harper's lighted office hoping the captain wouldn't look up from his desk, when the dispatcher buzzed Harper. "Long distance, Captain."

"Tell them—"

"It's New York. Some literary agent."

"A what?"

"Literary agent," she said. "An Adele McElroy."

Drawing back into the shadows, Joe listened with a thrill of interest. He heard Harper pick up and identify himself, then the captain was quiet for a moment. Then, "Of course I know Traynor. He's big news here in the village."

Joe didn't like hearing only one side of a conversation. He began to fidget. When Harper paused again, he beat it into the first empty office.

Leaping atop a makeshift desk of plywood balanced on sawhorses, he slipped the phone from its cradle.

Silence. Wrong line. He punched the lighted button.

". . . all right," Harper was saying, "as far as I know. Yes, Mrs. Traynor's here with him. They've cast his play and are starting to rehearse. What is this about?"

"Maybe nothing," the agent said. "Elliott is three months overdue on this book, and that's not like him. He's always ahead of schedule. And he's acting so very strange, he has me worried. We're good friends, Captain, social friends. But now suddenly he won't talk to me. Won't tell me what's wrong, yet I have the distinct impression something's very much amiss.

"I'm concerned about him, Captain Harper, and I didn't know who else to call. Elliott's always been so conscientious, enthusiastic about his work, always had the material to me months ahead of time—and he has always confided in me.

"I know about the cancer, of course, I know he's continuing treatments out there. It may be nothing more than his not feeling well, the depression that can accompany ill health. I can't get anything out of the medical people here. I've called his doctors but they won't talk to me.

"I can't help thinking there's something really wrong—more than the illness. I know it sounds strange, but—do you know him well?"

"No, Ms. McElroy, I don't. I really don't see that—"

188

"This—this may sound like nothing to you, but he's sending me chapters—a few at a time, which I asked him to do. Chapters that are . . . they have me upset about his mental state. They're so . . . so inferior to his usual work . . . "

"That really isn't—"

"We're talking a half-million-dollar advance, here. I don't think he's in any condition to write this book. But he won't talk to me. Nor will Vivi. This isn't like Elliott. And I . . . I need help here, and I don't know who else to call."

Harper was silent.

"I called a friend of his, out there, a Gabrielle Row, asked her if Elliott was all right. She said she really didn't know, that she didn't see that much of them, that they were only casual acquaintances. I had thought differently, from Elliott. I had trouble getting her number, and I still haven't reached Richard Casselrod, though I've left messages."

"You want to fill me in on your relationship with Gabrielle and with Casselrod?"

"Well, it's really Elliott and Vivi's relationship. Gabrielle was here in the city last fall. She had lunch with Elliott. And Casselrod was here in December for the antiques show. He contacted Elliott and spent some time with him, something to do with research on the new book."

As far as Joe knew, Casselrod hadn't socialized with the Traynors in the village. Now, Harper was cool to the agent. "Can you be more specific about the problem?"

"It's his writing, Captain. It's . . . I know this sounds silly, but these last chapters are so very different from Elliott's lyrical style, so different that I'm worried about his state of mind."

"Ms. McElroy, there's nothing the police can do about Mr. Traynor's writing skills or his state of mind. I'm not some literary shrink committed to treating writer's block. If Traynor should become violent or present some kind of danger. . ."

"Or, Captain, if he is in danger? I think that might be a possibility."

"If he's threatened or harmed, Ms. McElroy, of course it's our business. But he would have to file a complaint."

Why was Harper being so stuffy? And sarcastic! Joe felt a quick stab of anger at the man he admired. This woman sounded in real distress.

And he could understand why, having read Traynor's latest work. If he were Traynor's agent, he'd be worried, too. This Adele McElroy was three thousand miles away, trying to deal with a writer who seemed to have lost his grip, who seemed to be dumping a million-dollar novel down the drain. She needed some help here. Why wouldn't Harper at least be civil? Joe wanted to tell her she should hop on a plane, get on out here, deal with Traynor in person.

"Captain Harper, let me give you my number. Would you call me . . . if you find anything you think would be of help?"

Harper grunted. She repeated her number. Hastily Joe memorized it, saying it over to himself. The handicap of being unable to write didn't bother him often. But when a problem did arise, it really bugged him—just as Harper's attitude was bugging him.

Though to be fair, he had to consider the matter from Harper's view. This really wasn't police business. Not unless a complaint was filed, as Harper said, or something happened to Traynor that would bring in the law. Max Harper was a cop, not a social worker.

And yet, Joe thought, knowing Harper, and despite what Harper told Adele McElroy, he bet the captain would go the extra mile, that he'd look into Traynor's condition far more thoroughly than he had told Ms. McElroy he could do.

After all, there was plenty of indication that Traynor might be going funny in the brain. Like shooting raccoons in his pantry—some people might consider that strange. And Traynor's extreme irritability. And Traynor demanding that Fern Barth play the lead, instead of Cora Lee, a decision any fool could see was softheaded. And Traynor's two disappearing acts from local restaurants, apparently to avoid a face-to-face with Ryan Flannery. Added up, all this seemed to Joe Grey to amount to a decidedly squirrelly mental condition.

Sliding the phone back onto its cradle, Joe trotted down the hall, catching Dulcie's eye where she sat on the dispatcher's desk purring and preening. He watched Dulcie give the dispatcher an enthusiastic head rub, and drop to the floor meowing loudly.

Obediently Mabel Farthy came out from her cubicle. Maybe she had cats at home who had conditioned her to the imperative mew. Looking out carefully through the glass exterior door, she threw the lock and opened it.

The cats trotted through. Looking back at her, they had to hide a laugh. She stood at the glass watching them but when she saw them looking she grinned sheepishly and returned to her station.

The minute they were out of sight and earshot, Dulcie was all over Joe, lashing her tail, nudging him into the bushes so they could talk. "What was that about? What's with Elliott Traynor? His agent called? What's happening?"

191

Moving along through the bushes that edged the sidewalk, Joe was quiet. Dulcie nudged him harder. "What? Talk to me! Tell me what's happening!"

Joe turned to look at her. She looked so bright and sweet, peering at him through the camellia bushes—exactly like the first time he'd seen her. She'd been peering out at him, then, her dark tabby stripes blending with the foliage, her pink mouth turned up in a smile, her emerald green eyes flashing. In that one moment, he'd been hooked. Head over heels. He'd never regretted it.

"Come on, Joe. Talk!"

"Traynor's agent's worried about him. Partly because his work's overdue, partly because it isn't up to his usual standards—she's worried about his mental condition.

"She said she'd called Gabrielle, that Gabrielle said she hadn't seen them, that they were barely acquainted. The agent said Elliott had told her otherwise.

"And she said Richard Casselrod spent some time with the Traynors in New York last December."

Dulcie sat down beneath a camellia bush. "We haven't seen Casselrod with Traynor or Vivi. I don't—"

The kit appeared suddenly from nowhere, pushing under the bush beside Dulcie, batting at the fallen camellias. Pressing against Dulcie, she was very quiet. Dulcie nosed at her. "What, Kit? You feel all right?"

"Fine," said the kit in a small voice.

"You miss Cora Lee," Dulcie said. "She'll be home soon. Didn't you enjoy the library today?" Despite the success of Cora Lee's operation, everyone was concerned about her. "She'll be home soon, Kit. Home to Wilma's house until she feels stronger. Maybe you can sleep on her bed, if you're careful of her incision."

Dulcie looked at Joe. "We need to—"

"Check out Casselrod," Joe said. "See what we can find. Maybe letters or an address book, something to connect him to the Traynors. And don't you wonder about Gabrielle?" Joe gave her a long look, and sprang away, heading for the shops south of Ocean.

Buffeted by the wind, and dodging tourists' feet, within ten minutes they were across the village and up onto the roofs of Hidalgo Plaza. Here on the tiles and shingles, the wind blew harder. Unimpeded by the barriers of solid walls, it shook the tops of the oak trees, the gusts so violent that it flattened the three cats against the slanting peaks. They had to dig in their claws and wait for the hardest blows to ease. Pummeled and prodded, they at last reached the lighted attic window of Gabrielle Row's sewing workroom.

The open curtains revealed five sewing machines, three padded worktables as long as beds, and racks of hanging clothes and stacks of fabric. Beneath the fluorescent lights, Gabrielle stood alone leaning over a table cutting out a pattern pinned to a length of heavy white silk.

"Could that be Catalina's wedding gown?" Dulcie said. "Or her nightie? Spanish brides had elaborate nightgowns."

The kit wriggled close between them, her black-and-brown fur tugged by the wind. "So far away, that other world," the kit whispered.

"What other world?" Joe said uneasily. He didn't like the kit's dreaming. "That talk isn't going to get us Gabrielle's address book."

"Worlds beyond worlds," the kit said. "Centuries all gone, in another time. An address book? But we can just slip in through the window. Help me push."

"Not here," Joe said. "We just wanted to make sure her apartment was empty." And fighting the wind he took off again over the roofs, then along an oak branch above an alley; then up a peak so steep they slid as they climbed and nearly tumbled down the far side, approaching Gabrielle's small third-floor window.

Through the glass, they could smell spices, and coffee grounds. Three potted plants stood on the deep sill, between the dark pane and the drawn curtain. The room beyond was dark. They pawed uselessly at the glass. It looked like it had never been opened. All the other apartment windows but one were inaccessible even to a cat, all faced a sheer, two-story drop to the street. Not a vine, not a trellis, not even a protruding windowsill.

The larger window, which was tucked away around the corner among the rooftops, was heavily draped, too, emitting only the thinnest glow at one side, as if from a nightlight.

"Double locked," Joe said, peering sideways along the glass. "A heavy sliding bolt."

"Listen," Dulcie whispered. They all heard it, a click from somewhere deep within the apartment.

Another click, and a soft thud. No lights came on. They'd heard no door open and close as if Gabrielle had finished work and hurried home. She'd hardly had time to do that; they'd come themselves swift as the wind, blown by the wind straight across the rooftops.

From the kitchen, a stealthy sliding noise, like a drawer being pulled out. Another. And another. Then cupboard doors clicking open. Belatedly, a light went on in the kitchen, throwing a shadow on the opaque curtain; a shadow that rose tall, then dropped low as the searcher moved and knelt, opening cupboard doors.

Unable to see in, and unable to reach any other

window or try the front door, whose stairway they knew quite well opened from a locked foyer, the cats waited with tail-lashing frustration. The sounds ceased with a final click, and soft footsteps went away again, then a thud as of the front door closing.

Peering over the edge of the roof above the lobby door, they watched a figure emerge, a tall man in a tan coat, with a floppy hat pulled down low. He hurried to the corner and disappeared around it, a slim man with a long, easy stride.

Racing across the shingles they looked down at the side street where he moved quickly toward a tan Infinity. He pulled his hat off and slid in. He had light brown hair, neatly trimmed. The car was a sleek model with curving lines and a sunroof. As its lights came on, Joe leaned so far from the roof that little more than his rump remained on the shingles. When the car roared off he hung there a moment then backed away from the edge.

"2ZJZ417,"Joe said, smiling. "That's the car from the Pumpkin Coach that almost hit us." He looked away where the Infinity had disappeared. "Could be Augor Prey. The guy fits his description. Let's have a closer look." And they took off across the roof and down a pine tree to the street. Who knew what scent the tires may have left on the blacktop? Whatever might be there, Joe wanted to find it before wind and passing cars wiped it away.

22

THE STREET WAS EMPTY EXCEPT FOR TWO PARKED cars half a block away. Despite the wind, the smell of exhaust still clung along the concrete. Where the tan Infinity had parked, the pavement was patterned with fragments of crumbled eucalyptus leaves, already stirred by the wind, deposited in the shape of tire grids and decorated with crushed green berries.

"Pyracantha berries," Joe said, sniffing. "Don't get that stuff on your nose, Kit. It's poison." The tomcat sat down on the curb. "If that was Augor Prey, maybe he's renting a room, like Harper thought."

How many places in the village rented rooms, and had eucalyptus and pyracantha by the street or by a parking space? Two dozen? Three dozen? The cats looked at each other and shrugged.

"What else have we got?" Dulcie said.

Most likely the guy hadn't been lucky enough to get a garage. Garages in the village were scarcer than declawed cats in a room full of pit bulls. Even a single garage built for a 1920s flivver was a premium item much in demand. The first place that came to Joe's mind was up the hills on the north side. The other house was a block from the beach; both had a eucalyptus tree, pyracantha bushes, and rooms to rent.

"But before we go chasing after Augor Prey," Joe said, "let's give Casselrod a try. See if we can find a connection between him and Traynor." He was silent a moment, his yellow eyes narrowed, his look turned inward as if listening to some interior wisdom.

"What?" she said softly.

"I keep thinking we're missing something. Something big and obvious, right in front of our noses."

"Such as?"

"I don't know, Dulcie. Are the chests the connection between Susan's break-in and Fern's murder? Are a few old Spanish chests enough to kill for?"

"The chests, and Catalina's letters—at some ten thousand each. How many letters were there? Ten letters is a hundred thousand bucks." The concept of that much cash, to a cat, was surreal. Did you count that kind of money by how many cases of caviar that would buy?

"And there are not only Catalina's letters," Joe said, "but Marcos Romero's answers. According to the research in Traynor's office, those letters were smuggled back and forth for years—by travelers, the servants of travelers, by vaqueros herding cattle. Even by some of the mission Indians."

He rose impatiently. "We're not going to learn anything sitting here in the gutter." He headed up the pine tree again, and away across the roofs, Dulcie and the kit close behind him, fighting the wind, heading for Casselrod's Antiques.

In through the high, loose window they moved swiftly, and through the dusty attic presided over by the motionless sewing dummy. She stood stoic and silent, as if disapproving of their trespass. The kit stared at her, and hissed, then approached her cautiously. Sniffing at her iron stand, she turned away with disgust, and was soon caught up in the attic's jumbled maze, lost among Casselrod's ancient and dusty collections. Dulcie glanced back at her only once before following Joe, galloping down the two flights to the main floor.

The first order of business was to call Harper.

Because the information they'd collected was so fragmented, they had delayed that sensitive call, hoping to put some of the pieces together into a tip that was worth passing on. Joe couldn't remember when a case had been so frustrating.

He wondered sometimes if his phone voice carried some disturbing feline echo that made Max Harper uneasy; some unidentifiable overtone, some exotic nonhuman timbre that unsettled the captain.

Harper was an animal-oriented guy, attuned to the moods and body language of dogs and horses, to their subtle communications. What might such a person detect in the timbre of Joe's phone calls that another human might not sense?

Heading across Casselrod's dark showroom into the office, he leaped to the battered secretarial desk, slipped the phone off its cradle, and punched in the number of Harper's cell phone. Following him up, Dulcie pressed her face close to his to listen, her whiskers tickling his nose.

Harper answered curtly. His voice cut in and out as if he might be moving through traffic. Joe knew he could call the station for a better connection, but he never liked doing that.

"You are looking for Augor Prey, Captain. He may be driving a tan, two-door Infinity. Fairly new model. License 2ZJZ417."

Harper repeated the number, not wasting time on small talk. Long ago he had quit asking the snitch useless questions. Maybe, Joe thought, he was getting Harper trained.

"That man tossed Gabrielle French's apartment this evening," Joe said. "And there's another matter that might interest you."

"Go on."

"Elliott Traynor has sold at least two valuable old letters written by—"

"Hold it," Harper said, "you're cutting out. Wait until I turn the corner."

There was a pause.

"Okay," Harper said, coming in more clearly. "Letters written by who?"

"Catalina Ortega-Diaz, the heroine of his play. Traynor sold those two letters for over twenty thousand bucks to a San Francisco dealer."

"What does that—?"

"The history of Catalina tells not only about her letters but about the carved chests in which she kept them—like the three taken from the Pumpkin Coach window, when Fern Barth was killed. Vivi Traynor seems interested in similar chests, as is Richard Casselrod. The white chest that Casselrod took from Gabrielle Row at the McLeary yard sale could be one of the group of seven. Casselrod took it apart, and there was a secret compartment in the bottom, plenty big enough to hold a few letters."

Joe didn't wait for Harper to respond. That was all he had to tell the captain. He punched the disconnect, shoved the phone back in its cradle, and leaped from the desk to a bank of file cabinets, then onto the chair before the rolltop desk.

The lock was engaged, as before. Inserting a claw into the keyhole, he felt delicately for its inner workings.

He tried for some time to line up the tumblers, with no luck. From two flights above them, they could hear the kit leaping and playing among the stored furniture. The lock was more cleverly fashioned than Joe had

199

thought. Both cats tried until their paws felt raw, then Joe tried the metal file cabinets, with no more success. To lose against an inanimate object gave him the same feeling as being caged, a helpless anger gripping him. The drawers were as impenetrable as if Richard Casselrod had invoked some kind of office voodoo. Joe and Dulcie ended up hissing irritably at each other as they pawed through Casselrod's stacked papers.

They found no mention of Elliott Traynor.

"Maybe," Dulcie said, "it was Fern Barth who put Casselrod onto the letters."

"How do you figure that?"

"Say that Fern heard about the play last summer, when Mark King was writing the music. If she wanted the part, she'd have gotten a copy of the script the minute Molena Point Little Theater decided to do it."

"So?"

"Will you stop pacing those bookshelves! How can I talk to you!"

He sat down on the top shelf beside an ancient leather dictionary.

"Fern reads the play. She talks to Casselrod about the story and about Catalina's letters. Casselrod gets interested, begins to wonder if there really were letters. He does some research, finds that there were, and wonders how much more information Traynor has in his possession.

"When Casselrod goes to New York, he gets in touch with Elliott. Elliott has to know the letters are valuable. Casselrod's an antiques dealer, he could help Traynor search for them."

"That doesn't wash. Why, if Traynor thought there was money in the lost letters, would he deal Casselrod in?"

"He has cancer, Joe. He might be dying, or at the least is very ill. He wants to find the letters, but he doesn't have the time or the energy to pursue such a search. And he doesn't have a contact on the coast that he trusts."

"He has Vivi," Joe said. "He could send her out. He doesn't even know if the letters are still on the West Coast, after some hundred and fifty years."

Dulcie's green eyes widened. "Would you trust Vivi to run that kind of search? Competently? And not cheat your socks off?"

Joe smiled.

She said, "Casselrod is based here on the coast. He has contacts among the antiques dealers and wholesalers, he's in the perfect position to search for the chests and the letters. Traynor will supply the research, find out all he can. Casselrod will do the legwork.

"Casselrod comes home to Molena Point, starts talking to dealers, looking in other antiques shops, checking out the private collections. They figure collectors might want the chests, but probably very few people know about the letters.

"But then Fern finds out that Traynor and Casselrod have joined forces; that her own boss didn't include her, after she was the one who told him about the letters. She gets her back up."

"A lot of conjecture," Joe said. "And how do you explain Traynor giving Fern the lead in *Thorns of Gold?*"

Dulcie shrugged. "Fern gets mad, wants to get back at them. Say she can't find any hold on Casselrod. Maybe she starts digging into Traynor's past, and finds some dirt on him, maybe some illegal business dealings. She trades her silence for the lead in the play, for the chance

201

to be Catalina."

"That's reaching, Dulcie."

"Maybe. But you keep saying there's something we're not seeing. Maybe that's it."

"So, say you're right. What does—did Fern have on Traynor?"

"That's the mouse that doesn't want to come out of its hole," she said softly. She began to pace along the bookshelves lashing her tail, thinking, working off frustration.

When a scent caught at her, pulling her back, she sniffed deeply at a leather-bound set of Dickens.

"But Gabrielle was in New York, too," Joe was saying. "Maybe she's part of this, maybe . . ."

Dulcie wasn't listening. She crouched, frozen, staring at the old handsome set of classics. Her tail was very still, then began to twitch. Her whiskers and ears flat, she stalked the leather-bound volumes.

She paused. Carefully she pawed at the books' spines, trying to separate them.

The leather looked old, marred, and faded, but it wasn't crumbly like old leather. The books didn't smell like leather. Looking along the tops of the volumes, Dulcie smiled. Joe watched her with interest.

Dulcie wasn't a library cat for nothing, she knew how to hook her claws behind a book and slide it from the shelves. But these babies wouldn't budge. It was all the two cats could do, together, to pull the set out. Even as it balanced on the edge of the shelf, the books stuck together. One last hard pull, and they leaped aside as the set fell to the table.

It was only a two-foot drop, but the books sounded like a load of bricks dumped from the back of a truck. And they were still stuck all together—one of those clever "hide your valuables" numbers advertised in trinket catalogs.

"No one," Joe said, laughing, "certainly not Richard Casselrod, would be dumb enough to hide anything in this."

"So why is it locked? Maybe it's so obvious, he figured no one would bother to look."

Joe pawed at the lock, certain that this one, too, would resist them. But after four tries something snapped, a faint, clinking sound, and they slid the back of the set away to reveal a hollow brass interior, dry and clean and smelling sharply metallic.

A brown envelope lay within, a small, padded mailer.

"I don't believe this," Joe muttered. But carefully he clawed the envelope out, its cushioned lining crackling. They were working at its little metal clasp when the kit came charging down the stairs, exploding onto the table.

"What?" Joe said, alarmed. "What happened?"

"Nothing," said the kit, surprised. "I just got lonely." She brightened with interest as Joe reached a paw into the crinkling envelope and slid out a letter.

It was fragile and old and musty, the ink faded, the handwriting thin and beautiful.

"Cara mia," Dulcie whispered, picking out a few words she knew from the carefully written Spanish. The paper was so frail that she dared touch it only with the gentlest paw. Hesitantly she lifted the page and turned it over to the small, scrolled signature.

"Catalina," she said softly.

Joe sat looking, twitching a whisker. The kit was very quiet, sniffing the scent of old paper. Dulcie tried to find other Spanish words that she recognized, but she could not. The handwriting was fine and elegant and, in itself, hard for her to read. "What will we do with it?" she asked Joe. "We can't take it with us. If it blew away, if we lost it . . . Maybe we should put it back where we found it? So Casselrod won't—"

"No way. No matter what kind of monkey wrench we throw in the works, we're not leaving this here."

With misgivings, she helped him slide the letter back into the padded brown envelope and claw-closed the metal clasp. A letter worth ten thousand dollars, which they would have to carry between them, across the windy rooftops.

They spent a long time working at the brass box to shift it back into the shelves. They had to push books under to lift it up, tipping it to insert one book at a time until they had it to the height of the shelf, then shoving it back where they'd found it. The operation seemed to take forever. But maybe, with the fake set of Dickens back in its exact place, Casselrod wouldn't look at it for some time. At last they headed for the attic, Dulcie carrying the envelope in her teeth.

"Interesting," Joe said, trotting up the wooden steps, "that Casselrod put the letter there instead of in the big combination safe downstairs."

Her voice was muffled by the envelope. "Did he put it there? Or did Fern? It smells of both of them." As they dropped from Casselrod's attic window onto the windy balcony, she concentrated on keeping the envelope from being snatched from her mouth. Starting across the roofs, they held it between them, fighting the scudding gusts. When their passage startled a sleeping bird that flew up in their faces, the kit took a swipe at it; but she let it go and came chasing after them, her galloping paws thudding on the shingles. Only the kit could run the rooftops sounding like a herd of horses, yet could race, when she chose, as silent as a soaring owl. Twice the wind snatched the envelope nearly from their teeth; they could only pray that the letter wasn't damaged. At last the three cats were off the roofs, backing down a pine tree two blocks from Joe's house, Joe's teeth clamped into the edge of the envelope. As he looked ahead to the white Cape Cod, suddenly he ached to be inside his own house, warm and full of supper and settled down in his clawed and comfortable chair.

How lonely the house looked. Not even the porch light was on, and no car in the drive.

But no matter, it was home, he just wanted to be inside. Wanted his creature comforts—some supper, and a few hours snooze, and he'd be ready to roll again.

But then, padding up the dark steps, he imagined his home turned into a restaurant with lights burning everywhere and cars filling the street and crowds of strangers shouting and laughing in the rooms that were his own, and he didn't like that scene.

Hastily dragging the envelope, with Dulcie and the kit close behind him, he pushed through his cat door into the welcoming dark and the good familiar smells of home—smells of old Rube, of the household cats, of kibble and spaghetti and furniture polish and Clyde's running shoes, all the comforting mix of aromas that had never been so welcome.

23

THE FIRST THING THE THREE CATS SAW AS THEY entered Joe's darkened house, even before the plastic flap of Joe's cat door stopped slapping behind them, was the sheet of white paper that had been lodged securely under the foot of Joe's well-clawed lounge chair.

A note? Clyde had left a note?

Warily approaching, Joe saw the familiar handwriting. What could be so important that Clyde would leave a note in the middle of the living room, where anyone could see it? What if Ryan came back with him? That would be cute. How was Clyde going to explain a note left under the leg of the chair? Joe could imagine him rushing into the house ahead of her, snatching up the scrap of paper and shoving it in his pocket.

The message was cryptic enough. *I'm out with Ryan. Goodies in refrigerator. Don't make yourselves sick.*

Joe read it twice, looking for some concealed meaning. What uncharacteristic fit of generosity had prompted Clyde to leave treats for them? Probably some leather-hard remnant of an overdone hamburger that he wanted to get rid of.

But Dulcie was pacing and nervous. "Come on, Joe. We have to hide this thing."

"What about the bookcase? A bookcase is where we found it."

"Oh, right. In the bookcase where every housebreaker since books were invented has looked for hidden money, where half the doddering old folks in the world hide their cash."

"Where, then? The freezer, where everyone who doesn't read books keeps their valuables?"

She looked pointedly at his chair. "No sensible human wants to sit in, let alone touch, that monstrosity."

Joe shrugged. He'd hidden valuables there before, and not too long ago. Had hidden jewels and stolen money during that rash of thefts that accompanied the Patty Rose lookalike contest. What a week that had been, with all those beautiful would-be stars, and the retired movie star herself, all tangled up in two murders.

"Lift the cushion, Joe, so we don't damage the letter any more than we already have."

Nosing the seat cushion up, shoving his shoulder under it, he watched Dulcie lift the envelope in her teeth and gently slide it into the dark recess, accompanied by the faint crinkle of the bubble-wrap lining.

"That'll do until we find something better," she said. "Only Clyde would know to look there—and it's a sure thing no one will sit there." She paused to consider Joe. "No chance he'd be sending that chair to the Goodwill anytime soon?"

"No chance Clyde wants to meet his maker anytime soon."

When, some months back, Charlie Getz had helped Clyde redecorate his living room, Joe's chair had been a matter of heated discussion. Charlie had wanted to replace the chair with a new one and had talked Clyde into it, generating an argument so volatile that at one point Joe had had both Charlie and Clyde shouting at him.

Charlie said his chair belonged in the city dump. But she'd apologized later. She had been, Joe thought, truly contrite. Joe had prevailed, outshouting, outswearing, and finally shaming them both into acceptance. He'd had that chair since he was a half-grown kitten, since he first came to live with Clyde. That was the first time he had ever seen Clyde or Charlie promoting an act to hurt a poor little cat, and he told them so.

The Damen living room, in spite of being decorated around Joe's chair, had become, under Charlie's ministrations, a handsome, cozy, and welcoming retreat. Charlie's artful accessorizing had made his chair look more than acceptable. "It is," Charlie had decided, "the epitome of shabby chic." She had selected, to harmonize with it, a handsome group of African baskets and sculpture, all done in tones of black and brown. These, with Charlie's framed animal drawings, white-matted against the tan walls, gave the room additional style. And the black-and-brown African throw rugs over the pale carpet tied Joe's chair right into the decor as one more rare and valuable artifact. The carved bookcases and entertainment center and tables had cost a bundle, but Clyde had simply sold another antique car. The room looked great. The humans were happy. Joe was happy. The night Charlie completed the room by hanging the newly framed drawings, she had taken Clyde and the cats out to dinner. Celebrating the fact that they had all been able to agree, she had treated them to broiled lobster in the patio of their favorite seafood café.

Glancing up at the kit, always amused that her black-and-brown coloring fit so perfectly into the room, Joe thought it would be a pity to even think of selling this house, now that it was looking so good.

With the envelope safely hidden, the three cats headed for the kitchen, the responsibility of Catalina's ten-thousand-dollar letter weighing heavily on Joe. What, ultimately, were they to do with it?

They could make a discreet phone call to Max Harper or Detective Garza, then leave the envelope at the back door of the station. That would put the ball in their court. Except, with carpenters and painters still busy on the premises, the fate of a lone envelope could be uncertain.

They could drop the envelope at Dallas Garza's cottage door; or they could tell Clyde about it. Let Clyde take over, though this suggestion was totally against Joe's nature.

Maybe, after all, he'd just leave it where it was, wait to see what developed.

Standing on the kitchen counter hooking his claws in the refrigerator door, Joe pushed backward, wrenching it open. He caught it with a fast paw, before it swung closed again.

On the bottom shelf lay a take-out tray glistening with clear wrap to keep it fresh. This was no collection of dry leftovers, this was a work of art, an elegant and expensive party tray, a concoction from Jolly's Deli, meant for true indulgence. This was their little snack? Joe wondered if he'd read the note right.

But the tray had been placed in his personal area, on the bottom shelf of the refrigerator.

"To what," Dulcie said, "do we owe this? Has Clyde not been well?"

They removed the tray carefully and laid it on the linoleum. "Maybe he's trying to make up for past cruelties," Joe said, clawing at the plastic wrap. The tray contained an assortment as fine as any George Jolly had ever put together. There was imported Brie, Beluga caviar, Alaskan smoked salmon, king crab, shrimp salad, cold mushroom quiche, spinach soufflé, four small cannoli, and brandy-flavored sponge cake, a treat that most cats would give up eight of their lives for but would find dangerous to their digestion. Enough party food, in short, to give the three cats heartburn for a month if they did not employ some restraint. The two older cats tried to eat slowly, savoring each bite. But the moment the wrap was off, the kit plowed in as if she hadn't seen food in weeks, slurping, guzzling, smearing the floor and her whiskers.

Joe glanced at Dulcie as if she ought to teach the kit

some manners, but Dulcie was too busy enjoying her own supper. When at last they were sated, they pawed the plastic wrap back over the uneaten portions and, like the good cats they were, they put the tray back in the refrigerator. In case Clyde would like a bite later.

With their bellies full, they curled up together in a heap on Joe's chair, atop Catalina's hidden letter. They were asleep in seconds.

They barely woke when Clyde came in, didn't hear him go to bed. They slept until the small hours called to them, the bright and imperative predawn summons that routs all night predators long before the sun appears—that shot of psychological adrenaline that has belonged to cats since the world began. This was the witching hour, the hour when the village was its most silent and when, on the hills, the succulent little rabbits danced.

But tonight, they hunted human prey.

Pushing out through Joe's cat door, they galloped across the village watching for marauding raccoons and the occasional coyote that might wander the village streets. Overhead, every star that ever burned seemed to crowd the rooftops. They had chosen five locations where the man in the tan Infinity could be staying, all houses with rooms to rent and with the requisite eucalyptus tree and pyracantha bushes. They separated before they reached Ocean Avenue, Joe heading for a cottage to the south, the kit for the one nearest the shore, and Dulcie for a motel just beyond the courthouse. The kit had been given specific instructions and stern warnings about what not to do.

Many villagers didn't like eucalyptus trees, those handsome, aromatic imports from New Zealand that had so changed the face of California. In a high wind, their trunks broke too easily; and their wood was so full of oil that they created considerable hazard in case of a nearby fire. But other villagers loved them; and to a cat, certain varieties were excellent to climb, with open spaces between their wide-reaching branches, and clumped foliage that could conceal. And tonight those landmark trees might lead them to Susan Brittain's thief and maybe to Fern's killer.

Dulcie, trotting away from Joe and the kit, galloped by the courthouse, looking ahead to the tall, rangy eucalyptus that thrust above the cypresses and pines, its silver foliage pale against the night. Beyond it stood a small, old motel of ten cottages surrounding a patio. The softly lighted sign read, *No Vacancies. No Pets.* The only parking, besides the street itself, was around back, four spaces; first come, first served. Trotting across the neatly tended patio garden between massed blooms of geranium and lavender, and watching for the motel cat, who, being elderly, was probably still asleep, she scrambled up the six-foot gate. Perched atop the fence, she looked down at the bare-dirt parking strip.

A line of pyracantha bushes bordered the drive, and on the narrow space, parked two behind two, were a Ford convertible, a white Olds coupe, a blue Chevy S10 pickup, and a black Jaguar. No Infinity, tan or otherwise. And nothing of that description was out on the nearby streets when she circled several blocks looking. She gave it up at last, and went to meet Joe and the kit. Joe, meanwhile, was trapped in the bedroom of a young woman.

The lady had woken suddenly when Joe jumped to the dresser, though he'd made only a tiny thump. Looking sleepily around the room, she had pulled the blankets up against the early dawn chill, but then had risen to shut the window, effectively trapping Joe inside, unless he could slide the glass up again. She hadn't noticed the hole in the screen, or that it was unlatched. She had apparently been too sleepy to notice a cat blending into the shadows around the dresser. Joe wondered if all the young women of her generation slept in oversized T-shirts with pictures and statements of a personal nature stenciled on them. This lady liked champagne, diamonds, and hot cars. The room was on the first floor of an old, brown, shingled rooming house sheltered by a large eucalyptus. Joe had found the Infinity parked behind, license 2ZJZ417. Oily leaves stained its sunroof, and from the pyracantha bushes that grew along the drive, green berries were crushed beneath its wheels.

Sniffing along the edge of the driver's door he had detected the scent of a man, of shoe polish, and of sugar doughnuts. He had followed the trail to the front door of the building, which of course was locked. A small, demure sign by the door said Do Not Disturb Resident. This meant, in village jargon, that the owner rented out a room or two, possibly illegally, a common practice in Molena Point, where any kind of housing was at a premium. He had tried the first open window, had smelled sugar doughnuts within, and had entered.

He'd found the doughnut bag wadded up in the trash, and only the young woman in residence. Had Prey been here, visiting her, and already left? Joe waited until she was breathing deeply again, then fought the window open a few inches. He heard her stir, but he was out before she saw him.

Leaping to the next sill, peering in through the glass, he listened to ragged male snoring. Even through the closed window, he smelled the same male scent as on the car, as well as the sugarsweet doughnuts. Maybe the two tenants had shared a little snack.

He could detect no smell of dog—but the guy had dumped the dalmatian. Maybe the dog had caused trouble with the landlady, maybe dogs weren't allowed. Maybe the guy had tried to smuggle it in and got caught, so he left it somewhere.

What kind of a man would abandon a nice dog? Couldn't he find some other solution? Board the animal? At least take him to the pound if there was no alternative, not just dump him, frightened and hungry.

The man slept naked in the single bed, the sheet thrown back, one arm draped over the side. Enough starlight washed into the room so Joe could see his face clearly. Thin cheeks, muddy-brown hair, pale brows and lashes, his ears set close to his head. His nose was long and thin, with slightly pinched nostrils. His forehead was high, for such a young man, rising into a widow's peak. A fresh scar burned across his brow, red and puffy, pushing up into his hair just where Susan Brittain's intruder had been wounded.

The window was locked tight, Joe could see where the bolt had been thrown. But above him to his left, the high, narrow bathroom window was cracked open, the occupant assuming correctly that no human burglar could get through that small opening.

Scorching up a bottlebrush tree that crowded against the house, Joe jumped to the sill and hung, scrabbling onto the narrow ledge. Clawing a hole in the screen, he unhooked the latch and slipped inside.

He balanced for a moment on the sill, looking, then dropped to the cluttered sink among a jumble of shaving gear, antiseptic bottles, adhesive tape, and oversized Band-Aids. A tangle of wet towels hung on the two rods. The walls smelled of mildew. Slipping silently

213

down to the linoleum, without his usual heavy thud, he moved into the bedroom.

The mismatched furniture was scarred and old, possibly purchased from the Goodwill with just this rental in mind. A calendar of the Grand Canyon hung above the bed, a stone landscape without any hint of plant or animal life, so dry looking it made Joe's paws feel parched. A half-eaten doughnut lay on the dresser next to the guy's billfold. Leaping up, Joe nosed the billfold open and had a look at the driver's license.

The face matched that of his sleeping friend. The name given was Lenny Wells—Susan's dog-walking companion. The address was in San Francisco. He went through the billfold, stubbornly pulling out credit cards with his teeth. He found no other identification. But this guy with the fresh scar on his forehead had to be Augor Prey.

Using teeth and claws, he managed to slide the little plastic cards back into the tight leather compartments, leaving curious indentations for Prey to puzzle over, and coveting, not for the first time, the luxury of human thumb and fingers. He searched the dresser, easing the drawers open, trying his best to be quiet and not make scratching sounds, and glancing up frequently to be sure Prey hadn't awakened.

He needn't have worried; the guy slept like the dead, didn't make a wiggle. Maybe he'd OD'd on too many sugar doughnuts. Finding nothing in the drawers but a few pairs of jockey shorts and athletic socks, and nothing taped beneath the drawers against the rough undersides, he inspected beneath the dresser.

Nothing for his trouble but dust in his nose and whiskers. When he crawled beneath the bed, his inventory included five large dust balls, three gum wrappers, and a wadded-up paper bag, which, when he got it open, proved to be empty. He found nothing remotely resembling Catalina Ortega-Diaz's letters.

When he shouldered the closet door open, he found the interior bare except for a row of rusty wire hangers. Apparently Prey preferred the backs of chairs for keeping the wrinkles from his jacket and spare shirts. Not until Joe slipped stealthily up onto the bed itself and approached Prey by padding across the blankets did his search pay off.

Watching Prey, ready to leap free from grabbing hands, slipping to within inches of Prey's stubbled face and redolent night breath, Joe pushed an exploring paw beneath the pillow.

Under the pillow lay a gun, just beneath Prey's head. Joe could smell burnt gunpowder, as if the piece had been fired recently but not cleaned. The cold barrel lay against his paw; he touched along its length, careful to stay away from the trigger, then gingerly he pressed a paw against the back of the cylinder.

He could feel one shell casing, in the little exposed part of the cylinder that protruded out beyond the barrel. That could mean anything. A full load of five or six shots? A partial load? Only one bullet, in that particular chamber? Or even a spent shell. But surely no one would fire a gun and leave the empty shell casings in the cylinder.

He sure wasn't going to try to open the cylinder and eject the shells to find out, even if he could manage that. Not without some pistol training—which he didn't think was in his immediate future. And not while crouching on the bed with his face just inches from Augor Prey's face.

He had no way to know if this was the gun that shot

215

Fern—but it sure did smell of burnt gunpowder. Slowly he backed away, watching the sleeping man, moving softly across the bed. When his heart stopped pounding, he leaped to the dresser again and sat for some time studying Prey.

The wound on Prey's forehead was still angry, and darkly scabbed over. Joe could see the rectangle of sticky lines where adhesive tape had been pulled off. When Prey stirred and moved his hand, Joe dropped down to the rug again as silently as he could, and headed for the bathroom.

Onto the counter, among the jumble of toiletries, one leap to the high windowsill, and he pushed out beneath the screen.

Dropping to the grass, he headed through the village, for the house just beyond Molena Point's tallest eucalyptus tree, where the kit had gone to look for Prey. There must, he thought, be another two dozen houses in the village with eucalyptus trees and pyracantha bushes; and who knew how many of those rented rooms. He and Dulcie, picking the three they knew best, had gotten lucky. Trotting along the sidewalk beside the deep flower gardens of a handsome Tudor cottage, he wondered if his anonymous report of the revolver would be enough for Harper to get a warrant, either for Prey's arrest or to search the premises. Ahead stood the hundred-foot eucalyptus, at the edge of the little sand park.

The park, running between the Bakery Restaurant and the beach, was a block-square oasis of low sand dunes, twisted cypress trees, and patches of hardy shore plants. The eucalyptus stood on the corner, its pale bark peeled off in long rolls like parchment, its white arms stretching against the night sky. Among its clumps of long silver leaves, he could see something dark, high up; something alive and clinging, wriggling nervously from the highest branch. He caught the gleam of frightened eyes.

"Wow," said the kit from that great distance.

"Come down," Joe said softly. "Come down, Kit."

"Can't," bawled the kit. She clung like a dark little owl, high and alone in the night sky.

"What do you mean, can't? Why did you go up there? You're not afraid?"

"Tomcat chased me up. I've never been this high."

"Where's the tomcat?"

"I slashed his nose. He went down again, and Dulcie chased him."

Joe looked around for Dulcie but didn't see her. He didn't hear any anguished cries from the neighboring yards. "What tomcat?"

"A spotted tomcat, in that house I looked in. Came right through the window at me! Mad! Really, really mad!"

Joe Grey sighed. "Come on down, Kit. Come down now!"

She turned on the branch, heading down headfirst.

"No! Don't do that! Turn around, and back down. You know how to back down a tree with your claws holding you." He was shouting, angry and terrified that she'd fall, and praying that no one was out walking this late. Or that some homeless soul had decided to sleep in the sand park and would wake highly entertained by their little drama. Why was it that a cat who knew better would lose all good sense when high up in a tree? Why would any sensible cat insist on starting down headfirst, knowing very well that she would be unable to stop herself?

"Turn around, Kit!"

She turned, wobbly with fear, clinging onto one small branch. She started to slip.

"Get your claws in the tree. Back down with your claws! Watch where the bark is loose, don't . . ."

She backed straight into the loose bark and slid fast, the bark curling down with her. Frantically she scrabbled and grabbed and nearly fell, then got her claws into a hard place. He could feel his own claws clutching, trying to help her. But at last she seemed to have a good hold. She backed down slowly, though he could still hear her claws ripping the bark. Where was Dulcie? Why had she run off chasing some worthless tomcat? The bark slid again, and he crouched to leap up after the kit, to break her fall.

A voice stopped him. "You'll only make things worse."

Dulcie pushed against him, her whiskers brushing his, both of them staring up at that small, scrambling creature. "She has to do it on her own. She has to know she can."

"If she doesn't break her silly neck."

They waited, not breathing, watching the kit fight her way down. She dropped the last six feet into the sand, crouched there panting, then slogged across the sand to them, her paws seeming heavy as lead, her head and ears down, her fluffy tail dragging.

They praised her for coming down so cleverly, then scolded her for going up so stupidly high. They licked and nuzzled her and praised her again until she began to smile. Then they headed for Jolly's alley, just to cheer her. They were all three stuffed from Clyde's costly deli plate, but nothing else would delight the kit as much as that little side trip. Trotting close together, soon they turned onto the brick walk, beneath the little potted trees. Light from the two decorative lamps reflected in the stained glass doors and mullioned shop windows. The jasmine vine that hid Jolly's garbage cans breathed its sweet scent onto the cool night breeze.

But the bowls that George Jolly had set out last evening had been licked clean, the other village cats had been at them. They sniffed with interest the lingering scents of vanished smoked salmon and seafood salad, a little nosegay of mouthwatering goodness where no scrap remained. Facing the empty bowls, the kit hunched down with disappointment.

"You're not starving, Kit," Dulcie said. She leaped to a bench beside a potted euryops tree, and stretched out beneath its yellow flowers. Above the tree, the stars burned like the eyes of a million cat spirits. "You found Augor Prey," she said, watching Joe, amused by his smug look.

Joe Grey smiled. "Fits the description. Fresh scar on his forehead. Driver's license in the name of Lenny Wells. Revolver under his pillow, that's been fired recently." He looked intently at Dulcie. "It's time to call Harper. Time to find a phone," he said shortly.

Since he'd grown dependent on placing a call for certain matters, and since every human he knew had a cell phone, the inability to access a phone anywhere, at any time, had begun to make him irritable—instant phone access was now the norm. He didn't like being left behind.

Right. And he was going to subscribe to Ma Bell Cellular? Walk around wearing a phone strapped to his back like some kind of service cat all duded up in a red harness? Though he had to admit, phones were getting smaller all the time. Who knew, maybe the day of Dick

219

Tracy's wrist radio wasn't far in the future. Maybe he could wear one on a collar, designed to look like a license tag.

Though the electronic wonder that concerned him most at the moment was caller ID. How long would it be until Harper sprang for caller ID on his cell phone? That was going to complicate life. As would this new system that would give police the originating location of all cell phone calls via satellite. That would be more than inconvenient.

Wilma had subscribed to caller ID blocking, and so had Clyde, in both cases to give Joe and Dulcie some anonymity. But it didn't work very well. Whether the phone company didn't bother to maintain the service, or whether there was some electronic problem, the cats didn't know. But the fear of identification by telephone deeply bothered Joe and Dulcie, and these new developments presented a constant threat of discovery.

"*Maybe* Prey shot Fern," Dulcie said. "And maybe Casselrod killed her. If she knew about the letter that Casselrod found, would he try to silence her? Or hire Prey to do it?"

"For a letter worth ten thousand bucks? Not likely. Maybe for ten or twenty letters." Joe looked hard at her. "In all of this, Dulcie, there's still something missing. Something right in front of our noses. Don't you sense it? I can't leave that idea alone. Some obvious fact that's the key to everything else."

He began to pace. "Nothing's going to fit, nothing's going to make sense until we find it, or the department does." He stopped prowling to irritably wash his paw, then paced again. At the far end of the alley he turned to look back at her. "Let's go, Dulcie. Let's make that call—let's nudge Harper, and see what we can stir up."

24

AS THE COURTHOUSE CLOCK STRUCK 4:30, ITS chimes ringing sharply across the dark and silent village, the three cats galloped up Wilma's drive and in through Dulcie's cat door, their backs wet with dew from Wilma's flowers and splotched with primrose petals.

The dark kitchen smelled of last night's roast chicken. Hurrying across the slick, chill linoleum and through to the living room, Joe leaped to Wilma's desk. He felt shaky suddenly, and uncertain.

With this phone call, he'd be playing on pure hunch. No shred of proof, no real information. He'd fingered Susan's burglar, he was pretty sure—or had fingered one of them. But did this information point to Fern's killer as well? So far, all circumstantial.

And as to the other matter he meant to bring up with Harper, that might be all smoke dreams. He could, Joe knew too well, be dead wrong in his suspicions.

Glancing to the hall, he locked eyes with Dulcie, where she sat listening outside the bedroom door to make sure Wilma didn't wake. Wilma knew they used the phone; she wouldn't be surprised that he was calling Harper. It was the second call that would be the touchy one, that he would just as soon she didn't know about.

For a moment he wanted to back down, his bold tomcat chutzpah deserted him.

But he'd made up his mind to do this. And when Dulcie gave him a tail-up all clear and an impatient look to get on with it, he swallowed back his misgivings and reached a paw to knock the phone from its cradle.

Dialing Harper's number, he was glad Cora Lee

hadn't been released from the hospital yet, that he didn't have to worry about her overhearing him from the guest room. A surgery patient, who would surely be in some pain, probably wouldn't sleep too well. While tossing and turning, in the small hours, he wouldn't want her to discover more than she needed to know.

Harper answered crossly, on the second ring, irritable at being awakened. Joe knew from past calls, and from prowling Harper's ranch house up in the hills, that at night, the captain kept his cell phone on the bedside stand next to the house phone—Joe liked to think that might be because Harper had come to respect and value his two unidentified snitches, who preferred the cell phone number.

"Captain Harper, I can tell you where to find the tan infinity, license 2ZJZ417, the one I called you about last night."

Harper was quiet.

"And I can describe better now the man who drives it. I believe you'll recognize him." He gave Harper the location of the cottage and described the occupant of the rented room. "He carries a driver's license in the name of Lenny Wells." He could hear Harper breathing. Once in a while, Joe thought, he'd like to hear more than silence to the gems he passed on, would like to hear something besides Harper's smoker's cough and his gruff, one-syllable responses.

"Prey has a gun. A revolver, I don't know what caliber. It has been recently fired and not cleaned. He was asleep an hour ago, with the gun under his pillow."

He knew that this information would generate some hard questions with Harper. How had the informant gotten into Prey's room? How had he been able to look under Prey's pillow and not wake him?

He couldn't help that. Harper had to take him on faith. He had done that, so far, and had benefited from the exchange.

"Captain Harper, do you have the feeling there's something we're not seeing? Some piece of information that would tie all the pieces together? Something so obvious that we're blind to it?"

"Such as?"

"I wish I knew. I'd be happy to share it. This gut feeling I have, maybe it involves the Traynors."

Harper remained silent.

"Captain?"

Nothing.

Joe pressed the disconnect, keeping his paw on it to prevent triggering that annoying little voice that said, *If you want to make a call, please hang up and dial again. If you need help . . .*

He knew from his past calls that Harper's lack of response was usually positive. But this silence had seemed somehow heavily weighted.

Was Harper having the same nibble of unease that he himself was experiencing?

Call it cop sense or feline intuition. Didn't matter what you called it, those little irritating nibbles, for both Joe and Harper, had turned out more than once to be of value. He stared at the phone, trying to steel himself for the next call.

Beyond the window, the sky was beginning to lighten. The time on the East Coast would be about 7:40. He glanced out to the hall toward Dulcie where she lay relaxed, washing her shoulder, giving no indication that Wilma had stirred. He had no idea whether the number he had memorized would be the agent's office number or her residence. Or if, indeed,

223

she worked out of her home.

If he were a New York literary agent, that would be the lifestyle he'd choose. No office rent and no commute. He'd watched a miniseries once on writers' agents. A lot of stress there. But with an office at home, you could get up at three in the morning, if you felt like it, to take care of your paperwork. Plenty of time during the day to hit the street for lunches with editors. And then on other days, one might want to just schlep around ungroomed or unshaven with no one but the occasional delivery person to know any different.

He knew he was killing time, half scared to make this call. Carefully he pawed in the number. He was mulling over the wisdom of leaving a recorded message if she didn't answer, when she picked up. Her early morning voice was low and steamy, like Lauren Bacall in one of those old romantic movies that Wilma and Dulcie liked to watch. But she was even more irritated than Harper at being awakened. Hey, it was 7:40 on the East Coast.

Well, maybe New Yorkers didn't get up too early.

"Ms. McElroy, this is about your friend and client, Elliott Traynor. You've been concerned about him."

"Yes, I have. Who is this?"

"I won't identify myself. I'm calling from Molena Point. You'll want to hear what I have to say. I believe your questions about Traynor might be answered if you would take a photo of Traynor over to NYPD and talk to one of their detectives. Tell them your concerns about Traynor. I can imagine you haven't wanted to do that and stir up the press, but I think that time is past. In fact, the time may be growing short for you to trigger an investigation."

"Why would I want an investigation? Who is this? I don't understand what you're saying." She was silent a moment, then, carefully, "You think the police could help me? In exactly what way?"

"I have an idea that your questions about Elliott will be answered," he said obliquely.

"You realize that I have caller ID. That it won't be hard to find your name and address."

"Ms. McElroy, I'm doing you a favor. You'll understand that when you've followed up. You can return that favor by destroying any record of this number, by preserving my anonymity. Someday you may understand exactly why that is so important. In the meantime, you will be protecting someone seeking only to help you."

He hit the disconnect, feeling scared. The woman had, when talking to Harper, given Joe the idea that she kept careful records of phone numbers and names.

Dropping down from the desk, he sat a moment, carefully washing, getting hold of himself. He did not feel good about this.

He certainly didn't want Wilma dragged into this because he'd used her phone, didn't want Ms. McElroy phoning Molena Point Library, checking the cross-reference, gaining access to Wilma's name and address—or maybe getting that information from some Web directory. He'd sure hear about that from Clyde and Wilma. He prayed that Ms. McElroy would get herself over to NYPD and not waste time tracing calls, hoped she'd see a detective first thing this morning. Because if he was right, there truly might not be much time left.

Joe worried all day about that phone call, fretted over it almost to the point of losing his appetite—to the point where at the animals' suppertime, Clyde started

225

feeling Joe's nose for fever and smelling his breath. Talk about indignity.

"I feel fine! Leave me alone! I have things on my mind."

Clyde looked hard at him. "Do you know that cats can have heart attacks? That cats can suffer from debilitating, life-threatening stress, just like humans can?"

"No cat I know ever had a stroke."

"So now you're a vet, with unlimited research and information. How many dead cats have you autopsied? This sleuthing business is—"

"You talk about stress. Riding me unmercifully every minute gives me more stress than any kind of activity I might choose!"

"I'm not riding you every minute. I ask one simple question—"

"Two questions. Two questions too many."

They'd argued until Clyde made himself late picking up Ryan for dinner, then stomped out of the house swearing that it was Joe's fault. And all the time, Clyde didn't have a clue what was really wrong.

An ordinary cat expects the house person to know what's bugging him. An ordinary cat thinks that a sympathetic human is clairvoyant—that he knows when and where you hurt and knows what to do about it. Your everyday cat expects an able human companion to know what has upset him, what kind of food he wants, where he wants to eat his supper, where he wants his bed. The ordinary cat thinks humans can divine that stuff, that they just know. And he's royally put off when some dumb guy can't figure it out.

But when you have more than the usual feline cognizance, when logic tells you that humans aren't really that sharp, then you have to inform them. Though at the moment, Joe wished that Clyde could divine just a little bit of what he was feeling.

He hadn't wanted to go into a big thing of explaining about Adele McElroy, but it would be nice if Clyde could guess. Because he couldn't stop worrying about that New York phone call. He had the gut feeling that McElroy would be in touch with Harper this morning and that very soon, Max Harper would be asking Wilma about her outgoing phone calls. He was irritable all day and didn't sleep well that night, even after Dulcie told him that Wilma hadn't talked with Harper. He felt all pins and needles, was so filled with questions that two hours before daylight he slaughtered two moles in the front lawn just for the hell of it and conducted a complimentary vermin eradication marathon among the neighbors' gardens. Leaving twelve little bodies lined up on the front porch for Clyde, he headed for the Traynor cottage.

As Joe prowled a rooftop looking down into the Traynors' windows, and as the sun rose, sending a fiery glow across the bottom of the low clouds, Charlie stood at her apartment window pouring her first cup of coffee. Looking out at the first streaks of sunrise, and down at the village rooftops that always seemed fresh and new, she was thinking about Max as she did most of her waking moments. But she was thinking, too, about the job he'd given her to do, a sensitive bit of subterfuge that both amused and flattered her.

She hadn't the faintest idea why he wanted the evidence, and he hadn't offered to tell her. But the chance to play detective in the Traynor household had set her up, big time.

She took her time finishing her coffee, enjoying the sunrise, then showered and dressed and took herself out to breakfast, treating herself to pancakes at the Swiss Café. She did Vivi's grocery shopping and stopped by the drugstore, arriving at the Traynors' just as their black Lincoln was pulling out of the drive.

Waving, she turned in, parking by the back door. Using her key, which the rental agency had given her before they moved in and that Vivi had so reluctantly agreed she keep, she carried the groceries and her tote bag into the kitchen.

Putting away the canned goods, milk, salad greens, and cherries, she waited long enough to be sure Vivi wouldn't forget something and come hurrying back, then got to work with the evidence bags.

She left the house ten minutes later carrying her tote, which now contained six dirty glasses from the Traynors' dishwasher, each lifted out with a spoon and dropped into a separate bag. Out of six, Detective Garza hoped to lift prints for both Vivi and Elliott.

She wondered what Clyde would think of her doing this. Not that he needed to know. Last night, she and Max had planned to have potluck with Clyde and Ryan, but then Max and Dallas had received a call that sent them off to the station. Charlie had used the excuse to go home and curl up with a sandwich and a good mystery, sending Clyde and Ryan out alone for dinner—a far better arrangement, in her opinion.

Interesting, she thought, that Clyde's attraction to Ryan truly pleased her. And it wasn't that she was happy to dump him, to have someone take up the slack when she started seeing Max. It was more than that. She thought Ryan Flannery might be very good for Clyde.

Wheeling out of the Traynors' drive, she met Max two blocks away at the designated intersection. Both stayed in their vehicles. Double-parking beside him, she moved over to the passenger window and handed the bagged glasses through to him. He grinned at her, his brown eyes amused. "Will they notice them missing?"

"I bought six like them at the drugstore, it's a common style. When the agency furnished the house to rent, they didn't want to use the owner's crystal. The new ones are in the dishwasher, where Vivi left these."

Max gave her a wink that made her toes curl. She grinned back at him, did an illegal U-turn in front of him, and returned to the Traynors'. She felt so pleased with herself that before she began to clean she wheeled the vacuum into Traynor's study, to have an excuse for being there while she copped a peek at the latest chapter. Maybe this would be better, maybe these pages would be as fine as his old work.

She couldn't leave it alone; the flawed novel drew her, habituating and insistent.

But, starting to read, she was more dismayed than before. Even considering that Elliott was ill, the work left her perplexed. She didn't understand this writer who had for years charmed her with his prose. She was convinced his mind was deteriorating, and that was incredibly sad. She wondered if he might be in the first stages of Alzheimer's and wondered if Vivi understood how much Traynor's work had changed, if Vivi really knew or cared. Laying the pages back on the desk, she had a terrible, juvenile urge to grab a pencil and start editing, the way she would have done one of her own amateurish school papers.

The history was all there, but reading this was so dull. Elliott Traynor's words should flow, be alive, propel the reader along. She wanted to see these chapters as he should have written them. She felt strangely hurt that Traynor was ruining his own work. Aligning the pages, she had no notion that she was not alone. A thump on the desk brought her swinging around—to face Joe Grey. He stood boldly on the blotter, a smug smile on his gray-and-white face.

"At it again, Charlie."

"How did you get in? I fixed the vent."

"What did you take to Harper?"

She simply looked at him.

"What did you take to Harper? Something from the dishwasher, but you had your back to me. I couldn't see much through the window."

"How did you get inside?"

"Slipped in behind you when you got back from meeting Harper."

"That makes me feel pretty lame that I didn't even see you."

"I was on the roof next door when you came to work. Watched you through the window, digging around in the dishwasher. Bagging plates, Charlie? Followed you over the roofs. What's Harper after, fingerprints? All that fuss with evidence bags."

Charlie sighed. "Dirty glasses. I don't know what it's for, okay?"

He glanced at the pages in her hand. "When did Harper ask you for the prints?"

"He called me early this morning, if it's any of your business."

"What time this morning?"

"Why? What difference does it make? I don't know. He woke me up. Around five, I guess." She looked at him, frowning. "He said he was working on a hunch.

230

That he didn't want to make waves yet—that an early morning tip got him thinking."

Joe Grey smiled.

She reached to touch his shoulder. "What? What did you say to him?"

Joe glanced at the manuscript. "What do you think of the latest chapter?"

Charlie sighed. You couldn't force information from anyone, certainly not from a hardheaded cat. She looked down at Traynor's offending pages. "This should be a wonderful book; so much was going on in the early eighteen hundreds. He's done a huge amount of research, but he's going nowhere with it. This makes me want to write it the way it should be. How can he—"

They heard the back door close softly, though no car had pulled up the drive and they had seen no one approaching the house. At the sound, Charlie flipped on the vacuum. "Get lost, Joe. Hide somewhere." Maybe Vivi or Elliott had cut through the backyards from the side street.

"Open the window," Joe hissed.

Flipping the latch and sliding the glass back, she watched Joe leap through and vanish in the bushes below. She was vacuuming when Vivi appeared, pausing in the doorway to watch her. She was dressed in blue tights, a short denim skirt, a black halter top, and a black cap, her dark hair pulled through the back in a ponytail. Charlie turned off the vacuum.

"Why did you leave this morning, Charlie? You left just after you got here. What did you take away with you in the tote bag?"

"I went to get my purse, I left it in the grocery. I had trash in the bag," Charlie said, laughing. "Thought I had my purse. The house I cleaned last night—I dropped the trash in my bag and forgot about it. What's wrong?"

"You could have thrown it in our trash."

"I dropped it in the grocery dumpster." Unplugging the vacuum, she looped the cord up, to wheel it to another room.

"And why is Elliott's manuscript all mussed?" Vivi's eyes were wide and knowing; slowly they narrowed, never leaving Charlie. "Have you been reading this?" Her face drained of color. "Elliott doesn't like people reading his work-in-progress. What were you doing, Ms. Getz? And why is the window open?" She was suddenly so heated that Charlie backed away. "Speak up, Ms. Getz. What were you doing in here?"

Charlie looked Vivi in the eye. "I guess I brushed against the pages. I had no idea he was so—that he, or you, would be upset." Her look at Vivi was as puzzled as she could manage. "As to the window, I was warm. If you don't like me opening a window, I won't do that anymore." Closing the glass, she moved away down the hall to clean the bedroom.

Vivi didn't follow her; she remained in the study a long time. As Charlie made the bed and hung up their clothes, she heard Vivi unlock the desk, heard her open and close the drawers and shuffle papers, perhaps trying to see what else Charlie might have been into. So what was she going to do? Charlie thought, amused. Report her to Max Harper?

Vivi was gone when she finished vacuuming and dusting, had apparently left the house. Charlie supposed, if Vivi had followed her earlier this morning and had seen her meet Max, she would have been far angrier, would have confronted her with that information in a real rage.

Or would Vivi actually have confronted her? Maybe

Vivi had seen them, maybe she was desperate to know what Charlie had taken from the cottage.

She went about her work absently, leaving at noon to take care of a number of small household repairs for other customers while Mavity and her crew did their cleaning. She couldn't wait to see if Max had been able to lift two good sets of prints. She finished up at five and hurried home to her apartment to shower and start dinner, stopping first by Wilma's to pick a little bouquet from the garden, daisies and some orange poppies, simple flowers that should please Max.

Frying hamburger to add to the bottled spaghetti sauce, she made a salad and pulled a cheesecake from the freezer. Max got there early, coming directly from the station. He sat on her daybed drinking an O'Doul's, making no comment as she recounted the events of her morning. She left out only her conversation with Joe Grey. Moving from stove to table, and to the daybed, she sat down at the end tucking her feet under her, sipping her beer while the spaghetti boiled. She liked living in a small space, everything near at hand. This apartment was so compact she could almost cook her breakfast before she got out of bed.

She looked at Max comfortably, quietly relishing his presence here in her private space. "I've never felt quite the degree of anger and confusion that I do with Vivi Traynor. You're right, she's not a likable person. And she was so suspicious of me," she said, grinning. "I don't think she saw me meet you, but I can't be sure. She was so prodding and pushy."

"Don't you feel sorry for her husband?" Max said, amused.

Charlie shrugged. "He married her. Poor man. Maybe he got more than he bargained for. Did you get their

233

prints all right?"

"Two perfect sets. Unless they've had company in the last couple of days, we have prints for both Vivi and Elliott."

"And you're not going to tell me why."

"Not yet."

She rose to test the boiling spaghetti and to dress the salad of baby greens and homegrown tomatoes that their local market had been featuring. As she shook the dressing, Harper's cell phone rang. She drained the pasta quickly and dished it up as he talked, afraid he would be called away. She liked watching him, liked his thin, brown hands, his angled, leathery face. She liked the contrast between how he looked in his uniform, a very capable, no-nonsense cop, daunting in his authority, and how he looked in faded jeans and western shirt and hat, with a pitchfork in his hand, or on horseback. That same sense of ultimate control was there, only more accessible.

"Yes, I have them," he said into the phone. "I sent the card this morning, overnight mail. You'll let me know—you can guess we're wanting this one yesterday."

He smiled, glancing at her as he listened. "You bet it will. Answer a lot of questions. Was she dealing with it all right?"

Another pause.

"Very good. Maybe we'll get it sorted out."

He hung up, winking at Charlie, and poured another O'Doul's. He said nothing about the call. She was certain it had to do with the Traynor's prints. Across the table from him, she ate quietly, content in his silence. When he was ready to share information, he'd do that.

But, she thought, that sharing would present a prime

dilemma.

Because, was she going to pass on whatever he told her to Joe Grey? Or was she going to guard the confidence Max Harper had in her?

25

BEYOND WILMA'S WINDOWS, THE GARDEN WAS PALE with fog, the twisted oak trees and flowers washed to milky hues. Looking out from the desk in the living room, Dulcie enjoyed both worlds, the veiled garden from which she had just emerged and the fire on the hearth behind her. Near the warm blaze, Cora Lee was tucked up on the love seat, with the afghan over her legs and the kit cuddled on her lap.

Wilma had just this morning brought Cora Lee home from the hospital and gotten her settled in the guest room. It seemed to Dulcie that her housemate was always sheltering one, friend or another. Charlie had first come to her aunt when she fled San Francisco after quitting her commercial art job, convinced she was a failure, that she would never make it on her own. Then after Charlie started her cleaning business, she had come home to Wilma's again when she was evicted from her first apartment, dumping her cardboard boxes and bits of furniture back in Wilma's garage. And Mavity had come here from the hospital after she'd been hit on the head and left unconscious in her wrecked car—had come with a police guard, round-the-clock protection. And now another police patrol was cruising the streets, watching over Cora Lee.

Dulcie looked up, purring, when Wilma appeared from the kitchen carrying the tea tray—a final comforting touch on a cold afternoon. The little tabby looked around her at the perfection of their small, private world, with the fire casting its warm flickering light across the velvet furniture and over the shelves of books and the bright oil painting of the Molena Point hills and rooftops. As Wilma set the tray at the end of the desk, Dulcie sniffed delicately the aromas of almond bread and lemon Bundt cake; but she kept a polite distance. Some folks might not like cat noses in their dessert. Wilma flashed her an amused look and cut two tiny slices for her, slathering on whipped cream. Wilma was wearing a new turquoise-and-green sweatshirt, printed in a ferny leaf pattern, and her gray-white hair was sleeked back with a new turquoise clip.

"You spoil her," Cora Lee said sleepily, watching Wilma set Dulcie's plate on the blotter. "What about the kit? Can she have some?" She stroked the kit, who, at the sound of knife on plate, had come wide awake. Cora Lee was dressed in a creamy velvet robe, loose and comfortable, covering her bandages.

"Both cats will feast," Wilma said, preparing a second plate, "while you and I wait politely for our guests."

Cora Lee shivered, pulling the afghan closer around her. "A week in the hospital, and I still feel weird and disoriented."

"It's the residue of shock, from the surgery," Wilma said. "Plus the shock of what happened—of someone intentionally hurting you, and of seeing Fern dead."

Dead, Dulcie thought, after maybe Cora Lee had idly wished something of the kind for Fern. That wouldn't be easy to live with.

Certainly Cora Lee was still pale, her color grayish, her ease of movement, and lithe ways replaced by stiff, puppetlike gestures, though already she had begun a regimen of exercises designed to strengthen her injured muscles. Very likely painful exercises, Dulcie thought, stretching her own long muscles, extending her length with ease and suppleness. She thought of the distress Cora Lee must be experiencing—and was ashamedly thankful suddenly for her own lithe feline body.

"Growing up in New Orleans," Cora Lee said, "murder wasn't uncommon. It was ugly, but we accepted it. Even as a child, street murder, gang murder, drug-related killings, we were well aware of them.

"But here, in the village that I chose for its small-town gentleness and safety, murder and violent attack seem to me far more shocking." Cora Lee smiled. "I guess I haven't come to terms with that yet," she said lightly.

"We should not have to come to terms with it," Wilma said. "And if you hadn't been bringing the kit home—"

"I would have gone by the Pumpkin Coach anyway. You know I stop every Tuesday morning to see if anything in the window is worth getting in line for." She looked solemnly at Wilma, her thin, oval face drawn and serious. "I should have driven away when I saw the window was broken, when I saw Fern lying there.

"I got out to see if she'd fallen. I had this silly notion that she had been decorating the window—you know how they do, different volunteers taking a turn each week. Fern worked for Casselrod's Antiques; I assumed she'd be a natural one to ask. I was so focused on the idea that she had fallen and hurt herself that I didn't think at all to close the car door, to shut the kit in. I felt guilty afterward.

"When I was close to the window and saw the blood,

237

saw the terrible wounds, I knew I should get away. Like a dummy I stood there trying to see back inside the shop, looking for whoever had hurt her. So foolish . . .

"Then when I turned to the car to phone for an ambulance, there was the pack of letters on the sidewalk. I didn't know what they were but something, a twinge of excitement, made me snatch them up—and then that man leaped out of the window, from nowhere . . ."

"And you ran . . ." Wilma encouraged. It was good for Cora Lee to talk about it, try to get rid of the trauma. "The letters . . . Old paper, you said . . ."

"Old and yellowed. The ribbon was faded and sort of shredded. I got only a glance—the handwriting like old copperplate. Then he was after me. I ran, I got up that little walkway and around the corner before he grabbed and hit me and snatched the letters. The pain in my middle was so bad I knew I'd pass out.

"It's strange. Once I thought the kit was there with me. Then later when I woke in the hospital I thought about leaving the car door open and I worried about her.

Cora Lee smiled. "Detective Garza didn't know how I could outrun the guy as far as I did, could get clear around to the back street—I told him I run at the sports center. When the guy did catch me, when he grabbed me, I really don't remember all of that clearly. I don't remember how I got into the alley where the police found me."

She looked at Wilma, frowning. "Just . . . him hitting me, grabbing the letters, twisting my hand. I remember falling, doubling up with the pain, and I heard a car take off. I don't know who called the police. A woman, they told me. They said she made two calls. I suppose it was someone in one of the upstairs apartments, but no one knows who. I'd like to thank her."

On Cora Lee's lap, the kit rolled over purring and looked up at her with a little curving smile. And Dulcie thought, *Careful, Kit. Be careful.* She watched Cora Lee with apprehension.

If Cora Lee, in her deepest mind, remembered that the kit was there with her, licking her face, did she remember, in some lost dream, the kit speaking to her? Remember three cats crowding around her, talking about her? Did unconscious people hear and remember what was said in their presence? Some people thought so, even some doctors thought they did—but Cora Lee mustn't. Enough people already shared their secret, they didn't need anyone else knowing, even a person they liked as much as Cora Lee French.

Besides Wilma and Clyde and Charlie, Kate Osborne knew about them. They didn't see Kate often; and Kate would never ever tell their secret, one that was so close to her own. But one other person knew, as well—a sadist now locked in San Quentin, a man who had broken out once and followed Kate, surely meaning to kill her just as he had wanted to kill Dulcie and Joe.

Dulcie watched the kit, on Cora Lee's lap, licking the last specks of cake and cream from her whiskers.

"I'm surprised she doesn't make herself sick." Cora Lee said. "She ate like that at my house, too."

Wilma laughed. "Nothing seems to bother her. Apparently she has the same cast-iron constitution as Dulcie and Joe."

"Maybe they're a special breed." Cora Lee stroked the kit. "Certainly this little one is more intelligent than most cats, she seems to know everything I'm saying."

The kit glanced up at Cora Lee, then looked at Dulcie guiltily. Cora Lee seemed unaware of having said anything alarming; her expression was completely innocent. Watching her, Dulcie started when the doorbell rang.

Wilma rose to answer it, hurrying Mavity and Susan in out of the cold fog. Mavity's uniform of the day sported pink rickrack around the white pant cuffs and collar. Over this she wore a zippered green sweater, and her frizzled gray hair was covered by a pink scarf damp with mist.

Susan Brittain was snuggled in a brown sweatshirt over her jeans, and a tan jacket, her short white hair curly from the fog. Gabrielle came up the walk behind them, her smart cream pants suit well tailored, probably fashioned by one of her seamstresses. The three women crowded around the fire and around Cora Lee, making a fuss over her, though they had visited her in the hospital only the day before, taking her flowers and the latest magazines that Wilma had good-naturedly carted home again this morning. On the way home, Wilma had driven Cora Lee by the police station to talk with Detective Garza again. Then at home, she had had a nice lunch waiting. Dulcie herself had curled up on the afghan with the kit while Cora Lee had a long nap.

Gabrielle helped Wilma serve the coffee, then sat down at the end of Cora Lee's chaise. "Did the doctor say whether—say when you can go on with the play? I've started your costume."

"Will there still be a play?" Cora Lee said, surprised. "But they won't want me, they'll put out a call for new tryouts. Truly," Cora Lee said, "with Fern dead, in such an ugly way, I feel ashamed to think about the play." Coloring faintly, she looked up at Susan, where she stood before the fire. "Ashamed that I would still want to do Catalina," she confessed softly.

"Feeling guilty?" Susan said.

"I suppose. Because I did so want that part."

"You're not responsible for Fern's death," Susan said.

"I can't help feeling guilty, though, because I surely wished her no good the night of the tryouts."

"Wishing didn't kill her," Wilma said sharply.

"And whatever debt the Traynors owed Fern Barth," Susan told her, "to make them give her the lead, that's over now."

"Well, they won't want me," Cora Lee said. "Vivi Traynor won't."

"What did the doctor say?" Mavity asked. "How soon will you feel right? How soon can you sing again?"

Wilma said, "There's a lot of muscle tightening around the incision. She'll be stiff for a while, and hurting, and fluids will collect there. The doctor wants her to be careful so it doesn't go into pneumonia. He's told Cora Lee not to take any fill-in restaurant jobs until she's completely healed."

Cora Lee touched her side. "If anyone wanted me—if Sam Ladler wanted me bad enough to arrange it, I'd be ready. Two or three weeks, I could be ready to rehearse. But I . . ." Her face reddened. "That won't happen."

Gabrielle said, "Were you able to help the police? To give them information that would be useful?" She fiddled nervously with her napkin. "I hope Detective Garza doesn't feel that you were involved in Fern's death in some way?"

"Why would Garza say that?" Wilma asked. "Though, in fact, he has no way to know at this point. Until he's sorted through the evidence, he has only Cora Lee's word. He has to wait for the lab tests, has to remain detached."

"I suppose," Gabrielle said. "But Captain Harper knows Cora Lee."

"That really doesn't matter," Cora Lee said. "Wilma's right."

"But," Mavity said, "what exactly did happen? The part you can talk about? It was all so confusing. The paper said there were blood splatters in the back room and on those three wooden chests, that there was a fight back there. I don't—"

Wilma put her hand on Mavity's. "Cora Lee doesn't need to talk about this anymore."

"I'm sorry," Mavity said contritely. "Of course you don't."

"In fact there's very little that Cora Lee is free to discuss," Wilma added.

"But those three carved chests," Gabrielle began, "Catalina Ortega-Diaz's letters . . ."

"No one knows," Wilma said, "if any of the letters have survived all these years. Those letters could be nothing but dust."

Gabrielle put her hand on Wilma's. "I . . . have something to tell you." She looked shy and uncomfortable. "I didn't before because . . . Well, I hadn't intended to do anything about it—I didn't do anything about it, so I didn't think it mattered."

They all looked at her.

"When I was in New York and stopped to see Elliott, he was more than cordial. He fixed lunch for me—Vivi had gone out—and he wanted to talk with me about Molena Point." She sipped her coffee, looking down as if finding it hard to tell her friends whatever was bothering her.

"Elliott told me about the Spanish chests, about the research. He said he had been corresponding with a museum that had one of the chests, and that it had contained three of Catalina's letters. He thought there might be other chests still around, with letters hidden in them—a false bottom, something like that. He told me they would be worth ten to fifteen thousand dollars each.

"He wanted me to look for similar chests when I got back to the coast. He said that if I found any, he would handle selling them to the highest bidder, and we could split the money—that I would be acting as his agent.

"I didn't like the idea. The more I thought about it, the less I wanted to do that. I told him I'd think about it, but when I got home I wrote him a note, said I wasn't interested, that I was sorry he had told me.

"I was up front with him, I told him about Senior Survival and that we were shopping on our own for antiques. I said it wouldn't be fair to you if I were to be shopping for someone else.

"He never answered my letter. And then when they arrived he didn't get in touch. I felt awkward about it, but what could I do. I feel awkward about doing the costumes, about working with him. And I suppose I ought to talk with Captain Harper. Just . . . to fill him in?" she said, looking at Wilma.

"I think you must," Wilma said.

Gabrielle twisted her napkin. "Well, there it is. I knew all along that Elliott could be connected somehow to the theft of that white chest and to your break-in, Susan, though I'm sure Elliott wouldn't do anything violent. That had to be someone else."

The kit's eyes had grown so wide as she listened that Dulcie leaped at her, landing on the arm of Cora Lee's chaise, licking the kit's face until she had her full attention. The kit subsided, tucking her face under her paw.

"With all the violence these last weeks," Mavity said,

"I'm not sure I'll go to any more sales. That Iselman estate sale, that should be grand. But if the Iselmans had those old carved chests, what else might they have that would cause trouble?"

"I'm going," Susan said. "I'm not letting Elliott Traynor, if he is involved, or anyone else frighten me. We can make some money out of that sale, if we buy carefully. I think we should all go."

"And carry our pepper spray," Mavity said, laughing. Pepper spray was the one legal weapon a woman could carry without any kind of permit. After Susan's break-in, Wilma had bought vials for all of them, and taught them the safety procedures—including careful awareness of which way the wind was blowing.

"Why not with pepper spray?" Susan said. "I carry mine all the time. I don't like to be intimidated. If I'd been at home, with that little vial in my pocket, my house wouldn't have been trashed. I'd have given them something to think about, and so would Lamb." She looked around at her friends. "I've been selling on eBay all week. I've sold nearly everything on our shelves that wasn't destroyed. If we mean to go on with this, to keep putting money in the bank, we need to start buying again."

"Are we smart to go on with this?" Gabrielle asked hesitantly. "Or are we only fooling ourselves? Are we going to make enough money to do this? And is it going to work?"

"We've been over the numbers," Susan said. "We've already put ten thousand in the bank from our sales, and we've only been at it six months. If we do this for a couple of years, plus the money from our own houses . . . mine and Mavity's . . ."

"And mine," Wilma said, "if I'm ready to throw in

with you."

"And the profit from my two rentals," Cora Lee added. "And from that lot you own, Gabrielle . . ."

"I hope it will work," Gabrielle said uncertainly.

"It will work," Wilma said.

"We'll all have our privacy," Mavity said, "and our own space—maybe as much as I have now, in that little house. Plus a nice big living room and kitchen and a garden, maybe a nice patio.

"But then, it's different for me. I have to move." She looked around at her friends. "I got the notice this morning. The official condemnation. Thirty days. The letter said they made it such a short time because it's been talked about so long, because we all knew it was coming."

"You'll move in with me," Wilma said, "until you decide what to do. There's plenty of room for your furniture in the garage."

"By the time you're ready," Cora Lee said, "I'll be home again, and Wilma's guest room will be yours."

"We can move you," Susan said. "Rent a truck, maybe hire one of Charlie's guys to help us—make a party of it, go out to dinner afterward."

And on Cora Lee's lap, the kit was looking back and forth again, from one to the other, paying far too close attention. Dulcie tried to distract her. When the kit ignored her, she swatted the kit as if in play, forcing her off Cora Lee's lap and chasing her through the house to the kitchen.

Excusing herself to refill the cream pitcher, Wilma followed them, shutting the kitchen door behind her.

Backing the kit into the corner behind the breakfast table, Dulcie hissed and spat at her. "You didn't see yourself. You were taking everything in, looking far too

245

perceptive and interested."

"But no one would guess," the kit said. "No one . . ."

"Cora Lee says you seem to understand everything she tells you. They could guess, Kit! Charlie did! How do you think she found out?"

"I thought—"

"Charlie figured it out for herself. She watched and watched us. She figured out that we were more than ordinary cats, and those ladies—especially Cora Lee—could do the same."

"Oh, my," said the kit.

"Charlie would never tell," Dulcie said. "But those other ladies might, without ever meaning any harm. You be careful! If you're going back in there to sit with Cora Lee, you practice looking dumb! Dumb as a stone, Kit! Sleepy. Preoccupied. Take a nap. Play with the tennis ball. Have a wash. But don't look at people when they talk!"

The kit was crestfallen, her yellow eyes cast down. She looked so hurt that Dulcie licked her face. "It's all right. You'll remember next time," she said, giving the kit a sly smile. "You will, or you'll be licking wounds you don't want."

Wilma looked at the kit a long time, then picked up the two cats and carried them back to the living room. She gave them each another piece of cake, lathering on the cream, setting their plates side by side on the blotter. Watching the kit guzzle the rich dessert, Wilma was torn between frustration at the willful little animal and love and amusement. But always, she was filled with wonder, with the miracle of these small, amazing beings.

If the cats would only leave police business alone. Theft, armed robbery, murder, Joe and Dulcie were in the middle of it all, refusing to back off. And the kit was becoming almost as bad. The cats' intensity at eavesdropping among questionable characters and their diverse ploys when digging out hidden information left her constantly worried about them.

But maybe, this time, what appeared to be a tangled case would turn into nothing. Maybe Fern's death wasn't connected to Susan's break-in or to the carved chests. Maybe Fern had happened on some gun-happy youth looting the store and in panic he had shot her.

Maybe, Wilma thought. But how, then, to explain the three chests pulled out of the window, and, days earlier, Richard Casselrod snatching the white box?

Dulcie watched Wilma, half amused and half irritated. They'd been together a long time, she knew how Wilma thought. Wilma was hoping right now that this case would turn out to be a dud. Just as Clyde seemed to be hoping. What was it that so disturbed them? The fact that a famous personality was involved? Both Clyde and Wilma seemed to want present circumstances to go away. And that wasn't going to happen.

For one thing, neither Wilma nor Clyde had all the facts. Neither knew that Joe had called New York this morning, setting in motion a whole new string of events. Nor did they know that Joe had found Augor Prey and found the gun that may have killed Fern, or that Joe's subsequent phone call had prompted Harper and Garza to stake out Prey's room.

And no one, not Wilma nor Clyde nor the police, knew that a second stakeout had been set up on the roof next door to Prey. A twenty-four-hour observation post with instant communication to Molena Point PD. A surveillance operation, Dulcie thought, that was soon going to need a nice hot dinner—a little sustenance for a cold and hungry tomcat.

26

WHERE A STEEP ROOF ROSE FROM A FLAT ONE, THE space beneath the slanted overhang formed a small, triangular cave protected from rain and from the sea wind, and from the eyes of curious pedestrians. One last ray of the setting sun shone in, where Joe Grey lay on the warm shingles looking down at Augor Prey's windows. Clyde's cell phone was tucked on the roof beside him—a real mouthful to carry through the village for five blocks, during the dark predawn hours, and to drag up the pine tree and across the slippery shingles. Before he left home, at 4:00 this morning, he had turned the ringer off to avoid alarming any late-night pedestrians or street people. And certainly, here on the roof, he didn't want a shrilling phone to announce his presence. He'd been here all day; it was twilight now and he was hungry.

Peering down into Prey's room, he could see the bed and dresser and a pair of jeans thrown over the armchair whose back served as a hanger for Prey's shirts. Prey had just gone out, walking, leaving his car parked on the street. Joe had watched one of Harper's rookie cops, a young man dressed in jeans and T-shirt, idle along a block behind him, appearing as aimless as any tourist.

After Joe's call to Harper, the captain had made no move to take Prey in for questioning or to search his room for the gun, but he had put a tail on Prey. Maybe he and Garza didn't want to tip Prey too soon. Or were they not willing to take the word of their unknown informant that this guy was, in fact, Augor Prey?

Certainly when they did arrest him, if the guy's prints matched those in the Pumpkin Coach and in Susan

Brittain's breakfast room, they had more than enough to hold him. The delay in making an arrest had Joe digging his claws into the shingles wishing they'd get on with it.

But impatience wouldn't cut it. All he could do was wait, and back up Harper's surveillance by observing Prey from the roof, where a cop could hardly remain unnoticed. Crouched in the chill evening, he was hungry as a homeless mutt. He wished Dulcie would show up, before he had to snatch some sleepy bird from its nest. Tonight, with the cold wind parting the fur along his back and shoulders, sending its icy breath clear through him, he'd really rather have a nice hot, home-cooked supper.

By the chimes of the courthouse clock, it was nearly 7:00. During the fifteen hours he'd been on the roof, with only a few short breaks down to the garden, he'd followed Prey to breakfast and then to lunch, shadowing him from above. After lunch he had watched Prey as he sprawled on the bed entertained by a series of mindless sitcoms, snacking on candy bars and a Coke. He couldn't figure out why Prey was hanging around; why, if he killed Fern, he hadn't skipped.

And if Prey hadn't killed her, Joe didn't know who to look at next, among the several candidates. Besides Prey, who had attacked Cora Lee and whose scent was all over the charity shop, Vivi had been in the shop, sucking on frozen cherries. And quite possibly others. Scent detection in that medley of furniture and old clothes and shoes was no easy matter.

When Prey headed out again, likely for dinner this time, Joe tucked the cell phone deeper under the overhang, and followed across the roofs to the same restaurant where Prey had enjoyed his previous repasts, a plain box of an eatery that looked like it belonged not in Molena Point but beside some central California freeway catering to the camper trade. Prey's restaurant of choice had no garden blooming in front, no murals or elegant paintings on the walls, no potted plants inside. The harsh lighting illuminated a plain room with bad acoustics, chrome-and-plastic furniture, and the thick smell of a menu heavy on fried foods. No light California fare of the interesting combinations that Dulcie loved, but that, in Joe's opinion, was like mixing the garden flowers with the mousemeat.

Across the street and half a block away, the rookie cop who was following Prey stood huddled in a doorway trying to keep out of the wind. Joe, from his own high vantage, wondered who was watching the back door. Likely no one; Prey's shadow had him in plain sight.

Dropping to a low overhang above an art gallery, Joe hit the sidewalk, crossed the street among the feet of wandering tourists, and galloped half a block down to the alley behind the restaurant.

The kitchen door was ajar to let in fresh air amidst the hot smell of onions and frying meats. Trying not to drool as he pawed the screen open, he slipped in past the cook's heels, across the kitchen, and under an empty booth at the back.

At a front table, Prey was just ordering, glancing repeatedly toward the window. Did he know he had a tail? Watching him, Joe tried to figure out where he'd hidden the packet of letters that he snatched from Cora Lee. Earlier in the day, while Prey ordered his lunch, Joe had returned to his room to toss it again, checking all his pockets, slipping a paw between the mattresses and crawling in as far as he could reach without smothering himself. He had fought the dresser drawers open again and climbed in behind them, and peered up at the undersides of the drawers. He'd found nothing more valuable than a rusted bobby pin and an old gum wrapper.

So maybe Prey had the letters on him. Maybe they'd been under the pillow along with the gun, and he'd missed them. There was a limit to how familiar the searcher could get without waking the searchee and getting one's tail in a knot.

Or had Prey given the letters to Richard Casselrod, maybe to sell and split the take? Joe was yawning with boredom by the time Prey paid his bill and rose to leave. Jerking awake, Joe rose to follow. Slipping beneath the tables and around assorted pant cuffs and stockinged ankles, he left the restaurant by the front door directly behind Prey's heels; but dropped back when the rookie fell into line.

Prey stopped at the market to pick up a six-pack, then headed back to his room. Could he be waiting for someone? Was that why Harper was watching him and not making an arrest? Back at their mutual destination, as Joe scorched up the nearest pine tree to the roof, Prey's room light and the TV came on. Joe watched him pop a beer and settle down on the bed, again not bothering to remove his shoes or to pull the shade. Joe could still taste the meaty cooking smells from the cheap café. Crouched in the wind, his stomach rumbling with hunger, he began to worry about Dulcie. He kept peering over the edge of the roof to the sidewalk below and to the scruffy patch of garden that ran between the houses, but there was no sign of her. Every time he glanced up into Prey's dismal room, he felt like he was peering in at a captive. Prey had, for all intents and purposes, made himself a prisoner, or nearly so—

251

watching him had become as boring and tedious as watching paint flake from a rusting car.

Joe thought about the comfort of his own home, about his soft easy chair clawed to furry perfection, and the big, well-stocked refrigerator, and the wide, warm bed he shared with Clyde—but then his fear of Clyde's selling the house returned to haunt him. The idea of abandoning his home and going to live somewhere unfamiliar was totally depressing, the idea of a strange house filled with the unfamiliar smells of departed strangers and departed animals, where nothing fit just right or smelled right. The thought of moving and of starting over dropped him right down into a black well of dejection.

"You look limp as a fur rug."

He jumped, startled. Dulcie stood behind him dangling a paper bag from her teeth. He could smell pot roast, he could tell that it was still warm and succulent. She dropped the bag on the shingles, nosed it open, and clawed out a Styrofoam dish. It took her a moment to undo the little clasp, revealing a heap of sliced roast beef, crisp string beans, and au gratin potatoes.

"Hot from Wilma's microwave. Dig in. I had my share, didn't want to carry it all."

"Wilma puts up the best leftovers in the village."

"Not leftovers, really. She cooks a big roast, all the fixings, then portions it out for future meals."

"The blessings of a woman's touch."

"That's very sexist. Is that why you want Clyde to get married?"

"It couldn't hurt," Joe said with his mouth full. And when he came up for air, slurping and purring, he said, "Frozen suppers, ready for the microwave. We could do that when the rabbits are out by the hundreds, bring home a brace, portion them out into little dishes . . ."

Laughing, she lay down on the shingles, soaking up warmth from the vanished sun. "Not even Wilma and Clyde would dedicate their freezer to our hunting kill."

"Does Wilma know why she fixed supper for me? Does she know I'm up here?"

"Of course. I had to tell her something. She didn't say a word, except did you have Clyde's cell phone up on the roof because Clyde's pitching a fit, trying to find it. He thought maybe he'd left it at her house." Curled up in the shadows of the overhang, she began to wash her paws. "You could call Clyde and put his mind at rest— so he won't think he lost it and someone's going to run up a big bill."

"He doesn't need the phone."

"So call him. He's not going to come up here on the roof to get his phone back."

"I wouldn't count on it. He's been so grouchy lately—and nosy. But what's happening at the station? What did you find out? Did you get in all right?"

Dulcie smiled. "I'm a permanent fixture. The day dispatcher's just as much a cat person as the lady on second watch. She made all kinds of fuss over me, made a bed for me on her sweater. All the officers stopped to scratch my ears and chuck me under the chin like some hound dog. They're so funny. Don't they know how to pet a cat?"

"Harper doesn't think it strange we're suddenly showing up there?"

"He gave me a look or two. Said maybe I was getting bored with being the library cat. But what would he suspect? A cat could shout obscenities in his face, and Harper wouldn't want to believe it."

Joe shrugged and licked the Styrofoam one more time

in case he'd missed a drop of gravy.

"Clyde stopped by the department," she said. "Asking Harper about Fern's murder. Didn't even wait until they went out for coffee, just started asking questions. I think he's worried about you—about us. Maybe it's all this business of trying to decide whether to sell the house, maybe he's feeling insecure."

"Clyde's feeling insecure, so he takes it out worrying about us."

"Maybe, for humans, that's the way it works. Life gets uncertain, and every little frustration becomes a big problem. But listen to this," she said, her green eyes gleaming. "Garza brought the Traynors in."

"On what charge?"

"No charge. Just to talk to them. He couldn't hold them. Elliott was totally silent, didn't even complain about the inconvenience. You'd think he'd pitch a fit. You can bet Vivi whined; she said this would throw Elliott behind schedule, that he had to finish his book. She ranted on while Elliott sat there saying not a word and looking miserable."

"So how did the questioning go?"

Dulcie looked abashed. "I tried, Joe. I thought it would be a snap, that I could sit on the dispatcher's counter and watch the interrogation on her monitor, but I should have known better. Garza just took them into his office. And shut the door. Practically in my face. I lay down on my back against the door playing with my tail, but I got only part of it. Those doors are thick, maybe bulletproof. Garza asked about their leaving New York, about their movements just before their flight. Vivi sounded surprised, but then she got really mad."

Joe smiled. "Sounds like Adele McElroy did talk to the New York detectives. But why would Garza ask

254

questions and alert Vivi? If there is anything to my theory, they'll pack up and skip."

"My thought exactly. But I really didn't hear enough to make sense of it. Garza drove them back to their cottage himself.

"But he put a tail on them," she said, grinning. "So maybe that's his idea, too, to catch them skipping."

"Who did he send?"

"Davis. She's good, but I can find out more than she can. I can look in the windows to see if they're packing, and I can slip inside."

"Watch yourself, Dulcie. Don't forget Elliott has that 'target pistol' as he calls it."

"I don't think he'll use that again." She gave him a whisker kiss, and left him, leaping into the pine tree and scrambling backward down the rough trunk carrying the empty Styrofoam dish in its paper bag. She dropped it beside the steps of Prey's landlord, next to the trash can.

Prey had turned the light off; only the glow of the TV remained. Across his windows the evening sky reflected in a glut of slow-moving clouds. Joe could smell rain. He hoped it would hold off. Even under the two-foot overhang, a sudden downpour would splash up from the shingles, drenching him and playing hell with Clyde's cell phone.

He watched Prey pop another beer, sitting on the bed leaning against the pillows. Playing with the remote, Prey began to channel-hop, producing a staccato of jolting squawks and flashing light. As the evening deepened, the pine tree that rose beside the roof turned from separate green needles to a black and shapeless mass, and the house walls darkened to nondescript shadows blending with the ragged bushes. Only the pale sidewalk directly below retained its sharp edges, the concrete empty now except for a scattering of dead leaves skittering in the wind. Stretching out, Joe rested his chin on the metal roof gutter, looking down, half dozing, his bored gaze fixed on Prey.

He stiffened.

Something dark was sliding among the bushes; a figure was approaching Prey's windows noiselessly from the street, Joe caught a glimpse of jeans and a dark shirt. Was it the rookie that Garza had sent to tail Prey? Had he pulled a heavier shirt on over his pale T-shirt, and put on a black cap? The man moved along beside the shrubs below the window, making no sound at all.

At nearly the same moment, Prey flicked the overhead light on again. As the harsh glow struck the bushes like a searchlight, the guy ducked away. Joe picked him out of the blackest shadows, crouching, watching the window above him. He looked bigger than the young cop. Inside the room, the glow of the single bulb shattered across the dresser's oval mirror, picking out Prey as he opened a third beer, the scar across his forehead angry in the artificial light. Staring at himself in the mirror, he moved to the bathroom and rinsed out a washcloth.

Returning to the TV, he lay down and folded the cool compress across the healing wound. Outside the window the silent watcher waited. Above the dark treetops, the clouds lowered and extended, cutting away the last of the fading daylight, casting the village into darkness. The watcher moved closer, peering in through the glass.

Snap, his shoe broke a dead twig. He crouched, frozen, as Prey swung up from the bed and switched off the light.

Prey stood for some time peering out, picking

nervously at the scar, glancing behind him around the room.

When he pulled the blind, Joe could hear him moving, could hear drawers opening. Nipping across the roof, Joe dropped to the branch outside the bathroom window.

In the lighted bathroom, Prey was sweeping razor and toiletries into his jacket pockets, along with a pair of socks that he snatched from the shower rod where apparently he had hung his laundry. When he left the bathroom, Joe slid the window open. In a moment he heard Prey punch the phone, and listened to him ordering a cab.

Leaping back across branches to his own roof, Joe pawed at Clyde's phone, hitting the on button and the redial, the way he had set it up. In seconds he was speaking to the dispatcher.

"Augor Prey is getting ready to split, packing clothes and shaving gear in his jacket. He just called a cab."

"Will you repeat your message?"

"Prey's ready to skip. Tell Detective Garza, now! I don't know where the tail is. There's a guy watching him, but I don't think it's your man." Joe watched Prey lift the mattress, shouldering it up high enough to reach clear to the middle, deeper than Joe had been able to search without smothering himself. "Well, I'll be damned," Joe said. "I think—tell Garza that I think Prey has the letters."

He watched Prey carefully stuff a little packet wrapped in clear plastic, into his inside pocket. It looked like letters; he thought he could see a ribbon wrapped around the small bundle.

Garza came on the line. He was as matter-of-fact as Harper had been lately. As if maybe Harper had talked to him about this snitch, had told him this informant was eccentric but reliable. "Is Prey's car still there?"

"It's there," Joe said. "He's called a cab. Guess he means to leave the car, and leave his bag in the room, just walk away as if he's coming back. He's armed. If that is your man right outside Prey's window, he's too close for you to risk your calling him."

"There is no officer on duty."

"You've had a tail on him all day."

Garza hesitated as if not sure how much to trust this stranger.

"That officer is back at the station," he said at last. "We have not sent a replacement. You say someone is watching Prey?" Garza's voice was sharp.

Joe leaned over the gutter, peering down. The guy was still there. "You have no tail on him now?"

"No tail. If you'd give me your name . . . "

Joe watched the squarely built, darkly dressed figure, caught a glimpse of a pock-marked cheek.

"That's Richard Casselrod," he hissed suddenly. "Casselrod's tailing him—black sweatshirt, black cap and shoes."

Prey left his room and in a moment came out the back door of the house, looked around him, and quickly crossed the side yard.

"He's making for the back street," Joe said softly. "He's standing in the shadows of a cypress tree. I can hardly see him under the low branches. Casselrod's following him, moving in behind him."

Casselrod made not a sound. Nor did Garza. The phone sounded like it had gone dead.

"Are you there?" Joe whispered.

No one answered; Garza was gone. Joe watched a cab turn into the street, its lights reflecting across darkened house windows. As Prey started toward the taxi, Casselrod lurched out of the night and grabbed him, swinging Prey around and shoving a gun in his face.

Jerking Prey's jacket back over his shoulders to confine his arms, Casselrod took Prey's own gun. Joe watched him pat Prey down and remove the plastic-wrapped packet from Prey's shirt pocket.

Holding his gun on Prey, Casselrod backed toward the cab. At the same moment, police cars moved in from both corners, parking diagonally to block the narrow street. Detective Garza swung out, followed by three uniforms. They grabbed Prey, and Garza was on Casselrod. Kicking him toward the cab so he went off-balance, Garza swung him around, taking his gun and forcing him against the vehicle.

Within seconds, Prey and Casselrod had been searched and cuffed and secured in the backseat of a squad car. Garza had their guns, and he had the plastic-wrapped package. Joe Grey sat on the roof smiling with satisfaction as the black-and-whites pulled away, taking the two to their new accommodations. He hoped MPPD could offer them a long, extended visit.

27

THE SETTING MOON PAINTED A LINE OF BRILLIANT light along the clouds' ragged edges, a display so spectacular that up on the hills the two cats paused from devouring their freshly killed rabbit and sat looking toward the heavens, held by that burning stitchery.

It was only a few hours since Augor Prey and Richard Casselrod had been arrested, a positive event in an ongoing scenario that seemed, to Joe Grey and Dulcie, far more nebulous than the clouds shifting above them. The department had Prey's .38 revolver. By tonight or tomorrow the ballistics report should be in. With that thought to cheer them, the cats fell to again, sharing their warm, bloody kill.

They ate in silence, making a leisurely meal, then washed up, licking gore from their whiskers. Around them the tall grass shivered in the predawn wind. What concerned the cats at the moment was that Vivi and Elliott had been released.

They had no idea on what grounds Garza had picked up the Traynors and brought them in for questioning; but the thought that they were free again was not encouraging. They had no notion, either, what Adele McElroy might have learned from NYPD about the Traynors.

"If this comes down the way I think," Joe said, "Vivi and Elliott could split any minute—get edgy and pack a bag the way Prey did, and they're gone. Well, Harper and Garza will be expecting that." But still, he began to pace, looking restlessly down the hills toward the Traynor cottage.

"Relax," she said complacently. "You know Harper has an officer in place. And they weren't packing earlier. I watched until they went to bed."

"A tail won't know until they get in the car and take off."

"So, the law will pick them up." She licked blood from her paw. But then she rose, with a little half-smile. "You're not going to rest until we have a look." And she took off down the hills. Galloping through the forest of tall grass, the two cats could not be seen—only the thrashing line of their flight wildly tossing the grass

260

heads.

Dropping down off the hill, they raced beneath a rail fence and through a garden that had been decimated by grazing deer, its roses nibbled away until only ragged fragments of petals remained, scattered like potato chips. Down through the village gardens they sped, as the courthouse clock struck five, then swiftly across empty side streets. Approaching the Traynor cottage, they passed the department's surveillance car, an old blue Plymouth Rent-A-Wreck parked four doors away, its engine and tires still warm, the smell of coffee perfuming the air around it, though no driver was visible.

The Traynors' black Lincoln was gone. The house was dark. Scorching up the oak tree to the high living-room windows, they looked down through the glass.

"They haven't moved out," Dulcie said. "Vivi wouldn't leave that tangerine satin robe, it's too gorgeous. She wears it every morning." The room was its usual mess, the robe tumbled across a chair under Vivi's red sweater, a pair of sandals tossed on the coffee table next to an empty cup and a torrid-looking paperback romance, the heroine with enough cleavage to hide a sheep dog.

Dropping to a lower branch, they looked into the study.

The computer still reigned on the desk like a small electronic god. The stack of research was still on the shelf. Only the new chapter was missing; there were no freshly printed white pages aligned neatly beside the blotter. The cats waited for what seemed hours, and no sign of the Traynors. The sun was pushing above the hills when Charlie's old Chevy van pulled into the drive, its bright blue paint glistening, its rebuilt engine

261

purring. Last year Clyde had completely rebuilt the engine and fixed the rusting body, pounding out dents, applying filler and primer, then expertly sanding before it was painted—a labor not of love but in return for Charlie's carpentry work on the neglected apartment building that Clyde had purchased. Their exchange of work had been a fair trade all around.

They watched Charlie swing out of the van, hauling her caddy of cleaning supplies to the back door, to disappear inside. Soon they heard her loading the dishwasher, then opening cupboards.

But soon the study light came on, and she wheeled the vacuum in. Standing at the desk, she bent to try the drawers, her kinky red hair falling loose from its ribbon. Was she looking for the manuscript? All the drawers were locked.

"If the Traynors have skipped," Joe said, "maybe they mailed the manuscript to Elliott's agent, maybe hoping when they surface again the second half of the advance will be waiting?"

Dulcie sneezed. "Could they really believe that?"

When Charlie hastily turned on the computer, the cats hurried along the branch where they could see the screen, watching her bring up chapter 1 of *Twilight Silver,* then move to the final pages. They were so fascinated that when a mockingbird flitted boldly past their noses, they hardly noticed its rude taunting.

Taking a floppy disk from her pocket, Charlie put it in the computer and went through the steps to make a copy.

Glancing out toward the drive, she dropped the disk in her pocket, then went through the little ritual of shutting down the machine. "Nice timing," Joe said. The computer was chuckling its closing noises when the

Lincoln turned into the drive.

Vivi got out of the car alone; Elliott wasn't with her.

"He's not in the house?" Dulcie said, glancing through the study door to the empty hall.

The moment the car turned in, Charlie snatched up Traynor's research from the bookshelf and slipped it into the waistband of her jeans, tucking it out of sight under her sweatshirt. By the time Vivi crossed the drive and turned her key in the back door, Charlie was vacuuming the hall. And the cats learned nothing more until that night when Charlie and Harper, Dallas Garza and his niece showed up at Clyde's for sandwiches and a few hands of poker.

Harper and Garza were in a gala mood, their expressions as smug as Joe had ever seen. Clyde looked at them patiently, waiting for whatever big news they were holding back. When the officers said nothing but simply began to count out chips and shuffle cards, Clyde glanced at Joe, as frustrated as the tomcat. Couldn't people just come out and say what was going on with them, couldn't they simply tell a person why they were grinning? Ryan and Charlie remained expressionless, waiting to see what would develop.

The kitchen smelled of salami and onions, and echoed with the clink of poker chips. Harper dealt, fanning the cards with a thin, practiced hand. The cats, to keep a low profile, retreated to the laundry and cozied down on the bottom bunk next to Rube. The old Lab was sound asleep, softly snoring. Harper said, "That's a nice car, that Lincoln the Traynors drive. I understand they picked it up from the Ford dealer when they got off the plane, ordered it months ago, before they left New York."

Clyde looked at Harper, puzzled. "Are we supposed

to be impressed?"

Harper shrugged. "I don't know. You wouldn't expect a multimillion-copy best-selling author to drive a ten-year-old Mazda."

Joe couldn't figure out where this was leading. Apparently, neither could Clyde, and he was not amused. He sat staring at his cards, scowling darkly. Well, he'd been touchy all week. Joe knew that he'd called Kate several times and that he kept leaving messages but she hadn't returned his calls. At one point, worried about Kate, Clyde had called the designer's studio where she worked. She was there, they told him, but very busy.

At the poker table, Clyde said, "If Traynor's so rich, why did he opt for a Lincoln instead of a Jag or BMW?"

"You mean, why didn't he buy from Beckwhite's?" Harper said, laughing. "What, you're getting a percentage from the showroom now? I'll take two cards."

Clyde flipped cards around the table. "Second-rate car. And a wife young enough to be his granddaughter."

Ryan and Charlie were silent, glancing at each other.

"Forty years younger," Garza said, his square, Latino face not changing expression. "He and Vivi were—have been married three years." Garza slid two chips to the center. "His fifth wife. But the first time around for her—first time for a legal relationship." He glanced at Harper again, the faint gleam of humor sparking between them.

Joe stretched and curled up with his chin on Rube's golden flank. Beside him, Dulcie closed her eyes. They listened with keen interest; they'd never before heard Harper and Garza amuse themselves at Clyde's expense.

When Harper raised the bet, Garza slid two chips to

the center. "Vivi's first marriage," Harper said, "after a long line of live-ins and one-night stands. She's been busy for a girl of twenty-five. Apparently she's lived off rich men since she was fifteen."

Garza said, "I wonder if Elliott knew, when he married her, that she would be his last."

Clyde came to full alert. And in the laundry, Joe's and Dulcie's ears cocked sharply forward.

Clyde watched Garza raise the bet, then folded. Garza took the pot. No one said anything more, the table was silent, Harper and Garza stonefaced and ungiving. Joe wondered if a cat could expire from unfulfilled curiosity.

The poker players ran three more hands, talking only in monosyllables. "Raise you two." "Three cards." "I fold." Twice Clyde glanced across the kitchen at Joe, at first with the same unfulfilled curiosity, a moment of mutual sympathy—before he gave Joe that *none-of-your-business, why-don't-you-go-out-and-play-like-a-normal-cat* look that made Joe hunker down harder against Rube, stubbornly waiting for Harper's punch line.

28

HARPER RAKED IN THE LARGEST POT OF THE NIGHT, stacking his chips in neat rows. "That would have been tight," he said, "keeping a twenty-four-hour surveillance on the Traynors, pulling men off patrol."

Garza nodded. "Better off in custody. New York is sending Vivi's case file?"

Clyde stared at his cards and said nothing. And from the bunk in the laundry, Joe and Dulcie watched with

265

slitted eyes, pretending to be asleep.

Harper said, "Homicide put it in the mail this morning. No wonder Traynor's agent was upset."

"All right," Clyde said, "that's enough. Let's hear it."

"If not for Traynor's agent," Garza said, ignoring Clyde, "hassling NYPD, they might never have identified the body."

Joe had sat up, staring at the two cops so intently that Dulcie nudged him. He lay down again, tense with interest. At the poker table, Charlie and Ryan were quiet, watching Harper feed the story to Clyde piece by puzzling piece, the captain loving every excruciating minute.

And Joe and Dulcie looked at each other, buzzing with questions. Had the case come down like Joe thought? Was that what Garza and Harper were saying? Had Adele McElroy and NYPD found the missing piece? Did Harper and Garza have to he so damned oblique? They were not only teasing Clyde, they were driving two poor innocent cats nearly crazy.

"You're not saying," Clyde snapped, "that Elliott Traynor is wanted in New York? For homicide? You're saying he killed someone? This guy is famous. You're saying he—"

"He didn't kill anyone," Harper said mildly.

"Vivi?" Clyde said. "Vivi killed someone?"

Harper shrugged.

Clyde laid down his cards. "No more poker. No more beer. Nothing more to eat until you guys lay out the story."

The officers began to laugh.

Ryan said, ". . . he and Vivi *were* married three years? *Were* married . . .?"

Charlie repeated what Harper had said earlier. "*Did*

266

Elliott know that she would be last? That she would be Elliott's last wife, Max?"

Clyde said softly, "Elliott Traynor is dead. When did this happen?"

"Before we ever met him," Garza told Clyde.

Joe Grey felt his heart pounding, and felt Dulcie's heart pounding against him. He'd been right. A wild guess, a shot in the dark, and he'd pounced on the big one. Had nailed his quarry right in the jugular.

Clyde looked hard at Harper. "This is not Elliott Traynor, this guy in the Traynor cottage who's the spitting image of Traynor, who looks like Traynor's picture on his book jackets, who is supposed to he suffering from terminal cancer? Who is overseeing the production of Traynor's play and finishing up Traynor's novel?"

"Fry cook from Jersey," Garza said. "Dead ringer for Traynor."

Clyde shook his head. "And Traynor's agent was worried because his work was so bad? A fry cook is writing Traynor's book? And is Vivi a fake as well?"

"That's Mrs. Traynor," Harper said. "They came close to pulling it off."

"They killed him?"

"Not sure yet," Harper said. "New York's working on that."

"How did you . . . ?"

"Someone knew," Garza said. "Or suspected. Someone blew the whistle. Called the agent, told her it was time to take her problem to NYPD, to talk to the detectives."

Clyde shuffled the deck. "I'm getting lost here. It would be nice if you guys would start at the beginning."

"Talk about chutzpah," Harper said. "Fry cook with no literary talent, impersonating one of the country's top

267

writers."

"And you have them in jail."

"Brought them in late this morning," Garza said. "They were packing up, getting ready to skip. We're holding them on illegal disposal of a body, until New York decides if it was homicide."

Garza counted his chips, then looked up at Clyde. "Elliott Traynor died six weeks before they were to fly out here. No one knew, there was no report made of his death. For all intents and purposes, Elliott boarded the plane with Vivi."

"No one might have known," Harper said, "except that Traynor's book wasn't finished when they left New York. When they got out here, the writing suddenly turned inept. Apparently this fry cook can't write worth a damn."

"What did they do with the body?" Clyde asked. "You can't just—"

"Seems Vivi dressed him in old ragged clothes, old shoes. Elliott had lost weight, didn't look well, and that fit right in. She left him in an alley—a dead John Doe, one of New York's homeless."

"Agent got concerned," Garza said, "because Traynor's last chapters were so bad. She started poking around, then called Max."

"Agent was waiting for us to check on Traynor, when someone from Molena Point called her. Suggested she get over to NYPD and talk to the detectives, take them a picture of Traynor."

Clyde didn't ask who called the agent. Under the table, his foot was tapping. He eased back his chair as if he found it hard to sit still.

"The agent's visit paid off," Garza said. "One of the detectives remembered a John Doe that looked like

Traynor. Body was tucked away in the morgue waiting to be ID'd. The detective took the photo and ran with it. Got the agent to bring him some manuscript pages— some that Traynor sent before they left New York, and some later chapters that were sent from here."

Harper said, "Prints on the chapters Traynor wrote before they left the city matched the John Doe. The other set, on the chapters sent from Molena Point, are Vivi's, most of them. One or two that match up with the fry cook. And," he glanced at Charlie, "some prints where the housekeeper had moved the manuscript, when she dusted the desk."

"You had Vivi's and this guy's prints?" Clyde asked.

"We were able to lift them from the house," Harper told him, "sent them overnight to New York."

"Another few weeks," Garza said, "and Elliot might have been buried in a pauper's grave to make room for new bodies."

"But why would Vivi . . . How did Traynor die?"

Harper shook his head. "The body was found by a garbage collector behind a row of trash cans. Unshaven, dirty, shaggy hair. Nothing visible to indicate the cause of death. Usually, whether the coroner suspects murder or not, on a John Doe they'll take blood and tissue samples for later investigation.

"Even though he was really too clean, no thick calluses on his feet, no sores or signs of prolonged ill health, New York thought Traynor was homeless. They're a busy department. Overworked, backed up on investigations, as is the medical department. They didn't take samples. Tucked him away hoping they'd get an inquiry, someone looking for him."

"But why didn't they run his prints?"

"They ran his prints," Harper said. "No record. Even

if he'd had a driver's license, New York DMV doesn't take prints. Only a picture. Could be, they would never have made the connection except for Traynor's agent and whoever tipped her. I talked with her this afternoon. She's not taking this too well—they were close friends. She's convinced it was murder.

"She said Traynor had plotted a smashing ending to the book, a finale that fit the story yet would blow the reader away. Said Traynor plotted carefully before he began to write, and that he always adhered to his outline. She said the plot was followed in the last chapters, but the writing was not like Traynor's work. She thought for a while that it was the medication.

"She said that for several weeks after he sent the first chapters, while he was still in New York—when the writing first turned bad—Vivi wouldn't let her talk with Traynor when she called. Vivi claimed he had a bad cold, on top of the cancer and his treatments, that his condition was pretty serious, so McElroy didn't push it. Said she was leaving town for a week's conference. When she got back, Traynor did finally return her calls but he was forgetful and his voice muted, like the cold was hanging on. What upset her was that he didn't want to talk about the book, didn't seem able to talk intelligently about it. She wondered if he'd had a stroke, but Vivi denied that.

"Then," Harper said, "Traynor decided to come to California to oversee the play and finish the book, despite his illness. McElroy said she was worried about him doing that."

"But," Clyde said, "if Traynor died naturally, from the cancer, if Vivi didn't kill him, why wouldn't she have a bang-up funeral and collect his estate?"

"If the book wasn't finished," Harper said, "she might

270

have to give back his advance. And the guy had four previous wives. Maybe he didn't leave much to Vivi."

"Then you're saying she had no motive to kill him? That he died a natural death, but she didn't want anyone to find out?"

"That remains to be seen," Harper said.

Joe and Dulcie exchanged a glance of smug satisfaction. But they lowered their eyes when they saw Clyde watching them, and began diligently to wash— the age-old ritual of pulling a little curtain of disinterested preoccupation around themselves.

Garza said, "Apparently she met this fry cook some six months ago. Willy Gasper, working in a little hole-in-the-wall in Queens." That made Joe swallow back a laugh. This tall, well-dressed, elegant-looking man that everyone thought was an author of international fame— this guy's name was Willie Gasper?

"Think about it," Garza said. "She discovers a dead ringer for Elliott. Elliott's ill, she assumes he's terminal somewhere down the line. She knows that when he dies, the writing income is reduced, and that very likely four ex-wives could have some claim on his assets. Willie presents a ready-made way to keep Elliott in the picture, convince everyone that he's still alive. Not hard, she thinks, if she offers Willie the right deal.

"She'll have to take over Elliott's writing, but she has his research, and this book's three-fourths finished. She figures she can do that."

Garza smiled. "Apparently it didn't occur to Vivi that she might not be able handle the literary side of the matter. The opportunity was too good. How could she pass it up?"

Harper said, "The New York medical examiner should have an answer in a day or two as to whether she killed him or he died of natural causes. Meantime, the two of them are in jail raising all kinds of hell.

"When we get this sorted out," Harper continued, "we may find a link between these two and Augor Prey. We picked Prey up last night. Prey and Casselrod."

"On a tip," Garza said quietly. "From this phantom snitch of Max's, that no one has identified."

"Last night," Garza said, "I'd pulled off the officer I had watching Prey. We had a party to break up south of the village, a free-for-all fight—kids—and someone fired a few shots from a twenty-two. We had everyone down there. Maybe Prey knew the officer had been pulled back. Maybe not. But whoever called in was close enough to Prey to see him packing up—and to see Richard Casselrod follow him."

Garza frowned, aligning the cards into a neat stack. "I'd like to find this informer. See what other information he might have—see what his interest is in all this."

Harper was quiet. Clyde was quiet. Charlie rose to refill the plate of cold cuts. And in the laundry, crouched on the lower bunk, Joe Grey smiled. *Don't waste your time,* he thought, glancing at Dulcie, and he put his head down on Rube's leg, feeling pretty good about life.

If he hadn't called Adele McElroy, she might not have gone to the New York police until it was too late, until the body had been disposed of—if he hadn't had that niggling little itch that wouldn't let him rest. Cop sense, Harper called it.

And apparently Harper, too, had felt that a big piece of the puzzle was right there, looking him in the face.

Though Harper, constrained by certain ethics and codes, might not have been able to take the freewheeling approach that a cat could employ.

Joe knew it wasn't smart to get smug about a case until there was an arraignment, a court date, and the wheels of the law were grinding, but he couldn't help it. Dropping off the bunk to accept a plate of snacks from Clyde, he found himself rumbling with purrs. And when he looked up into Clyde's eyes, the two shared a rare moment of perfect understanding. Clyde was proud of him, and that made Joe want to yowl.

All he and Dulcie had to do now, he thought, giving Clyde a purr and a head rub, was wait to see whether Vivi, maybe with Willie Gasper's help, had indeed killed Elliott. Or whether she simply took advantage of the situation at hand.

Or, Joe thought suddenly, had Elliott himself done the deed? Had Elliott Traynor, following the philosophy of some other terminally ill folks, unwilling to deal with increasing pain and weakness, taken his own life? Had he stepped out of the sickness, perhaps with the expedient use of some powerful and legally prescribed pain medication? Joe was thinking so hard about this possibility that he didn't wonder until later about Willie Gasper's "target pistol," about the .38 with which Willie had killed the raccoons. He didn't wonder until late that night if Garza had searched the Traynor cottage and found the weapon.

As he curled down on the pillow beside Clyde, he knew there must be more to the story that Harper and Garza hadn't yet told, and he began to wonder, anew, what the two officers were holding back.

Maybe there was something they were feeling edgy about, not yet certain how the facts were unfolding? Well, if Harper and Garza wanted to play that hand close to the chest, that was their call. Maybe they knew where the gun was, and weren't spilling that part just yet.

29

THE LADIES OF THE SENIOR SURVIVAL CLUB MET early Saturday morning to stand in line for the Iselman estate sale and ended the day falling in love. To their great dismay, the object of their affections was not available, but was spoken for by another. The day was breezy, streaks of clouds blowing so low over the hills that, high up where the Iselman house rose, they seemed to catch on the rooftops. Mavity and Gabrielle and Susan waited in line at the door for the tickets. The house stood on a steep street of expensive residences at the east side of the village, a large two-story structure of stucco and rough-hewn timbers, with multiple wings and patios, and angled tile roofs. At precisely 7:00 a.m. John Tharp, manager of Tharp Estate Sales, opened the front door from within and, holding a large roll of blue tickets, began passing out numbers to be presented three hours later for admittance. Already the line snaked to the street and half a block along the sidewalk. The three ladies took their numbers and greeted Clyde and Ryan, who stood behind them some ten places.

"Will you join us?" Susan asked. "We're having breakfast at La Junta." La Junta Hotel's patio breakfasts were a village favorite.

"Wilma and Cora Lee are meeting us. After the sale, we're going to look at houses."

Clyde raised an eyebrow. "I didn't know you were that far along in your plan."

"Neither did we," Susan said, "but the marsh houses are being evicted since the city finally made up its mind. Mavity has thirty days to get out, so we thought we'd have a look."

"Well, it's a buyer's market," Clyde said. "But we'll take a raincheck on breakfast, we're going to the state park—deli picnic, and a hike before the sale begins." He moved up beside Ryan to accept their tickets and the ladies turned away to Susan's car.

They read the real estate ads over breakfast, and marked the most desirable houses.

Walk to the village from this charming five-bedroom home . . .
One-of-a-kind design, separate guest quarters . . .
Secluded setting, large house delightfully crafted . . .
Bathed in sunshine, four bedrooms, two baths, and large office . . .
Spectacular ocean views. Solarium. Two fireplaces . . .

It would take a lot of looking before they found the house that suited, and in their price range. The ladies lingered over the ads, enjoying their breakfast, then hit Iselman's estate sale shortly before 10:00. Shopping for only an hour, they covered the ten rooms that were open to the public carrying away cloisonné bowls, Haviland china, ebony carvings, and some nice old brass pieces that should do well in the eBay auctions. Packing their purchases into Susan's and Gabrielle's cars, they unloaded them in Susan's garage with only faint unease. With both Augor Prey, aka Lenny Wells, and Richard Casselrod out of circulation, their purchases would be perfectly safe. The first open house was a residence so immaculate, with its creamy fresh paint and white carpets, that they all were afraid to set foot inside. The garden was equally well manicured, each tree and rosebush

275

trimmed to a perfection seldom found in nature. The house had five large bedrooms and four baths, and a kitchen to die for; but no one felt comfortable.

"Too picture perfect for me," Mavity said. "I'd be afraid to breathe."

"And me," Susan agreed. "Not a home for a dog, even as well mannered as Lamb."

"I like it," Gabrielle said, imagining herself in the largest, front bedroom, the one with the fireplace. Neither Wilma nor Cora Lee showed much interest. The house was beautiful, with its large living room and sunken seating area, its white satin draperies and white tile fireplace; but it wasn't the home they wanted. Anyway, the price was out of their reach. They moved on to the next open house, and the next, traveling in two cars in case Cora Lee should grow weary.

Some of the houses were elegant. Some showed the love marks of hard wear by large families. Some had good space, an appealing kitchen, or a welcoming garden, but none quite fit. Not enough bedrooms. Rooms too small. And of course the universal complaint: too much money.

Mavity, at the end of thirty days, would receive a cash payment, the city taking out a low-interest loan for its investment. The council had voted to turn three-fourths of the land back to the marsh as a bird and wildlife refuge, and to sell the remaining acre at a profit for a small, tasteful condominium in the heart of the sanctuary. The "nature" units would be much in demand. Mavity made no comment about the city's intentions. She walked through the open houses with little enthusiasm, caught in the trauma of dislocation, feeling insecure and off-center and frightened. Wilma put her arm around her friend, knowing that when her own time came to move, she'd feel the same.

Wilma didn't intend to leave her stone cottage anytime soon, but it was nice to have a plan for the future, a place to go if she should become ill. And now, driving to the next open house, she couldn't get her mind off Dulcie and Joe Grey.

The cats had made a point of asking when Cora Lee might be going home, but they wouldn't tell her why— only a sly little smile from Dulcie. They were preparing some surprise. Knowing those two, she remained uneasy. As she pulled up in front of the last open house on their list, two cars were leaving, and a black BMW was parked at the curb.

This was probably the ugliest house in the village, a brown wooden box with a flat roof, cracked siding, and peeling trim, the fascia boards pale and discolored. On top of the large main floor stood a second, smaller cube, apparently a single room, resembling nothing so much as the wheelhouse on a Mississippi riverboat. The structure was, in fact, very much like Mavity's little fishing cottage, in a larger and more sprawling version and without the stilts that held Mavity's home above the muddy marsh.

The house backed on one of the wild canyons that bisected the Molena Point hills. Maybe, Wilma thought, the view from the back would be nice, out over the canyon and across Molena Valley to the low mountains that edged the rocky coast. These fissures that cut through the hills had, eons past, been deep sea canyons, this whole neck of land lying beneath the ocean. It was the canyons, in part, that kept Molena Point from becoming overpopulated. One couldn't build in them, and the lush terrain, with wild bushes and grasses, offered food and shelter to deer and coyotes, to occasional bobcats, and, just this last spring, to a large male cougar. How interesting that the house stood between the two worlds, the rear decks forcing out into the wild land, the front of the house solidly a part of manicured human civilization.

The front yard was enclosed by a tall wooden fence and belonged apparently to one or more large dogs that were not at the moment in residence. The earth was trampled bare beneath a few sickly bushes and dotted with their chewed rubber toys. At least the owners had cleaned up the dog do; and probably they had taken the dogs away for the day—the sight of canine pets could cause a prospective buyer to look twice as hard for interior damage, for chewed door moldings, scratched floors, and stained carpet. The ladies gathered in front, beside the "Open House" sign.

"I don't think . . ." Gabrielle began, looking the house over, "I don't think this one . . ."

Wilma took her arm. "Come on. It won't hurt to look, it's the last one on the list. Nearly four thousand square feet, Gabrielle, and it has enough water credits to start a hotel."

The ad read, *five bedrooms and five baths, five custom-built fireplaces plus two sunny, legal basement apartments.* The word *legal* should mean not only that the land was zoned for two apartments, but that every water fixture on the premises had a proper permit.

All over Molena Point there were unobtrusive apartments tucked into a hillside basement or over a garage, some legal, some not. All were in demand as rentals. Molena Point's water code mandated an official permit for any household fixture that used water in its functions, from a king-sized shower to a bar sink. New credits were not an option; your house had just so many.

278

If you wanted another washbasin, you had to give up a fixture in exchange.

"There's plenty of parking space," Susan said. "Three-car garage and this nice wide drive. And the front planting, between the fence and the street, is nice, where the dogs don't play." That wide area was lush with native bushes, succulents, and large volcanic boulders. Susan's Lamb, though he, too, had a fenced yard, had in his poodle dignity allowed Susan's garden to flourish and even the lawn to present a respectable green carpet.

The front door was open. They saw no one inside. Entering, they formed a divergent group, Mavity in her maid's uniform, Wilma in jeans and a red T-shirt, Gabrielle wearing a linen suit and heels, and Cora Lee in stretch pants and the oversized shirt that hid her bandage. Susan wore a calf-length denim jumper over a white T-shirt, and leather sandals. They moved into the foyer.

"Oh, my," Mavity said.

"Oh!" Cora Lee whispered.

They stood in a wide entry, its tile floor and skylight bathing them in brilliance. Potted plants filled the corners. Through a door to their left, they saw a young couple in the large, light kitchen, talking with realtor John Farmer. Glancing up, he waved to Wilma. A stairway rose to their right. Passing it, they moved ahead into a large living room dominated by a fireplace of native stone.

The gray-blue walls wanted paint, and the carpet still showed stains despite an apparently recent cleaning. But the ceiling was high, with tall windows, a spacious room very different from what the exterior implied.

The three bedrooms on the main level, two to the

right of the living room and one to the left past the dining room, were all large. Each had a private bath, and two had raised fireplaces.

The oversized kitchen was done in cream-and-white tiles. Opening off this were an ample laundry and storeroom, before one entered the garage. All the walls needed paint, and some needed patching. The doors were marred with claw scratches, made, apparently by a very large dog. Returning to the entry hall, they climbed the stairs.

The upstairs cubicle, that looked so small from without, offered a large master suite with another raised fireplace, a private deck, an ample study that would do for another bedroom, and a view straight down into the canyon. Three levels of decks overlooked the canyon. The ladies glanced shyly at each other, but no one spoke. They hurried down again, to the basement apartments.

Both apartments were fusty and needed work. But both had their own small kitchens. Either would do for a housekeeper, a caregiver, or as rental income.

Returning to the living room, they could see John Farmer still in the kitchen with the young couple. Farmer was in his forties, a man with surprisingly round cheeks, a pink-and-white complexion, a slim, sculpted nose, and dark hair in a military cut. He sat at the dining table with the blond young woman and the slim, redhaired young man. Their voices were low, their conversation solemn, the couple's expressions excited and serious.

"They're too young to afford this house," Mavity whispered.

"And whose BMW is that at the curb?" Susan said softly.

The sight of the young man making out a check wilted the ladies. When the couple had left, shaking hands with John Farmer and tucking away a deposit receipt, Farmer joined them.

"Did they offer full price?" Wilma asked.

John Farmer nodded, and put his arm around Wilma. "You folks were serious."

"We were," Wilma said. "Very serious. Are they requesting an inspection?"

"Yes. And the sale, of course, is contingent upon their getting their loan. If you'd come half an hour earlier . . ."

Wilma looked at the others; she didn't know what had come over her, she wasn't ready to sell her house, but they couldn't let this one go. Maybe the loan would be refused. Maybe the inspector would find some disastrous seepage problem that the couple wouldn't want to bother repairing.

"You can make a second deposit," John said. "Contingent upon their not completing the sale."

An hour later, after walking around the outside and inspecting the furnace and the ducts and wiring as best they could, and writing in several contingencies to their deposit, the checkbooks came out. The ladies split the deposit five ways and called their attorney to help set up the venture. The legal work seemed tedious, but they were caught up in the thrill of the purchase and in the trauma of not knowing whether they had actually made a purchase.

While Wilma and her friends agonized over their hunger to own this particular house, across the village in Wilma's guest room, Joe Grey and Dulcie were pawing a few scattered cat hairs from the dresser, where they had left a brown, padded envelope. They had placed a computer-printed note on top, weighting it down with Cora Lee's bracelet so it couldn't be missed.

Cora Lee,
The letter in this envelope belongs to you. You bought the white chest at the McLeary yard sale. Richard Casselrod took it from you by force, even if he did shove some money at you. He took the chest apart and removed this letter from the false bottom, so it should be legally yours, to keep or sell.

A friend

The letter had been Dulcie's longest effort at Wilma's computer. Her paws felt bruised, and her temper was still short. It took a lot of squinching up to hit only the right keys, and took far more patience than patrolling the most difficult mouse run.

They had gotten Catalina's valuable letter out of Joe's house before Clyde might, in fact, decide to pack up and move. Before he fell prey to the hunger for change that had gripped the ladies of the Senior Survival club. At least three of those women seemed fairly itching to box up their belongings.

Now, following Joe out through her cat door, Dulcie said a little prayer for him, a plea that Clyde wouldn't sell their house, that there would be no move for the tomcat, that Clyde and Joe would stay where they belonged, and Joe could quit worrying so foolishly about homelessness and displacement.

30

THE FRONT PAGE OF THE *MOLENA POINT GAZETTE* was deeply shocking to citizens who knew nothing of recent events. But to Joe Grey and Dulcie and to the Molena Point police, the headline was satisfying, the indication of a job completed. The national noon news on TV and radio may have scooped the *Gazette*, but still the paper sold out in less than two hours. Every daily across the country carried the story.

AUTHOR ELLIOTT TRAYNOR MURDERED
VISITING AUTHOR AN IMPOSTOR

The handsome gray-haired author living among us while his play, *Thorns of Gold*, was being cast, has turned out to be an imposter. The man whom villagers assumed to be Elliott Traynor is, in fact, a New York fry cook from Queens bearing an uncanny resemblance to the author. The real Traynor died six weeks ago on the New York streets, in a drama more bizarre than any of Traynor's many works of fiction.

The debonair and charming fry cook who impersonated Traynor was able to deceive the entire village, including director Samuel Ladler and musical director Mark King. Only Traynor's wife, Vivi, seems to have known the truth.

The body of the real Elliot Traynor was identified late yesterday by New York police after it had lain for six weeks in cold storage in the New York City morgue, tagged as a John Doe. Molena

Point police are holding Vivi Traynor and the fry cook, Willie Gasper, for transport back to New York where they will face murder charges. Until this morning, Traynor's death was considered a possible suicide. Police now have a witness to the murder.

Traynor was found dead in early March, in an alley frequented by the homeless. There was no identification. He was dressed in rags. The fingerprints lifted could not be matched in any New York State or federal records. On Friday, Traynor's widow and Gasper were arrested and held for possible illegal disposition of a body, but early today a witness was located claiming to have seen the author's wife smother him with a pillow and dump him in the alley.

Early this month, Elliott and Vivi Traynor were thought by Traynor's publisher and his New York agent to have flown to the West Coast, where Traynor meant to complete his latest novel, and oversee the production of his play. According to New York police, Traynor died the night the couple's flight left John F. Kennedy Airport. Gasper, impersonating the world-famous author, accompanied Mrs. Traynor on the flight to California using Traynor's identification, then posed as Traynor, even acting as consultant on the production of Traynor's only known play.

New York medical examiner Holland Frye told reporters that Traynor's body contained a large dose of Demerol laced with alcohol, a potentially lethal combination. Traynor had a legal prescription for Demerol, which is a powerful pain reliever. The pillow with which Traynor was smothered was

284

hidden by the witness to his murder. Subsequently turned over to police, it was booked as evidence and sent to the state crime lab for identification of hairs clinging to the fabric and DNA testing of possible saliva stains.

Max Harper and Dallas Garza watched the evening newscast while standing in Clyde's living room. The three cats lay on the back of the couch behind Charlie and Ryan, pretending to doze but Joe was so interested he could hardly lie still. Both the *Gazette* and the newscasters had mentioned only one New York witness.

So, Joe thought, smiling, NYPD had been able to keep some of the details under wraps.

Besides Marcy Truncant, the bag lady who had awakened to see Vivi kneeling in the alley holding a pillow over Traynor's face, a neighbor of the Traynors, living upstairs from them in their midtown apartment building, had come forward. She had told detectives that she saw Vivi and Elliott leave the building early the evening of his death, five hours before the Traynors' flight. She remembered the date because it was her wedding anniversary, the first since her husband had died. She saw the couple go out the front door of the building and down into the parking garage, then in a few minutes saw their car pull out of the garage. She told police she saw both of them inside the car as they turned into traffic and sat waiting for the traffic light.

She said that approximately twenty minutes after the Traynors left the building, Elliott returned, coming into the lobby through the front door, and that he was dressed differently. He had left the building dressed in a suit and tie and had returned wearing chinos, a T-shirt, and a frayed denim jacket, attire devoid of the meticulous care that Traynor always exhibited. She didn't see their car return, but an hour later when she went down to the garage, the Traynors' black Jaguar was in its slot.

Joe imagined a scenario where Vivi and Elliott left in the Jaguar, then Vivi had somehow gotten Elliott into Willie's car, maybe had feigned car trouble. She had gotten some liquor into him and perhaps additional Demerol. When he passed out they had changed his clothes and dumped him in the alley, and apparently smothered him to make certain he was dead. Crude, Joe thought. But effective.

Willie had driven the Jaguar back to the building and put it away, so it would appear that Elliott and Vivi were at home. In Elliott's place, he had gone up to the apartment. He had changed clothes, called a cab, and headed for the airport to meet Vivi, to catch their red-eye flight out of JFK. Willie's car had not yet been located. Joe wondered what they'd done with Elliott's dress clothes. Had they been stained or torn when Vivi dispatched Elliott?

When the TV news switched to tensions in the Middle East, Harper turned the volume down. Joe could hear Clyde in the kitchen tossing the salad and stirring the spaghetti sauce. The house smelled of Italian sausage and garlic. Elaborately, Joe stretched, trying to get the kinks out. His whole body felt tense. He'd rest easier when the two detectives had arrived from New York, and had taken Vivi and Willie Gasper away with them. He kept thinking, without any logic, that all the confusion with the Spanish chests and Catalina's letters wouldn't end until Molena Point had seen the last of Vivi Traynor—as if Vivi's switch-and-bait game had somehow contaminated everything she touched in the

286

village.

Catalina's hidden letters, if the ladies of Senior Survival had been able to buy all the chests and found all the letters in them, would have contributed nicely to their future security. But that hadn't happened. Too many people knew about the letters. Of the seven chests that Marcos Romero had carved for Catalina, five were now accounted for. The white chest that Casselrod took from Gabrielle, in which he found the hidden compartment; the three chests that the Iselman estate gave to the Pumpkin Coach; and the chest that Susan Brittain had bought on eBay. Susan had examined it carefully, but had found nothing inside.

Five chests. And nine letters—the one Casselrod found in the white chest and that Joe and Dulcie had returned to Cora Lee, and the eight letters taken from one of the chests donated by the Iselman estate, that Augor Prey took from the smashed chest in the Pumpkin Coach. Those would remain with the police as evidence until after Prey's trial, then would be returned to the Pumpkin Coach to sell. Eight letters, each valued at some ten thousand dollars, though both the curator at the museum of history where Susan inquired, and an official at Butterfield's, thought that at auction they would bring more. Forty to eighty thousand clams, Joe thought, for the boys and girls clubs, the Scouts, and Meals for the Elderly—and maybe the local Feline Rescue. That would be nice, to see some of it go for indigent cats. After all, without a cat or two, Augor Prey might have slid out of Molena Point with the letters, as slick as a greased rat.

When Joe heard Clyde dishing up the spaghetti, he dropped off the couch and melted into the kitchen, rubbing against Charlie's ankles, then leaped to the far end of the counter beside Dulcie and the kit.

Curled up on the cool tile, impatiently awaiting their turn, the cats watched Clyde serve the plates. Charlie unwrapped garlic bread hot from the oven, as Ryan popped cold beers. The Italian feast smelled like the cats' idea of heaven, making them drool with greed.

Humans wind their spaghetti between spoon and fork, but cats slurp it—in this case while listening guiltily to Rube whining at the back door. The old dog's digestion could no longer handle spicy food. Clyde fed him a special diet about as appealing as tofu burgers.

But hey, Joe thought, *the stuff is good for him.* He watched Charlie and Harper at the table, observing the sense of shared sympathy between them. And he had to smile, that Clyde and Ryan seemed to be hitting it off. Certainly Clyde was scrubbed and neatly dressed in a V-neck sweater over a white turtleneck and freshly washed jeans, and he hadn't grouched once—he was, in fact, observing impeccable behavior. That never hurt, Joe thought, amused.

"When is Augor Prey's arraignment?" Charlie asked. "Are you sure he'll be indicted?"

"Time and patience," Harper said. "You can never be certain of anything, but I see no reason why the grand jury won't hand down an indictment. We have the gun that killed Fern, with Prey's prints on it."

Charlie nodded. "Along with Willie Gasper's prints, and Vivi's?"

Harper nodded. "It was apparently Willie's gun or hers. There was no registration. And no way to know if that gun killed the raccoons. It was the same caliber weapon, but with a hollow point that spreads all over, you're not going to see any riflings. If it was the same gun, Gasper apparently wiped off the trigger. It showed only Prey's prints.

"Prey's story is that, the morning Fern died, Vivi followed Fern in through the broken window, into the back room, and pulled the gun on them while they were fighting over the wooden chests. That he snatched it from her and it went off, killing Fern. We have evidence that Vivi was in the back room at some point." Joe thought about the cherry pit that Garza had picked up, and about Prey's sworn statement putting Vivi there. The cats, playing up to the night dispatcher, had found a copy of Preys signed statement that Garza had left for Harper. Easing the door of Harper's office closed and flipping on the desk lamp, they had crouched on the blotter, reading.

Not only had Fern tried to grab the chests from Prey—a real fistfight, as Prey had described it—but Prey said that one of the chests had been smashed, and that Fern managed to snatch up the letters that fell out of it.

Joe assumed there had been some gentle pressure from Garza or Harper to obtain the rest of Prey's statement. Prey said that when Fern ran toward the window he lost his head, went kind of crazy, as he put it, and shot her again, firing at her in a fit of confusion.

He said that Vivi had disappeared; and that when he saw he'd likely killed Fern, he jammed the gun in his pocket and ran for the back door, jumped in his car, and took off. He said that, driving away, he wanted to go back and talk to the police, that he heard the sirens and wanted to tell them what had happened, but he was afraid to. That had made the cats smile. Anyone who thought Prey was trying sincerely to make amends for an innocent mistake ought to think again. For one thing, both shots had been from behind, entering Fern in the back.

"It's interesting," Garza said, "that Vivi saw him shoot Fern, but didn't try to blackmail him. Likely she didn't want to call attention to herself at that point. Apparently she just went home and laid low, but then she got nervous and started to pack."

Harper leaned back in his chair. "Not too nervous to send those chapters she was writing off to New York before she and Willie tried to sneak out. Maybe she hoped that in the next few weeks, New York would dispose of Elliott's body and no one would ever know he was dead. She may have planned for Willie to keep right on being Elliott Traynor, she may have really believed that Elliott's publisher would think that what she wrote was Elliott's work. It takes," Harper said with a lopsided grin, "some kind of talent to write like Elliott Traynor."

The shadow of a smile touched Charlie's face; and she rose quickly to dish up more spaghetti. The cats watched her with interest; but it was not until the next morning that Joe was certain of what he suspected.

It was just after ten when Joe trotted in through Dulcie's cat door; she met him in the kitchen, her green eyes bright, her tabby tail lashing with excitement. He'd seen Charlie's van out front, and Gabrielle's and Mavity's cars. In the living room, Charlie and all the ladies of Senior Survival were gathered; all seemed to be talking at once. Joe sniffed the good smells of coffee and chocolate and sweet vanilla, and twitched an ear toward the animated female voices.

"They're celebrating," Dulcie said. "They got the house. They really got it, they're so happy they're almost purring."

"What house?"

"The last one they looked at, the one they've all been talking about, the one above the canyon. Don't you listen? Tomcats," she said, flattening her ears with annoyance. "It has a had water problem, so that young couple didn't get their loan. Anyway, they didn't want to do the repairs. The ladies are so thrilled."

"Right. That's just what they need, a huge house with a water problem. Plumbing? Leaking basement? What? Do you know how much it costs to—"

"Ryan looked at it. She said she can fix it."

Joe narrowed his eyes. "Saying something and doing it are not always the same. The drainage on those hills—"

"Come on, Joe. They're so happy. It'll be all right— let's stay for a little while. Charlie's here. She will be one of the trustees. But she's—I don't know what's wrong with her. She's acting as nervous as a mouse at a cat show."

Heading for the living room beside Dulcie, Joe glanced up at the buffet. "Is that the chest Susan bought, the one that was in her car during the break-in?"

"Wilma's keeping it for her."

"Out in plain sight?"

"Since Augor Prey and Casselrod went to jail, why not?"

"I wouldn't leave it lying around. You don't know who else . . ." Exasperated with Susan and Wilma, he leaped up to have a look.

The box smelled just like the others, of old, seasoned wood. The geometric carvings were primitive and handsome, each side with a rosette in the center. Pawing the top open, he sniffed at the empty interior.

The walls and bottom seemed too thin for a false compartment. Likely this was just a nice collector's

291

piece that would bring maybe four or five hundred dollars, he thought, dropping to the floor. Heading for the living room, the two cats slipped into the cave beneath Wilma's desk beside the kit, where she lay on her back playing with one of Cora Lee's slippers, holding it between her front paws, killing it violently.

Moving deeper in beside her, Joe and Dulcie listened to the ladies' plans, to Susan's decision to put her house on the market, and to their discussion of the legal aspects of a joint purchase that their attorney had outlined. All the numbers and percentage points made the cats' heads reel. Curled up together, they were almost asleep when Charlie's cell phone rang.

Answering, her face colored. She glanced around at her friends, then rose, heading for the kitchen, cradling the phone to her ear, her sudden excitement seeming almost to send sparks. Quickly the three cats slipped out to follow her, pushing through the kitchen door before she closed it. Leaping to the table, they crowded around her. The voice at the other end reached them like a bee buzz. Charlie listened for some time, going pale; absently she petted Dulcie.

Slipping close to her, Joe put his face next to Charlie's. She didn't push him away. The woman's voice at the other end was husky and familiar. ". . . totally unprecedented. There are a lot of well-known writers who would like to step into this contract. I can't make any kind of promise, but I have to say, I like this very much. Really, I find it difficult to separate your work from Elliott's. I'm hoping Elliott's editor will feel the same.

"I'm taking it over to her this afternoon. This whole thing has been upsetting to everyone—and you can imagine that several writers' agents have already contacted Kathleen Merritt and called me."

Nervously, Charlie hugged Joe.

"If she does like it, can you meet the August tenth deadline?"

"Yes," Charlie said, looking with panic at the cats.

"You said you're not a writer by profession?"

"I'm an artist. I do animal drawings. I'm represented in Molena Point by the Aronson Gallery. And I . . . I own a cleaning and maintenance company."

"So you work full-time?"

"I can meet the deadline. I have reliable crews. My time is my own." She didn't mean to sound defensive. Beside her, Joe and Dulcie were smiling and purring. The kit looked wide-eyed and puzzled. When Charlie hung up the phone, she grabbed the cats in a huge hug.

"Our secret," she said softly, glancing toward the living room.

Joe listened to the faint sound of the ladies' voices, preoccupied with loan points and interest rates. Strange, he thought, that loud, giggling Vivi Traynor, when she brought her ugly little secret to Molena Point, might have launched Charlie into a new and exciting venture.

Though if Charlie hadn't been so nosy, as curious as a cat herself, even Vivi's subterfuge wouldn't have made that happen. And it was Charlie's love of Traynors work that had truly set her on this path.

"Not even Wilma," Charlie whispered. "Don't even tell Wilma. Not yet. Not until I see if this will fly."

"It will fly," Dulcie said softly.

Charlie looked at them uncertainly. "Maybe. And maybe this is all foolishness, maybe I'll fall on my face." She grinned. "But I've done that before, and gotten up again."

Joe twitched a whisker. He could imagine Charlie sitting up late at night, into the small hours, in her little

293

one-room apartment, working on a borrowed computer at her breakfast table. Stopping work sometimes to stand at her window looking down on the rooftops as she formed, in her thoughts, her own kind of magic for the last chapters of Elliott Traynor's novel. And he rubbed his face against Charlie's, raggedly purring.

31

IT WAS OPENING NIGHT OF *THORNS OF GOLD*. AMONG the shadows above the dimly lit theater, Joe and Dulcie lay stretched out along a rafter, watching the crowd streaming in below them laughing and talking, the seats quickly filling up. The villagers were dressed all in their finest, in coats and ties, and long gowns. Dulcie was wide-eyed at the lovely jewlery and elegant hair arrangements. Despite Elliott Traynors death, despite the fact that Vivi Traynor and Willie Gasper were back in New York and had been arraigned for murder, the producers had moved on with the play—finding Elliott's agent far easier to deal with than Vivi in matters of production and casting.

Elliott's move, in making Adele McElroy recipient, in trust, of his works, had been a surprise to everyone. In Joe's opinion, considering the number of ex-wives in the picture, that had been very wise. He wondered, when Traynor set up the trust two years earlier, if he'd guessed how soon it would take effect. One thing was certain: Vivi hadn't known about the arrangement.

Joe and Dulcie had watched as Vivi and Willie Gasper were marched from Molena Point jail handcuffed, and locked into the backseat of the New

York detectives' rented car, for the ride to the airport, and they had witnessed her vile language. There were no giggles now, nervous or otherwise. Certainly the New York grand jury's ruling indicting Vivi for murder had set off enough national headlines and prime-time news to he heard even by Elliott himself wherever he was in heaven's high realms.

Joe supposed that if the New York police hadn't had an eye witness to Elliott's murder, Adele McElroy herself, because she was trustee and partial heir, might have been a suspect.

In Molena Point, Augor Prey had been convicted for breaking and entering and vandalism. That had netted him two years in county jail and two thousand dollars restitution to be paid to Susan Brittain. Though very likely, Susan wouldn't see much of the money. Prey's upcoming trial for Fern Barth's murder should, if all went well, put him behind bars and out of the workforce for some time to come. Joe Grey smiled, feeling greatly at ease with the world, feeling much the same as when a brace of fat mice lay lined up before him—a nice finish to a day's hunting.

But the Kit, though pleased that justice had prevailed and that Vivi was behind bars, wasn't nearly finished with related matters. Nor was she up among the rafters, tonight, with Joe and Dulcie, watching the house fill with eager theatergoers.

Sprawled across Cora Lee's dressing table, her black-and-brown tattered coat looking like nothing so much as a ragged fur scarf, the kit watched the star of the play button her satin gown for the first act. They could hear from the audience tides of hushed voices echoing back to them where folk were laughing and greeting friends.

The proximity of a real audience excited the kit so much it made her paws sweat.

Sitting down at the dressing table, Cora Lee drew on eye makeup and applied mascara while leaning over the kit, and blushed her cheeks brighter than the kit had ever seen. When she slipped on her wig of long, shining black hair, those sleek Spanish tresses curling around her shoulders, she wasn't Cora Lee anymore.

She rose from the dressing table as a young, vibrant Spanish woman, splendid in cascading folds of pale ivory satin. Catalina stood stroking the kit, her hands shaking.

"You bring me luck, Kit. You are my luck." Her fingers were so cold that the chill came right through the kit's fur, making the little cat shiver. Cora Lee stood still for only a moment, then began to pace the small dressing room, singing softly the lines of her opening number—whether to calm her nerves or to warm up, the kit didn't know. She sang part of a song from the second act, the verses so hurt and lonely they made the kit want to yowl—Catalina's lament touched the kit so strongly that she mewled, lifting her paw to her friend.

"Does that number make you sad, Kit?" Cora Lee tilted the kit's chin up, looking into her eyes. "Say, 'Break a leg,' Kit."

The kit's eyes widened with alarm, making Cora Lee laugh.

"That's what theater people say, for good luck. Break a leg. If you could talk, that's what you could say to me." Careful of her costume, Cora Lee picked up the kit and hugged her. "I'm so nervous. I haven't done this since New Orleans—not a musical. Well, it's not a musical. Experimental, Mark calls it. But for so long, I've only done speaking parts. And then I used to sing

296

sometimes in small clubs. It still hurts to sing, Kit—like a knife in my middle. I don't care, this is Catalina's night, Catalina is alive, tonight, and she will be wonderful."

She will be wonderful, the kit thought. *You are Catalina, and you are wonderful.*

The music began. There was a knock at the door. Cora Lee set the kit on the dresser. "Stay here, Kit. Think good thoughts." And she left the dressing room, heading backstage behind the sets.

The kit waited only a moment, then followed her. Staying among the shadows, she hid herself in the wings behind the long curtains where she had a good view of the stage. Above her in the rafters, high over the gathered audience, Joe and Dulcie saw her. Dulcie smiled, but Joe Grey tensed. "What's she doing?"

"She's just watching," Dulcie said quietly. "She loves Cora Lee. And she loves the play; the songs seem really to charm her. She'll just sit there purring," she said complacently.

But Joe's yellow eyes shone black in the shadows, burning with unease.

"Not to worry," Dulcie said. "What could she do? She's a sensible little cat."

"She's too close to the stage. Why doesn't she come up here?"

"She wants to be close to Cora Lee, she wants a front-row seat." She gave him a sweet look. "It's opening night, everyone's talked about opening night. Of course the kit's excited." She peered down over the rafter below them, where Clyde and Ryan were taking their seats. Clyde was dressed in a dark suit, white shirt, and tie, and was holding Ryan's hand. Ryan wore a long emerald green dress. Dulcie loved all the pageantry and elegance. It would be no good to have a play, if the audience didn't dress up, too.

To the cats' left sat Wilma and Susan, and Gabrielle and Mavity, all wearing long dresses and whispering among themselves. Three rows in front of them, Max Harper and Charlie were finding their places.

"Can you believe that Harper sprang for front-row seats?" Dulcie whispered. Harper was dressed in a well-tailored, dark sport coat, tan slacks, pale shirt, and tie. Charlie wore a long, rust-toned skirt and a brocade jacket in orange and turquoise that was, Dulcie whispered, "stunning with her red hair."

The house lights dimmed and the orchestra shifted from a soft tango to the opening strains of Act 1. The curtain opened to the patio of the Ortega-Diaz hacienda, filled now with angry, arguing rancheros—with Don Ortega-Diaz and a dozen of his contemporaries, resplendent in Spanish finery, discussing with Latin passion the sudden foreclosure on their lands. Not until the American, Hamilton Stanton, appeared in their midst offering to pay Ortega-Diaz's commitments, did the mob quiet. What was this? What a fortunate turn of events, that their friend could marry off the eldest of his five daughters to a rancher of obvious means and, at the same time, save his lands.

But when Catalina's hand was promised, she stepped from the shadows fiery with rage against her father; the angry violence of her song shook the audience. When the lights came up at the end of Scene 1, the theater was silent. Applause, when it broke, was like sudden thunder.

It was Scene 2, as servants locked Catalina in her room, that her saddest lament rose—and that a small movement in the shadows drew Cora Lee's attention.

The cats saw her glance into the wings though her singing didn't falter. Dulcie caught her breath. Joe Grey crouched, ready to leap across the rafters and down, to haul the kit off the stage.

Dulcie stopped him, her teeth gently in his shoulder. "Wait, Joe. Watch—look at the audience."

Catalina's voice faltered for only a second as she reached out to the dark little cat that had slipped up onto her couch beside her. As Cora Lee's song held the audience, she drew the kit to her in a gesture natural and appealing. Singing with a broken heart, she cuddled the kit close. Every person present was one with them, not a sound in the darkened theater. Cora Lee and the kit held them all.

The kit appeared in two more scenes, both times when Cora Lee glanced into the wings to draw her out again, the two seeming perfectly attuned to one another. Cora Lee might be amazed at the kit's behavior, but she was a child of the theater. And the audience loved the small cat. When Cora Lee glanced into the wings at Sam Ladler, he was smiling—Cora Lee played the kit for all she was worth. When Catalina was fed on bread and water, the kit slipped in through the window grate to keep her company. The kit disappeared after the wedding and did not return until Catalina's lover, in desperation, began to ravage the Ortega-Diaz lands, stealing cattle and burning the pastures. Now again the kit was there, with exquisite timing, as Catalina herself set a trap for her lover.

In the last scene, when Marcos escaped Hamilton Stanton's vaqueros and came to take Catalina away, and when Stanton was there in her stead, Catalina stood in her chamber holding the kit in her arms, weeping for Marcos, for her part in his death, as the curtain rang down.

Among the cats' closest friends, response to the kit's theatrical adventure was frightened and guarded. While everyone in the village raved about Cora Lee's performance and about the wonderful part the little cat played, and the kit had front-page newspaper coverage, her friends worried for her and wanted badly to put a stop to her foolishness.

"You're racing too close the edge," Dulcie told her. "Don't you think people will wonder?"

"But no one—" the kit began.

"Kit, this scares me. Don't you understand what could happen?"

The kit looked at Dulcie sadly, filled with misery.

"You're lovely in the play, Kit. You're exactly what the play needed. Everyone loves you. But, Kit, you know that not all humans can he trusted. Even if they believe you're no more than a trained cat, the way Wilma and Clyde have tried to convince people, don't you know how many no-goods would steal such a cleverly trained kitty and try to sell you."

"But they wouldn't hurt me. And I would escape, I would get away."

Dulcie just looked at her. Life before the kit had been so peaceful and predictable—and, compared to life *with* the kit, seemed in retrospect deadly dull. "If we stick with Wilma's plan," Dulcie said, "maybe it will come right." It broke her heart to scold the kit, the kit took such joy in the play. But when she licked the kit's ear, the kit brightened.

By the next morning, Wilma and Charlie and Clyde

had convinced Cora Lee that it would be best to tell admirers that she and Wilma, together, had trained the kit. They set up a scenario for the remainder of the play that included Wilma taking the kit to the theater each night, standing in the wings with her, and giving her hand signals like a trained dog. Cora Lee followed the plan, understanding quite well the danger to the kit—as far as she knew it.

But the wonder of the kit's creative performance didn't pale. To Cora Lee and to her audiences, the kit was a four-legged angel, a magical creature.

Wilma told Sam Ladler that onstage, when Cora Lee's emotions built through song, the young cat was naturally drawn to her in a powerful response. She said that was how she trained the kit. Ladler said the kit's appearance had been a nice surprise, that the kit added just the fillip the play needed. "This couldn't have happened," he said, laughing, "if Vivi had been present. She would have pitched a fit."

The play was to run for six weeks. Dulcie told the kit, "Except for performances, you'll stay in the house. When the play's over, you'll stay in the house until, hopefully, people forget about trained cats."

"If they ever forget," Joe said darkly.

"I will stay in the house," the kit said dutifully, her round amber eyes glowing with the magic of the theater, with a wonder and dimension that stayed with her each night long after the last curtain had fallen, so it was hard for her to fall asleep. She prowled the house worrying Dulcie, prompting Wilma to rise and warm a pan of milk for her then stroke her until she slept. If Wilma began to look haggard, people put it down to her demanding cat-training regimen.

Thorns of Gold, with the kit's added magic,

contributed to the village of Molena Point a warm and glowing experience; and maybe the magic spilled over to anoint others. It was a week after opening night that Charlie made her announcement, at the engagement party at Clyde's house in honor of her and Max.

Ryan came early to help Clyde lay out plates and glasses on the seldom-used dining table. Mavity and Susan arrived just before Charlie and Max, bringing trays of canapes. Wilma and Gabrielle and Cora Lee of course were at the theater. Mavity had dressed in a powder blue pants suit that was not a uniform. Susan wore a long skirt and a hand-knit sweater. Soon after Detectives Garza and Davis arrived, loaded down with ice buckets and champagne, and before the engagement announcement, Charlie broke her news.

"Looks like the last chapters of Elliott Traynor's *Twilight Silver* will be published after all," she said quietly.

Garza frowned, "How did that happen? I thought Vivi couldn't write her way out of a paper bag. That's what alerted her agent in the first place."

"Vivi won't be writing the last chapters," Harper said.

"Who, then?" Garza said, waiting for the punch line. "Not Willie Gasper?"

"Charlie will be writing them," Harper said. "She talked with Traynor's editor yesterday. They like her work very much, they're sending her a contract."

"And," Charlie said tremulously, "I guess I have a literary agent. If I . . . if I decide to write something more."

Dulcie glanced at Joe, remembering how frightened Charlie had been when she first learned that her drawings had been accepted by the Aronson Gallery, how nervous she had been before the gallery opening—then how bubbly

302

with excitement when everyone loved her work.

She was just as frightened now. But that didn't matter. Charlie did fine under pressure.

Harper put his arm around her, grinning down at her, then looking around at their gathered friends. "We've set the wedding date—four months from today, then we're off to Alaska. When we get back, maybe I can talk Charlie into supervising Charlie's Fix-It, Clean-It from her studio at the ranch, and spend the rest of her time working on whatever projects she maps out— provided she makes spaghetti once a week, and helps me with the horses."

Champagne corks were popped, toasts offered up, and the party food was attacked with enthusiasm. A dozen more officers arrived, some with their wives, and most of the librarians who worked with Wilma, and soon other friends began to straggle in. With the party in full swing, people crowding in wall-to-wall, the two cats, having eaten their fill, retired to the bedroom. It was perhaps half an hour later that Clyde appeared to ask Joe's advice. He shut the door behind him.

"You want my advice?" Joe said. "You're asking for my opinion? What's the catch?"

"Just be quiet and listen. Do you always have to be so sarcastic?" Clyde stood scowling down at him. "What would you think, if I didn't sell the house?"

Dulcie mewed softly. But Joe's heart gave a leap as violent as if he'd swallowed a live mouse.

"What would you think if Ryan added a second-story bedroom and office, with a view over the village—so we could see the ocean? And redesigned the backyard into a walled Spanish patio with those outdoor heaters, and a raised barbecue and fireplace?"

"Be okay, I guess," Joe said noncommittally. He

didn't dare glance at Dulcie for fear he'd lose his cool. He wanted to do back flips, to yowl with happiness. "With, say, one of those cupola things on top of the new bedroom, a sort of cat tower? Could she do that?"

"She could do that," Clyde said. "But of course we'd have to live with a restaurant next door, with all the traffic, and people going in and out."

"We would," Joe said carefully, keeping the conversation lowkey. He looked hard at Clyde. "Let's give it some thought. Think about our options." And for the first time, the idea of moving didn't seem like the end of the world. If he had options, and if Clyde was including him in on the decision making, then it wasn't like being thrown out homeless, back into the alleys. For the first time, the various possibilities held such interest for the tomcat that he couldn't help but purr.

Amazing what a difference it made when Clyde softened up a little and asked his advice. Joe felt like he'd fallen right back into his secure and comfortable life, as cozy as his own easy chair. Smiling up at Clyde, and then at Dulcie, he was caught in a warm froth of family sentimentality. "After all," he told Clyde, "if we did decide to move, we have the whole village to choose from."

Clyde grinned and picked Joe up, setting him on his shoulder, then tucked Dulcie under his arm. "You two did all right with the Traynor case. That phone call to Adele McElroy was, I have to say, a stroke of genius."

He looked down at Joe. "I don't want to know how you knew about her, or how you two softened Max Harper up to the point of allowing you in the station. The dispatchers seem quite taken with Dulcie.

"And Harper doesn't want to know, ever," Clyde said, "why there were gray and white cat hairs in the window of the Pumpkin Coach, among the broken glass." And he headed back for the party, dropping the cats on the couch beside Charlie. Harper, sitting close to her, turned to look at the cats, his expression stern and withdrawn—but there was, deep in the captain's eyes, something uneasy, something questioning.

Joe looked back at Harper as blankly as he could manage, and kneaded Charlie's knee, keeping his claws in. Charlie looked down at him, her eyes filled with amusement, and reached over him to hold Max's hand. And Joe thought, no matter how many thieves and deadbeats there were in the world, there were far more good folks. No matter how many tarty little murderers like Vivi Traynor, with her frozen cherries and her giggles, there were many more humans who were totally okay, folks a cat could count on.

All a cat had to do was right a few wrongs when he could, ignore the human transgressions he couldn't change, love his true friends, and always, always have the last laugh.

Dear Reader:

I hope you enjoyed reading this Large Print book. If you are interested in reading other Beeler Large Print titles, ask your librarian or write to me at

Thomas T. Beeler, *Publisher*
Post Office Box 659
Hampton Falls, New Hampshire 03844

You can also call me at 1-800-818-7574 and I will send you my latest catalogue.

Audrey Lesko and I choose the titles I publish in Large Print. Our aim is to provide good books by outstanding authors—books we both enjoyed reading and liked well enough to want to share. We warmly welcome any suggestions for new titles and authors.

Sincerely,